NO
ROMEO

T0130919

OTHER TITLES BY DONNA ALAM

Stand-Alone Titles

The Interview

No Ordinary Men

No Ordinary Gentleman

Love + Other Lies

Before Him

One Night Forever

Liar Liar

Never Say Forever

Love in London

To Have and Hate

(Not) The One

The Stand Out

Phillips Brothers

In Like Flynn

Down Under

Rafferty's Rules

Great Scots

Easy

Hard

Hardly Easy

Hot Scots

One Hot Scot

One Wicked Scot

One Dirty Scot

Single Daddy Scot

Hot Scots Boxed Set

And More!

NO ROMEO

·MY KIND OF HERO·

DONNA ALAM

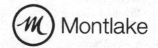
Montlake

Text copyright © 2024 by Donna Alam
All rights reserved.

Published by Montlake, Seattle

www.apub.com

Amazon, the Amazon logo, and Montlake are trademarks of Amazon.com, Inc., or its affiliates.

ISBN-13: 9781662521027
eISBN-13: 9781662521034

Cover design by @blacksheep-uk.com
Cover photography by Michelle Lancaster

Printed in the United States of America

I was in the middle before I knew
that I had begun.
—Jane Austen, *Pride and Prejudice*

Chapter 1
EVIE

Pockets. The one day in a woman's life she's denied a purse, she should at least have pockets.

This gown was probably designed by a man.

Words hum around me like a tune I can't catch, the papers jammed down the front of my dress prickly and annoying. I should've decreased the font and printed them out again or just used my phone. I should've—

"Marriage is the union of two people . . ."

I shake off the unfinished thought as the celebrant's declaration yanks me back to the moment with such clarity. *I shouldn't be here at all.*

". . . voluntarily entered into for life and to the exclusion of all others."

A wave of rage washes over me. I thought those were the rules too! It takes everything I have not to burst She-Hulk-style from my dress. Hulk smash! Hulk maim! Hulk rip off the groom's testicles and wear them as dangly earrings!

"Are you, Evelyn, free lawfully to marry Mitchell?" Her tone is sweetly resonant as she turns a warm smile my way.

She-Hulk needs to concentrate.

My gaze slides to the man at my right, my fiancé, as handsome as he's ever been, in an impeccably cut dark suit. His hair gleams russet in the light, his faint smile meant to reassure as he mistakes the tears that suddenly well in my eyes.

Oh, honey, that's not love shining there. Try murderous intent.

It's good for him that I, as a veterinarian, swore an oath to use my skills for good, because I was sorely tempted to swing by the clinic this morning to pick up a little something to put him out of *my* misery.

"Evelyn?"

Jerked from my thoughts, I notice the celebrant's worried frown. "I'm sorry, what?"

"Are you free to marry Mitchell?"

"I am." My husky-voiced answer is technically correct. I am free to marry him. Whether I *will* is another question.

"And are you, Mitchell, free lawfully to marry Evelyn?"

"I am." He smiles again, because ignorance is bliss. Ask me how I know.

"Now that you have both declared . . ." The celebrant's words trail away, the room suddenly echoing as I raise my hand. "You have a question, Evelyn?"

"Um, yeah." So many, the first of which is, *How did it take me until this morning to see Mitchell for what he really is?* You might say the veil was plucked from my eyes right before its pearl-encrusted comb was poked into my head.

"Evie?" Mitchell's expression falters, his eyes darting over my shoulder to Jen, my maid of honor. She needs a new title. A few unflattering options spring to mind, but first:

"Before we get to the 'I take thee' part, I'd like to read my vows." My answer carries clearly through the hall.

"That part comes in a moment, dear." The celebrant's eyes rico-chet between us before she adds a quiet "Remember?"

"I do—" I almost roll my eyes. "I mean, I know. But I need to read them now." I reach into my neckline when Mitchell tries to stop me.

"Babe, there's a way this has to be done."

"There's what's meant to be," I say, snatching my hand back, "and then there's what is." My fingers tremble as I unfold the sheets of A4 paper with the ridiculously large print as I prepare to make what my mother would call (gasp, horror) a scene. "Mitchell"—my voice is clear and calm—"you are the french fry to my chocolate shake."

The congregation hums a collective "*ahh*," and Mitch blows out a relieved breath. I'd call his smile tentative. Short lived, anyway.

"What a shock it was this morning to find you've been sticking your *french fry* into other milkshakes. In other yards." I shoot a glare Jen's way. She looks like she's about to barf.

A giggle or two echo from the small crowd, but when the punch line doesn't arrive, you could hear a pin drop. Meanwhile, Mitchell looks confused. *Time to ditch the subtlety.* I give the papers a shake and scan the long line of anonymous text message screenshots I'd gotten this morning.

"Apparently, 'that thing you do with your tongue is *uh-mah-zing.*'"

"What?"

"That's exactly what I said. I feel shortchanged."

"Evie?" He reaches for me, but I pivot away. Balling up the first sheet of paper, I aim it at his head. *Bull's-eye!*

"'I have never had this kind of connection before,'" I kind of yell. "That one's from Jen. Which is weird, given I'm the one in the damn dress."

Color leeches from Mitchell's face right before I bounce another ball of scrunched paper off his head.

"It's not what you're thinking." His words come so quick, they almost trip over themselves.

"I'm thinking you're a deceitful, two-timing, unfaithful piece of shit!"

Cue an intake of breath from our audience. It seems Mitchell isn't the only one a little slow on the uptake today.

"Sweetheart, you've got this all wrong."

"I have?" I hold the paper in front of me. "So, when you said you 'couldn't wait to get your mouth on Jen's pussy,' you were talking about her cat?"

"Give me those." He grunts as he reaches for the papers.

Oh, hell no. I snatch them away. "Do you think Jen's cat would be into—oh, wait. Jen only has a dog. I guess she has two now."

I step backward into the aisle, thankful I didn't choose a dress with a train. Dropping the first printout, I glide between our guests, who are silent and gawping in their jaunty hats and pastel dresses. *Is it weird how I'm only just noticing they're mostly Mitchell's friends?*

"'I can't wait to give you my rock-hard eight inches,'" I announce, flicking the next sheet away. "I hope one of you thought to gift that man a new ruler. Whatever he's using right now is lying to him."

Someone snickers. Another barks out a laugh. At the end of the aisle, I swing around to face my lead-footed groom, delivering my finale with, I like to think, aplomb. *If my mother was here, she'd probably have a coronary.*

"This one's a doozy . . . 'Next time I see you, I'm gonna suck your brains out from your dick.'" I press a pondering finger to my chin. "I do wonder if Jen achieved her aim. Your brains have *obviously* migrated to your balls, so that's like, what?" Holding my finger and thumb a little apart, I add, "Four inches to travel, give or take?" Done, I throw the rest of the printouts up into the air.

I see the moment that this all sinks in—the moment Mitch realizes this isn't a bad dream. The color that drained from his face moments ago comes rushing back with a vengeance. My heart leaps in my chest as, through the flutter of oversize confetti, he begins to move, sidestepping those who'd stop him.

"Ladies and gentlemen, I am done with this man. Done with this wedding. But please help yourself to the champagne being served in the anteroom. Raise your glasses to close calls and anonymous text messages." I swing around and tug the door open, my heels ringing against the marble floor as I brush past a server and his silver tray.

Mitchell bellows my name, and a burst of adrenaline courses through my veins.

"Not today, whorey Satan," I mutter as I pick up my pace, caterers rocking like pins as I bowl past them.

Dammit, I was looking forward to those Thai-spiced prawn canapés.

The sun is almost blinding as I explode from the town hall's Victorian front doors and almost roll my ankle as I slip on the steps I'd imagined having beautiful wedding photos taken on. I tug off $600 worth of Jimmy Choos, regretfully pitching them behind me.

"Evie, come back!" Mitch yells as the doors bang open a moment later.

I don't spare him the breath of an answer as I gather the front of my froufrou dress and burst into a barefoot sprint.

"Please, let me explain!"

Not on your life. And *his life* is right. I'm not running away because I'm afraid of him. It's more like I'm afraid of what I might do to him. There is no rationalizing this. It's just a choice between undignified behavior and homicide, and he's not worth going to jail over.

Where the hell is the car? The wedding venue is on a busy inter-section in a no-parking zone. Not that a 1928 Daimler would make any kind of high-speed getaway.

"Evelyn!" Mitchell bellows with a change of tone. "Get back here—we need to talk about this!"

Where is a bus when you need one?

I scan the two lanes of traffic, the lights up ahead set to red. Without a second thought, I slide between two stationary cars and edge my way along the row of vehicles.

"Look, Mummy, a princess!" squeals a little girl from the open window of a car.

"Oy! Cinders! Did your carriage turn back into a pumpkin?" A burst of deep laughter sounds from a nearby van, but flipping them off would be unprincessly. *No need to ruin everyone's day.*

When the asshole shouts my name again, I panic and stumble, catching myself on the door handle of a car. I barely register my reflection in the darkened window as I pull myself upright, but I do register the door isn't locked. I don't know which of us is more surprised when I tug it open.

"What the—"

"Please help me," I plead, channeling my best damsel in distress as I throw myself across the back seat, only to realize the man I'm looking at isn't a driver. He's *the* driver. And the man whose lap I've literally just thrown myself into?

Well, hot damn.

Chapter 2
EVIE

I find myself staring into the most striking eyes I have ever seen. They're too vivid to be blue—that they seem violet can only be a trick of the light. Or maybe it's the frame of the thickest, sootiest lashes I've ever seen on a man.

"Are those extensions?" I tighten my grip on what I realize are his lapels.

He looks like the kind of man who takes care of himself. Feels like it, too, thanks to the broad chest I'm currently pressed against. But I'm going to take that wintry, unimpressed twist of his lips as *no.*

"Wow, real? Mother Nature sure is a joker." Taking a deep breath, I refocus. "I'm sorry for bursting in on you like this—"

"Quite literally."

"—but this is an emergency."

"And this isn't an ambulance." His voice is deep and refined and feels like the brush of velvet along my spine. "It also isn't a wedding car."

"I'm not going to a wedding," I snap, my damsel-in-distress act slipping. I glance out of the rear window and spot Mitchell on the sidewalk, scanning the spaces between the idling cars. My gaze narrows. He should be on his knees thanking God for tinted windows because I won't be forced to strangle him with my veil.

"Contrary to appearances, you mean?"

"What?" I swipe the gauzy lace out of my face, and when I turn back, I find we're almost nose to nose.

"Did you run off with the contents of the collection plate?" His brow spikes like an elegant question mark.

"There isn't a collection at a wedding." I frown, pulling back and pressing up onto one palm to put a little distance between us. I shouldn't notice the fine fabric of his pants or the thick muscle of his thigh flexing under them.

Get it together, Evie. The man is wearing a three-piece suit, for gosh sake.

"There is usually a bride."

As the pretty man's gaze flicks over me, I decide *pretty* is doing him a disservice. His face must be a photographer's delight, all broad strokes and sharp angles, square jawed and with those supermodel cheekbones. His dark hair is glossy and thick, and his eyes are the most unlikely shade of . . . whatever that is.

"I might be going to a party," I object. "A princess party."

"Except you're wearing a veil, not a crown, and you're clearly not six years old. You're either running to or from a wedding." His eyes skate over me. "Or running from someone at a wedding."

Would it be too much to hope that he might be rich and sympathetic? Not traits that often go together, but what choice do I have?

"Yes, okay. I'm running away from a hall of guests and a cheating groom." I slide my fingers across his chest to straighten his abused lapel, not ready to see pity in his expression. *Gosh, his torso seems almost geometric.* I wonder if there's a red *S* under here, except that whole eyebrow thing he does makes him look more like a villain. "Please, I just need a ride. Anywhere." My fingers

8

halt as I come back to myself, realizing it might seem like I'm feeling him up.

A car nearby sounds its horn, and the traffic begins to creep forward, thank God. The knot in my stomach begins to loosen, until his arm moves behind me. The buttery leather seats barely murmur as he settles me against his side, his fingers folding around my shoulder to hold me close. My heart creeps up my throat as he reaches for the door, and the locks click as they engage.

This could be why children are warned not to get into strangers' cars.

"Ted, we must get the locks examined."

"Yes, sir," the driver replies.

"Meanwhile, something tells me that would be your groom."

"What?"

"Evie!"

My body jolts, my unease spiking at Mitchell's voice. The stranger's fingers tighten as I turn, finding the window open and that shithead staring at me from a gap in the traffic.

"Evie, please!" His eyes flick to the man beside me, and his expression turns sour. "What the fuck is he doing here?"

"You have got to be kidding me," I mutter at the accusation in his tone. He's got some nerve after what he's put me through today.

My companion's arm tightens, giving my shoulder a reassuring squeeze. "Pure chance, Atherton. A pleasant quirk of fate. But I see you're still undertaking your life's work to screw over everyone around you."

"You two know each other?" My head whips around as the car begins to move again. Tires squeal, and my heart shoots into my throat. I glance back just in time to see Mitch slam his palms onto the hood of a black cab.

"Pity." The stranger slants me a look. "Don't you think?"

"That he wasn't hit?"

9

"You'd rather run him over yourself?" When I bite my tongue from answering *yes*, he gives a graceful shrug. "Violence. It might not be the answer, yet it doesn't stop certain individuals from begging the question."

"Believe me, I know."

"Babe, I'm sorry." Mitch appears at the window, his fingers curled around the glass.

"Sorry you got caught, more like."

"Please don't do this." His throat bobs with emotion.

"You did this, not me. You. And don't you ever call me *babe* again." Balling my fists in my lap, I swing away. I doubt I could get a good shot from this angle, anyway.

"Evie, we need to talk about this. I know I've hurt you—that you deserve better."

I make a derisive noise. I so want to punch him in the face. Why isn't this car moving? The traffic in London is the absolute worst! As horns honk, and angry Londoners yell their displeasure, I glance out the window and realize we're not crawling because of the traffic—we're causing it.

"What we have is too good to throw away. Just give me five minutes," Mitch pleads. "Let me explain."

"I got all the explanation I needed this morning in fifty-two anonymous texts." My voice sounds supremely cool, yet inside, my blood is boiling. *Why won't this stupid car just move?*

"Please."

"Go fuck yourself." Making a scene *and* using vulgar language. My mother would be so proud.

The stranger's fingers tighten again as though in reassurance. "Still against death by cabbie?"

"This has nothing to do with you, Deubel," Mitchell grates out.

"And yet, here sits your fiancée."

"Ex," I correct. "Can we please go?" This time, my distress is not an act.

He turns to the driver. "Ted, we're done here."

And with that, Mitchell's hands are forced to let go as the car speeds up.

◆ ◆ ◆

"Only I would climb into the car of someone who knows Mitch," I mutter, watching as the city passes by the window. Buildings and figures blur, the afternoon sunshine a haze that glints from store windows.

"For a city of nine million people, London often feels like a small town."

I glance up and study his almost-perfect profile. He's a little older than I first imagined, and something tells me those lines at the corners of his eyes weren't made by a life of laughter.

He shifts slightly in his seat, the movement stirring up the subtle scent of a cologne that's all spice and no sugar. It ignites a highly inappropriate tingle between my legs, which is unfortunate because I know men like him. They're all three-piece suit and no substance, like a gift basket prettily wrapped to disguise disappointing contents. I bet his name is double barreled, or maybe he's the fourth in his line to use it. His wealth is probably inherited, which is just another way of saying he's entitled, and when it comes to giving head, I'll bet he doesn't reciprocate.

Yet those aren't the connections my brain makes as I stare at him. He smells nice, which makes me notice how smooth his cheeks are. It might be wrong to imagine him draped in nothing but a towel, his skin shower slick, but it's better than replaying my clusterfuck of a day. Which is (thanks, brain) exactly what my mind does as it slides to the image of Mitch standing at the altar. I'd never seen him in a suit. Rugged boots, jeans, and a perma-cocky grin were more his thing. Whatever. He's still gift-wrapped dog poop.

Do I just have terrible judgment when it comes to men? My gaze flicks over the man next to me, and I stifle a sigh. *Can't fault my taste.*

"It's better that I do know him."

I startle as I find the man looking down at me. "I'd prefer you didn't." Just as I'd prefer to erase the last two-plus years from my brain.

"But then you'd still be standing on the pavement, arguing with him."

"What? You're only helping me because you don't like him?"

"The enemy of my enemy is my friend?" The corner of his mouth tips sardonically.

"What happened to good old-fashioned chivalry?"

"Romeo or the villain. Those are my only choices?"

He's sure as heck not Superman, though he does remind me of Henry Cavill playing the villain in whatever movie that was. "How about plain-old human kindness?"

"Try putting yourself in my position," he says, adjusting the knife-sharp pleat in his pants. "What would you do if a stranger in a wedding dress hijacked your car?"

"Hardly hijacked—"

"Then praised your eyelashes."

"That was a genuine compliment!" It might've been worse, given I almost landed in his lap. *Is that a gun in your pocket or were you just blessed in that department?* Not that I should be embarrassed. Or imagining him seminaked. Again. *Dear amygdala, have you gone offline today?* "So it probably sounded a little random, but trust a man not to understand."

"I understand well enough why you'd leave Mitchell Atherton at the altar." As he stares down at me, I realize two things.

One: He hasn't moved his arm.

Two: I don't mind one bit.

Who would've guessed at the surprises on my wedding bingo card? A cheating groom, a slight mental break, the loss of my gorgeous shoes, and this man, my reluctant hero. Maybe my night of hot revenge sex?

"I appreciate your honesty, if not your reasoning," I begin. "Obviously, there hasn't been much of that in my life lately. But I promise, I'm not deranged. Though I'm not sure my guests would agree." *Guests,* I think, plucking at a seed pearl in my lap. *Faces I barely recognized.*

"Weddings are boringly predictable, I find. So full of empty promises."

"Love, fidelity, and other lies," I add, ignoring the impulse to rub the sudden ache in my chest.

"I'm sure your guests will say it's the most entertaining ceremony they've ever attended."

My stomach turns uneasily. "I guess if they're talking about me, they're leaving some other unfortunate alone." Despite my blasé tone, it's not a position I relish.

"If they're talking about you," he says, suddenly lifting my chin, "it's because they aren't half as interesting."

"I'm not sure about that." I find myself blinking into those mesmerizing eyes. "But thank you. For not leaving me on the sidewalk, at least."

"It was my pleasure." I feel the loss of his fingers immediately. "Now that we've established you're not bound for a lunatic asylum, where would you like to go?"

"You can drop me off the end of the earth," I whisper at the sinking realization that I hadn't planned this far ahead. Not just for what happened earlier, but also for my original expectation—my so-called happily ever after.

Had I anticipated something like this?

I loved being with Mitch, but when I accepted his proposal—a cute but unoriginal giant cookie iced with the words *Marry me?* on Valentine's Day—I knew in my heart things had already started to change. I told myself it wasn't that he was emotionally uninvested but that he just wasn't the type to talk about his feelings. Now I see he just didn't have any.

As for me, I'm sorry to find my mother was right. I mean, she was way off about a lot of things, but I think I wanted this wedding more than I should have. I wanted to be right, maybe more than I wanted to be with him. Because, look at me. I'm so angry right now, and not even a little heartsick!

"Oh, my gosh," I whisper, sliding my hands to my cheeks. "I'm a frog. A frickin' frog." It's an unnerving realization because, like the proverbial frog, I've been stewing in a pot of my own wedding apathy for months.

Unaware of this—the ickiest of eureka moments—my reluctant hero gives my shoulder a friendly shake. "I think you mean you've been kissing one. I haven't heard you ribbit once."

I laugh and force back a prickle of tears. Kindness might be what I need, but it's also what I can't afford.

"You do realize you've just saved yourself years of trouble? Isn't it better to find out what kind of man he is before the wedding?"

"It would've been even better to have found out last week before I gave up my lease and moved into his apartment."

"Ah."

"Try *arghhh!*" As the enormity of my situation hits me, I fall forward and bury my face into my hands. I don't love him—maybe I never loved him—but I deserve better than this. "Pockets! Why the hell didn't I choose a dress with pockets?"

"Do you need a handkerchief?"

I spring up again, his eyebrows joining me in the motion. "I'm not going to cry over that asshole! If I had pockets, I would've filled them with rocks. Then when I threw my vows at him, I would've hurt more than his pride!"

Okay, so maybe I'm not quite done with anger yet.

"Rocks aren't as final as vehicular manslaughter."

"Do you think I'd get away with it?" I only half joke.

"With a good lawyer we could make it look like an accident."

We. It feels good not to be alone, no matter how temporary. "What did Mitchell do to you?"

"A more interesting question is, How did you *throw* your vows at him?"

"I found out he was cheating before the ceremony," I murmur, ignoring the hot twist in my stomach. "Someone sent me screenshots of some very explicit text message exchanges. So I printed them out, and I read them at the altar instead of my vows." I shrug. "It felt kind of fitting. I might also have balled up the printouts and thrown them at his head."

"Ah, the rocks," he adds, trying to curtail his smile. "What I would've given to have seen his face."

"I probably shouldn't have done it. That's not remorse, by the way. Except for my shortsightedness."

"It sounds to me like something you needed to do."

As a glow rises through me, I tell myself it's the remains of my righteous indignation rather than about the way he's looking at me. "You're right, and I do feel kind of vindicated. If I'd called off the wedding before the ceremony, it would've saved us both the embarrassment, but then he would've gotten off scot-free."

"Not completely," he adds softly. "In either circumstance, he loses you."

"He should've thought about that before he screwed my maid of honor," I answer, the glow taking on a heated edge.

15

"A double betrayal."

"More like a betrayal and a half. She was a stand-in, but I thought she was my friend." My brow creases as I process the truth in this. "Not an old friend, but I guess it now makes sense why that asshole was so keen on us hanging out."

I met Mitch on vacation two years ago. Though, more accurately, I was working and traveling. I'd been living that way almost since graduating from college. We'd been doing the long-distance thing when he proposed, and I'd loved London instantly. I knew no one in the city but Riley and was so glad Mitch was happy to share his friends.

I just didn't know how far the sharing went.

"My maid of honor was more my *male* of honor. Riley is my oldest friend, but he broke his leg last week in a nasty rock-climbing accident in France. If he had been here . . ." *At least it wouldn't have been him Mitch was fucking.* "You know, it was only when I stepped out into the aisle that I noticed how small our wedding was. How few of the guests were my real friends. That's weird, right?" I don't wait for his response, especially as it might include pushing me out of a moving car. "I told myself it was because it was such short notice—my visa conditions meant we had to be married quickly." *Within six months.* "That I couldn't expect my real friends to travel. But the truth is, I never invited them. I half assed my own wedding. Can you believe that?"

"Hindsight is a wonderful thing," he murmurs.

"I guess the silver lining is there were less people to witness the travesty." I blow out an unsteady breath. "I wish Riley was here."

"What would he do for you?"

"Get me drunk. Let me vent. Help me plot Mitch's death." The enormity of my situation hits me in a heavy wave. "Be here for me, because, right now, I don't have . . ." *Anyone to turn to.* ". . . my phone or my wallet or anywhere to go. I don't even have shoes!"

My eyes sting as I hold out my feet and stare down at pink painted toes sheathed in grubby silk stockings. "All I have is this damn dress and veil, and a thousand dollars' worth of lingerie!" I cry, throwing up my hands. Then I cringe. Boy, do I cringe. "Forget I said that."

"I don't think I will."

"Try. Please."

"You've already established I'm not chivalrous. However, if you'd like to know if you overpaid, I'd happily offer my opinion."

"Good try," I say with a soft chuckle. "You know, contrary to popular opinion, women don't buy underwear to please men."

"Not even for their wedding night?"

"You're still not looking."

"My offer stands. Meanwhile, perhaps I can stand in for your best friend."

"How do you mean?" I turn to face him.

"I could do what Riley would do for you."

"I think I've inconvenienced you enough." I'm desperate, not a charity case. Or maybe what I am is a desperate charity case. "You said yourself, you would've left me on the sidewalk five minutes ago."

"That was before we were friends." His tone suddenly turns velvety.

"Friends." I sound less convinced. "Well, Riley would supply alcohol."

"We'll toast to your close escape."

"And hold my hair when I vomit."

"I think I might make a more responsible friend than Riley," he answers with another wintry twist of his lips.

"How can we be friends when I don't even know your name?"

"Oliver Deubel." He holds out his hand.

"The fourth?" I blurt out.

"There's only one of me."

"Right. Good. Evelyn Fairfax. Evie to my friends."

"Also to your ex-fiancé." His thumb slides over my knuckle, and I force back a shiver. "I'm pleased to make your acquaintance, Evelyn." Something in his delivery seems to dare me to protest, but I can't muster a retort, his gaze licking at my insides like a flame. "I should probably warn you, I make a terrible friend."

Chapter 3
OLIVER

"Welcome back, Mr. Deubel." The doorman bids us welcome with a wide smile as he pulls on the door.

"George." I incline my head, pressing my hand to the small of Evelyn's back as I steer her into a darkened interior. She'd removed her veil in the car, leaving her neck and the graceful slope of her sun-kissed shoulders bare. As if her silky-looking skin wasn't temptation enough, she has a tiny beauty spot partly obscured by the lace of her dress. It makes me wonder what other treasures her dress is hiding.

Like that thousand dollars' worth of underwear.

Was her reveal accidental or a blatant come-on? I force my head from her underwear. I'm not going there, figuratively or . . .

"Looks fancy," she whispers over her shoulder.

Ignoring darker impulses, I take the opportunity and press my lips next to her ear. "At least we won't have a problem with the dress code."

She looks so delicate. So small. She'd look so delightful riding my cock.

Or not.

"There's a dress code?" Her lashes flutter as though disconcerted by the news rather than the shiver that ripples through her at my tone.

"Yes." My answer makes the tiny, escaped curl at her temple dance. I curl my hand into a fist to stop myself from touching it. It's an automatic reaction, I tell myself. A small pleasure. Damsels in distress are not my thing, especially ones foolish enough to be taken in by Atherton. "No denim, no canvas, no shorts or T-shirts, nothing outlandish."

"Because wearing a wedding gown for no reason isn't at all over the top?" The corner of her mouth tilts before she looks away again.

"It's better to be overdressed than under. In most situations." The latter I add in an undertone, surprised to find myself imagining the fiancée of Mitchell Atherton naked.

Former fiancée, my mind unhelpfully supplies.

How the hell did he capture such loveliness? Curves in all the right places, luxuriant strawberry blonde hair, and soulful brown eyes that, in a blink, can burn like gold-flecked flames. I push the images away. I'm not interested in my nemesis's sloppy seconds.

We pass the club steward who, like the doorman, is wearing a curiously wide grin. How strange. While always pleasant, the staff at my club aren't given to an excess of happiness. *This isn't Disneyland.*

"Most situations?" my companion teases.

"It wouldn't do to visit the beach in a three-piece suit."

"I think you could probably get away with it." She slides me an appreciative look. "I'm almost offended by how good you look given I'm the one in the fancy dress."

A surprised bark of laughter bursts from my chest. *That* was a little more obvious. What a pity she's not for me.

"Just don't let the staff know you're not wearing shoes, or we'll be shown the door."

"Something tells me they wouldn't dare." True, but I don't say so. "What is this place?" she whispers as I steer her into the lounge, where dust motes dance in the sunlight. For the first time, I notice how the smell of whisky and old books overlays the scent of beeswax polish. At least the place isn't busy at this hour.

"It's my club." I indicate seats in the bay window overlooking leafy Saint James's Street.

"You mean, like a gentleman's club?"

"They prefer *private members' establishment*."

She glances around, taking in the Adam's era fireplace and the dark paneled walls hung with portraits of long-dead members and frowns at a bronze bust.

"That's a Samuel Joseph, I believe."

"It looks like something from Harry Potter," she says, sitting in one of the pair of oxblood leather chairs I indicate. "Or maybe a museum."

"It is often full of old relics."

"More original than poles."

I pause. "Poles?"

"The kind with half-naked women swinging around them."

"Ah."

"Ah." Her mouth turns up at the corners, her lips pink and lush in between. "Do you have membership to one of those clubs too?"

"I might've walked past a place like that once or twice."

"Only past? Don't worry, I won't tell."

"Who'd be interested?"

"Me." She lifts her palm upward, a shrug of sorts. "Because then I wouldn't be the only one embarrassing myself today."

"You've nothing to be embarrassed about."

"Debatable." Her nose wrinkles. She has the most animated face. Odd that it seems to add to her beauty, not detract from it.

"If there's anyone who ought to feel shame, it isn't you."

21

"When my future holds so many mornings of waking up, seeing your face, and reliving the whole undignified moment again?"

"It's going to be that kind of friendship?"

"I mean, who just climbs into a stranger's car?" she blusters on, her cheeks flushing pink. "You didn't even have candy or kittens!"

"Just enticing lashes."

"Not helping," she groans, pressing her hand to her forehead.

"If it's all the same to you, I'll remember the experience differently. You're the most interesting thing that's fallen into my lap this year."

"Don't be nice to me, Oliver. I'm still running on rage and adrenaline. I can't believe I threw my beautiful shoes into a bush!"

"I'm a firm believer in forgiving those who've wronged us." Her eyes flash gold as they cut to me. "But not until we've evened the score."

"For a minute, I thought I wasn't going to like you."

"You already do like me, Evelyn."

"What I don't like is being called *Evelyn*." Lowering her tone, she draws out the sound of her name.

"That is not how I sound." I smile, unable to help myself.

"Isn't it?"

"Not, *Evelyn*. It is not," I say, dropping my tone a little more.

"Everyone calls me Evie." She adorably scrunches her nose. "Only my mother calls me Evelyn."

"When you're in trouble?"

"Oh, I'm always in trouble with Muffy." As she answers, she rolls her eyes.

"Muffy?" I turn to a harrumph and the sound of crushed paper, Viscount Radler slicing me an unhappy glance over his now-crumpled copy of the *Times*. As I turn back, I find Evelyn leaning closer, as though she has a secret to share. I resist the impulse to meet her halfway.

"Does that man have muttonchops?" she whispers, delighted.

"Possibly." Whereas *this* man has the urge to push his hands into her hair and pluck out the pins to watch it curl around her bare shoulders. It's good that she sits back. "He's here so often, he's almost part of the furniture."

"I bet you're wondering why she didn't help me today. My mother, I mean."

I make a noncommittal sound, which is better than admitting the truth. I don't care.

"London is a long way from Connecticut, but so is across the street when you're marrying the wrong man." With the reluctant reveal, she turns her attention to the window, offering me her profile. Her upturned nose and the way the light hits her evoke the look of another era.

"A mother's intuition," I venture. *A pity she hadn't shared it, because Mitchell Atherton is a grade A prick.*

"Her objection wasn't personal. They'd never met. Just as well, I guess," she adds with a sly grin. "Hadley women never do anything as lowbrow as cause a scene."

"Apparently, most Hadley women don't know what they're missing."

"Fond of making an ass of yourself, are you?" Both skepticism and a smile leak into her words.

"Fond, no. But it has happened." And I have her bastard of an ex to thank for that.

"It's no surprise I'm living on this side of the pond. My parents are so . . . emotionally constipated. Meanwhile, *I* seem to be suffering from the opposite of that affliction." She presses her hands to her face as her shoulders begin to shake.

"Eve?" Her name springs from my lips. *Eve*, not *Evelyn* and certainly not *Evie*. I like it. It feels appropriate.

"Oh, man." As she sits up, I realize she's not crying but laughing. "And I thought I was done embarrassing myself today."

"Where is George?" I glance in the direction of the door.

"George was the doorman, right?"

"Yes, but I meant George the waiter. He's not usually so slow."

"Wait." She cants her head to one side. "The waiter and the doorman are both called George?"

"Everyone who works here is referred to as George. They answer to the name for convenience."

"Theirs or yours?"

"I imagine that could run both ways. It's a tradition. Nothing else."

"What about the women? Are they called George too?" she asks, unimpressed.

"Georgina." I stick to a one-word answer. Better I don't mention that women, both as guests and as employees, are a relatively new concept here.

"Who would've thought there was somewhere more elitist than the country club," she mutters flatly.

"I don't make the rules. I just follow them." When I feel like it. "The men of my family have been members of this place for generations, and while it wouldn't be at the top of my list of places to take a guest, I thought it might be the place that would provoke the least attention." My gaze dips briefly to her gown, and she doesn't miss my meaning, that rush of heat burning up her pale throat again.

"You're right, that was rude. I'm not usually so—"

"Fractious," I offer at the same time as she adds, "Crotchety."

"Good afternoon, Mr. Deubel." George the waiter appears, as silent as a wraith. A widely smiling wraith.

"Ah, George. Would you mind answering a question for me?"

"Not at all, but I think I can preempt it by saying steak-and-kidney pudding—and honestly, I wouldn't. There's also wild duck with an orange *jus*, which is"—he presses his gathered fingers to his lips.

"Chef's kiss," Eve supplies.

"Exactly!" He turns a smile her way.

"Thank you, George, but my question wasn't about the menu. I was wondering if you mind being referred to as George while you're at work." A pointless question. Of course he'll say it's not an issue. But if it makes Eve feel better . . .

"It's better than being called Cyril."

"Was that the other choice?" Eve asks.

"No, that's my actual name. Unfortunately."

"Oh, well, you don't look like a Cyril," she soothes.

"That's because I've got all my own teeth." The thirtysomething gives a resigned shrug. "I was named after my grandfather." He takes a deep breath before beginning again. "On behalf of the establishment, may I offer you both my congratulations?" He beams Evelyn's way, but she's already shaking her head.

"Oh, but we're—"

"Keeping it to ourselves for the time being," I interject. "And thank you, George. That's very kind of you. We can count on your discretion, of course."

"Of course," he agrees, puffing his chest out. "You'll want champagne?"

Eve's eyes dart my way. "That is . . ."

"An excellent suggestion."

"I have just the thing," he announces before bustling off again.

"The smiles begin to make sense," I murmur, plucking an imaginary piece of lint from my trouser leg. A woman in a wedding dress? Of course that must mean I've gotten hitched! As if I'd bring my bride for a pint and a cheese-and-pickle sandwich to celebrate. As if I'd ever shown interest in tying myself to one woman.

When I glance up, I find Eve looking at me, doing her inquisitive-terrier impersonation again. "Why did you tell him we're married?"

"Did I? I thought I just went along with his assumption."

"Yeah, but why?" she asks, lowering her voice to a whisper.

"I didn't want to cause you any more discomfort." It's a simple explanation but one I find, on reflection, is true. I acted on instinct rather than with any kind of ulterior motive. I did it because I find I want to make her day a little better. Or at least, not any worse. How uncharacteristic of me. I suppose everyone has an off day now and again.

"Well, thank you." She presses back into the seat, and I watch as her teeth begin to worry at her lip. "What happens next time you're here and they ask how your wife is?"

I glance the viscount's way. "I'll just pull that face. He's been married for fifty years and has spent forty-nine of them in here hiding from his wife. I can get away with the ruse for at least that long."

She gives a tiny shake of her head.

"You don't believe me?"

"I was just thinking how, less than an hour ago, you were going to ditch me. Now look at me, your sham bride."

"I told you—you're the most interesting thing that's fallen into my lap this year."

"As opposed to the kind of lap action available in those other gentleman's clubs?"

Desire tightens my skin. Eve in my lap would be something. She'd be hypnotic, my hands on her hips, encouraging her gentle rhythm. Mouths sliding, skin slipping against skin. The insight is blissful and short as I blink. Atherton's ex should not interest me. "That's not my style."

26

She doesn't answer for a beat, though she studies me. Which suits me fine. It allows me to reciprocate.

"Why are you being so nice?" she asks.

"Curiosity probably." There is bound to be some use in it for me.

"Are you hoping to get back at Mitchell by fucking me?"

"Are you?" I volley back, ignoring the flare of heat in my gut.

"What did he do to you?"

"Let's just say as well as understanding why you'd leave him at the altar, I'm also coming to understand why he'd chase you."

"Flattery?"

"Honesty." Even I hear the note of alarm in my answer.

"Honesty is entry-level human behavior, Oliver."

"In the quest for the truth, then. Allowing George to misunderstand wasn't a purely noble gesture. I find there's still a thousand dollars' worth of reasons lurking at the back of my mind."

She gives a delightfully dirty laugh. "Lurking, huh? Well, try not to dwell *too* long."

"Where's the fun in that?"

"Might it help to know I recently considered neutering my ex-fiancé?"

I press my elbow to the arm of the chair and my chin to my fist. "You know, I think I might be perverse."

This time, it's Eve's hearty laughter that disturbs the viscount.

"You know you can take that." Her eyes sparkle over the top of her old-fashioned champagne saucer as I ignore the incessant buzzing of my phone.

"I don't want to."

"That's clear." She sets the glass down. "It's been ringing on and off since we got here."

"You're right. I should just turn it off completely." I slip my hand into my jacket pocket, pulling out my phone.

"That's not what I meant. I don't want to completely hijack your day." Despite three glasses of champagne, she looks genuinely distressed at the prospect.

"Hijack away," I say, powering down my phone, though not before I see a text from my business partner, Fin.

Did you hear about Mitchell Atherton? The fucker got dumped at the altar earlier today.

It's not even the most remarkable thing about the situation, because how in the hell did he land a woman like this? She's attractive, funny, and doesn't seem at all stupid. There must be something I'm missing.

"I hope you're not missing anything important because of me."

"Nothing that can't wait. You were telling me what happened to the poodle." Mitchell is a dog. Perhaps that's the connection, given Eve is a veterinarian.

"Weird, I thought you were telling me what my ex did to earn your hate."

I raise my foot to my opposite knee. "Hate is such a strong word."

"Your feelings aren't strong?"

Weapons-grade titanium hate, not that I'll say so. "Do I look enraged to you?"

Her gaze falls over me with the invitation, and pleasure surges through me.

"You think I'm projecting," she says, reaching for her glass. As she sets it to her lips, sunlight turns the bubbles the color of her hair.

"It wouldn't be without good reason."

She gives her head the tiniest shake. "Except when I mention his name, your jaw tenses and you get a tiny twitch here." She taps a fingertip to the corner of her eye.

"A twitch? I don't think so." My denial is all drawl and no substance. I won't allow that arsehole to get under my skin. I satisfy myself with the knowledge that I'm a patient man. He'll get what's coming to him eventually.

"Fine, you don't have a twitch," she replies without an ounce of conviction. "Maybe I should have one, given my imminent future might include deportation."

"We don't deport people for throwing balls of paper in wedding ceremonies."

"No, but you do for being here on the wrong visa." With the stem between her fingers, she twists her glass this way and that, her words almost absently delivered. "I've got to get married to stay here. Don't worry, that wasn't a proposal."

"I'm relieved," I murmur as I give in to a half smile.

"I'm here on a spousal visa." She shrugs. "A spousal visa without . . ." *A spouse.* She sets down her glass as though the summary means nothing to her. I make a sympathetic noise, not having a suitable answer. "But the upside of that," she adds, relaxing back in her chair, "is that I'm free to do what I want on my nonexistent wedding night."

The way her eyes skate over me makes it almost impossible to miss her meaning. It's not a question of *what* she's free to do, but *whom.*

It was brazen, and I like it. I like her.

But I'm not going to fuck her.

Am I?

Chapter 4
EVIE

"Thank you." There's an undeniable zing of electricity between our fingers as I hand him back his phone.

"Did it help?" Cool blue eyes match his tone, but I know he noticed as he slides his phone back into his pocket, keeping his gaze deliberately from mine.

"Yes. Riley replied." I might not remember anyone's phone number, but I've had the same email address and password since I was thirteen. "The spare key will be under the planter by the front door tomorrow morning. I'm just sorry I couldn't arrange it before." His roommate, Lori, is away for the weekend. Just as well, as she doesn't like me. It also means I'll get to raid her closet. Miss Havisham is not a look to cultivate.

"It's not a problem—the hotel is nearby." A gentle breeze ruffles Oliver's hair, the summer sun still hanging in the evening sky, shimmering through the leaves to make a lacy pattern on his jacket. His lips look too soft for that face of chiseled granite. Another of Mother Nature's jokes, I guess. *I'll make him so good looking, he seems untouchable, but I'll give him lips made for kissing. Licking. Biting.*

What is going on in my head today? Champagne usually gives me a headache, not make me desperately horny.

"Do people really do that?"

"Um." I roll my lips inward, not sure of the answer. I saw the shapes his pretty mouth made, but that was the limit of my attention. *Hot. Horny. Keys. Plant pot?* Ah! "Sure." I paste on a bright smile. "You've never done that?"

"I can't say I have."

"You sure you're a property developer?" I give my head a slow shake. "I thought it was standard practice to leave the contractor a key under a pot or a doormat."

"Perhaps London is different than Connecticut."

They sure breed the men a little differently here. Maybe the weather makes for broodier types. "Well, Riley better find a way, or I'll be sleeping on the streets from tomorrow." Another strange entry on my wedding bingo card. Honeymooning in the Maldives or sleeping in the doorway of Zara?

"I'm sure it won't come to that."

"Not once I get my purse back." *My credit cards, my phone, my clothes.* My mental list goes on. *Pack my bags. Face him who shall not be named. Avoid going to jail for murder.*

"Would you like some help?"

"With Mitchell?" I shake my head. Maybe he'd like to dig the hole. "No, thank you." My next undignified performance will happen without an audience.

"He seemed . . . very insistent."

"Probably his ego," I add briskly. "I'm not a violent woman, but I've found I can be inspired to violence."

"Oh, I'm very sure you can take care of yourself."

I like that he said so, whether he means it or not.

"Well, I appreciate you letting me take advantage of our new friendship." *I'd appreciate it if you let me take advantage of your body too.*

Considering the many things I have to worry about, flirting with Oliver should not be at the top of my list. It's fun though. The man is very good at it.

"A friend in need," he answers prosaically.

"Is a pain in the ass indeed!"

He laughs, throwing back his head to expose the strong line of his throat and the masculine rise of his Adam's apple. A ripple of *yes please!* washes through me.

"What?"

I give my head a tiny shake in the face of his curious expression. "Huh?"

"You're looking at me strangely."

Try thirstily, friend. Is it him? Is it the champagne? Is it because I don't want yesterday's wax to go to waste? I am currently as smooth as a dolphin from the brows down, and it was *not* a joyous experience.

"I was just thinking." Lusting. Wondering if you're my gift from the universe. *I deserve one, don't I?* "Oh, ow!" I step on a stone—stupid me, I'd been so careful all this way not to—then stumble over the hem of my dress. I don't fall though, as Oliver reaches out to grasp my arm.

"You should've eaten more." Concern pinches his brows as he pulls me against him, brushing my hair from my face.

"It was a stone," I protest laughingly, taking the opportunity to touch him up. I mean, straighten his lapels. "If you add a steak dinner to all that champagne, I might get the wrong idea, *friend.*"

"And what idea would that be?"

"That I might need to sell a kidney to pay you back."

He chuckles as the late-setting summer sun crowns his dark head in a halo of bronze. Something shifts inside me, something with heat and substance, the suddenness of it robbing me of my breath. If men can be beautiful, Oliver Deubel is the epitome of the ideal. Tall, dark, and more than handsome, he wears a suit like it's a lethal weapon, and I am *so* attracted to him.

Mitchell is lower than a rat for what he's done, but this isn't one bit about him. When I look at Oliver, I get this awful yet heavenly twist deep inside. I can almost taste his kisses—anticipate the experience. But if I make a move, would that look like I'm pursuing pity sex? I'd rather Oliver rail me good and hard as a way of getting back at Mitchell. On some level, wouldn't I be doing the same?

"Eve?"

I find myself blinking heavily. "Sorry, I was miles away."

"Anywhere nice?" His words end in a provocative curl. "Judging by your expression . . ."

"This is just my thinking face." *It's good you can't see into my head, because I was imagining how incredible you'd look naked.* "Maybe I shouldn't have had that last glass of champagne."

"Or you should've eaten more," he says again.

"Like I said, I stood on a stone and tripped over my stupid dress."

"It isn't stupid. I'm sure I'm not the first person today to say you look very beautiful."

My insides suddenly feel like they're filled with Pop Rocks. I dip my head to hide my delight. Wait—does he think I was fishing for compliments? I wasn't, but I'm very happy to land them.

"Give a girl a fancy dress." Lace whispers as I swish the skirt, and his shiny oxfords appear in my line of vision.

"Accept the compliment in the vein it was given." His voice is soft as his finger finds my chin.

"I never learned how," I whisper. Compliments make me feel uncomfortable.

"We'll practice. You're perfect. Right here in this moment. It's easy, see?"

Perfect is an ideal I've never sought, but my body enjoys its resonance as he cups the side of my neck.

"Now thank me. Say it like you mean it."

If his compliments resonate, his demands detonate, heat pulsing through me in their wake.

"Thank you," I whisper, coy suddenly.

"Thanks may be shown as well as spoken." His thumb is a sweet hint that slides across my lips.

I wrap my fingers in his lapels and rise to my toes, brushing my lips against his. "Thank you, Oliver. For everything."

"You're welcome, beautiful Eve."

"And you really do have the loveliest lashes I've ever seen." I move my hands across his superhero chest to flatten his lapels. *Allegedly.* "Even if you don't follow your own rules."

"I didn't accept the compliment gracefully, did I?"

"As I recall, you didn't accept it at all."

"Lift your head. Look at me." His words are a purred command, one I find impossible to resist. "Thank you for the compliment, Eve." He leans in, his husky words a bare breath across my lips. "The accolade just took me by surprise." The second meeting of our lips is no brush. His kiss is warm and unhurried, but all too soon, he pulls back. "How was that?"

"Nice." My voice sounds rusty. I lick my tingling lips. Oliver's eyes darken as he watches me taste his kiss.

"Then I mustn't have thanked you properly."

The sounds of the street fall away as our mouths meet again. His body comes up against mine, his tongue licking lushly into me, his fingers quick and clever as they work down my spine. I ball my hand in the back of his shirt, willing it to disintegrate, my hearing reduced to the pulse of my blood as time stands still, and space becomes irrelevant, as—

"Get a bridal suite!" A yell from a passing car. Cackling, distant laughter.

I make to pull away, but the way Oliver cradles the back of my head prevents me. *Makes me feel protected.*

"A little more inventive than 'Get a room,' I guess." I bite the inside of my lip. Did that sound like a hint?

"Idiots," he mutters without venom.

"We were kind of going for it."

He takes my face in his hands, his thumbs gliding across my cheeks. "I've wanted to kiss you for hours, no matter how inappropriate the notion."

"We get to make our own boundaries."

"And I just straddled mine."

"So I guess inviting you up for a drink would be a waste of time." I sound unimpressed and feel like he just poured cold water all over our vibe.

"Beautiful Eve," he groans. "Please don't make this any harder."

Oh, I could. I could make it so much harder. "It doesn't have to mean anything."

His head lifts, his eyes scanning the street behind me. "How can it not, after the day you've had? I don't want to be someone you look back on and regret."

"Don't humor me, Oliver." The early evening is cool, yet my skin burns. "I'm not some damaged damsel in need of protection."

"Good, because I'm not the hero type."

"So, if you want me and I want you—"

"It's the nature of regret," he says, cutting me off. "It happens after the fact. Haven't you been through enough today?"

35

The burst of laughter that spills from my lips sounds like it belongs to someone else. "You don't have to make excuses." I pull away until his strong fingers curl around my forearm, his grip firm.

"This isn't just about you. I want you—I want to fuck you so well, you'll cry out my name. But I won't be the instrument of your revenge. If you're in my bed, you're there for me alone."

He might have had the last word, but we're not done here.

We turn into a street of Georgian town houses, their stuccoed frontages tall, formal, and as white as wedding cake, their window boxes brimming with colorful begonias.

"This is it." Oliver, my amiable companion, lifts our clasped hands as his pointed finger indicates our destination. A boutique hotel.

Holding hands is okay. Kissing too. But sex is out of the question. We'll see.

I'm impulsive, but I've never been the type for one-night stands. I'm determined. Obstinate, I guess. I also know I'm not for everyone, but Oliver is into me, and I'm not trying to put a Band-Aid over my horror of a day.

We're still holding hands, and I'm still pondering *how* as we approach the entrance, and my pace slows when the thoughts I've been trying to arrange manifest themselves into words.

"Hey."

He turns as I tug on his hand, his expression guarded.

"I just want to say thank you for today. I will pay you back for all this." I give a vague wave to the hotel. "I also wanted to say what you said earlier about regrets, it cuts both ways. When you walk away this evening, you'll regret this. You'll regret me."

He frowns, reaching to rub his right eyebrow. His answer, when it comes, seems almost reluctant. "Yes, that's very likely."

"And when I close the door to my hotel room tonight, I can choose both how I feel and how I want to spend my night. I can ride the roller coaster of the betrayed, tap into all that embarrassment and foolishness and make myself feel sick to my stomach. I might hit the minibar, then cry myself to sleep—choices that are guaranteed to come with regrets.

"But what I'll never regret is good company. That's not to say I don't understand. Today has been tainted by Mitchell for us both. And I'm sorry for that. I'd liked to have met you under different circumstances is what I'm trying to say."

I don't wait for his response as I turn away. I'm not done, but I'm not about to announce my intentions in the middle of this leafy London street. Instead, I smile at the doorman as he bids me good evening, and I step inside.

The hotel is much larger than the outside suggests, the interior stylish, moody, and masculine. Vintage chandeliers, parlor palms, and vermilion velvet walls; it's all very bohemian, Roaring Twenties style.

At the desk, Oliver is greeted by name by a stunning brunette, her winged eyeliner both subtle and perfect.

"Good evening, Mr. Deubel."

"Natalia, good evening."

"Your usual suite?" Her gaze darts my way, the split-second glance taking in my dress and my hair. I can't make out if she's more perceptive than the multiple Georges or she knows Oliver better than I'd appreciate. I begin to wonder, *Have these two . . .* and if so, *What has she got that I haven't?* Apart from perfectly winged liner, I guess.

Maybe the question should be, What have I got that she doesn't? *A white dress, obviously. And a connection to someone he clearly hates.*

"That would be wonderful, Natalia."

"Just for the night," I interject. As Natalia's gaze drops to her keyboard, I regret her assumption. And her red cheeks.

"That's not what I meant," I mutter, ignoring Oliver's low chuckle of amusement. I was thinking about how expensive a night here might be. I have a good job and a decent income, but I'm also newly homeless, and God only knows what I'm going to do about my visa. How do you stay in the country on a spousal visa without a spouse? Maybe I can get the clinic to sponsor me, though I'm pretty sure that means I'll have to go home in the meantime. There must be a way. Nothing is insurmountable if you set your mind to it. Like my man here. He's totally *mountable*, given a little time and persuasion.

As Natalia continues to type away, I file all those worries away for Future Evie as I find myself wondering why a man who said he lives in London has a *regular hotel suite*. For regular assignations? He probably gets more ass than a toilet seat.

"Enjoy your evening." Natalia's smile is nothing but professional as she moves a key card wallet across the gleaming desk, but I still can't help but wonder. Has Natalia experienced Oliver's kisses? *The kind of kisses that make a girl swoon and want things she wouldn't ordinarily?*

Oliver turns, pressing the key into my hand.

"Add this to my tab," I say, tapping it to his chest.

"There really is no need." His smile is measured, the space between us deliberate, but his stiff upper lip tasted too good to ignore.

"Friends pay their debts, Oliver, and I really can't thank you enough—"

"Careful." Heat pulses through me at his silky delivery.

"Always."

The glint in his eye seems almost wicked, and we stare at each other for several long, loaded beats.

"You know it's not because I don't want you."

That was not what I hoped he'd say. I don't answer because I don't accept his rejection.

"Let me walk you to the lift."

"Why thank you, kind sir." I press the backs of my fingers under my chin, my accent turning ridiculous and southern. "Because I surely couldn't find the *elevator* on my own." In for a dollar, in for a dime, I give my lashes an exaggerated flutter.

With a lopsided half smile, he offers me his elbow. "Come along, Scarlett."

I slant him a confused look. Is Scarlett the usual reason for his hotel suite?

"O'Hara? I thought that was who you were trying to impersonate."

"You would make a terrible Rhett," I reply, sliding my arm through his.

"True. I don't have the ears for it."

We pass the hotel bar, which looks like the kind of place you'd find red-lipped starlets drinking dirty martinis.

"Looks fancy," I say. "But do you think I might be overdressed?"

He frowns and looks like he's about to say something when the universe intervenes and his phone vibrates with a text.

"You should get that," I say, stepping ahead to the elevators. A group of men stands in front of the doors. One of them slides me a cursory look over his shoulder, then does a double take. And suddenly I have a plan.

"Don't worry, the hotel isn't holding a wedding," I offer with a pleasant smile. "At least, not mine."

39

"Sorry?"

"You won't be kept awake by a cut-rate Céline Dion, I mean."

"I like a bit of Céline myself." His eyes follow my fingers as I slip the key to my room into the top of my dress. His mouth kicks up in one corner. Something tells me I've captured the attention of the cocky one of the pack.

"You struck me as someone with different tastes."

Welcome to flirty level one: I might be interested.

"Did I?" He turns to face me, sliding his hands into the pockets of his pants. "You didn't get married here, then?"

I give a soft laugh. "I didn't get married at all. I mean, that was the plan, but . . ." Cue a hesitant smile and a coy shrug.

Level two: we've established I'm single.

"What happened?" His gaze moves over me, taking particular note of where I've stashed my key.

"A slight miscalculation," I say holding my thumb and index finger almost together. "Turns out, he's been banging someone else."

Level three: I might just be up for it.

"No fuckin' way!" His eyes almost fall out of his head as his companions exchange a look, their ears straining to listen in to the conversation.

"That was pretty much my reaction." I sigh, in kind of an *Oh, well. Who needs a groom when you're this cute?* way.

"But you're gorgeous!" There goes his wandering gaze again.

Level four: he's pretty much confirmed he'd like to see me naked.

"That's sweet of you to say so." I push an artfully curled lock of hair behind my ear, shivering as I anticipate Oliver's presence behind me.

"What are you gonna do now?"

Here we teeter on level five: making plans.

"I haven't decided," I say, pondering. *Ponder lonely as a cloud.* I almost snicker. Wordsworth I am not. "My choices are run a bath, have a long soak and a drink or five. Or hit the bar and let my hair down."

"The bar, definitely," he asserts, grabbing the opportunity with both hands as the doors to the elevator slide open. "And as an apology on behalf of my gender, your drinks are on me."

"That won't be necessary," Oliver answers for me. His voice sounds like it should come with a yellow warning label. *Caution. Volatile when under pressure.*

"This is Oliver," I offer as his fingers curl possessively around my hip.

The man frowns.

"He's not staying."

"Gav. You coming?" one of the group calls from the open elevator.

Poor Gav. So conflicted. And Oliver? I can practically feel the heat of him simmering.

"I'll see you in the bar?" Despite the question in his tone, Gav isn't giving up hope.

"Maybe you will," I say.

He steps into the waiting car with the kind of swagger that would've dissolved my guilt, had I been feeling any. "Room for a little one," he offers suggestively as he turns.

"We'll wait." Oliver's grip tightens, his words dripping with a frightening civility.

My stomach turns over with excitement.

Well, look at that. Game on.

Chapter 5
OLIVER

"You're quite proud of yourself, aren't you?"

She smells like gardenia and secrets, yet she looks like butter wouldn't melt in her mouth. *I know she'll melt under mine.*

"I don't know what you mean."

"I need a drink," I mutter. Lie. What I need but shouldn't is my mouth on her pussy.

"So you'll be in the bar too?" She turns to me, her face a beautiful, blank mask. *A ruse.*

"A drink might help me appreciate your brand of humor."

"Who's joking?" she says, twisting away from my hand.

"I don't do funny." I find myself straightening my cuffs to stop myself from reaching for her. This infuriating woman needs some sense fucked into her. My mind bends to that image, my heart thumping loudly once in my chest, my throat growing dry as I see myself kissing her, holding her down, fucking her until her cries rock the room. "And I don't do women in wedding dresses."

"I thought it was just this bride you objected to."

"That's not it," I snap. My temper isn't the only thing frayed.

"That's right. You objected to the groom. Like I said, Mitchell *has* tainted the day. My day. This is my way of fixing it."

"Whatever can you mean?" I find myself drawling.

"Rebound sex." She shoots me a look I can only describe as hostile.

"Of all the asinine . . ."

"Haven't you heard? The best way to get over someone is to get under a new someone else."

"And that's your plan?" My gaze drops over her curves, desire buzzing through me now like electricity without an outlet. "You're going to hang around the bar in your wedding dress?"

"Don't tell me. There's another dress code."

"I'm not sure whether it reeks of desperation or fancy dress." I saunter closer as though I haven't a care in the world, let alone a care for anyone else having her. "Poor Gavin will be surprised when you turn up still wearing this."

"And that's your concern how?"

A good question, because despite my cool tone, the thought makes me feel murderous. Eve is not my responsibility—the fact that she was about to marry my nemesis six hours ago should've been reason enough to leave her at the curb. Instead, I canceled my meetings and set aside my whole day, telling myself I might learn something useful about Atherton. That I might discover a way to ignite the pyre I'm building for him. Instead, the day was an exercise in self-restraint as an invisible force built and twisted between us. A force I acknowledged but intended to ignore. *Even as I kissed her.*

The lift chimes its arrival, and the minx has the temerity to offer me her hand.

"Well, I guess I'll be seeing you."

I should pity her attempt at manipulation. Somehow, it just makes me want her more.

"Yes." My jaw tightens, my balls along with it, as my palm meets her much daintier one. Would she still look at me this way

43

if she knew the depths to which I'd sink to in order to ruin her ex? *You're dancing on a cliff's edge, and I am no savior.*

"Oh!" She makes the tiny exclamation as I tug her into my chest.

"It looks like you'll be seeing quite a bit of me." Crooking a finger beneath her chin, I lift her gaze. "You win, darling." *You also lose, you beautiful, blind fool.*

"Do I?" Her lashes lower, veiling her triumph.

"Unless you'd prefer to spend the night drinking Jägerbombs with *Gav*?"

"You know what I want."

"Whom. Whom you want."

"It's not like I'm taking advantage of your virtue."

"Admit it. To yourself. To me." *Tell me this isn't all my fault.*

"Sheesh, all right." Her gaze lifts, her eyes golden in the light. "I want you. Though God knows why."

"Eve." Ignoring her disclaimer, I make a sigh of her name. "You are a shameless floozy." *And I am sorry you'll come to regret taking this step.*

"I prefer *go-getter*." Her lips twitch, then give in to a grin. "Which would make you . . ."

"Hard to get?" Taking her hand, we make the lift before the doors begin to close again. "I'm certainly part of that sentence, in any event."

I don't reach for her as the doors slide closed. Instead, I watch her trembling hand as she hits the button, then enjoy a ride upward that's silent and anticipation filled. As we step out into the hallway, I push my hands into my pockets and slow my pace, encouraging her to walk ahead.

"I thought you had a *regular* suite." She delivers her taunting words over her shoulder.

"Which suggests what?"

"Well, you're following me like you don't know the way."

"Perhaps I'm just enjoying the view," I purr meaningfully.

Her laughter is girlish and unrestrained, her gait altering, her hips swaying hypnotically. As she reaches the door, she lifts her hand to the neckline of her dress. A whisper of air separates our bodies as I slip my hand over her shoulder and two fingers into the top of her dress.

"Do you have anything else hidden down there?"

"That all depends."

I press a kiss beneath her ear, relishing her tiny gasp. The resulting shiver as I slide the key card out. "On?"

"How nice you are to me."

"Oh, Eve." Wrapping my arms around her waist, I pull her back against me. "I'm not going to be nice to you."

"Oh!" Her answer is little more than a flutter of air as I press my lips to the curve where her neck and shoulder meet.

"Not even a little bit. What's more, you'll thank me for it."

I swipe the key against the reader and turn the handle as Eve gathers her dress and practically shoots inside.

The suite is reasonably sized. Stylish rather than outlandish, a tasteful nod to the 1920s in a palette of cream, gold, and black. A fireplace, a velvet sofa setting, a cherry dining table, and in the next room, if I'm not mistaken, a four-poster bed large enough to hold an orgy in.

As the door clicks closed behind me, I slip off my jacket and drop it onto the sofa.

"How about that drink?" Eve couldn't get much farther away if she tried. She stands by an old-fashioned drinks trolley, her eyes widening as I reach for the buttons on my waistcoat.

"What are you having?" Heart palpitations by the looks of things, but not second thoughts as she watches me slip it off.

"Whisky." Her attention swings away. "I'm having whisky." I bite back a chuckle as her fingers fumble with the heavy decanter stopper and it thuds to the carpeted floor. "Dammit." Pivoting, she drops to scoop it up. If she finds me a little too close as she stands, she doesn't say so.

"Allow me." My forearm glances her waist as I reach for the decanter, tendrils of her perfume a temptation twining its way around me. "Will two fingers satisfy?" I ask silkily, splashing a little into the glasses.

"After the trouble I've taken to get you here?" Her answer is soft and amused, though she can't quite look at me as I press the tumbler into her hand.

"Trouble?"

"I've never worked so h-hard"—she stutters as I arch a brow but valiantly carries on—"to get what I want."

"Let's toast to that." I touch the rim of my glass to hers.

"To working hard?"

Oh, you'll work, darling.

"To getting what you want, and not what you deserve."

We both bring our glasses to our lips, then Eve laughs. "Wait, you think I don't deserve—"

"Sometimes, the key is not to think." Lifting her glass from her hand, I set them both down. She sucks in a sharp breath as I slide my knuckle across the smooth wing of her collarbone. "There's no need to be nervous."

"I'm not."

"It's in the way you tremble." My touch skates across her bare shoulder and down her arm. "And the way you look at me." She's not the only one affected. Desire tightens my belly, muscle sinew taut and aching with the need to seize, to touch, to speed this up. It's been a long time since I've reacted to anyone like this.

"Look at you how?" Her voice is soft as I loop my fingers around her wrist, lifting her hand to the back of my neck. The other follows naturally.

"Like I'm a wolf in the chicken coop."

Her laughter is soft, then stuttering as I span my hands around her ribs. *Touch. Hold. Feel.* I slide them slowly upward.

"And yes, that does mean I am going to eat you." As my thumbs glide over her nipples, her breath hits my lips in a tiny, jagged exhale. "I'm going to put my head between your legs and eat your pussy until the entire floor knows my name."

"Only the floor?" Her voice quivers in a tiny tell I'm sure she'd hate.

"Give me your mouth, lovely Eve."

Soft eyed and expectant, she is slices of sunshine, champagne froth, and creamy lace, but as I press my mouth to hers, I'm reminded of how looks can be deceptive as I experience the darker depths of her. She tastes of whisky, of woman, and of a base desire that meets my own in a sweet yet bitter ache.

"I have a question." My tone husky, I press her body between my hands and my cock, and she arches against me.

"Consent *is* sexy." Her lips fighting the shape of a smile.

"Presumptuous," I playfully admonish with a squeeze of her arse. "After your diligence in getting me here?"

She gives a tiny smirk.

"I was thinking about this underwear of yours."

"What about it?" she purrs, and my cock aches as she stretches against me like a cat. Her breasts, pressed lushly against my chest, almost spill from the top of her dress. My mouth waters. I want to use my tongue to trace the rise and fall of her flesh. Press my teeth into the unblemished flesh. But this isn't going where she thinks it is.

"I wondered if you'd dressed before or after."

47

"I found out? What does it matter?"

"It matters if you dressed for him. Or not."

"And if I was already dressed when I read those texts?"

I tighten my fingers on her arse, and her exhale feels like liquid fire through my veins. "It would mean you dressed for him, and I'd have to insist you take it off. All of it."

Her smile is infectious, her words laughingly expelled. "That *is* where this is going."

"Eventually. You're far too lovely to rush."

Chapter 6
EVIE

"Tell me, Eve." His demanding lips trail my neck, licking and sucking, teeth tantalizing. Pleasure pulses through me as I arch against him, luxuriating in the thickness apparent through my dress.

"I dressed to spite him."

"Are you fucking me to spite him too?"

I take his face in my hands to make certain there can be no mistake. "I've never wanted someone so much that I physically ache. Happy now?"

Oliver's blue eyes burn like twin flames, his arm slipping around my waist to deposit my butt onto the dining table. His palms press either side of my hips, and his deeply masculine purr curls around my ear. "Deliriously."

"So the underwear?" My voice turns smoky at the rasping brush of his dark bristles, twisting the question from casual.

"It stays. For now."

"Dammit." My smile is almost audible. "Isn't it better to be under- than overdressed in this situation?"

His response is a low rumbling laugh. God, he smells so good, like dark spice and whisky and so unforgivingly male. My fingers shake as I reach for his tie and begin to undo the knot. He doesn't object and, if what I felt against me moments ago is any indication, he's as ready for this as I am.

"Though I must admit, I can't wait to see what a thousand dollars can buy."

"Not a lot as it happens." Can he hear the tremble in my voice? Feel it in my fingers as I struggle to coordinate them. "Fabric-wise, anyway."

Schlick. The sound of his tie sliding free from his collar drowns out my tiny, desperate breaths.

"Don't stop there." His voice is velvet and smoke as he catches my hands, pressing them to his chest. "Do the buttons next."

My insides turn molten at his direction, and I begin with the top of that line of tiny hindrances. His breath brushes my lips, and cool air slides around my ankles as he begins to gather my dress up my legs. The lower I move with the buttons, the more my legs are exposed, until his pristine white shirt hangs open and the hem of my dress is laid across my waist.

"Nice." I press my fingers to his chest. Taut pectorals. A smattering of dark hair. I gasp, my hand falling away as he grasps the back of my knee, spreading me wide.

"Fuck." His utterance is like a prayer of thanks as he stares at the triangle of gauzy lace. *All that's left between me and immodesty.*

I want to run my hands over his body, follow that downy trail from his navel like it's a ribbon wrapped around a gift. But Oliver seems content to torment us both as his thumb sweeps over the skin bared above my stocking top.

"Worth every penny." His eyes lift to meet mine.

"I'm pleased you think so." My voice sounds shaky. I feel touch starved. I ache for contact.

"Lovely Eve, the things I am going to do to you." The sensation is almost electric as his thumb slips under the garter. "The things you're going to scream."

50

"Oh, good. I was worried you were polling for suggestions."

"Do I look like I lack imagination?"

I gasp as the garter snaps, his free hand snaking into my hair. It should feel painful, not like a dark kind of pleasure.

"Because I don't." He angles my head to his liking, his tongue swiping my bottom lip.

"Good . . . good to know," I almost moan.

"Better to experience."

Holy heck, his mouth is clever, his lips soft yet commanding as he holds me in place. As he sucks and bites, studying my reactions, watching my breath. I whimper as his mouth slides down my neck, my insides pulsing like I'm about to come on the spot.

"Oh, God."

"You like that," he asserts, shaping the words to my skin.

"If you have to ask . . ." *Then you didn't hear my ovaries explode.*

I tighten my thighs on his hips, pulling him closer, welcoming his tug at my scalp. My hands rove, pulling at his shirt, my nails digging into his skin.

"Will you wriggle this much when I suck on your clit? Should I pin you down while I lick it?"

His words burst inside me, and I bite against a reply of *yes.*

"While I make it shiny and pink."

"You can try," I counter, not sure where the words come from.

"A challenge?" His mouth returns to mine, and struck by a sudden impulse, I suck on his tongue. The husky sound he makes sends a thrill through my bones. I roll my hips, rewarded by a grind of his, the thick press of him sending a wave of pleasure through my insides.

"Harder," I rasp, trying to pull him closer.

"What makes you think I take orders?" The dark note in his reply feels like another wave of pleasure. *Another of my body's demands.*

"I can't tell you what I like?" I goad as I undulate softly against him.

His gaze narrows before his hand drifts to my breast, cupping the weight. His thumb circles my nipple once, twice. It stiffens under the lace, though I refuse to make any sound. Until his fingers firm and he tugs. I gasp. *The reveal of my enjoyment.*

"You were saying?" The look in his eyes could burn down whole buildings.

"Beginner's luck."

"That must be why I can feel you pulsing for me."

My denials are short lived as his hand slips between my legs. My body jolts, and I moan as his thumb massages me over the silk of my panties. "No one likes a show-off."

"Oh, I don't know." There's a concentration to his gaze, a dark intent as he toys with me. As his thumbnail scrapes against the fabric and he swallows my next sound. Feasts on it. "I'd say you like me well enough." His hot words travel up my jaw, and I suck in a sharp breath as his teeth find my earlobe. The rest is lost as his hand slips into my panties. I arch with a cry, my flesh giving so easily to the press of his fingers.

"Seems we're both a little perverse." His tone is all praise as his fingers glide through my arousal. "I've barely touched you, yet you're *so* wet."

My response is a soft whimper as he paints my pleasure to the rise of my clit.

"What was that?" he purrs, circling a light touch. "I didn't quite hear you."

"Don't tease." I fall back on my palms as he fills me with his fingers, the violence of the motion bringing with it such relief that I cry out.

"You're such a good girl for me," he purrs, ignoring me as my body contradicts my complaint. I arch against him, desperate to satisfy the need that wants to twist me inside out. "Look at you, taking my fingers."

Holy Lord. His praise hits some secret pleasure button I didn't know I possessed.

"Sweet, sweet Eve." Slow and rhythmic, his fingers coax and dance. But his gaze is nothing short of predatory. "You make such pretty noises for me."

"I'd be . . . be more into this if you stopped talking." The words rush from me in a broken breath.

His laughter feels like a brush of velvet against my skin, my lie called out by the way I arch against him. "You think I should use my mouth for something else?"

My body reacts to his words before my mind can process them, my thighs beginning to twitch like they don't belong to me.

"Yes." He spears me deeply, and my fingers curl around the edge of the table as though to hang on. To the sensation, the moment, or my wits, I can't be sure, as he swallows the sounds of my relief. In my line of vision, his bicep contracts, and my breath leaves my mouth in three powerfully connected bursts.

"So slick."

I mewl, distressed as I find myself empty and pulsing, with his glistening fingers in the air between us.

"I suppose you're going to say this isn't for me either." He rubs the evidence of my pleasure between them.

I have no answer, everything south of my navel contracting as he presses his fingers to his lips. He sucks them deep.

"Certainly tastes like mine." Pleasure spirals through me as he gives his thumb one final catlike lick. "In fact, you taste like I might lose my mind."

"You're still talking."

"Oh, that mouth." He gives a disparaging shake of his head. "It needs occupying. The question is, should I kiss it or fuck it?"

There's something about those coarse words in that accent. His diction so sharp, it seems to slice to my core. *Layers, my God, the layers.*

He dips, and I suddenly find myself over his shoulder. Instead of protesting, I give in to a delighted giggle because no one in the history of me has ever gone caveman on me. Are there really men like this outside of movies, or is it just him? But then my heart jumps as I notice him swipe up his necktie.

"What's that for?" Did that sound like panic or excitement?

"Can't have you running away."

Not twice in one day. The thought is an unwelcome reminder, the malicious sprite on my shoulder sounding suspiciously like my mother. I guess Oliver must sense some change in me because, in the bedroom, he sets me gently to my feet.

"What is it?" His tone is gentle, the setting sun rendering him a mixture of shadows and deep bronze.

Not trusting myself to speak, I give a small shake of my head.

"You've had a big day." His knuckles tenderly glide down my neck. "We don't have to do this. We could . . ." His eyes drift to the contemporary four-poster bed behind me, with a dozen pillows, its linens snowy white.

"Cuddle?" I pinch in a delighted smile. "Go on, say it. Make it sound convincing."

"And you think I shouldn't talk." He frowns. "We could order room service and watch a film?"

I laugh—he looks so out of his element. Try as I might, I cannot see this man watching a rom-com, chowing down on french fries. With a tiny throb of longing, I realize I would not kick him out of bed for making crumbs.

"Are you trying to be my friend?"

"I did warn you I'm terrible at it."

"I think you're doing pretty well so far."

"That's because you can't see into my head." He gives the kind of sigh that makes his chest heave. "It's a ruse. Subterfuge. You see, I still have every intention of getting you out of your underwear."

"I have no idea why I like you." His ego? That confidence? Because he's super easy on the eyes? *Especially almost shirtless.* Maybe he would make a terrible friend, but I don't really believe it. He put his whole day aside to be with me. He hasn't judged, pried, or looked at me with pity. He saw beyond the sad story dressed in lace and made me feel like myself.

"Perverse." Reaching out, he hooks a finger around my ear as though sliding away a curl. "You really shouldn't."

"You don't get to tell me what to do," I whisper, leaning back against the bedpost.

"As if I'd dare presume." His eyes dip as I slip my finger into the waistband of his pants. He presses his hand over mine, sliding it lower to the thick outline of his cock.

"Liar."

His dark glance slices up, and heat slicks between my hips. His eyes turn midnight as I fasten my fingers over his thick outline, and he hums a masculine sound as he leans in. Our mouths meet, his tongue dark and clever as it licks into me. Kissing, kissing, but then I'm hauling in a breath as he breaks the kiss. His breathing doesn't seem much easier than mine, those violet eyes almost black now.

"Turn around." His words are rough, almost a command. I dip my head, not wanting to share what they do to me, and fight a shiver as he moves my hair over my shoulder. He sets his fingers to the buttons running down the back of my dress, my body instinctively undulating into his touch.

"Stop squirming." The point of his tongue flicks lightly at my bared nape.

"When you stop teasing." Need rushes through my veins in a sweet, urgent agony at the press of his teeth. Several torturous moments later, my dress parts from my skin, my breath catching as he slides it from my ribs.

I stare at the lace as it pools on the floor when he turns me to face him again.

"What's the verdict?" Maybe vanity prompts me to ask, because the way his eyes devour me will be forever burned into my brain.

"Exquisite." His gaze meets mine, full of heat and promise.

"Worth the money?" I'd thought my choice achingly pretty. A delicate demi-cup bra shaped like oyster shells, a garter belt to hug my hips, and tiny, triangular panties. And of course, silk stockings.

"It's not the lingerie." His finger trails my collarbone, then down between my breasts. Slipping into the gauzy cup, he bares my nipple. "No need to gild the lily," he whispers as he lowers his head. My insides turn fiery, his words blowing across my skin. "Or paint the perfect pearl."

I whimper as his tongue licks the pebble of my nipple. My body convulses, my next breath ragged as he sucks it hotly into his mouth. Anticipation washes across my skin, the attention he lavishes resonating sharply between my legs.

"You're so lovely. So delicate." His fingers make manacles of my wrists, pulling my hands above my head. "Bones so easily broken." He folds my fingers around the bedpost behind me. "But your spirit? Not so."

His words and the reassuring squeeze bring tears prickling to my eyes. But as he settles his hand between my legs, my thoughts scatter. With one swift tug, he rips my gossamer panties from my body.

He drops to his knees, and *oh, my*. I close my eyes to the sight of his dark head as he presses his mouth to me. I cry out, my spine arching at the first swipe of his tongue.

"You're so sweet." His compliment washes through me like a shower of stars. His tongue finds my clit. *Circling, petting, loving.*

"So wet and pretty and all for me." Oliver's hand slides behind my knee, lifting it to his shoulder as his fingers spear me, as he whispers the kind of compliments I never thought to hear. "That's it, darling." He grunts, working me rougher, faster. Making me wetter. "You're so close."

Pleasure begins to spiral, the air around me somehow complaisant to it. I've never felt this kind of intensity, never needed to come so hard, as Oliver makes good on his earlier promise, burying his head to make a meal out of me.

"Oh, God." *There.* "Yes!" I cry out.

"Don't come."

My answer is a tortured rasping laugh. Like that's even possible. Until . . . "What? No!" I protest as his tongue begins to slow.

"Who does this night *belong* to, Eve?" His voice and his fingers are both rough and tender at the same time. "Whose mouth is going to make you come?"

I almost levitate, chasing the fleeting swipe of his tongue. "Stop, that's—"

"Mmmm."

My eyes roll to the back of my head at the vibration against my clit. I was going to say *cruel*, but . . .

"I could drown in you."

"Don't," I whimper, pressing my hand to his dark head. Too late. He pulls away. His eyes crawl up my body, his mouth lewdly wet and his blue eyes burning.

"Do I have to use my tie?"

"No." My voice is hoarse, and my body throbs as I withdraw my hand. "No. At least, not the first time . . ."

He smiles like the devil, his tongue lewdly licking into me. "Who, darling. Who is going to eat you out until you scream?"

"You. You're going to make me come. Can I, please? Please and thank you."

His laughter is possibly the dirtiest thing I've ever heard. Then he presses his mouth to me and begins to eat me like a starving man at a feast. I can't process a thing as my orgasm begins to crawl through my insides, gathering and building until I'm fit to burst. And I do—I implode, explode, come so hard I definitely lose brain cells. When I come back to myself, I'm sure the only thing keeping me upright is Oliver's fingers and slow, lapping tongue.

"No. No more!" I twist, every swipe feeling electric.

He stands, wiping my pleasure from his chin with the back of his hand. "I do so appreciate good manners." His gaze sweeps over me, bold and possessive. I blink, not quite following. Then his arms come around my waist, and he lifts me up, then lays me across the bed as he whispers *"Please, please, please"* in my ear.

"I did not . . ." My words trail away as he begins to strip off the remains of his shirt, his cuff links making a dull sound as they hit the floor. His skin looks like he's been dipped in honey, his nipples copper colored and almost flat. My eyes slip down the ladder of his abdominals as his pants come off next.

Thick thighs dusted with dark hair, black boxer briefs and—

His knee hits the mattress between my legs, his cock jutting between us, long, thick, and ruddy. *In the name of the Father, the Son, and the Holy smokes I'll be lucky if I ever walk again.*

My gaze slides upward to find his eyes glittering in the lowering light. He looks otherworldly, like some dark beautiful creature making plans to feed on me.

Oh, wait. He already did that.

"What are you smiling about?"

"I'm not smiling," I whisper . . . smiling. "I don't have the energy."

"You'll rouse." He drops onto his palms, his lips a hot trail up my throat, the length and heft of him apparent against my skin.

"Condom?" whispers the sensible side of me.

He hums, and something sharp drags against my shoulder. But his mouth is on mine, and I'm tasting myself from his tongue, and we're licking the salt from each other's skin, touching and squeezing and—so good.

"Please, I want—"

He pushes onto his knees. A tiny tear. A grunt. My breathy "Yes" as I stare.

"Darling, the way you watch. Like you're desperate to suck me off."

Everything inside me twists, the images he paints blooming inside me like heat. But as the solid masculine weight of him follows, my thoughts dissolve.

"*Oh . . .*" I shiver at the brush of his sheathed cock as, with a broken groan, he moves lower.

"*Fuck, yes.*" His silky crown nudges against me, his heated words brush past my ear. It sounds like he's just hanging onto his sanity.

"Please!" I pant, knowing I am.

I hold my breath as he pushes inside me, his soft grunt exhaled against the skin of my neck. "Eve, this is . . ."

I nod—my God, I know. *The sensations. The feels.*

His hand grips my hip as he surges into my body as though it belongs to him. The stretch is exquisite, his tortured groan everything. He moves over me, once, twice, pinning me to the bed as my moans layer over his, my whimpers over his whispered compliments.

He rises over me, hooking his hand under my knee. The slick sight of his cock as it works me makes me unspool. My hands, grasping and greedy, drag him down, and I press my teeth to the skin of his neck as it hits.

There. Oh, God. There. My soul twists from my body, euphoric.

He stills as I grind against him, crying out, everything around me ceasing to make sense. There is only Oliver over me, inside me, as I'm consumed by pleasure.

Chapter 7
OLIVER

"Hey."

"Is dried grass. Is not an appropriate greeting," I reply.

"Thanks, *Mom*." Fin, my friend and business partner, saunters into the suite. "I'll try for polite next time."

"Liar." I swing the door closed. "I thought we were meeting downstairs."

"I was early." He pauses midturn, unable to resist his reflection in the wall mirror. He slides his hand through his fair hair and, satisfied all is as it should be, drops negligently onto the end of the sofa. "Actually, you were late. But don't let that minor detail bother you."

"By five minutes," I murmur, making my way across the room to the credenza. "And it's breakfast, not a merger."

"It was breakfast, now it's brunch."

"Any excuse for a mimosa." With my back to him, my mouth curls as I swipe up my wallet.

"I'm not your girlfriend."

"You're almost pretty enough," I reply, shooting him a look over my shoulder.

"Flattery will get you nowhere, *Mr. My Time Is Valuable.* Where's my apology, huh? You give me shit for my timekeeping."

"Because it's mostly an alien concept to you."

"Why are you staring at your wallet? Did last night's date clean you out?"

I turn to face him as I slip it into my back pocket. "Paying for companionship is more your thing, isn't it?"

"One time." Finger in the air and grin unrepentant, Fin adds, "It happened one time. And she told me she was a model." His finger becomes accusatory. "And I didn't pay for it in the end, so it doesn't count."

"If you say so." Leaning back, I fold my arms across my chest.

"Speaking of women"—he glances over his shoulder in the direction of my bedroom—"where is the delightful Selena, anyway?"

My answer is a nonverbal *who?*

"Or is it Elizabeth this weekend? Carolina? Whichever horsey woman you're boning this week."

I slide him a bored look. Fin has never met Selena, Elizabeth, or anyone else coming out of my bedroom.

"One of these days I'm gonna catch you out," he says with an admonishing wag of his finger.

"Unlikely."

"I know women are the reason you live in a hotel."

"I live here because it's convenient."

"Exactly what I said."

"And because I own it."

"You also own an apartment block in Knightsbridge, commercial space on Canary Wharf, a huge chunk of the Docklands, but I don't see you bedding down at any of those for the night."

My chest expands, though I stifle the sigh. "No one lives in the Docklands, Fin."

"No one you'd speak to, you mean."

I push off from the credenza. "Shall we?"

"Wait. All this conversation, and you haven't said a word."

"I'm sure I've said several. And I'm about to say several other less-pleasant ones."

"About yesterday."

I'm startled for a moment but then remember Fin doesn't know about Eve or the tension bunching my shoulders that has nothing to do with him and everything to do with waking to an empty bed. An empty bed and a scribbled note on hotel stationery.

Oliver, thank you for your friendship.

Those were some benefits . . .

Eve x

Friends.

I've never had a friend I wanted to fuck my name, my finger-prints, into.

It's been a long time since I'd woken alone after a one-night stand. Living in a hotel has many conveniences. The door is always open. I don't need to maintain extra staff or security. The location is convenient and very secluded, given I live in the penthouse with my own elevator, and if I require anything—from a coffee at three o'clock in the morning to condoms at that vital moment, the concierge is just a phone call away.

Despite Fin's assertions, my private life isn't conducted out of this suite. I book another, then explain to my companion that I have an early meeting but that the room has a late checkout. That they should order breakfast or whatever. Meanwhile, I just pop upstairs unseen.

It's a win-win situation. A sexual connection without the need to suffer through that awkward morning after. I feel my brows pinch. I would've settled for awkward over alone this morning.

"I expected to find you doing cartwheels."

"What was that?" I glance up, realizing I'm standing halfway between the credenza and the door and Fin is eyeing me narrowly.

"You haven't heard? Ah, man." He rubs a hand across his mouth as though to hide his delight. "This is gonna give you such a fuckin' hard-on."

I rotate my wrist. *Please, go on.* Or get to the point.

"You know Atherton was supposed to get married yesterday?"

The sound of his name usually makes me want to curse, but this time I find it hard to curtail my smile. "Was he?"

"You've heard," Fin retorts flatly.

"No." I give a quick shrug, not wanting to be too disingenuous. The fact is I hadn't known. Not until I'd slid my arm around his would-be bride. "I take it he didn't?"

"The bride came to her senses."

About a week too late, if I remember.

"Caught him with his pants down. But that's not even the fun part."

"Because finding out your fiancé is cheating is always fun."

"Pah! Like you've ever dated anyone for longer than a week."

"Not true. Also, kettle"—I tap my chest, then point my finger at him—"meet pot."

"Do you want to hear this or not?"

Altering my path, I take a seat opposite him. "I'm all ears."

"Make it eyes too," he says, pulling out his phone. "Because it went viral."

"What did?" I sit straight. I would've known if we'd been recorded. I took her to my club, for God's sake—that place is like a vault. A fuckin' crypt! Then I booked her into her own room at the hotel. *I just hadn't meant to stay there with her.*

"Just a clip of the ceremony." He stares down at the screen of his phone. "Dude was definitely punching."

"Yes, wasn't he?" Mitchell Atherton is a posh boy with an empty head who once got lucky at my expense. He's greedy and rash, and I've no doubt in my belief he'd be idiot enough to screw up his life over a quick fuck. And Eve? Well, Eve is just . . . I find myself trailing my forefinger across my bottom lip as though I could still taste the depth and complexity of her. That balance of her sweet and bitter notes.

"She's hot."

"Mm." Like a flame dancing in my hands. *And just as dangerous.* She'd intrigued me, but I hadn't intended to act on it, no matter how her eyes darkened or her breath hitched at my whispered commands. It was the best night of my life, yet it's left me with the worst feeling.

Because I woke alone?

"Wait, do you know her?"

"An educated guess," I add, my tone clipped. "It's all such a cliché."

"And she looks the type."

My attention slices up. "What's that supposed to mean?"

"Gorgeous. A killer rack." He gives a meaningless shrug. "A bod made for wet dreams." With that, he pitches his phone into my hands, which saves me from wrapping them around his throat. "Play it," he demands. "Then take me to breakfast for making your day."

◆　◆　◆

"For the love of everything that's holy," I mutter, throwing down my napkin. I hook my elbow over the back of my chair and turn to the table of women seated behind. "Do you mind?" I glance pointedly down at the phone the blonde is holding in one hand. In the other is a half-drunk mimosa. She has the good grace to blush as

64

she flicks from the social media app blaring out yesterday's travesty at Shoreditch Town Hall.

When I told Eve I'd pay to see her throw rocks at her ex, I didn't for one minute think I'd get the chance. But then Fin had thrown me his phone and I'd watched the minute-long recording of the moment she rejected him so spectacularly.

It was good, for at least the first dozen times. She'd blazed incandescent, and it made me want her all over again. But I'm not the only voyeur, the likes, saves, and shares of the video increasing by the hundreds every few seconds. It seems like the whole of the UK has watched it, including the group of women in the same restaurant, playing it on repeat.

"What's your problem?" demands a brunette from the far side of the table, her words slightly slurred. "Is the dick groom a friend of yours?"

It used to be that London's streets were full of drunken football hooligans on Sundays. Now it's women, teetering on their heels after bottomless brunches.

"I just find it hard to stomach how society revels in the suffering of others."

"He deserves to suffer," she says, her eyes daring me to contradict her.

Fin smothers a chuckle, knowing how I feel about Atherton. While I might've suggested death by cabbie yesterday, I'm not about to discuss that with a group of half-drunken strangers.

"I was talking about the bride." The very lovely bride who snuck out of my hotel this morning, leaving me with nothing but sore abdominals and the flavor of her pleasure on my tongue.

Smarting? Me? Definitely.

"You should stop talking," Fin mutters in a tone meant only for my ears.

"Bad enough to discover her fiancé's infidelity," I say, ignoring him, "but then to find herself the viewing pleasure of half of London seems cruel, don't you think?"

"We're applauding her," the brunette announces, raising her glass. "Read the comments." She thrusts her phone in my direction.

"She's a boss-ass bitch!" interjects her friend.

At a strangled noise, I glance behind me to find Fin slunk low in his seat, his hand covering his eyes.

"You're on your own," he mutters.

"She's a motha-fuckin' queen!" yells the redhead, turning suddenly street. And American. "If she was here, I'd buy her a drink. Hell, we all would."

If she were here, I'd probably drag her back upstairs, and not just to protect her from being gossip fodder.

"You should get your sister to interview her for her blog," says the woman who'd been playing the video. "It's all over the socials. It's only a matter of time before the news gets ahold of it."

"By all means, humiliate her further," I mutter as I turn back.

"Holy patriarchy, Batman! You just don't get it, do you?"

"What has feminism got to do with it?" My words drip with derision as I whip around again.

Fin makes a noise as though he's in pain.

"How could you possibly understand?" one of the women demands.

But I comprehend better than anyone because I felt her tremble. Heard how she disparaged herself. I'll be damned if I sit here allowing others to make her the topic of the day.

"Ah, man. The *City Chronicle* already posted about it. Listen to this!"

I tell myself I'm not as bad as them as I pull out my phone and search for the newspaper's online article. No, not an article of news. A fucking gossip column.

about a scandalous scene at a Shoreditch Town Hall wedding yesterday when a bride read out her cheating fiancé's salacious text messages in the place of her vows. Guests (and the—allegedly— unfaithful groom) were left speechless as the bride extracted her savage revenge at the altar before taking off.

Did you see the viral video? A Little Bird suggests you check out the link below, because there's five hundred big ones waiting for the first person to tell us the names of the (un)happy couple.

"Of all the vindictive, vengeful . . ."

"He got off lightly." The woman directly behind me pokes me angrily in my shoulder, completely misinterpreting my meaning.

I turn to their glares, but before I can respond, Fin is on his feet, rounding the table.

"Ladies, please forgive my friend. The truth is, he feels deeply." His hands are clasped, and his gaze touches each of them, his expression the mask he wears when he's tasked with giving our clients bad news. He's bloody good at winning over hearts and minds, so I let him get on with it. "And, well, he won't want me to say this, but he was recently hurt in love." I snort and shake my head. "What you've just seen was a human reaction in defense of another's pain. I'm sure we can all understand that. Which of us hasn't been hurt in love?" And then he comes in with the perfect close when he orders the women another round of mimosas.

"You were recently hurt in love, right?" he says, sliding back into his seat. "Weren't you handcuffed to a bed and the metal chafed your wrist? Left you with a graze?"

"That sounds more like you."

"Nah. If it wasn't you, it was probably Matt. Where is he, anyway?" Matt is the third partner of our private equity company, Maven Inc., which largely deals in real estate investments.

"He's in Dublin this weekend. Was that really necessary?" I say, indicating the guzzling coven behind me.

"I guess I could've just watched. Waited until you were wearing one of their drinks. We all know how you feel about your clothing."

"By all means, arm them with more liquid bullets."

"Just keep your mouth shut and eyes this way, and you'll be fine."

"I'm not allowed an opinion?"

"How can I put this . . ." Steepling his fingers, he peers at me pensively. "It's not your opinion that's the issue. Those women have the wrong impression, thanks to your goddamn miserable face."

"That seemed to require a lot of contemplation."

"You're always a fucker, you're just not usually so tetchy."

"I'm stoic."

"Like someone pissed on your cornflakes. I mean, I can't imagine why I thought seeing your archenemy be humiliated might make you smile," he mutters, reaching for his own glass.

"He's not my enemy," I reply loftily. "He is below my notice. Mostly."

"If only that were true. Sometimes I think the world would be a better place if you two just hate fucked and got over yourselves."

Chapter 8
EVIE

"What do you mean he can't be my unicorn?" I drop the phone from my ear, bringing it back just as quick. "Who died and made you the boss of me?"

"I wouldn't be your boss for all the bourbon in Kentucky." Riley snorts. "You are unmanageable."

"Doesn't stop you from trying."

"I think the word you're looking for is *counsel*. You know, like a friend worried for you and your mental health."

"My mental health is just fine." I glance up, distracted as a group of teenagers passes by the front window. Riley lives in a mews house in a super bougie part of Chelsea, on a narrow street of pastel facades and overflowing window boxes. Lined with buildings originally intended as coach houses—to accommodate the horses and servants of those living in much grander spaces—the cobblestone lanes were laid for hooves rather than quaintness. These days, the inhabitants are more likely to own five-hundred-horsepower Aston Martins than coaches with two high-stepping grays. Home to London's artsy and affluent, the street is also an Instagram hot spot.

"If you want the truth, last night was just what I needed."

"I can't get my head around it. A one-night stand is so unlike you."

I hum a noncommittal sound and cross my legs, running my finger around the hole in the knee of my leggings. Well, not *my* leggings, but what Lori, Riley's roommate, begrudgingly loaned me. Gosh, her face as she opened the front door for her morning run and found me about to stick the key in her mouth. *In my wedding dress, with my hair bedraggled and my skin beard-burn pink.* Trust Riley to have gotten it wrong because his roommate hadn't gone away for the weekend after all. *So much for raiding her closet in peace.* But at least Riley got his cleaner to leave her key. Without it, Lori might not have let me in.

"It's not every day you get humiliated at the altar."

"I think you have that the wrong way around, Evie. Just do yourself a favor and avoid the hair salon."

I reach up, snagging a lock of wayward hair and sliding it behind my ear. How spooky; I'd just been contemplating booking an appointment after I'd grown my hair out just for yesterday. "Why?"

"The effects of a revenge bang are usually short lived. Revenge bangs on the other hand . . . Remember the great tenth-grade hair experiment?"

"How could I forget? But last night wasn't revenge." It was an experience like no other—an experience I won't ever have again. "I see it more as just returning the favor."

Riley chuckles. "Oh, I bet Bitchell will just *love* that."

"I don't really care what he thinks. I am so over thinking about yesterday and what an idiot I've been. You know, when I read those texts, my love for that asshole was snuffed out like a cheap candle." I click my finger and thumb together. It's the truth but not the whole truth.

"I'd like to snuff him out," Riley mutters.

"I mean, if I never really knew him, how could I have loved him?"

"Evie, honey. Love is like an orgasm. If you have to ask yourself if you felt it, the answer is, you didn't."

"Maybe we both fooled ourselves into thinking we were in love, or else why did he cheat? And if I really loved him, wouldn't I still be distraught?"

"I don't know. I'm still trying to figure out a reaction to your one-night stand."

"Is the air a little thin up there on your high horse? Because I recall a certain someone taking twins home recently. Twins! That's just nasty." I frown as the doorbell rings. "Who can that be?"

"Sadly, my psychic powers are on the fritz, along with this damn leg."

"You're so crabby. Do you need better pain meds?"

"Put it this way: if you were here, I might ask you to put me out of my misery. Let Lori get it in case it's *him*."

"He doesn't know where you live." *Never cared to ask, I guess.* "Besides, Lori is upstairs, probably sticking pins in the puppet that looks like me."

"She doesn't hate you."

"Then why is there a note on her bedroom door that reads *The We Hate Evie Club—Meeting in Session?*"

Riley laughs as the bell rings again.

"Who the heck visits on Sunday?" I complain, climbing from the couch.

"Wild idea, go find out, because we're not done here."

"We are so done. Telling you about last night wasn't an act of confession," I mutter, trudging my way along the hallway. "I don't need your absolution, Father Filthy." But I do need my new bank card to arrive. I reported it and my credit card lost this morning.

71

They said three business days until a new one is mailed out. It'll be good to be solvent again.

"I just don't want to see you hurt." Riley's sigh is audible down the line.

"I don't need to know him," I reply as I unlock the front door. "I'm not seeing him again. One and done."

"Yeah, but—"

"Riley, I am not all heart-eye emojis over the guy. As usual, you're missing the point, because when I said he was my unicorn, I was referring to his magical horn. And by horn, I mean—"

"His dick!"

Riley's pronouncement is shrill as I swing the door open, and my entire stomach flips, somehow landing on my ovaries. Because out in the street stands Oliver, looking like he's just stepped from a yacht in Saint-Tropez. His jet hair is sun dappled, and the hem of his linen shirt flutters in the summer breeze.

"His magical dick," Riley repeats, oblivious to the man with the magical member standing in front of me. "Come to think of it, I think I heard you yelling last night. From all the way over here. In France. Harder, pony boy, harder!" he cries in some approximation of Evie ecstasy. And then he whinnies.

"You were enthusiastic." The vision in front of me is all smoky tone and devilish grin as he slips off his sunglasses, those strangely lovely eyes pinning me where I stand. "Hello, Eve."

"Who is that?" Riley demands from somewhere near my hip because I almost dropped the phone.

"What are you doing here?" My heart seems to slide through my insides, settling in the space between my legs. I cross my legs at the ankles, oh so casually, as though he might hear it thrumming away down there.

"Isn't it obvious?" His gaze moves over me, stroking like a caress.

"Oh my God!" Riley squawks. "Is that the unicorn?"

"Shut up," I hiss into the phone as I swing back to the hall. "If you wanted to know who's at the door, you should've installed a Ring doorbell." I end the call, setting my phone on the thin hall console.

Oliver moves back a pace as I step into the front street, pulling the door almost closed behind me.

"Seriously, what are you doing here?" I strain to keep my tone even, conscious of passing foot traffic as my heart pounds away in its highly inappropriate resting place.

"Ah." Oliver slips his hands into his pockets, his gaze dipping to the cobblestones. "I see," he murmurs as he scuffs the sole of his expensive loafer. "I'd hoped you might be pleased to see me."

Pleasure pokes me in the chest. "That I am not buying." I'm digging it, but not buying it.

"I'm sorry?" His gaze lifts, and he blinks almost owlishly.

"This whole . . ." I wave my finger over whatever this is meant to be. *"I'm so adorably embarrassed, floppy-haired rom-com male lead."*

"My hair is not floppy." His eyebrow spikes. "And I was aiming for bashful."

"Doubtful." I try not to grin as he straightens. Maybe Riley was right. Maybe I'm not cut out for one-night stands, because I'm not exactly unhappy to see this amount of tall, dark, and handsome on my (borrowed) doorstep. "Have you ever been?"

"No, not for a while."

"Color me surprised," I deadpan, crossing my arms across my chest over Lori's threadbare T-shirt. *The girl loves me, what can I say?* You can practically see my bra through the worn cotton—the only bra currently in my possession, the same one he peeled from me last night. It's only a hop and a skip of his thoughts for him to realize I'm not wearing panties. *Thanks to him destroying them.* And that's hardly a Sunday afternoon conversation.

"You didn't seem too concerned about my personality yesterday. Aren't you going to invite me in?" His gaze drops briefly to my mouth.

"Not until you tell me how you found me. And probably not even then."

"You took a hotel car. I asked the concierge for the address after I woke this morning. *Alone.*"

"And you thought, what? My leaving must've been a mistake." Check me out, all cool and feisty, as though I totally wrote the one-night stand rule book.

"Why did you leave, incidentally?"

"To save us this." I gesture between us.

"Are you embarrassed?" He shifts his weight onto one leg and makes a *V* across his chin with his hand. "Because I remember you being much less inhibited last night."

His tone vibrates under my skin. At least until a passerby does a double take, no doubt catching his meaning. "Hush!"

"You *are* embarrassed," he says with a low, delighted chuckle. "How charming."

"The concierge wouldn't have told you where the car took me," I retort, ignoring my burning cheeks. "Unless you bribed them."

"Bribery is unnecessary when you own the hotel."

"You—*what?*"

"I own the hotel. Relax, Eve. This isn't the start of a stalking campaign."

"That's exactly what a stalker would say."

The look he slides me isn't exactly complimentary. Can't say I blame him as I stand here in my borrowed, unattractive activewear, my face free of makeup and my hair resembling a tumbleweed. A serious stalker would probably run the other way.

"I'm here because I need to speak with you."

"Why?" Disquiet pokes at me as he reaches to his back pocket, pulling out his phone. *Better than my torn panties.* He hands it to me wordlessly, and my eyes dip to the screen. "Pulse Tok?" The popular social media app is already open. "I wouldn't have pegged you as the type."

I have it on my own phone, mostly for video makeup tutorials and people doing crazy dances. Maybe I'm expecting something like that, and that's why it takes my brain a moment to compute. To make sense of what I'm seeing. The sound isn't on, not that I need it, as I recognize my wedding dress. Yep, that's me, full of vengeance and experiencing (what looks like) a mental break.

"Oh. Oh no." I press a hand to my mouth as a wave of nausea rises through my insides. Oliver reaches for me as I sway, but I'm not about to faint. Or maybe I am, as my butt hits the door and I find myself sitting heavily. "This is . . . so bad."

"Is it?" He crouches down, his gaze level with mine, but there's no sympathy in those striking eyes.

"You're kidding, right? Look at the number of times this has been watched!" I demand, extending his phone. So much for consoling myself that a small wedding meant fewer people witnessed my disgrace. *What a joke.*

"Six million, last count." His hand retracts when it becomes clear I'm not ready to give it back to him. "But I'm sure most people watch it more than once."

"How is that helpful? And it's eight million now! Is there anyone left in London who hasn't seen this?"

"I'm told viral can mean regional or worldwide."

"Oh my God." *Home?* My heart begins to bang against my rib cage like it's trying to escape. "Hey, no! I haven't finished," I complain as, this time, he successfully tugs the phone away.

"You're familiar with how it ends."

"Me and half the world!"

"That's not really true. There were only two of us in the hotel room last night." There's a smoky hint in his voice, yet his words seem vaguely threatening.

"Your hotel, you mean." I'm annoyed he didn't say, though I'm not sure why I find the news surprising. The rich are such an untrustworthy bunch.

"Would it have made a difference had I said?" When my eyes meet his, I get that telltale little flutter between my legs. "I thought not."

What the hell was I thinking? Just because Oliver isn't all about the flex doesn't mean he's different.

"Last night isn't the issue, not when I've made a spectacle of myself in front of an audience of millions."

"You should read the comments. You have a lot of fans."

"Don't." I hold up my hand like a stop sign, because nothing good can come of this. Or from him being here. "Tell me what you want. I know you didn't come all this way to show me that." Nausea rises as I glance down at his phone.

"I have a proposition to put to you."

"A proposition?" My tone makes a passing couple turn abruptly.

"That's *not* what I was proposing."

So maybe that was wishful thinking. A night with him was a fun distraction, but I'm not making the same mistake twice.

"Look, Oliver, I don't have time for any of this. I have no money," I say, beginning to count my problems off against my fingers, "no phone, no clothes, no idea how much longer I can stay in the country, and now the cherry on the shit show that is my life is a viral video that makes me look like bridezilla on crack cocaine!"

"As I've been trying to tell you, I can help."

I laugh. Manically. It's better than giving in to the alternative.

"Shall we go inside and discuss it?" he says once I've calmed. Outwardly, at least.

I glance up at the sky as though seeking divine intervention, but I'm just stalling. "No," I answer, dropping my head. I don't need Lori to hear how my life is falling apart. And then there's the small matter of how, when he crouched in front of me, I caught the scent of his cologne. *And we know how that went yesterday.*

"This is not a conversation to have in the street," he prompts.

"In case I run away?"

"Yes, well." He spikes a brow. "You find me not wearing a tie."

Was that a low blow or an enjoyable one? It's hard to tell, given the way my body throbs. "I can't invite you in."

"Can't or won't?" When I don't answer, he glances to the end of the street, where the shopping pavilion begins. String lights hang and colorful bunting flutters between the quaint buildings, home to artisanal bakeries, traditional cheesemongers, and upmarket eateries, all overflowing with tourists and bougie locals on this sunny summer's day. "Why don't we do this over a drink?"

"Sure. How about the grill place?" Somewhere I'm likely to stay vertical and fully clothed. *Not that we'll get a seat anywhere today,* I think with a frisson of malicious glee. It'll make this meeting short, if nothing else.

"Wonderful." He rises gracefully, the breadth of him setting me in the shade. "Shall we?"

"You go on ahead. I need to freshen up," I answer, ignoring his outstretched hand. And by that, I mean "find out if Lori is the same size shoe" because I'm not sure I can claim shoeless is the new boho.

"I'll see you soon."

My mouth twists. "Because that didn't sound like a threat. Nope, not at all. I get it. You know where I live."

"For now," he answers cryptically. He turns then, reminding me he has the kind of ass made for jeans. But you can't truly appreciate what you don't trust.

Chapter 9
OLIVER

Fifteen minutes later, Eve looks annoyed as she's shown to the booth at the back of the restaurant. When I arrived, I asked for somewhere we wouldn't be disturbed. Perhaps that's what's bothering her.

"This place is busy." Her tone is tellingly light as she slides into the pale-green banquet seating opposite.

"You say that like it's not a surprise."

"I knew it would be busy."

"Too busy, you hoped?" A fifty slipped to the hostess had not only remedied that problem but also provided us with a table out of the way.

"If I wanted to table block you, I would've come along with you. Nothing says *premium allocation* like hobo chic, and this thing is one wear away from a wardrobe malfunction," she adds, plucking at the worn cotton.

As she redirects her glower, I'm allowed a moment to look at her. She does look different. Yesterday, she shone like a newly polished pearl, and today, in place of the bride is a woman who looks barely old enough to be married. Her face is makeup-free, and her hair is a little wild. Different, yes, but just as lovely.

"A man can hope." I shoot her an unrepentant grin that's not likely to help my cause. I'm saved from further blunders as the waitress sidles up to the table with our drink order. "One Macallan," she singsongs, placing the lowball glass in front of me. "And a glass of Ruinart for the lady."

"Ordering for me?" Eve snipes from across the table.

"You didn't seem to mind me taking charge last night." I lounge in my seat and slide my hand along the velvety back as both women's cheeks flush with color. The waitress, though attractive, does nothing for me, yet the scowl Eve is wearing makes me want to lean across the table and lick it from her face. I find her opposition a level of pleasure all its own.

"Well, enjoy!" The waitress spins on her heel.

"You embarrassed the poor girl."

"You're not embarrassed."

"No." Both her scowl and her color deepen. "I give as good as I get."

"Yes," I agree, tempering my smile. "I like that about you."

"What do you want, Oliver?"

My answer is in the way my gaze sweeps over her, lingering in some of the spaces my lips had savored last night. The hollow beneath her ear. The sensual curve between her shoulder and her neck. Those lips in a mouth so full of denials yet so perfect wrapped around my cock. Sadly, there are more pressing matters, but you can't blame a man for getting sidetracked.

"You mentioned your belongings and your phone. I can help you get them back. Money and a place to stay too."

"You want to help?" Her brows knit with distrust. "Why?"

The offer is a means to an end, my first point of bargaining. "In exchange for something."

She leans forward, her eyes suddenly gold in the light. "How could I forget? You're not the chivalrous type."

"That *also* didn't seem to bother you too much last night."

"Last night I didn't have many options."

"Have things changed?" I ask, ignoring her implication—an insult that doesn't land. She chased me. In some ways, she only has herself to blame. Had it not been for the night we spent together, I mightn't have reacted as I did to the Pulse Tok recording or those drunken women. Or dwelled on Fin's assertion that Atherton and I hate fuck this out. He fucked us both—that's the reality. First me, then Eve. I just wasn't expecting her to be a reluctant partner in this.

"Well, I'm not homeless." She presses her elbow to the table, propping her cheek on her hand. "So, as fun as it was, I don't need a repeat." She brings her glass to her mouth, her eyes sparkling over the rim.

"Need is such a tricky thing."

"Is it?" She sets her glass down, sliding her thumb and finger down the dainty stem.

"When it's tied so closely to desire." I watch as she continues to toy with the stem, wondering if her actions are deliberate. "You didn't need to manipulate me into bed last night. You already had use of the room." My answer betrays neither the tightening in my belly nor the discomfort of my stiffening cock.

"I don't remember you being *too* hard to persuade."

I swirl the amber contents around the bowl of my glass. Nothing to see here. Just two people tormenting each other. "I suppose that depends on your perspective." I put it to my lips to conceal my smile. Or to prevent me from admitting how hard she's made me.

"Oliver Deubel. You are a one-off." But it's a smiling kind of insult, accompanied by a slow shake of her head.

"I could say the same about you."

"Oh, but you wouldn't mean it as a compliment." As her gaze dips, a curl springs free and dangles against her cheek. Unable to help myself, I lean across the table and hook it with my finger before brushing it behind her ear.

"You're wrong. I have nothing but good things to say about you."

She inhales a breath, then stills, the tiny, telling motion going off like a lightbulb in my head. Despite her denials, she's not as immune to me as she'd like to be. The second reveal comes as I take in her expression: she doesn't like that fact one bit.

"I'm not sure I need your help." Pulling away, she slices her finger through a streak of condensation on her glass, the motion marking a change in the tone of our conversation. "I expect he'll be off on our honeymoon tomorrow. I'll be able to get into the apartment then."

I don't think so. Not after seeing his plans unravel after yesterday.

"What a charmer. How on earth did you end up with him?"

"It's a long story with a shitty ending, as you've seen."

"I'd argue the ending was the right one," I say with a casual flick of my hand. In response, she says nothing. "How will you get into the apartment without a key? Shoreditch, wasn't it?"

"I'll manage."

"Unless he's grown vindictive."

"Because cheating on me wasn't cruel enough?"

"He seemed very remorseful when he chased you."

Eve flounces back in her seat with a snort.

"But I'm not sure he'll stick to the same narrative once he sees the impromptu wedding video."

"You're assuming he will." She folds her arms, her jaw taking on a stubborn set.

"One of your guests loaded it to the platform. It can only be a matter of time. I expect he'll feel quite demeaned."

"And that's supposed to make me unhappy?"

"He more than deserves it," I agree.

"And it's not like I'm responsible. I didn't record or load it."

"True, but humans are a funny bunch. It's strange how we can take our own mistakes and turn them into the fault of someone else."

"He can have at it."

"His wrongdoing and shame will likely turn inward to stew and froth into a sense of injustice. Of being wronged. Humiliation can make people very unreasonable in the aftermath."

"I'm aware what humiliation feels like, Oliver."

"Yes, you exacted your revenge." At the venue. Then in my bed. "It was quite spectacular, but you should probably prepare for him to attempt the same."

"He's the one in the wrong," she says, with less zeal this time. "I've done nothing to deserve . . ."

Her words trail off as I place my phone on the table between us. "He didn't come off very well in this." Idly touching the screen, I make a show of searching the app for it, like I haven't already saved it. Or watched it a dozen times. Hell hath no fury like a woman scorned. *No magnificence either.* "Few men would take this kind of embarrassment well. On the other hand, you really should take some time to read the comments," I add, glancing up. "You seem to have created quite the sisterhood."

"It won't be my fault if women start heckling him in the street."

"But will he see it like that? No matter how accidental, you've created quite a platform. He's become the poster boy for fuckups. The impact will invariably leak into his personal life and his business." I pick up my glass. "I wouldn't put it past him to seek some kind of retaliation."

"He can try." She shoots me a hot glare.

"You and I are reasonable people. Mitchell, in both our experiences, is anything but. After all, it takes a special kind of bastard to cheat on the woman he loves."

"He never loved me." Her answer spills from her mouth in a bitter laugh.

"According to him, he did. He does."

Her posture stiffens. "What do you mean?"

"Don't worry, I haven't spoken to him. He doesn't know about last night."

"I don't care," she grates out.

"I do," I say softly. "I wouldn't allow him to sully such a beautiful memory." My mind bends to a fragment of the experience. Her breasts pressed against me, so lewd and lush as I slid my hands into her hair. *Gold. Amber. Red. So many colors.* My fingers tangling in the silky strands as she threw her head back, rocking against me. I can almost hear the soft sounds she made, feel her breathless pleading against my cheek. But this won't do. "Would you like to hear the messages he left on my phone?" Using my forefinger, I swipe away from the app. "There are quite a few." I won't mention the articles in the online press. At least, not yet.

"He called you?"

"Dozens of times after we drove away." No doubt appealing to my better nature. Sadly for him, I haven't got one.

She rolls the edge of her cocktail napkin between her thumb and forefinger before glancing up. "Why didn't you tell me?"

"He'd ruined your day already." I give a one-shouldered shrug. "I didn't want to be put in the same category." A pause. "Would you have wanted to speak with him?"

"I never want to hear from him again." Like a statement of fact, there's no emotion in her answer.

"Then I'll delete them." I do just that as she watches me.

"Block his number."

"If you want never to have to deal with him, you could always return home," I suggest, picking up the thread of something she'd hinted at yesterday.

"To Connecticut?" She shakes her head. "He's not forcing me away from my life, from a job and a place I've come to love. I've made friends. I have responsibilities. No," she adds more forcefully. "I'm going nowhere."

"Visa issues notwithstanding."

"Obviously." Her answer is casual, but the pinch between her eyes gives her worries away.

I give her a little time to dwell on that as drinks are sipped but not really tasted before I speak again. "I've no cause to really know, but he sounded quite convincing."

"He's had a lot of practice," she answers flatly.

"Love, like humiliation, makes people do stupid things."

"Nothing but being an asshole makes you lie and cheat. Look," she says, making a triangle of her fingers around the base of her glass. "I don't care what he does. I've decided he can donate my clothes to Goodwill, throw my belongings out of his third-floor window like it's raining my stuff. Whatever. I'm over it. I just need my purse, my phone, my passport, and a few personal documents. Now, how about you stop telling me about my problems and just say what you brought me here for."

"Straight to the heart of the matter?"

"Give the man a prize."

"All right. I want three months from you."

"Three months of what?"

That scowl. I think I'd bite it before smoothing it with my tongue.

"Of your time, quid pro quo."

"That makes no sense."

"Something in exchange for something," I reply, not so much laying it out for her as annoying her more, apparently.

"I know what it means. I just don't know what it means in this instance."

"Your belongings, your phone, I'll get them back for you—today, if you like. You won't have to stay with your friend . . . or whoever that was yelling at you earlier." As she'd shut the front door, I'd lingered a moment. Those old mews houses don't offer much in the way of soundproofing.

"You heard that," she says wearily as she drops her head to her hands.

"It sounded quite contentious."

"I only asked her if she'd loan me a different T-shirt."

"You wouldn't have to borrow anything." *Though I'd loan you my cock, mouth, and fingers as often as you'd like.*

"If I throw my lot in with yours," she says with a snort. "For three months of . . ." Her eyes move over me speculatively, and I almost laugh.

"Yes, that might be one benefit, I suppose. And money. I'll pay you for your time." A startled noise sounds from her throat as her mouth falls open, but I push on. "Just name your price."

"This sounds a lot like the kind of deal that ends with at least one of us going to jail. Can you spell *solicitation*, Oliver?"

"That's not what I'm offering."

"Good, I'm not an escort. I'm a veterinarian."

"A noble way to earn a living. While fucking you was a delight, that isn't the purpose of my proposition."

"Would you keep your voice down!" she whisper hisses, her eyes sliding over my shoulder.

"I'm asking for your help, not access to your body," I retort, craving both. "I need the appearance of a relationship—a

85

stable relationship. There's a building coming up for sale in Surrey. Unfortunately, the seller has quite an antiquated outlook."

"Antiquated how?"

"He doesn't want to see it pass into the hands of a developer."

"You especially," she somehow intuits.

"He mistrusts my motivations."

"I can't think why," she mutters. "Oh, wait, yes I can."

"He wants the building to remain intact and believes the best way to ensure that is to sell it to a private buyer. Someone in a settled relationship. He also wants to be courted. Wooed like a debutant."

"When you just want to strip the old girl out of her underwear. I can see how that would be a problem for you," she adds, biting back a grin. "Given you prefer to be the one being chased."

"I think you're confusing courtship with manipulation."

"Either way, all this sounds like a *you* problem." She happily pokes the air with her forefinger. "One easily solved with a call to an escort agency, I'd say. Or if sex isn't part of the deal, you could try for an actress." She holds up her hands: a triumphant shrug in miniature. Like she's solved all my problems.

"When did Mitchell propose to you, Eve?"

"What has that got to do with anything?" Her hands fall, her expression turning guarded.

"He's interested in the same property."

"I don't know where he'd get the money from." Her eyes drift over my face, unsure.

"We're both in the same business. You know that."

"But not in the same league. You own a hotel. Mitch flips houses. You have a driver and a Bentley, and he—"

"Is not quite so wealthy," I agree. Pressing my elbows to the tabletop, I steeple my fingers in front of me. "But he's not so very far behind. Yesterday, you asked what I had against him. Well, last year, he outbid me on a parcel of land earmarked for regeneration."

"That's it? That's why you don't like him?" She sounds unimpressed, as though millions lost in profit is not enough to be upset about.

"What's important about what I'm telling you is that the land sold for ten million."

She begins to shake her head. "Mitch doesn't have that kind of money. I would know. He lives in a rented one-bedroom apartment. He drives an electric car that's on lease."

"He lives in the apartment, but he doesn't pay rent. He owns the building. He not only had ten million to buy the land, but he's also successful enough to attract investors. That means he has a track record of returns."

"I don't know where you got that information from, but you're way off."

"Why? Because he didn't tell you? Because he didn't ask you to sign a prenup? There would be no point," I add as her head rears back in shock. "They're not worth the paper they're written on in the UK. Besides, all his money is funneled through foreign shell companies. You'd never get a penny of what he's worth."

"I don't want his money—I didn't even know he had any!" Color rushes to her face, her eyes wide and pleading.

"Still, it looks like he's been lying to you on more than one front. He's quite cunning. You see, the parcel of land went to tender, and I happened to know my bid was the most competitive."

"Because that doesn't sound suspect at all."

"Yet I was outbid."

"It happens," she says uncertainly. "Maybe he just bid more."

"My point is how he knew what to bid because I later discovered he was sleeping with my personal assistant, Lucy." My jaw tightens. One of these days, my molars will likely turn to dust as I remember. What happened with Lucy was the most painful factor in the whole sorry, sordid business. The repercussions . . . well, I just don't want to think about any of it.

Eve grows pale and quiet, and as she reaches for her glass, I notice how her fingers tremble.

"I'm sorry," I find myself murmuring. Stranger still, I mean it.

"You didn't fuck me over. Lie to my face for an entire relationship."

"I can still be sorry. I don't like to see you sad."

"I'm not sad," she retorts sharply. "That asshole doesn't deserve my tears."

"I'm sorry because I'm about to make you feel worse. The property Mitchell and I are both interested in is owned by a man who'd like to see his legacy endure. He has no family of his own, and in his aging state, he believes the best thing he can do is to sell it to someone who has. Or at least has plans of settling down. I happen to know for a fact that Mitchell has played up to that."

"I don't know what you're trying to say."

"I think you do, Eve. When did he propose?"

"February."

"A short engagement?"

"Long enough." She frowns.

"Was that his idea or yours?"

"What does it matter?"

"The timeline ties in." I give a careless shrug, knowing it won't take the sting from my words. "If you're sure it's not love he professed"—I touch my phone for emphasis—"then perhaps it was need that prompted him."

"You're suggesting he asked me to marry him to get his hands on a house?" Her words are meant to be incredulous, but I hear the hurt in them.

"It is a very lovely house. An ancient estate, more appropriately." One with nine thousand acres of land. It's a symbol of the status that Mitchell covets, one that he no doubt imagines could be the crown of his success, were I not about to tear it out from under him and make it into a hotel.

He'd made no secret of his interest. Conversely, his wedding was almost a national secret. The first I'd heard of it was when Eve flung herself into my lap, which, of course, makes sense now. She's the perfect woman to help him get his hands on Northaby House and all that it encompasses, and I'm sure he wanted to be certain I wouldn't reach that same conclusion.

Too bad. His plans won't be going ahead. I'll have this monstrosity of a house. Truth be told, I'd raze it to the ground out of sheer spite, but English law tends to be very protective of its heritage. I'll do a lot for revenge, but that doesn't include wearing a prison uniform.

I'll settle for ruining him.

Step 1. Steal the woman he needs.

Fuck with his head. Make him wonder: *Is it real between them? Does Deubel know why I proposed? Does Eve?*

Step 2. Steal Northaby from under him.

I doubt he'll ever recover financially. And never professionally. He'll be utterly humiliated in the eyes of his investors—ruined. *Like he almost ruined Lucy.*

"It's still ridiculous."

I pause before answering. How do I explain this without giving away the most unusual facet of the estate—without revealing her place in this whole scheme? It wouldn't help either of us for her to know the whole truth.

"It has the potential to make him famous. It's a celebrated piece of history. Unique. He'd likely become a national celebrity. Not that I'm suggesting he doesn't also love you," I add.

"He doesn't know the meaning of the word."

"You have to admit, there could well have been an element of convenience in his proposal."

"No one proposes marriage for a business deal." She sounds like she's trying to convince herself.

"A few days ago, I'm sure you would've said the same about his cheating. Now you know differently. Your bridesmaid and my PA." With a sigh, I sit back.

"Excuse me." There's no swift removal from banquet seating. Her movements are ungainly and jerky—my own a little less so as etiquette dictates I also stand.

"Eve." I wrap my fingers around her forearm, and she stills, but she doesn't give me her gaze. "I am sorry." Sorry that it had to be her tangled in this mess. "I promise there is good to come out of this."

A sudden ache blooms in my chest as she swipes at a tear with the back of her hand. I just want to take her in my arms, but that would make me as bad as him. And the truth is I'll hurt her much worse than this to get what I want.

"Where are the restrooms?" she asks a passing waitress, an older woman, not the same girl from earlier. The woman's eyes dip to my fingers, her eyes an angry shade of blue as she misreads the situation.

"Follow me, hon." Her attention moves to Eve with a smile. "I'm going that way."

The pair leaves without a backward glance.

Chapter 10
EVIE

"This is so stupid," I mutter to my reflection as I wipe the tear from the corner of my eye. I'm reacting like a kicked dog, which is ridiculous. None of what Oliver just told me is worse than what I discovered yesterday. I mean, it would kind of make sense; if Mitchell cheated on me multiple times, then he's definitely the kind of man who'd marry for convenience.

But why the heck am I wondering if Oliver's assistant was more to him than an employee? He looked so cut up about it. Maybe that's why I feel so . . . urgh! And the fact that he wants to . . . what? Hire me? To pretend to be his girlfriend? *The new Lucy?*

"Collude," I huff into the mirror. Conspire. *Whatever. It's not the same as wanting me.*

I turn away from my reflection and lean against the vanity. I felt so different this morning, the hotel door handle cool in my hand as I paused to glance back at Oliver, splayed across the bed. His hair stark against the linens, his skin gilded by the rising sun. He had temptation stamped all over him. *My fingerprints too.* I'd felt a tiny thrill wash through me: I'd wanted him, and I'd had him. It all seemed like part of a grand plan—Evie getting her groove back.

I guess it's no surprise that when I opened Riley's door to him, my body throbbed with remembrance. Unfortunately, my heart also went pitter-patter.

"Men!" I grate out. Worse still, the rich kind. It figures that Mitchell was hiding more than his extracurriculars, because I was straight from the start—money was a turnoff for me. He knew I didn't get along with my family, that I couldn't agree with their outlook or their lifestyle. Money corrupts, and that's one of the reasons I left Connecticut. I said it was for adventure, but my mother was already applying subtle pressure. To her, the only good husband is a rich husband. As long as he provides, she's happy to turn a blind eye. But deep pockets do not excuse a stinking attitude. Same goes for a pretty face.

The bottom line is, I am disappointed. For Oliver to seek me out for this bull goes in the face of everything he did for me yesterday. Yet, underneath the bottom line lurks a painful postscript in tiny text that I can't help but acknowledge.

He doesn't want me, and that hurts my pride.

"Fuck it," I mutter, swinging back to address my reflection. "And fuck him." Playacting isn't in my repertoire, and one-way desire is a short road to hell. I take a deep breath: what's one more disappointment? *Nothing that I can't cope with.* Pulling on the door, I step out into the darkened hallway.

"Eve."

I turn at the velvet sound of my name. "I wasn't sneaking out," I begin, immediately defensive.

Oliver pushes languidly from the wall, moving closer, all sinuous stalk and prowl. "I just wanted to make sure you're all right." His words are pitched low, spoken like secrets, but they don't stop my ugly huff.

"I'm fine."

Another step, and the breadth of his shoulders blocks the light from the end of the hallway. "Let me help you."

"So I can help you?"

At my tone, his teeth flash. *White like a shark's.* "You say that like it's a bad thing."

"It's a thing I'm not interested in."

"Whether you believe it or not, Mitchell thinks he loves you. Either way, he's not going to leave you alone."

My stomach flips, but my reply is cool. "That's not your concern."

"Do you think he might be a narcissist? He certainly seems to lack empathy."

"You're giving him too much credit," I snap. "He's just another of the world's rich, cheating assholes."

"Money is the root of all evil? How Old Testament of you."

"If the sandals fit." I look him up, then down, but he doesn't bite.

"Hasn't he punished you enough?" He slides his hands into his pockets.

"There's nothing more he can do to hurt me."

"You underestimate him."

"Because I don't really know him?" I don't give him time to answer. "I'm well acquainted with his type." *With your type,* my gaze says as it flickers over him. He'd be my *Jeopardy!* specialist subject. *I'll take Rich Assholes for four hundred dollars.*

"What about your visa? You're no longer his fiancée. What if he makes that official? If he cancels it?"

"I'll manage something." Though my heart rate does a little skip at the thought.

"Help me, Eve," he says, stepping closer. "Move in with me."

"So you can be my fake visa fiancé?" I scoff, even as the hairs on the back of my neck begin to prickle. "That is such a terrible idea." But then his hands are on my waist, and wildfire is rushing through my veins as he eases us into a shadowy alcove.

"Bad ideas seem to be our specialty. I might even make a better fake fiancé than the real one." His lips are shockingly warm on my throat, my insides turning molten as he sucks at my skin.

"That wouldn't be hard. The bar was set pretty low."

He grunts. The sound reminds me of last night—of the sound he made as his body worked over me. "Say yes, Eve."

"Careful." I press my hand to his chest. "That sounded almost like a proposal."

"Shall I propose all the things I'd like to do to you?" he purrs, staring down at me.

Yes. "No." Both responses pulse inside me, my brain and my body at war. "I don't even like you."

He pulls my hips closer, the thick line of his cock pressed to my stomach. His body is so large and so hard, and he perfectly reads the hunger in mine as he holds me there, hard pressed to soft. His hand glides up my ribs, his thumb finding my nipple over the top of my T-shirt.

"Don't you?"

He tugs, and I swallow back a whimper as a throb starts up between my legs.

"Doesn't mean anything. It's just biology." And my brain cells disintegrating as he watches me.

"It's chemistry."

Is that why I sink into him like quicksand, the density of this thing greater than my will?

"You keep saying things I can't trust."

"Trust that I want you. Trust that my mouth would've worshipped you if you hadn't crept out this morning."

"Don't sweet-talk me, Oliver. Not when I know you would've left me on the sidewalk."

He pulls back, his gaze sliding over me, hot and heavy. "I lied. I lost my breath the moment I found you on top of me."

"Sounds like you're calling me fat."

His blue eyes glint without generosity or humor as he slips his free hand under my hair, tugging back my head. "What part of *perfectly formed* don't you comprehend?"

I gasp as much from his words as his hold. I hate how he seems to know exactly just what to say. *Hate it as much as I love this push and pull.*

"These fingers, this mouth. They would worship you."

"In the quest to ruin him." This is what I need to hang on to. His motivations, not the Oliver voodoo he works on me.

"Wouldn't you like to be part of the fun?"

"I'm not vindictive." Despite what that video says.

His dark laughter creates a rush of goose bumps along my arms. "You are such a lovely liar." He lowers his mouth to mine, his kiss just as I'd tried not to remember it. Lips soft yet sure, tongue licking into my mouth as though it's a source of deliciousness.

Whatever my plan was, he wasn't supposed to sweep me away like this as my hands grip his biceps, the muscles flexing under my fingertips. I turn my head, and he makes a sound of approval, his mouth trailing across my jaw, making a path down my neck. His hand slips under the hem of my T-shirt, and I arch against him like a cat, my body turning hot and liquid as he exposes my nipple— here in the hallway of a restaurant.

"Come back with me, Eve."

"No," I whisper, swallowing over the thudding of my pulse.

"Let me—"

"No." I push at his arms, self-preservation, that other animal instinct, taking over.

His thumb retracts from the lace of my bra, slipping away from my nipple. My T-shirt falls as his hand smooths it over my hip, but he doesn't move, our bodies still touching entirely too much.

"I don't need revenge."

Now he steps back, the air between us suddenly cool. "You're sure about that?" His question sounds barely curious.

I nod and press my back against the wall as he reaches out, his thumb passing over my collarbone.

"That's a shame," he says, his gaze following the movement. "Because I'm afraid I do." His charm is a satin sticky web, easy to fall into. Which is probably why it takes a beat for his next words to compute. "You will do this for me, Eve. You will give me three months of your time. Three months of you."

"You don't want me, not really."

He chuckles. It sounds unkind.

"You just want to use me."

"It doesn't have to be so sordid. Why can't we call it 'helping each other'?"

"Whatever you call it, I don't want any part." I swipe at his arm, only for him to catch my wrist.

"Not even as a means to keep you in London?"

Anger zips down my spine. *Romeo or the villain?* he'd asked before. The man is no Romeo.

"This is ridiculous. I won't do it." I pull against his hold, but he doesn't let go. So I force my arm to go limp, inadvertently acknowledging his power over me.

"You can, and you will because you're the kind of person who can do anything they set their mind to." He slips his fingers through mine as though we're a courting couple.

"Don't patronize me."

"That was a compliment."

"I'd sooner stick toothpicks under my toenails, then kick a wall, than be your fake anything." Because he's proving my point perfectly: rich men are nothing but trouble. And I already have enough.

"You'll enjoy some of the benefits." He lifts my hand to his mouth, pressing his teeth over my knuckles. I swallow, ignoring how everything pulls tight as his tongue flicks out. "Think of last night."

"The difference is last night I wanted you. Past tense." I dislike the wobble in my voice as I tug my hand away.

"We both know that's not entirely true." As his hand falls, his knuckles ghost over the pebble of my taut nipple. "We both know you'll do what it takes to remain in London."

I begin to make a show of patting over invisible pockets. "Gosh, why is it you can never find a crayon when you need it? You know, to draw little pictures to explain."

The corner of his mouth kicks up, his only answer to my insult.

"Mitchell isn't going to cause problems with my visa. It's not his style."

"Lovely Eve." His words feel like a pat on the head. "You seem to be laboring under the misapprehension that I won't."

Chapter 11
OLIVER

A Little Bird Told Us . . .

hell hath no fury like a woman scorned!

Or a group of women scorned on behalf of our Shoreditch Pulse Tok bride, after a comical scene was reported at Brick Lane Market today.

A man (who looked suspiciously like the Pulse Tok cheating groom) was forced to abandon his takeout and run when an angry mob began to bombard him with fruit snatched from a nearby market stall.

Bystanders report the women had been celebrating a friend's upcoming nuptials (bottomless brunch, maybe?) when they spotted him and reached for their weapons of choice. Some also struck up a chant of "dirty [expletive] french fry" while taunting him with their pinkie fingers.

Do we have our first sighting of our husband-not-to-be?

Did somebody catch it for posterity? Or us? Please say you did!

Come on, my lovely London flock—name that bride and groom!

Perhaps . . .

I put down my phone, conflicted. It's only a matter of time before the gutter press are camped on Eve's doorstep, given weddings are a matter of public record. *Even the ones that don't quite go through.*

It still baffles me how Atherton managed to get her to the altar. Still, there's nothing like a little outside persuasion. It can only help my cause, though it pains me to see that Atherton has put another woman through shit for his own means.

But Eve is made of altogether sterner stuff than Lucy.

Lucy. I put down my whisky glass, my thoughts turning as fiery as the liquid sliding down my throat. The man is a snake—a waste of flesh and air—and I have no fucking idea how women are continually taken in by him. *Even if the messages he left on my phone do sound quite sincere.* Not that I believe them for a minute. But it made my heart glad to hear him beg, because what he did to Lucy, involving her in his schemes, tearing us apart, makes me want to return the favor. It also makes my fingers itch with the desire to squeeze his windpipe, to make him feel some sense of the pain he caused.

As I pick up my phone, Lucy's words echo in my head. *But I love him.*

I'm not sure if love turns people blind to reality or just temporarily stupid. Probably the latter.

Flicking to my voicemails, I recall the desperation in his tone.

"Please, Deubel. Let me speak to her. If you've touched her, I'll—"

"I fucking love her!"

Had he professed to love Lucy with the same intensity? I put my phone away, disgusted with myself. With him. My own love for Lucy turned me blind for a while. I've since had my eyes opened. *Very wide.*

Reaching for my drink, I throw the rest of it back.

Now, Eve is an interesting proposition. A different kettle of fish. She's strong, feisty, and lovely. She can be quite determined, with the right incentive, I know.

She will bend for me. *I'll make sure of it.*

It will be such a delicious justice, turning Atherton's plan back on himself.

Chapter 12
EVIE

Wednesday morning, I decide to go to work. I'm not rostered on shift for almost three more weeks, thanks to my supposed honeymoon, but Lori's put-upon sighs and sulky glances are driving me crazy. I'm so tired of tiptoeing around her.

Besides, idle hands are the devil's playground. Not that I'm giving into any kind of manual dalliances when it comes to thinking about Oliver Deubel and his pretty face. I'm also not giving his lazy threats headspace or remembering how I allowed him to feel me up in a public restaurant. Or at least I wouldn't be thinking about it if I hadn't been forced to spend the afternoon hiding out in the break room.

"I'll cancel your visa," I mutter darkly to myself. All he was missing was a mustache to twirl. Maybe a bout of maniacal laughter. And this is the man who saved me from the street—the one I practically had to trick into bed! That sounds worse than it should. I mean, I understood his reluctance, but *this* I do not understand!

"I should probably warn you, I make a terrible friend."

I feel myself frown at the remembrance. It's such a crappy defense.

"You seem to be laboring under the misapprehension that I won't."

The man I spent the night with, the only person who helped me that day—he didn't seem the type to hold my visa over my head. But I know men like him, rich men. The kind my mother has a taste for. Men like my stepfather who will leverage just about anything to get what they want.

Which is probably why this all feels like such a head fuck.

Work hasn't been the distraction I needed—my colleagues can barely look at me! At first, I took it for concern. Maybe they thought I would be too upset to hold a conversation. That maybe I wasn't allocated a treatment room for fear I wasn't in the right mindset to make sound clinical decisions. But it feels more like the issue is theirs, like they're embarrassed *for* me. Like they don't know what to say or how to act in front of me.

It's like a bad farce out there—lots of forced laughter and scary smiles when I walk by. I mean, people, come on! Infidelity isn't catching—you can't contract it through a third-party host.

Even if some of them were guests on the day.

So here I sit, hiding out in the break room, eating my body weight in cookies. Weirdly, there is comfort to be found in these familiar surroundings. In the ever-present whiff of disinfectant and in the low hum of voices and animal sounds. It's better than the loneliness that lurks outside these walls.

"What are you doing here?"

I glance up, my heart suddenly glad as Yara's head appears around the door. "Helping myself to Rachel's cookies." I pull another chocolate Hobnob out of the packet—one of the UK's best inventions, for sure. "Snitches get stitches."

"I don't want you coming anywhere near me with a needle," she says, closing the door behind her. "You left that Labrador's paw looking like Frankenstein's monster last week." She makes a sad face, imitating a feeble paw wave.

"My sutures aren't that bad."

"Not when you remember where you've put your glasses, at least."

"Ha ha." My hand lifts until I recall my glasses are on the top of my head. The one good thing to come out of today was finding them. Well, that and seeing Yara. "I thought they were gone for good this time," I say as I dunk the Hobnob into a mug of tea the color of red bricks. I heap the soggy deliciousness into my mouth.

"You didn't come back for your glasses." Leaning her slender frame against the door, she folds her arms.

Yara is gorgeous, all high cheekbones and amber, feline eyes. "Bollywood eyes," I once heard someone in the clinic say, to which she'd laughed and said she wished she had the brows to match instead of inheriting Bollywood villain brows from her dad.

"No." My heart gives a painful little jig. "Turns out, Ivo put them in his drawer last Thursday. I wouldn't have them at all if he—"

Yara holds up her index finger. "Question. Why aren't you being sexed on a beach somewhere?"

The jittering stops, and my heart drops into the pit of my stomach. "Because sex and sand aren't a good combination."

"What?"

"Could it be you're the only person in London who hasn't seen my viral Pulse Tok video?"

My tone is less than joy filled. I thought being at work would give me something else to concentrate on, because Lord knows I've spent enough hours thinking about that stupid thing. At least thinking about it is all I have done, given I don't have my phone. Not that I couldn't have borrowed a colleague's phone, because I'm pretty sure a couple of them have it saved to their favorites.

When I find out who loaded it, I'm going to give them an elephant-size dose of ketamine.

I should've stayed home—I should've turned around when I reached the coffee shop this morning. Courtesy of Riley talking Lori into loaning me a little cash, I decided to treat myself to a latte and a muffin at Coffee & Carbs. The barista had the radio on in the background, and I almost swallowed my tongue when I heard the presenters talking about my so-called wedding ceremony. They'd laughed over the Pulse Tok—worse, they'd asked listeners to call in if they knew the bride and groom. Then, when I reached the clinic, I found Rachel, the vet nurse, and the new receptionist huddled over one of their phones, watching it.

Revenge is *sweet when I'm eating her Hobnob cookies.*

Borrowed scrubs, borrowed money, and brittle dignity—I've had the day from hell. Even the few patients I've seen weren't exactly run of the mill. From the seven-year-old kid who had a full tantrum when he argued his guinea pig wasn't dead, just hibernating (rigor ain't no hibernation), to the elderly couple who didn't appreciate being told their puppy wasn't suffering from a growth . . . unless they considered his newly discovered penis such a thing. *It's his. Let him lick it!*

"What's a Pulse Tok?" Yara asks with a frown.

"Seriously?" My first smile of the day is wide and comes with watery eyes. "You know I love you, work wife, but you are thirty going on old lady."

"Already got the elastic pants," she says, pinging the waistband of her pale-blue scrubs.

"Pass it over." I point at the shape of her phone, obvious in her pocket. "Let's get this over with."

Opening the browser, I quickly type bride uses cheating—scarily, the rest auto fills—text messages as vows. I hit search, ignoring the sinking realization that people have actively looked for this video outside of the Pulse Tok platform.

Though the image of the back of my veil-covered head is still the first result, there are dozens of new offerings in the search list. Digital media companies, newspaper mentions, blogs. The list goes on.

I swallow over the burn in the back of my throat as I select the Pulse Tok video from the preview. As my voice fills the room, my anguished tone hits me like a shock of freezing water. "Deaf like an oldie too," I say as I turn down the volume and hand back her phone. Then I try to turn off my brain. My attention. My anger. Everything.

I swear the clip gets longer each time, two minutes morphing into a lifetime as I watch my friend's reactions flicker and fade across her face. Her arm drops heavily as the clip ends, and she flicks her phone off before it has a chance to reload and play again.

"What the actual fuck." Pulling out the chair opposite, she drops into it, her dark eyes as wide as dinner plates. "Evie, oh my God." She presses her hand to her mouth, and I hate the look she gives me as her gaze morphs into soft-eyed pity. "Was that . . ."

"Jen? Yep," I answer, popping the *p*. She'd been to dinner with Yara and me a bunch of times. With me and Mitch too. It's not even funny how, in retrospect, I see exactly what Jen and Bitchell were up to. They weren't just affectionate in their contact. They were flaunting it, right under my nose.

"But she seemed so nice."

"I guess Mitchell thought so," I say, as numbness washes over me.

"What a pair of toxic ho bags! I wish I'd been there," Yara suddenly growls, hand balling into a fist. "I don't know who I would've punched first, but I definitely would've landed one right in that fucker's smug face."

"You thought he was smug? Actually, don't answer that. He's a total c-bomb."

"You won't turn into a pillar of salt for using the word."

"Not when he deserves it."

"Only, vaginas *are* the bomb, while he lacks the warmth and depth. That turd deserves to wear a wooden onesie. Let's put him in a fucking coffin!" she adds to clear my possible confusion.

"I know scrubs are *kind of* like prison wear, but I don't want to wear them all of the time."

"Not murder, then. Seriously maim."

"I'd rather just move on." I give a half-assed shrug.

"What we need is the Gulabi Gang."

"The what?"

"The stick-wielding aunties in pink saris? Vigil-aunties!" She snorts. "We could start a London group. I know Tasneem would be in," she adds, mentioning her sister's name.

I shake my head with a smile.

"My God, Evie. I'm *so* sorry I wasn't there," she says, her expression turning serious as she reaches for my hand.

"At least you know you can catch the playback all over the internet."

"That's so fucked up." Her brow creases with the kind of sympathy I need to keep at arm's length. There will be no tears today.

"I bet my wedding was more eventful than yours." Her cousin got hitched in Leeds on the same day, which is why she wasn't there. On reflection, that might've been a good thing. For Mitchell, at least.

"What the fuck was he thinking?" She scrubs her hands over her face, pushing the dark bangs away.

"You might need to ask his penis that. Book ahead. I hear it's been pretty busy." My maid of honor, Oliver's PA . . . "Also, take tongs," I add, scrunching my nose.

"More like a scalpel. I just don't get it." She slumps back in her chair, her long legs inelegantly angled. *A little like a chalk drawing of a murder victim.* "Why do men cheat? Surely the fucking you get is not worth the fucking you take."

"Take your house, your kids, half of your 401(k)?" I give a bitter shake of my head. "You have to be married, and I swerved that one good."

"He lost *you*, Evie," she says with such intensity.

I swallow over a knot of emotions tangled too tightly to separate. Yara is the kind of person you'll meet once in a lifetime, if you're lucky. Loyal, honest, real. For me, London and Yara go hand in hand. I can't imagine one without the other, and I know without a doubt both will always be part of my life.

"He was about to win big, and he lost everything. People will remember what he did for a long time. It'll totally fuck him over—fuck him up."

Her words seem to echo something Oliver said. Oliver, urgh! Why am I thinking about him? The rich are so self-involved. They will always put themselves first.

"So sweary today." I hold a crumbly Hobnob between us like a peace offering, when the reality is, I'm just done with this conversation. If I'd known Mitch the lying asshole was rich, I wouldn't be in this predicament. "Anyway, who needs a tropical beach setting when you can treat a husky with a suspected obstruction?"

"Fun," she deadpans.

"Or a Persian kitty vomiting on your shoes because you didn't move quickly enough?"

"Good times."

"He's hooked up to an IV now."

"Seems like a fair punishment."

I give a fond shake of my head. "For fluids while we wait on his blood workup."

"Of course."

"I'm leaving Prince Fursal in your tender care," I say, pushing to stand.

"People should be birched for landing their pets with stupid names." A pause. "You okay?"

"It's been a day." Arching my back, I give in to a stretch. "The looks I've gotten . . ."

"Cats are such suspicious creatures."

"I was talking about the people."

"Eh. People. So overrated. Zero stars. Would *not* recommend. Present company excepted."

"Same."

"So, do you want me to neuter him?" she asks, snatching another cookie from the packet.

I know she's not talking about the cat, so I appear to consider it for a beat. "Would I have to help? Because I don't ever want to see those testicles again."

"Fair," she says, then crams the cookie into her mouth.

"I thought I might just overdose him on ketamine."

Yara coughs, laughs, and then begins to choke. "Whatever works," she croaks. "What's discussed in the break room stays in the break room."

"Except for the crumbs." Leaning over, I brush the remains from her face.

"And the drugs we steal to off a certain someone."

Twenty minutes later, I pull on the hoodie I'd raided from Riley's closet this morning and step out into the rainy afternoon.

"Give me a break," I mutter, my brows lowering as I notice the shiny Bentley in the parking lot. I forcibly ignore the way my stomach flips. Those swanky wheels are probably just a coincidence.

The clinic is in Knightsbridge, which is a pretty tony area of London. We deal with a lot of pet advocates (not *owners*, because the term was judged demeaning to pets last year. Pets are people too . . . even though they're not) worried about Fido's gluten intake or inquiring if we offer cat Reiki. We see a lot of poodles in Gucci sweaters and fluffy cats in bejeweled neckwear, so the lot is no stranger to fancy vehicles.

So why am I squinting through the rain while fluffing my ponytail? *Because you don't want to look like shit when you see him again* should not be the answer, but it's the one my brain offers.

Oliver Deubel makes me feel . . . hot and bothered. Antsy and annoyed. I'd say he's the human equivalent of stinging nettles but for the flicker of *yes, please!* that starts up whenever I think of him. Even after his threats. *Well, I'm not going to let him cause problems for me. My visa can't be that hard to fix.* My stomach roils as I mentally push away the results of my earlier Google fest. It's just a temporary problem. It has to be. *Same goes for my fascination with him.*

Meanwhile, it looks like this rain is here to stay. I sigh, wondering if I should leave Nora's for another day. It's not like she's expecting me. I'm supposed to be on my honeymoon.

Nora is kicking eighty, and her cell phone is a brick. I doubt it has that ancient snake game, never mind access to the web. Even if she had the internet at her little animal sanctuary, she wouldn't ask questions. She has zero interest in any creature that wasn't born to walk on four legs.

"It's bloody chucking it down!"

I turn to the sound of the door opening behind me and of Ida, the practice manager's voice.

"Yep, good old British summertime."

Top tip: when seeking safe conversation in London, always opt for the weather.

"Better the rain than honeymooning with that waste of space."

109

So much for *safe.*

"I hope he gets crotch rot and his todger falls off." Ida gives a decisive nod, and I find myself laughing unexpectedly. *And tearing up, unfortunately.* "Anyway, I meant to give you these," she says, passing a bunch of colorful sticky notes into my hand. "Messages that came in for you today." She presses one age-weathered finger to the bridge of her glasses, prodding them higher on her nose. "Said they were journalists, all but one of them." She adds a distaining sniff. "That call was from someone called Lori complaining about a bad smell hanging around the front of the house."

"What?" Why would she . . .

"It was the waste-of-space shit bag," Ida adds.

A heavy brick sinks to the pit of my stomach. *Where did Mitch get Riley's address?*

"It's only a question of time before he turns up here. You know that, don't you?"

"Yeah." I thought, well, I thought he might not bother, given I'm supposed to be on vacation. *With him.*

"If you want to keep management off your back, I say you take your holidays."

I guess that's Ida speak for "they wouldn't appreciate a scene."

"Anyway, I neither confirmed nor denied you worked here," she summarizes, pulling the sides of her chunky cardigan tighter across her small frame. "Data protection, so I said. Then I told them to push off and get a proper job."

I shove the sticky notes into the pocket of Riley's hoodie. "Thanks, Ida."

"You're welcome, love. You okay?"

"Mostly." The word hits the air as wobbly as my smile.

"Poor lamb." She makes a sympathetic click of teeth and tongue. "Let me pass on something my dad told me a long time ago, God rest his soul. He said that if a man shits himself in public, it's usually because he has a bigger stink to hide."

I resist the urge to wrinkle my nose. Ida's dad was no poet, but I guess he wasn't wrong. Marrying me to get his hands on a property. Screwing Oliver's assistant. It could be the tip of the iceberg.

"Your dad sounds like a smart man."

"Not really. He fell down a manhole, drunk. Broke his neck. Anyway, you take care," she adds brightly as she disappears behind the closing door.

Well, okay. Head down against the deluge, I step out into the rain . . . and straight into a puddle. "What in the name of—"

A car door slams in the distance, but I'm too busy to pay attention as I try to determine if that's mud stuck to the sole of my wet sneaker (or something worse) as I curse the stars, the universe, and humanity in general. I've even forgotten the parked Bentley as someone calls out my name.

"Evelyn Fairfax?"

I lift my head and narrow my eyes at the woman with a polka-dot umbrella walking toward me. She holds out her free hand, but not in greeting, as she flashes me some kind of ID.

"My name is Una Smith. I'm with the *City Chronicle.* I wondered if you have a few minutes to chat."

"No." And hell no. "I'm in kind of a hurry." Gaze averted, I move past her, wet sneaker and all.

"'Savage Bride Reads Out Cheater's Text Messages Instead of Vows.'"

I pivot with an incredulous "What did you just say?"

"There's also 'Bridezilla's Revenge.'"

My feet shuffle against the wet ground. I'm unsure if I want to know what she's talking about or if I want to run away.

"Those are only two of the headlines I've seen. We at the *City Chronicle* would like to give you the option to tell your side of the story in our London society column, A Little Bird Told Us."

"There is no story." I turn away quickly. *I'm not the only bride to have changed her mind, to have stood up for herself.*

"It wasn't that you changed your mind, but the manner of your retaliation."

Shit. I said that? I only thought . . . "I have nothing else to say."

"Evelyn," she calls after me. "Women everywhere are cheering for you. I won't be the only journalist interested, but I'll be the best to tell your story!"

"Hello, Eve." Another voice, one that shouldn't feel like a swallow of whisky in a cold, empty stomach. *Warm. Intoxicating. Welcome.*

The pull of him is inevitable as I turn to the rear window of the Bentley, Oliver's fire-bright gaze fixed on me.

"Go away," I mutter, forcing myself into an undignified wet-foot limp past him. Tires hiss against the wet asphalt, but I don't stop. I'm pretty sure he's not about to mow me down. I haven't annoyed him that much. *Yet.*

As the Bentley pulls alongside me, I keep my attention ahead.

"Get in the car."

My, what a drawling command. Maybe I should try that tone for myself. "Oliver? Go suck my lady dick."

"I did. We both liked it."

"Are you serious right now?" I think my jaw just unhinged as my feet come to a stop and I glare at him. Mostly to cover how my body doesn't seem to have gotten the memo that we don't like him.

"I never joke about sex. Get in the car. Please," he adds as an obvious afterthought. Damn his perfect jawline; the universe is *unjust*, because if Oliver's looks matched his personality, he'd have a face like a troll. *Or maybe the devil, because wasn't the devil an angel once?*

"Can't. I have an appointment, and I'm late." I swing around and begin to walk again.

"All the more reason to accept a ride. Or should I go back and have a word with your friend? Was she a journalist?"

My sneakers squeak as I halt. Again. The Bentley's tires do not do the same. "You would not," I utter icily, my head turning like the turret on a tank. From what I'm coming to understand, he probably would, but . . . *Think, Evie. What benefit would it be to him? Just another manipulation. Whether he will or won't carry through isn't the point.*

"Probably not," Oliver concedes with a little lift of one shoulder. "But it got you to stop."

"And now I'm starting again." With a mean, closed-lipped smile, I pivot away. "Goodbye, Oliver. Let's not meet again."

I take a left out of the car park, and the Bentley follows, its pace matching mine. I hate the tiny spark of excitement inside me, and how it feeds the needy part of my soul.

"We can carry on our conversation like this, but only one of us is getting wet," Oliver says from the window. "And not in the fun way."

"You make me wish I had my headphones." I could get Ted, his poor driver, to wear them.

"Hop in, and we'll go and get them. Your phone, your belongings—everything."

"Oh, you'd just love that." I throw the words over my shoulder.

"Yes, you're right. I'd love to help you."

I hate that I glance his way again, but not as much as I hate the expression he's wearing. It's an incitement to violence.

Yes, Officer, that is *my knife sticking out of his chest.*

Yes, sir, I did say he had it coming to him.

"While we're at his apartment, I should get you a wooden spoon from the kitchen to help you with your stirring."

"Or I could spank you with it for being so obstinate."

"In your dreams."

His laugh is dirtier than the break room's microwave. "Eve, I would *love* the opportunity to describe my dreams to you."

That tempting little flutter starts up between my legs. It's not right or appropriate, as far as responses go, but I can't help how my body reacts to him. It makes no sense. He threatens me, trails me in his car, and I go all gooey? It's so wrong that my body is all *Oliver, just go full dark-book boyfriend, and throw me in the car!*

"For someone so spirited on Saturday, you seem very fretful about facing your ex."

"No one looks forward to seeing their ex. Unless that ex happens to be in a coffin."

"I did suggest death by cab. Let's make him green with jealousy instead."

I grit my teeth and brush my rain-wet hair from my face. I take it all back. Book boyfriends aren't supposed to annoy the heroine into exploding. "Not gonna happen."

"How unfortunate for your fluffy clientele. I'm sure they'll miss you."

"That's the best you've got?" I demand, spinning to face him. "I guess you must be running out of those idle threats."

"They're not idle, darling. I mean every word."

I pause, because his expression absolutely belies his drawling delivery. "You're not going to mess with my visa." I hate the lack of conviction in my words, the upward inflection at the end.

"No. I'll just have you deported."

"Unbelievable." At least, I want it to be.

"Have you even looked into how difficult it will be to remain in this country?"

I did. In the break room. And, honestly, it doesn't look easy. I'll probably need to leave the country to apply and start the process afresh. I guess I'd refused to believe it because I'd closed the web page and filed the issue for the attention of Next-Week Evie.

"The path you're on currently leads to deportation."

"So says you."

"I'm glad you were listening."

"Urgh!"

"Do you know the Home Office will hold your passport and only return it when you reach the door of your plane back to the US? You might even be held in detention if you're determined a flight risk. Which you obviously are."

My heart flaps like a sparrow in a cage as I spin away, forcing my chin high. Oh, but it's hard being dignified when you're filled with panic, your socks are soggy, and your borrowed sneakers are rubbing at the heel.

I'm aware of the car coming to a stop behind me, but I force myself to hobble on, ignoring the stupid pang in my chest lamenting that our moment is done. Then the rain suddenly stops, though the dark shadow of a cloud passes overhead.

No, not a cloud. A huge black umbrella.

"You are the most obstinate woman," says a familiar yet resigned voice as Oliver's large presence appears by my side. I totally ignore the way his biceps flex under his jacket as he gently lifts my hand, placing it there.

"Did I say you could touch me?"

"Yes, on Saturday. Repeatedly."

I laugh even though I don't mean to.

"If I remember rightly, you demanded it. 'Yes. Harder. Here.'" Dipping his chin, he slants me a look. "You really were a dominant little thing."

I shake my head. I guess my heart is just a traitor for this pretty face, because Lord knows it can't be his personality that stops me from setting him on his ass.

Chapter 13
OLIVER

"Why are you doing this to me?" Eve glances up, her pace not altering.

A smile touches my lips. That scowl . . .

"You know why."

"You would've saved yourself a journey if you'd listened to me Sunday. How'd you find out where I work, anyway?"

"Haven't you ever googled yourself, doctor?" While Eve had said she was a vet, I'd been surprised to discover she is both a doctor of veterinary medicine and a member of the Royal College of Veterinary Surgeons. This is no reflection on her—she's clearly an intelligent woman. It's just a pity her choice in men seems to make her appear otherwise, myself included.

"Can't say I have," she answers without glancing away.

"But you've googled me."

Eve's cheeks take on a hue that has nothing to do with the damp air.

I remind myself the only reason I'm here is because of Atherton. *Nothing to do with her.* "I see you have."

"It was a slow day at work. What can I say?"

If she's spent time cruising the internet, she might have also discovered how challenging it'll be for her to remain in the country. Unless you can engage the services of the country's leading immigration lawyer. Which I can.

"Were you sad to discover I wasn't one of the devil's minions?"

"Especially when I read about all those orphanages you built and the puppies you rescued."

"Saint or sinner." I sigh. "Romeo or the villain. There are middle grounds, you know."

"When we're talking about blackmail?" She slants me a less-than-complimentary glance. "Not in my book."

"Tell me, what would work, in your book?" Ignoring her bark of laughter, I add, "It's not like you've nothing to gain. You want to stay in London. I can help you. You want your life back. I can help you with that too. Improve it, even."

"Delusional! How could having you in my life possibly improve it?"

"I could think of a few ways," I find myself purring.

"Thanks, but I'll pass." She swings away, her damp ponytail swishing like an angry kitten's tail. "I can solve my own problems."

"Undoubtedly. You're very resourceful." She doesn't bite. "But I could alleviate a lot of the stress." And not just with sex. "I have connections. The best law team in London at my service."

"Oh, my Lord," she says, suddenly affecting the southern tone she'd used at the hotel Saturday evening. "I am just so honored that you'd take an interest in me, a poor, hapless, *helpless* little woman."

"Again, there's nothing helpless about you." My words don't sound very complimentary. "With my help, the outcome would be guaranteed."

Eve opens her mouth, but her response is overcome by chattering teeth. She clamps her jaw together forcefully.

"Serves you right for not getting in the car."

"Who died and made you king?"

"I'd gladly offer you my crown and my scepter, my rod and my staff, but something tells me you're not in the mood."

Nothing.

I sigh. "Life would be much easier if people listened to instructions." And poorer, too, considering how lovely angry looks on her.

She sniffs, and as she turns, I realize she's soaked through.

"Stop." I tighten my fingers on her arm. "Hold this." Thrusting the handle of the umbrella into her hand, I quickly tug on the zip of the oversize hoodie she's wearing.

"Hey! Stop that!"

I have it open and one arm free before she can complain with any great effect. Spinning her in the other direction means she almost takes out my eye with the umbrella spokes. "Don't worry, I'm not trying to get you naked," I mutter, jerking back.

"I got that memo, thanks."

"Not in the street, at least." The sweatshirt dangles from one wrist, and the expression she's wearing? We'll call it *how rude!* But not for long as I strip off my jacket, and her eyes slide hungrily down my chest. They linger in the vicinity of my belt, when she rolls in her bottom lip, rendering it pink and shiny. Bloody hell. If she doesn't stop looking at me like that, my rod and crown will announce themselves.

"Why do you keep tormenting me?" she whispers.

"Because you think I'm pretty," I murmur, reaching out to tidy a lock of her rain-frizzed hair, "and I'm nothing if not persistent."

Her brows knit. "I didn't say you were pretty."

"Yes, you did." I relieve her of the umbrella and lean the handle across my shoulder. I shake out my jacket from the collar, ready for her to slip it on. "On Saturday afternoon you said my lashes were pretty."

"I was in a state of shock," she mutters as she turns away. She slides in one arm, then the other. Then her breath hitches as, from behind, I drop my mouth to her ear.

"And on Saturday evening," I whisper as softly as a curl of smoke, "you said my cock was the prettiest you've ever seen."

"I did—I *don't* remember."

"Liar." I bite back my enjoyment as she spins and snatches the wet hoodie from my hand. I lift the umbrella, and resuming our positions, we begin to walk again. "Compliments are always welcome."

"I'm sure you get so many." Her tone is the verbal equivalent of side-eye as she swishes the hoodie back and forth by her thigh.

"Are you surprised?"

"Such modesty." She snorts.

"'You're so thick. So hard. I want you inside me,'" I utter perfectly pleasantly—as though commenting on the weather.

"Oh my God," Eve splutters, glancing up at me as though I've grown another head.

"Those are the usual. 'Your cock feels so good' is also nice. 'I feel so full, you're going to split me in two' is also special to hear."

"Stop! I get the picture."

"But 'Oh, God, your pretty cock. Please, please, I need it inside me' took things to a wonderful new level."

"I did not beg."

"You looked so beautiful, breathless and slightly desperate." I don't think I meant to sound so wistful.

"Please stop."

"*That* you never said. Your compliments are my new favorite. My current go-to."

"Go-to?" Her attention slices my way, a tiny throb of connection joining us for a beat. Her body perceives my meaning, her brain catching up a moment later when she glances away. "This is so inappropriate."

My feet slow to a stop. "I can thank you for your compliments, but I can't tell you how I enjoy them?"

"No, you cannot."

"You're saying masturbation isn't a general topic of conversation. We should change that. Have dinner with me."

"So we can talk about you jacking off?" she splutters.

"If you prefer, I could demonstrate?"

"Do you have a split personality? Because I am seriously beginning to doubt which is the authentic version."

"Every version of me wants you."

"Wants something from me, more like." Tugging gently on my arm, she steers us around a corner. At least she's not running away.

"I want your help, and I want you in my bed." *And you have no idea the lengths I'll go to.*

"Stop saying that."

She turns to the pressure on her arm.

"All right." Taking her hand, I press it to my chest. The air around us is flat and damp, but the space between seems to pulse with anticipation. I angle my head, and her lashes flutter, her cool lips yielding to mine, accepting the brush of my tongue. Rain begins to hammer against the umbrella as her fingers tighten on my biceps, everything around us forgotten. Our surroundings, her resistance, our cross-purposes, all gone. My palm glides over the curve of her hip, taking hold of the heavenly roundness of her arse. I press her to me, soft to hard, her moan so sweet I could bottle it.

"Eve." Her name is all gravel. "Come home with me." *Fuck my plans, at least for a little while. Just let me worship between your legs.* Her lashes flicker open, and a burst of heat floods my veins. Then dissipates as her fingers retract in the space of a blink.

"I wish you'd leave me alone." Her face is flushed, and my jacket, though huge on her frame, doesn't conceal the rapid rise and fall of her breath.

"No, you don't."

Which is a problem for at least one of us.

◆ ◆ ◆

"Shut the gate." Her tone is perfunctory as she strides up a weed-strewn path, taking my umbrella with her.

"*No more kissing,*" she'd said as she strode away. "*That doesn't work on me.*" Eve then issued me an ultimatum: she had a client she needed to check on, someone called Nora. I could behave and come along, or I could be gone. Like a lapdog waiting for the right moment to stick my nose between her legs, I followed, finding myself at a rustic-looking gate, fashioned from wooden pallets fixed with hinges and a lock.

I close it behind me as an unholy racket strikes up. Dogs—dozens of them, by the sounds of things—bark a discordant frenzy. They're either very excited to see Eve or about to tear her apart. I begin after her, running—skidding, thanks to the wet ground and the leather soles of my shoes.

Bloody English weather. Bloody women, throwing themselves in harm's way—

"Shut the fuck up!"

I almost halt at the sergeant major–like tenor of a woman's voice.

"What the hell are you doing, setting them off?"

I round a corner to find an older woman, Nora presumably, standing over Eve, who is sitting on the wet concrete, being mauled by a large, fluffy teddy bear. Or a large, fluffy teddy bear's tongue.

"Eww, Bo," Eve complains laughingly. "No face kisses—I don't know where your tongue has been!"

On second glance, the teddy bear appears to be a dog. If my tailor could see the muddy paws on his masterpiece of a jacket, he'd probably faint.

"He hasn't had his tongue on his nuts. Not since you chopped 'em off," mutters the other woman—her accent is pure East End, her tone a husky twenty-a-day habit. She has steel gray hair that looks like wire wool and wears faded jeans, the legs half-obscured by black Wellington boots. The woman leans down against the shovel she holds. "If I was him, I wouldn't give you the time of day." She pushes a sleeve of her puddle-brown cardigan to her elbow. "What you doing 'ere, anyway?"

"You talking to me or Mr. Bojangles?" Eve asks without looking up.

"I know what he's doing here. The little shit has escaped his run again. I ain't never had a dog that could climb fences like a squirrel," she says. "You, what are you doing here, girl?" Her thick accent renders the word *gel*. "Why ain't you on your honeymoon?"

Eve turns my way, her cheeks flushed. If she's thinking about kisses, I hope she's remembering mine rather than the dog's more recent attempts.

"I had a change of heart."

"So I see." The woman's mouth pinches, her eyes skimming over me in an uncomplimentary way. "Change of Heart gotta name?"

"Oliver Deubel." My name rings across the small yard, and I'm almost certain the woman curses under her breath.

"Oliver, this is Nora."

"A toff, Evie," the woman laments. "Where'd you pick 'im up?"

"It was more the other way around." She murmurs her response into the dog's fluffy pelt. "Oliver was my escape."

"Men." The word leaves the woman's mouth like *bah!* "Rich men." She eyes me like I smell offensive. "His type will bring you no joy."

I spike a brow. Saturday night was the embodiment of joy. It strikes me that joy might be part of the reason I'm pursuing her. *A welcome, secondary reason.* I know she feels it. I see it in the ways she looks at me. Even when she seems like she doesn't know whether to hug or strangle me.

"Don't I know." Eve chuckles unhappily. "But don't let that accent fool you. Oliver here is the salt of the earth. Or was it more *salt the earth?*"

My mouth twists, though her assertion reminds me of my purpose today. Why do I find it so easy to become sidetracked by her?

"Anyway, it's not like that. Oliver here helped me escape." She smiles sadly as she stands. "Things didn't go quite to plan on Saturday."

The woman frowns. "I warned you that Mitchell was ten pounds of shit in a five-pound container."

"I know you did," Eve responds in the kind of tone that suggests this isn't the first conversation of this kind.

"More dick in his personality than I bet he has in his pants." She pauses as though awaiting confirmation.

"You made that clear too. Try not to be offended," Eve says, turning briefly my way. "It's not just men. Nora is an equal opportunity hater. Isn't that right?"

"People." She sniffs. "Only good for spare parts."

"Speaking of parts . . ." I push the dog away as he sticks his nose into my crotch.

"Don't be flattered," Eve says. "Bo isn't very selective."

The older woman's shoulders jump and fall with her laughter as she shuffles away, only to stop as though remembering something. "What did he do anyway? To make you change your mind?"

"I found out he was cheating."

"Huh." The woman seems disappointed rather than sympathetic. "So no leather or handcuffs and stuff?"

"What?"

"Said you needed an escape." Nora nods my way.

Eve's nose delightfully scrunches. "Mitch didn't tie me up."

She's definitely disappointed.

"I just left when I found out he was cheating on me. In my wedding dress."

"A runaway bride?"

"And now the press are hounding me."

The woman sniffs her disinterest. "Yesterday's news is tomorrow's kitty litter. Just don't bring 'em here," she says as she turns away. "Don't want the newspapers knocking on my door."

"It's not like I'd do it intentionally."

"I mean it." The old woman swings back, pointing her finger at Eve.

"Okay. I get it. Do you want me to put Bo back in his kennel?" Eve adds hesitantly.

"What's the point?" Nora shrugs. "He'll just get himself out again." And with that, she trudges off.

"So, that was Nora," Eve observes.

"She's charming." The corner of my mouth twitches.

"Not even a little," she says as her lips curve. "But don't let her gruff exterior fool you. She's a good person, and a wonderful advocate for anything four legged."

"And that's why you're here, I suppose."

"Yeah. This has become a labor of love for me. The kennels aren't exactly to code." She gestures to the ramshackle buildings off to the side.

"Which would make this a . . ." A shambles? A dumpsite? Somewhere in need of condemning?

125

"An animal sanctuary, though Nora gets no funding, no charity status. It's privately run, financed by luck, goodwill, and donations. She basically does this out of the goodness of her heart."

"I can see she has a very big heart," I reply doubtfully.

Eve laughs. "There's only space in there for the four legged." Which seems the ideal opportunity for a three-legged sheep to hobble past. "And those born to walk on four legs."

Nora has a soft spot for animals, and Eve, while a veterinarian, has a soft spot for both animals and people. *I wonder which category you fall into,* whispers a dark voice in my ear.

"She seemed to have other interests," I say, sliding my hands into my pockets and sauntering closer. "Like whether Mitchell is into BDSM."

"Trust you—"

"—to pick up that Nora has a vivid internal life or that Mitchell is a slave to vanillaism?" I stand so close that if the rain were continuing to fall, it wouldn't pass between us.

She scoffs.

"He doesn't know what he's missing." Her eyes are all pupil as I take her chin between my fingers. "You'd be such a beautiful little slut for me, bound and on your knees."

"Just try it." Her whispered words feather across my cheek. "And you'll end up like Mr. Bojangles here."

"Slobbering and climbing all over you?" *I'm already partially there.*

She tries not to smile. *Tries and fails.* "Minus your testicles."

"Don't knock it unless you've tried it." Releasing her, I draw my forefinger down between the open sides of my jacket. "Just imagine, being helpless to my touch and my praise."

"While you demand I thank you."

"For my fingers and my tongue. My pretty cock as I feed it to you."

"You're the one with the fetish." Reaching out, she pokes her forefinger into my chest. My flex is deliberate; the way my nipple protrudes is just good luck, considering the way her gaze remains glued to it. "You get off on being thanked." Her words are puffs of warm air I want to swallow.

"A gratitude kink?" I purr, spiking a brow. "You should subscribe to my OnlyFans."

"You have OnlyFans?" Her eyes rise with a mixture of shock and interest.

"Where all good girls get to come, and they thank me for it. Do you know why?"

Eve gives her head a tiny shake.

"Because the pleasure is all *mine*."

Chapter 14
EVIE

If the pleasure is all his, then why am I vibrating from head to toe as he watches me? Oliver and OnlyFans. That would be an obsession in the making. He wouldn't even have to get naked, just sit there in his Savile Row suit and his shiny handmade shoes, straightening his cuffs and telling me what to do. I mean, I wouldn't do it. But I think we'd both get off on the tension.

"Was Saturday an off day for you?" I ask, ignoring the subtle scent of him drifting up from his collar. We're in the shed now, and I'm still wearing his jacket. I can't believe I almost let him kiss me again. It was only a deep warning *woof* from Bo that brought me back to my wits.

It's so bad that the dog has more sense than me.

I turn my head when Oliver doesn't answer and find him staring out over the kennel run, arms crossed, one broad shoulder leaning against a wooden column. I allow myself to drink him in. It's kind of thrilling that I know what he looks like under those expensive threads of his. The long, graceful muscles of his thighs, the wide expanse of his back. *That ass.* I know the sounds he makes. Where he likes to be touched. *Where I like to touch him.* And now I'm sniffing his jacket like an addict denying her problem.

Come on, Evie. Get it together. The man is no Romeo.

I begin to slip out of his jacket when he appears to come back to himself.

He glances around the space the volunteers use as a base. It's even more ramshackle than the rest of the sanctuary. "What makes you ask?"

"You were nice to me." I throw his jacket across the space, and he catches it effortlessly.

"Was I?" His purring tone catches me off guard, his earlier words echoing in my ear. *I'm not going to be nice to you. You'll thank me for it.* "You must've caught me on an off day," he adds, dropping his jacket to the blue plastic office chair, the one with a wonky leg.

"That I can believe."

"Because my powers of persuasion are winning you over?"

"Oliver, seriously. You're looking at the wrong person. You need an actress."

"Why, when we already have a relationship."

"What relationship?" I ask, my tone flat.

"We're friends. Friends who really like to—"

"Hand me that bag," I demand loudly—the Evie equivalent of *la-la-la-laa!* as I point to the bag of doggy treats on top of a battered filing cabinet. I'm kind of surprised Bo hasn't beaten me to them. Oliver closes his mouth with a smirk and does that spiky brow thing he does. The one that makes me want to shave it off. "Please?" I tag on heavily.

"My pleasure." He throws the liver treats my way. "You're missing the point. The involvement of an actress wouldn't hurt Mitchell nearly enough. That's what makes you perfect for this."

"I'll keep saying it if I need to—I'm not interested in revenge."

"A fact I find astounding after what he did to you."

"I just want to move on." I take out a couple of treats, shove the bag into one pocket of my damp scrubs and the treats into the

129

other. "I'm sorry about your jacket," I add, noting the smear from Bo's paws. "I'll take it to the dry cleaner."

He eyes it impassively. "Dump it. It's ruined."

"It's just a little mud," I chide, but he dismisses the topic with a flick of his hand.

"This animal sanctuary—does Nora take only dogs? And sheep?"

"Cats. Dogs. Sheep," I reply, glad the topic of conversation has turned. "All kinds of things." As I make my way into the yard, Oliver follows, and the din starts up: low barks and high yips, the puppies excited for company. "She had a llama a few months ago that someone was keeping on the twelfth floor of a high rise."

His expression, it's like that won't quite compute. I guess in his world people aren't given to flights of fancy. Or mental illness.

"She found him a home on a farm in Kent, but it's mostly dogs she gets." Shooing Bo out of the way, I turn to the first kennel run and unlock the gate. "Sadly, a lot of them have been through some kind of trauma. Isn't that right, Mouse?" The improbably named Mouse might be the result of a three-way between a lurcher, a Shetland pony, and a wolf. And right now, he's all teeth and growl.

"Eve, I think—" Oliver holds out his hand, his mouth beginning to form a word that looks a lot like *stop*. I don't, slipping quickly into the pen.

"It's fine. It's you he's growling at. He doesn't like men, thanks to his last owner. Me and Mouse are buddies, aren't we, sweetie?" Thick gums cover his teeth as I slip a liver treat between them. His tongue lolls as he chews, and as I pat his head, I swear he gives me the doggy version of a goofy grin. "It's not everyone you'll let stick a thermometer up your tushy, is it?"

"You're close friends, then?" I laugh at that one. "Nora pays you to do that?"

"No. Labor of love, remember?" My hands move over Mouse, my assessment thorough but brief. "He had a couple of broken ribs when he arrived. Some nasty cuts and bites, but everything is healing nicely. Next week you get your booster," I baby talk, taking his face in my hands.

"He's got a head like a battering ram."

I make a show of covering Mouse's ears. "Hush! You'll hurt his feelings."

"Are they all abandoned?" he asks as I slip out from the kennel, throwing Mouse another treat.

"Some are surrendered voluntarily: change of circumstances—homelessness, new babies and partners. Some come from the local pound, saved from euthanasia in the nick of time. Then there are the ones picked up on the street. They're usually in a terrible mess. Fleas, worms, sores, infections, and matted coats."

"Until you come along."

"Not just me. There are a couple of us who pitch in, also groomers and other volunteers. Dogs need to be walked, their runs and kennels cleaned, and then there's the training. Cats need social-ization, and then there's the admin."

"The cats take care of admin? How efficient."

I catch myself smiling at his silly joke. Sometimes, I just don't know whether I'm on my ass or my elbow with him.

"Nora would love the cats to work for their keep," I answer brusquely. "She hates dealing with paperwork."

"And the aim is to find all these animals new homes?"

"The ultimate aim. With medical help and a little TLC, most of the animals are ready for a family pretty quickly. For others, it's the damage we can't see that stops them from being pets. Psychological damage that can't always be healed, though we try, don't we, Mr. Bojangles?" I bend to pat his head as he dances between us.

"He's a very different-looking dog," Oliver says, his gaze sweeping along the kennels full of terriers, hounds, and our myriad of mixed breeds.

"Bo here is a designer doggy. A labradoodle that has found himself here through no fault of his own." If you discount his intelligence and his willful nature.

"And he hasn't been easy to rehome?"

"He has, but he's like a boomerang. He just keeps coming back."

"I wonder why," Oliver mutters, moving Bo's nose from his crotch again.

"He does seem to like sticking his head there." I press my hand over my mouth, but it does nothing to stem my giggles.

"Do you suppose I should be flattered? Buy him a thank-you gift?"

"Maybe you could just adopt him? He's already *so* fond of you."

"Not a chance," he deadpans.

"Nora wouldn't let you, anyway. He's staying until she finds a family who can convince her they're going to keep him."

Next, I slip into Bella's run, the elderly beagle waddling her way over to me.

"What's wrong with the way she walks?"

"Bella has cruciate ligament damage."

"A torn ACL?"

"More like a chronic wearing," I reply as I run through a quick checkup. *Eyes. Ears. Teeth. Fur.* No need for the works. She hasn't been ill since she escaped and helped herself to a whole bin of kibble a few months ago, the greedy pup. It was touch and go as to whether her stomach would need to be pumped, and I'm sure she had the worst case of tummy ache, but that's greedy beagles for you.

"You can operate to fix that, can't you?"

I make a noncommittal noise as I pull out a liver treat. "She's doing okay on anti-inflammatories, which is good, because Nora doesn't have the funds to cover her surgery. Never mind a recovery."

"What's Change of Heart still doin' here?" Nora's strident question arrives before she does, rounding the corner with a chipped but steaming mug in each hand. She directs her beetle-browed look toward Oliver.

"I beg your pardon?" he asks blandly.

"You heard."

"Nora," I half laugh, half correct as I turn her way. "Oliver is not a volunteer."

"If he's here, he's working. Them's the rules," she retorts, ignoring my gentle rebuke.

"I'm not sure you can afford my rate," Oliver murmurs, though Nora pretends not to hear.

"There are a dozen fifteen-kilo bags of kibble that need moving into the stores. The pet shop on the high street donated it this morning." The first she says to Oliver, the latter to me.

"Well, that's great!"

"Would be even better if those bags could shift themselves." She glares Oliver's way.

"I take it you'd like me to move them," Oliver asks with a completely straight face.

"Well," she says, thrusting one of the steaming mugs in his direction. "Let me think. Does Barbie have a plastic fanny?"

Oliver blinks, taken aback.

"Is a duck's arse watertight?" She glances my way. "You're sure this one's firing on all cylinders?"

"My cylinders fire just fine," Oliver drawls. Thankfully, he doesn't add, *Just ask Eve.*

"He looks like a chameleon in a packet of Skittles," she says, disregarding his answer. "Confused. But they don't have to be clever when they look like that, I suppose."

"Nora!" I give in to a delighted snicker.

"You know that one stubborn hair you have on your nipple?" she asks out of nowhere. "The one you pluck, but no matter what, it just comes back?"

"No." My answer sounds like a rusty violin string as my cheeks begin to burn hotter than a thousand suns. *Lord, this woman!*

"Well, I reckon your last one couldn't have had more hair on his chest than me, but he was pretty." Glancing over her shoulder, she gives Oliver a thorough once-over. "But this one, he's something else."

"Oh, my good Lord," I mutter. *Please teleport me someplace else. Say, Timbuktu?*

◆ ◆ ◆

Less than an hour later, and my four-legged charges are all fine and locked away, except Bo, who makes it clear he's not going anyplace he doesn't want to.

"I see she had other jobs for you to do," I say with a smile as Oliver appears in the shed again. His shirtsleeves are folded to the elbows, and the hems of his dark pants are mud splattered. My body prickles with pleasure that he helped. He isn't the kind of man who takes orders well, as my orgasms well know.

"The pleasure is all mine."

The echo of his words curls around my ear and bursts pleasurably a lot farther south. I've never had sex with a man like him, one who made my pleasure the aim, rather than a sideline to his. As movement catches my eye, I'm yanked from my smutty memories.

"I think she's under the impression I'm here as community service." Oliver whacks his hand against his elbow, as though it's a successful means to clean.

"Yeah." I blink heavily. *What the hell is wrong with me? This is the man who's trying to blackmail me.*

"I'm usually paid for what I know, not for what I do." Oliver stalks across the space, the smile playing on his lips suggesting he can see right into my head.

I give myself a metaphoric shake. "No one here gets paid. Ever."

"I feel like I should ask you to take a picture for proof. My partners will never believe this is how I've spent my afternoon."

"Getting sweaty?"

"That they'd believe." He slides me a look that makes my skin sizzle. "Especially if I said I was with you."

"It was Fin and Matt, right?"

"Yes." He kind of frowns and smiles at the same time.

"You mentioned their names once. Their names also came up in association during my Google search."

His smile deepens, and I feel like all my screws rattle loose. I might've lied to Riley when I said I don't feel all heart-eye emoji when I look at him, because I do. *Sometimes.* And sometimes I imagine myself shaving off that annoyingly haughty eyebrow.

"Why would I need an actress?" he murmurs. "Someone to pretend they like me. When I have the real thing."

"Stretching."

"You're saying your heart doesn't skip a beat when I'm near?" His words are as hot as the devil's whisper and twice as tempting. "Mine does when I look at you."

Nope. Non. Nee. Nein and nyet. Do not listen to that.

"Ignore everything else. Labels, reasons, my methods of persuasion." I snort at that, but he carries on. "To spend time together would be so good."

My stomach dips at his sultry tone, but to give him his due, he doesn't reach for me. Doesn't pull me against him, making my wits scatter. I'm not sure if I'm happy or disappointed.

"Sorry, say that again." Because my brain just checked out to happy humpy land, the place where you can have all the sex you want without the reasons, repercussions, judgment, and heartache.

"I said don't do it for you. For revenge, or because I forced you to. Do it for good. Do it for Nora."

"I . . ." Know she'd probably love to live vicariously through the tales of Evie and Oliver in happy humpy land, but that's not what he means. My heart sinks—I know what he's going to say before he even opens his mouth again. *Dammit, this right here is the trick the universe loves to play on all her unsuspecting children.* Lead the suckers down one path, then pull the rug out from under them.

"Fifty thousand pounds, deposited to Nora's bank account. For the benefit of the animals."

"Bribery, Oliver?" My response brims with disappointment. He just had to prove the stereotype, didn't he, the rich, exploitative fucker?

"Think of it as an act of charity."

"This is not a sponsored walk you're inviting me to." *And sadly, not a sponsored screw.* "You're asking me to move in with you, to pretend we're in a relationship. I think you're also suggesting I lie to the authorities about my visa."

"Yes, to the first. No to the latter. I've spoken to my lawyer, and she's already engaged an immigration specialist."

"I didn't say yes!"

"She's very experienced, I'm told."

"I don't care."

"And extremely optimistic regarding your position."

"Then I'll hire her."

"You'd have to find her first." He smiles like the devil. "She generally deals with oligarchs and the ultrawealthy. She keeps a very low profile."

"You mean she works for the corrupt. I guess she must if she's working for you."

"It means she works for those who have the means," he replies without bite. "I hope you have a heavy piggy bank if you want to retain her services yourself."

"You are such a—"

"All in all, her fees are well worth it, especially as she's confident your visa doesn't have to be dependent on a relationship with me."

"Except where you want me *to lie.*"

"Yes." His voice is clipped. All business.

"What is it that makes you want to grind Mitchell's nose into the dust so bad?"

"You say that like you find it unappealing." At the mention of Mitchell's name, he rakes a hand through his hair, leaving a wave of dark furrows. "For God's sake, Eve, we should be united—Mitchell Atherton fucked us both."

"My revenge is to move on and live my life well," I choke out, shocked by his sudden vehemence.

"You call living in a house shared with strangers, waiting until that bastard feels like giving back your belongings 'living well'?"

"None of this has anything to do with you."

"Fifty thousand, and I'll pay for the beagle's ACL repair, plus the surgery of any other needy animal." I open my mouth, but he cuts me off. "And medical bills for any and all animals admitted to the sanctuary for the next twelve months."

"It's still bribery."

"I don't know whether to commend or pity you for your convictions." He slides his phone from his pocket, throwing it to me without warning. I grab it, instinct taking over for logic, because I should've let it tumble to the floor.

"What's this?"

"Look at it."

I glance down—a mistake—the screen reacting to the accidental brush of my thumb. Shock immediately twists under my breastbone at a flash of Mitchell's face and a heading that seems somehow familiar. *A Little Bird.* "No." I thrust out my arm. "I don't want to."

"Come now, Eve. Willful ignorance never helped anyone."

Chapter 15
EVIE

A Little Bird Told Us . . .

What the flock!

The cheating groom of the Pulse Tok Shoreditch saga is none other than Mitchell Atherton, a contestant of the 2015 dating show *Millionaire Mates!*

Posh boy Mitchell, now a London-based property developer, was voted out of the house in the fourth episode after he was caught kissing one of the film crew.

A Little Bird thinks she can spot a pattern!

We'd love confirmation as the *groom that wasn't* has gone to ground and our runaway bride, Evelyn Fairfax, a veterinarian working at a swanky Knightsbridge clinic, has disappeared.

"What the hell?" Less demand and more plea. I glance up to find Oliver's expression impassive. "They used my name." I swallow over another wave of nausea. "I didn't agree to this."

"Freedom of the press means they don't need you to. I wonder how long it will be before a new column is out. One that mentions a mystery man in a Bentley."

"What?" A thorn wedges itself in my sternum.

"They not only know your name; they also know where you work. Perhaps she saw me follow you."

"Stop. Just stop."

Help us find them. That sounds almost threatening. Why do they want to speak to me? To humiliate me all over again?

"I can protect you. No one will find you at the hotel."

"This plays so well into your plans, doesn't it?"

"If only I were that imaginative," he adds witheringly. "I didn't contact the press, Eve. But I am offering you your visa and fifty thousand pounds for the sanctuary to soothe your scruples. In exchange for three months of your time." His attention flicks down to his watch. "You have two minutes to decide. London or Connecticut. A legitimate visa or a nasty visit from immigration."

Frustration bubbles inside me. One minute, he's shielding me from the rain, forcing me to wear his coat—helping Nora! And now this . . . this is blackmail!

He would do this to me?

My gaze slices his way, and understanding washes over me like frigid water, waking me up.

And I realize, yes. Yes, he would.

Chapter 16
EVIE

A Little Bird Told Us.

A little bird, my ass. That thing is more like an albatross, something bigmouthed and with the propensity to shit on your head.

"Are you listening to me?"

"What?" Rain lashes against the car window as I turn to Oliver. "Yeah, I'm all ears." All ears, annoyance, and anxiety.

"So you'll move in. Today, preferably."

"What's the hurry?" Not that I have any real problem moving into his hotel. I guess it means I won't have to hear Lori whine about the press when they turn up.

After reading the stupid A Little Bird column, I went back and read the previous ones. Then I googled the dating show Mitch had taken part in. I still don't know what to think about that, except that it's just another level of bullshit, and it adds another level of disbelief that I almost made it to the altar with that man.

I didn't touch the other articles, blogs, and mentions because I already felt like the media and the internet had chosen to evacuate their bowels on my head. I never wanted to be famous, but I think it might beat infamy, hands down.

"You're not listening. Again."

"I am!"

"What did I say?"

"Something about . . ."

"I said we have a very short timeline in which to achieve our aims."

"Yeah, three months." I remember that tidbit from before. "Also, not my aims. Yours." My stomach flips. This has got to be the craziest idea in the history of crazy ideas. And worse, I said yes to it.

"Well?" he demands.

"Yes, Oliver. I'll move into your hotel. But just so we're straight, only because you're holding the threat of deportation like a cartoon anvil of calamity over my head."

Sticking with the analogy, I'm Wile E. Coyote, wedged in a canyon where Mitch and Oliver are my rock and my hard place.

"Not just into the hotel, but my suite."

"What?" This time, my stomach swoops . . . not unpleasantly. "No." I shake my head. *No way.*

"It's a large suite. There's space for us both, and if it helps, the bedrooms are at opposite ends."

Another tummy swoop at the mention of beds. I glance out the window, afraid my face might betray me, because what in the fish cakes is wrong with me? Have I developed some kind of manipulation kink?

"You know, only assholes make their driver stand out in the rain."

"He has an umbrella," Oliver retorts tersely, barely sparing a glance for his driver. "He's there because you didn't want to go somewhere else to discuss this, while insisting on privacy."

"I didn't think you'd make him stand out in the rain!" Why am I surprised? I need to remember this is who Oliver is.

"The sooner we have this discussion—"

"Fine!" I snap. "I'll move into the hotel but not your suite." But he's already frowning. "It's not like anyone will find out."

"That's not a chance I'm willing to take. For the next three months, we need to look like a couple madly in love."

"No one's going to believe that. Not after I was about to marry someone else—they'll say you're my rebound."

"Then you'll just have to convince them otherwise."

"Me? Why do I have to convince them?"

"Because you're the one with the resistance."

"I'm not having sex with you." The words seem to burst from nowhere.

"Sex isn't crucial to our agreement." *Way to pour a bucket of cold water over my irresistibility.* "The person you most need to convince won't be aware of your recent troubles. I very much doubt he reads the gutter press. The story, as far as he's concerned, is we're in love, living together, and looking for a more permanent home than a hotel. Ours is a whirlwind romance."

"You put the *d* in *delusional* if you think anyone will buy that."

Better he puts d *in delusional than the* d *anywhere near me.*

"I have every confidence in your abilities."

I don't know why, when life just keeps taking chunks out of my ass. But there are fifty thousand reasons to keep me here. Bella will have her surgery. The oldies who are likely never to be adopted will have meds for their arthritis, plus a little more comfort. There might even be money for the traumatized puppers like Mouse to access behavioral therapy.

Your scruples versus the animals.

Your care for and of them.

Stay or go, Eve. Help the animals or go back to Connecticut.

Blackmail is his slap, and that fifty thousand the caress of his velvet glove.

I just can't believe I'm on the verge of moving in with a man who has more cash than scruples—a man I can't trust. But I need to know more of what I've signed on for.

"Why three months?" I ask casually, as I watch a rivulet of rain track down the car window.

"The property is going to auction in the autumn. My plan is to secure it before then."

"Won't the owner hang out for the auction? More bidders usually means more money."

"He isn't motivated purely by money. He's selling a piece of history and wants to do right by it."

"Then he should find a totally different buyer," I mutter, glancing his way. *Screw it, I'm not holding back.* "From where I'm sitting, neither of you deserve it."

"We're nothing alike," he utters icily.

"Except when it comes to manipulating me."

"He put you in this position," he grates out, straightening his cuffs.

"And you're just taking advantage of it, right? Totally different." Folding my arms, I give my head a reproachful shake.

"The suite. Preferably today."

So much for that tactic. "Fine. We'll be roommates." He might take advantage of me, but that doesn't extend to my body. Not that he seems all that interested. "What else is on your nefarious agenda? Am I supposed to pretend to be some doe-eyed sycophant—a rich man's airhead?"

"I would like you to be yourself. Without the attitude, preferably."

Myself? I give a huff of disbelief.

"Two reasons." He glances down, tweaking the pleat in his pants. "First, you'll need to convince my friends."

"They don't know about your taste for blackmail, I take it."

"If they find out, you'll be on a plane back to the US quicker than you can say 'forcible deportation.'"

"Got it. Keep up the pretense in front of your friends."

"Good."

"They really aren't in on this thing with the house?"

"It's a private matter."

"What's it called, anyway?" These types of buildings usually have names. Castle this. Mansion that. Never 123 Easy Street.

"I'll tell you when you need to know."

"Whatever." I feign indifference. *I guess I won't be googling the heck out of that.* "When will Nora get her money?"

"When I get my house."

"What happens if I can't swing it?"

"Then the deal is off."

"But that's not fair—I can't guarantee I'll be able to carry this off."

"Then you'd better try very hard."

Asshole.

"After a period of being seen together," he begins.

"Define *together*," I demand, interrupting him.

"Dinners, outings, that kind of thing. Once I'm satisfied you're up to the task, I'll introduce you to the owner."

"Can't wait," I mutter flatly. "And then what? You want me to dazzle him so he doesn't notice what you're up to?"

His smile seems reluctant. "That would be something to see."

"Seriously, Oliver, just tell me exactly what you expect me to do."

"Adore me."

I roll my eyes so hard, I'm sure I see the inside of my skull.

"It won't be a problem for you," he says smoothly. "You've convinced me before. Against my better judgment."

"Sex is not adoration."

"Then just look at me like you want to fuck me." Reaching out, he tips my chin, those mesmerizing eyes boring into me, corkscrew sharp. "No, darling," he murmurs. "Not fuck me up."

"What else?" I overstress.

"Just be yourself. I think you'll get along with the owner. You likely have lots in common."

"Was he recently cheated on? Blackmailed? Forced to pretend he's into someone too?"

"From the woman who manipulated me into bed." He smiles. "Try not to forget I'm not the only one getting something out of this."

"My visa," I mutter.

"And help for Nora. Managing the narrative of your split. Protection from anything Atherton might throw your way." He presses his elbow to the leather armrest between us, leaning in. "Believe me, Eve. There are many benefits available to you."

"And believe me, Oliver. I'm not having sex with you."

Chapter 17

A Little Bird Told Us . . .

Mitch Atherton, former reality TV star turned property developer and—who could forget—the Pulse Tok groom London loves to hate, was spotted out on the town with a familiar face last night.

"Is she a model?" a Little Bird hears you ask. "A starlet? A minor member of European royalty?"

A Little Bird wishes she could say yes, because the truth is much more salacious. She's familiar because she also starred in the Pulse Tok as the bride's maid of honor.

Can there ever be smoke without fire, my flock?

Let us know what you think.

587 comments

IloveLads: Agreed. No smoke without fire and that twatwaffle deserves to fry.

MissPickle: I hope they both get herpes.

Zara_A: Smoke? I'd f-ing burn him!

GreenOreo: Sir, you are a scumbag. Therefore, eat shit and die.

HideYoKids: Him? What about her? WHAT A TROLLOP!

MicroP33n: Takes tow to tango.

HoppyGoLucky: And half a brain to spell

DanteClaus: Name checks out. Tiny mind. Tiny todger.

Rope-a-dope: Marcus, is that you?

TheHallouminati: I saw him getting blasted by the brunching brigade at Brick Lane market. It was well sick!

McLuffin: I would've paid to see that.

JimBeamMeUp: That poor woman. Hasn't she been through enough?

LOAD MORE COMMENTS . . .

Chapter 18
EVIE

"Eve, I'm downstairs." Oliver's clipped words ring through the handset of my new phone. It has my old number—Mitchell's number is blocked, obviously—and I have my new bank cards, and passport, thanks to reporting it lost, which isn't really a lie. But just as importantly, I have this:

"Good for you!" I say into the phone, as though speaking to a toddler.

"I am downstairs. You are not."

"No flies on you, Olly. That must be why you earn the big bucks."

"The plan was for you to be down here by the time I returned," he replies, audibly tamping down his frustration and ignoring his hated nickname.

Was that the sound of a molar chipping?

"I don't know what to tell you. Plans change. Fashions change. Weather and hairstyles too. Nothing in this life is static." Which is total bull, because I hit pause on my life the day I moved into this suite. The day I turned up at his door and asked, *"Is this hell? Wow, I love what you've done with the place."*

It's been two weeks of chauffeur-driven rides to Nora's. Two weeks of yummy room service lunches, fancy spa visits, and late-afternoon siestas. Two weeks of champagne cocktails and fancy dinners out, all in Oliver's quest to build our backstory.

"Thank you for sharing your philosophy. However, we agreed you'd meet me downstairs for dinner."

"Did we agree?" I press my index finger into my cheek as though he can see me. "Wait. Was that before or after I said you'd regret blackmailing me into living with you?" My footsteps are barely audible as I cross the room to the French doors, pushing back the stylish window dressings. I step out onto the small Juliet balcony and look over the wrought iron railings down into the street. A sleek town car pulls up at the hotel entrance, the liveried doorman sedate in his progression to the passenger door. To the left of me somewhere is Buckingham Palace, to my right a hundred ritzy stores. Across the street, a man double-parks his bright-red midlife crisis Lamborghini as a woman in head-to-toe Gucci passes, using her $30,000 Birkin as her fluffy Pomeranian's pet carrier. I love London, but this spot right here is a crazy-pants level of wealthy.

"Do we have to go through this every day?" he mutters as I move back into the suite.

Poor Oliver. *Not.* He sounds so weary. *Yay!*

"Every day? Maybe just until I get used to the idea." It hasn't been at all hard to get used to unlimited spa visits, bougie afternoon teas, and room service. If you're going to decompress, where better than in a luxurious boutique hotel?

The break has given me time to think, to process things, and while I might not have been aware of Mitch's wealth, it makes sense now. It's not that I think all wealthy people are dirtbags and all the poor are virtuous, but I do know the rich live in a different kind of reality. It's one that often leads to a disregard for those around them. *Not to mention an inflated sense of self.* Sweeping statements, sure, but they ring true when I look at what has happened, and what is happening, to me.

So here I am, keeping up a campaign of subtle annoyance. Nothing too damaging, because fair *is* fair. Ariana, the immigration lawyer Oliver set me up with, is amazing. And he was right—there's no way I could've afforded her fees, let alone accessed them.

The acronym iykyk *was probably created for her.*

Anyway, yesterday I received notification that my visa application had been received. I've had my fingerprints taken, and I've submitted a photograph for my biometric card, the modern-day version of a visa stamp to a passport.

All systems are go: two weeks down. Ten more to go.

"Well, get used to it quickly," Oliver bites, "or that fluffy-arsed monster is going back to the kennel."

"Mr. Bojangles?" At his name, the labradoodle lying in the middle of the couch pauses in the act of cleaning his toe jam and looks up. "He's no monster."

"He's a testicular terrorist in a fluffy suit." Oliver's clipped consonants shouldn't dance along my spine like fingertips, but they do.

"Mr. Bo, it's good you can't hear what Olly is saying." The dog tilts his head like he understands everything. And doesn't give one single shit.

"To think I considered myself a dog person until he moved in."

"Well, see, Bo is more person than dog. Except, people don't punish you by peeing in your shoes for not sharing your hot dog."

"He'd better not even think about it," he mutters darkly.

Honestly, Bo looks like he's plotting much worse, and I'm *here* for it.

"Oh, Mr. Bo." I scratch his fluffy ear as I baby talk to him. "What did you do? Stick your nose in the mean ole man's crotch again?" *Jealous? Moi? Maybe a little bit.* I don't think I have a manipulation kink. I just have a thing for bossy-assed men like him.

"I am not old or mean, and he did not frighten me."

I make a doubtful noise. "You're kinda old, and there's no disputing you have a mean streak. I mean, hello!"

"A matter of opinion, again. Unlike the mutt's unbridled interest in my crotch."

It is quite special, as I recall.

"But now that I come to think of it, I was feeling quite unkind this morning, waking to find I wasn't alone. Again." My shoulders move with silent laughter. I count that as the third time this week that he's woken to Bo's doggy breath. "Somehow this time the light was on."

"Well, I didn't do it."

"You're sure about that?"

"Yes, Oliver, I'm sure I didn't come into your room while it was still dark and turn on the light." If I had crept into his room, it wouldn't be the light I'd be interested in turning on. *It's good that I'm a rule follower, especially my own.* "I mean, why would I? Such fun was had that one time I oh-so-wickedly turned on a light!"

"There's no need for sarcasm."

"I warned you Bo isn't the kind of dog who does well in confined spaces."

"That's on you," he gripes. "You insisted on making him part of this."

I bite my knuckle gleefully. I love that I'm getting under his skin. I did make Bo part of the deal, but what isn't my fault is how he's too smart for his own good. Or how he's a failed therapy dog. It's also not my fault he was trained for his therapy role by inmates of an open prison, even if his delinquency can be traced back to there.

Nope, it's totally not my fault a thief taught Bo all he knows.

"You can't have expected me to just sit here all day long by myself." Besides, he was driving Nora crazy. It was like a battle of wills at the sanctuary. "Bo is good company for me." My gaze drops to the mutt. He's a good listener. I especially like how he offers no opinions.

"A hotel is not a suitable environment for a dog."

"Some hotels make exceptions. Especially hotels that you own."

"At this rate, I won't own it for long. Do you know he was found in the kitchens again yesterday? I'm told he devoured a tray of Wagyu steaks—"

"Ouch." I've seen those on the menu at two hundred a pop.

"He also made short work of a whole Hereford rib eye before he was apprehended."

"That must've happened when I was at the spa." I thought he looked all lip-licking satisfied when I got back.

Oliver makes an interested noise in his throat. "What I'm hearing is it's not so terrible living with me."

"There are perks," I agree reluctantly. "Though I guess you could snore less." Wandering to my open bedroom door, I prop my shoulder to the frame and stare over the no-man's-land of the living room toward the matte-black double doors to Oliver's bedroom. We're like opposing teams or enemies. Except for the fact that, after fourteen days of watching (and annoying) him, I sometimes think I would crawl naked to his bed if he asked me to. Not that he's going to. I stipulated a no-sex arrangement, and those are the vibes I've been giving out. Even if it sometimes feels like self-sabotage. *I have never wanted to screw someone so badly.*

"No one else has ever complained before." His implication pokes at my sternum like a sharp pin—other women. "I could stop breathing altogether, I suppose."

"Let's not rule it out," I mutter, pushing away from the doorframe.

"Don't you want to do it yourself?"

"Like, strangle you?"

"You could wrap your hands around my throat while you—"

"Nah. I'd just pick up the appropriate drugs from the dispensary?"

When he shoots those shots, I bat them away. It wouldn't do to admit I still find him hot.

Lines might be crossed.

Rules might be broken.

And I'd most certainly be screwed—in more than one way.

Oliver is nothing if not imaginative.

"Meanwhile, perhaps you could make your way down to dinner. That wasn't a suggestion, by the way."

"Oh, a demand? Yes, sir, Mr. Deubel, sir. Right away! Oh, wait. You're not the boss of me."

"Eve." He makes a warning of my name. It feels like a brush of delicious punishment. *Ohhh, do it again, Olly. I kind of like it.* "Sometimes I wonder if you truly want to stay in London."

His meaning is like a coconut to the head—as in, not at all subtle. It's a reminder of what's at stake.

Yet I refuse to give him an inch. "Can I bring Bo?"

"Not unless you want the kitchen closed down by the health department." He sighs heavily, and I press my hand to my rib cage to stem a strange pang. Is he about to terminate our agreement? "I have guests waiting." His answer is oddly hesitant.

"Guests?" My heart lifts, like a balloon with cut strings. "Who?"

"My business partners. My friends."

The balloon deflates, farting its way to the floor as I immediately understand what this is. He's just building on the foundation stone of his deception.

Which is exactly what you signed up for, stupid.

"Sounds nice." I try not to sound lukewarm as I glance down. "I'm in sweats." Cute, cashmere sweats, thanks to my new capsule wardrobe, as curated by a stylist at Selfridges. Mitchell is still holding my belongings hostage, and hell will freeze over before I'll be manipulated by him. I don't often spend money on myself. I like clothes and try to buy things that will last over fast fashion. I'm also a fan of thrifting.

"Sweats?"

"Yes, lazy wear. And I haven't washed my hair."

"It doesn't matter, and sweats are fine."

"Only a man would say such a thing. Besides, your restaurant has a dress code."

"The nice thing about owning places, as you pointed out, is I get to make the rules."

"I'm not turning up in sweats while you and your friends sit there looking like you just stepped out of a *GQ* menswear feature, probably captioned 'Hot Bros: Summer in the City.'"

"Like we what?" His answer is tremulous with laughter.

"Suit porn, Oliver. It's a thing." An annoying thing that makes me think very hot and naughty things. "Give me ten minutes."

"It's not a parade, Eve."

"Oh, honey, how are you going to fool people into believing you have a fiancée when you talk like you've never even met a woman?"

"Fine," he utters resignedly. "Just try not to be too long."

"As sure as fiber forces flatulence from Mr. Bojangles's bowels, I'll be there within ten minutes."

He harrumphs again, and just as I imagine he's about to hang up, I add, "Oliver?"

"Yes?"

"I got there first!" I say as I gleefully hang up on him.

Chapter 19
OLIVER

"See, I told you he could wheel and deal while taking a leak."

I look up from my phone, annoyed to find my mind still on Eve, but more annoyed to find Fin wearing that shit-eating grin of his. "It's called multitasking," I retort, pulling out the chair opposite him. "You should try it sometime."

"I prefer to dedicate myself to one cause at a time."

"Except when it comes to women," Matt retorts somewhat under his breath.

I can't believe that Eve bloody well hung up on me! That she beat me to it, at least. The corner of my mouth twitches reluctantly, because the woman delights in getting a rise out of me. It's basically overkill. If she cared to tip her gaze south, she'd realize I've been walking around half-cocked since she moved in.

"Speaking of women," Fin says, leaning over the arm of his chair. "That wasn't a work call, because that smile you're fighting . . ." He circles a finger as though I don't know where a smile belongs. "It looks obscene."

"Don't be asinine." I put my phone down next to my knife, not sure which I'll end up reaching for first. Sometimes it's hard to believe Fin is in charge of investor liaisons, given he so often brings out the worst in me. He spends much of his time soothing the brows of the überwealthy and generally being affable. This niche he's carved out for himself as a lovable rogue makes him popular with our stakeholders, who'll forgive him (and consequently the company) of almost anything.

He's good for business, popular with people in general, women especially, and a darling of the gossip columns. I find myself frowning as I anticipate Eve taking an inevitable shine to him. This is not like me. I'm not jealous of that peacock. But in the short time I've been living with Eve, my mood has turned . . . unpredictable. *Fucking unstable.* And there's only one person to blame.

Evelyn Hadley Fairfax, according to her passport. She and her attitude drive me to utter distraction. What's more, I seem to have reverted to my teenage masturbation schedule. *As in, morning, noon, and night.* Or maybe morning, early evening, and midnight . . . or whenever she's done with her torment for the day.

"Ah. There it is. The Brit got back his stiff upper lip."

"Fin?" I inquire pleasantly.

"Yeah?"

"Kindly fuck off."

Tonight is important, and I arranged the dinner without advance warning for all parties concerned. I haven't mentioned Eve to my friends, mainly to avoid their plague of niggling comments. I also kept my plans from Eve. Giving her any kind of notice risked resulting in her arriving at the table looking like the hooker she says sex with me would make her.

Chance would be a fine thing.

There's nothing wrong with sex. Except when you're not getting any. Like me. Like now. Sadly, there seems to be little I can do to change her mind.

Outside of that, I've found living with her to be diverting. Both amusing and frustrating. I'd say the same probably goes for Eve.

Certainly, she always seems on the verge of delight when she gets the last word. *Or when the dog's antics piss me off.*

The strange thing is, I think I like having her around. I'd be lying if I said the fascination didn't begin with Atherton's expression that fateful day. I could see he was annoyed, but he was also genuinely distressed. At the time, I put it down to whose car Eve was in, but now I see it was that she was leaving. *It must've felt like the sun going out.*

I dismiss the whimsical thought. The opportunity to serve him a spoon of his own medicine was just too good to ignore. Steal his bride as revenge for Lucy, then use her as a means to snap the estate out from under his nose. While Eve didn't exactly jump at the chance for revenge, the viral video, her visa problems, and the resulting media interest were enough to persuade her.

Along with a little old-fashioned blackmail.

Atherton's life must be so awkward right now. Vilification in the gutter press, his investors pulling away day by day. Northaby only an idea in the distance.

Meanwhile, I live a cloud-walking existence. *If only.* Sex would definitely help the situation, but that's not to say I'm not enjoying the challenge that is Eve.

I think about that night more than is healthy. The feel of her silken skin and the pleasure of her soft sighs. I tell myself my interest in her doesn't need to be defined, that base lust is part of it. Revenge another. That her resistance piques my interest. But mostly, I think it's just her.

"Oliver, you okay, there?"

Matt's soft Irish lilt brings me back to the moment, and I realize my gaze has strayed to the entrance of the restaurant. I'm tense, I realize, but also oddly looking forward to what Eve will bring. *Will she be the sunshine or the hurricane?*

"Yes. Fine. I just have a lot of plates in the air in the moment."

"Speaking of plates," Fin puts in, "want to tell us why there's an extra place setting?"

I lift my glass to my lips, then answer, "Not particularly."

Fin's posture changes, his expression suddenly animated. "You haven't gotten Bellsand to come."

At the man's name, my stomach tenses. *If Eve can't convince my friends of our relationship, what chance will she have of convincing the man who owns Northaby?* I push the thought away. She can, and she will.

"Look at him, creaming his knickers." Matt chuckles. Leaning over, he smacks his hand to the back of Fin's head. "Sometimes I think if you were any less clever, I'd have to water you twice a week," he says, sounding distinctly Irish despite Matías Romero being a distinctly un-Irish name.

"Fuck off," Fin retorts.

But Matt's right. Mortimer isn't going to turn up to an impromptu meal. He wants to be courted—wined and dined in style. I know of at least five other parties who've done exactly that only to be served a polite *no thanks* at their purchase attempts. But at least they got that far. I haven't been able to get him to answer his phone.

Atherton, no doubt, had a hand in that.

"No offense to this place," Matt adds.

I wave his apology away. None taken. We're hardly sitting in a fleapit. The best of boutique hotels are noted for their sense of style, their character. They are an experience, not just a place to lay your head. I flatter myself that we have this here. But Mortimer is old guard. He thinks anything less than the Dorchester is slumming it. I'd wager he wouldn't deign to drink from our cellar on principle.

No matter. I have something else lined up to impress him. *Someone else.*

"Well, what have we here?"

159

An awareness slides down my spine at the exact same time as Fin opens his mouth. Resisting the urge to drive my fist into his face at his tone, I push back my chair. As I turn, everything seems to slow for a moment, the sight before me whipping my breath away.

Eve's red-gold tresses are piled to the top of her head, and she wears a dress of emerald silk that cuts across her clavicles. Cinched tight at the waist by a thin belt, it drops to her calves, where it swishes to and fro with every step she takes. My eyes devour her from the top of her head to the lofty heels I'd like to fuck her in.

"Sorry I'm late," she murmurs, sliding me a coy look from under her lashes. Chairs shuffle, and my companions stand, not that I have an ounce of attention for them. Eve Fairfax is fucking beautiful—but that's not news. And it's not the whole of her. She's a mixture of irreverence, mystery, drama, and sheer goodness. She's the whole fucking package, and she's far too good to be caught up in my scheming. But here she is, lovely and oblivious. And just for a moment, I hate that it had to be her.

"Ten minutes, you said." My reply sounds like a playful reprimand. It could be the essence of our relationship, if it weren't all pretend. Surprise causes a ragged breath from my throat as she presses a light hand to my shoulder, grazing her lips across my cheek. The scent of her is like fucking delirium, the tendrils of her perfume like beckoning fingers. "But I forgive you."

Will you forgive me?

"Because I'm worth waiting for, right?"

"Absolutely." I take her hand as it slips from my shoulder. I expected a performance—theatrics. Shenanigans. What she's delivering seems to be, on the outside, the perfect girlfriend experience.

160

"Like my dress?" She gives a small, graceful swing of her hips: a demonstration of how it sways. "It has pockets."

"Did you fill them with rocks?" I think her smile must reflect mine, the inside joke going back to that fateful Saturday.

"Should I have?"

"Not for me," I murmur, pressing a kiss to her knuckles. "Sadly," I add, turning back to the table and the stunned faces of my friends, "I can't vouch for these two. Fin, Matt, allow me to introduce Eve Fairfax. Eve, these reprobates are my business partners and so-called friends."

"He's talking about him," Matt laughingly protests as he gestures Fin's way. "I'm a Boy Scout. Just your average guy next door."

"What he fails to mention is he lives next door to a brothel," Fin retorts.

Eve giggles, and Fin flashes her that pretty grin of his, so I pull out Eve's chair as an alternative to punching him.

"You'll find I'm the pleasant, respectable friend. The one who is—"

"Prone to exaggeration," I mutter as Eve takes her seat between Fin and myself. I obviously didn't think this through. Maybe she should've brought those rocks.

"You guys are too funny," Eve says happily. "Oliver didn't tell me that."

"I'm surprised he told you anything."

"He's told me so much about you."

The men exchange a glance as Eve bursts out laughing. If sunshine had a voice, it would sound like her laughter, I decide.

"Not a thing!" she admits.

"Well, that is a relief." Fin smiles widely. "Or we might be forced to spill a few beans of our own. Like how he hasn't mentioned your name to us once."

"I was keeping her all to myself," I murmur, angling my gaze her way. Though her lashes veil her thoughts, I get a visceral kick from her pink cheeks.

"Is that a New England accent I detect?" Fin asks, leaning back in his chair.

"Connecticut," she agrees with a small nod. "Fairfield County."

"Westport?"

She flicks a shoulder. Not quite a yes.

"Swanky," Fin replies anyway.

"Says the man who owns half of a resort in Thailand," Matt mutters in the vein of *Just get a holiday home like regular people.*

"Westport is old money." Fin sends me a querulous glance. "And now Oliver is, I'm sure, about to remind me that a hundred years is a long time to a dumb 'Murican."

"And a hundred miles is a long distance to a Londoner," Matt finishes.

"Hilarious," I drawl as Eve watches the pair happily. *I am going to need alcohol.* "And I didn't say Americans were stupid. I believe I said that, for all your Ivy League education, *you* can be reckless."

"You're confusing me with Mr. Extreme Sports over there." He hooks a thumb Matt's way.

"Fine, he's reckless, and you're stupid. Happy now?"

Fin turns to Eve. "If I'm stupid, and he's reckless, then Oliver is . . ."

"Oh." She scrunches her nose delightfully. "Short tempered? Arrogant? Self-important?"

Fin gives a satisfied twist of his lip. "Just checking you knew what you were getting into."

"You of all people know I never pretend to be what I'm not," I retort.

"And what he is," Fin says, folding his arms against the tabletop to lean in, "is the devil. Isn't that right?" he adds, his gaze meeting mine.

"By name and by nature," I drawl, unimpressed.

"What am I missing?" Amusement lightens Eve's voice, though she refuses to look my way. She's not missing anything, given she's called me that herself.

"*Deubel*. It means 'devil,' right, Oliver?"

"'Devil of a man,' if I'm being pedantic. Swiss German in origin." I swirl the whisky around my glass before lifting my eyes to Eve. "Do you want to add that one to the list?"

Her eyes sparkle with delight. "The devil has the best disguises. Sometimes, he even pretends he's a gentleman."

"I'm so glad you can see me beyond the cloven hooves."

Eve throws back her head, her laughter unrestrained. God, she sends my head spinning. Or she might if I were a different kind of man.

The waiter's arrival is timed well. Drinks are ordered, and menus are delivered.

"Was I right?" Fin then asks. "About Westport?"

"Well, that depends," she counters. "The rest of the county would say Westport is filled with upstarts. Besides, real old money is often more like *no money left* these days."

"Rich in assets, poor in cash. Keep darning those tweeds but hang on to that Rockwell!"

"I don't own a Rockwell, and there won't be one in some future inheritance. As for inheriting tweed, my sutures are better than my darning skills."

"A doctor?" Fin sounds impressed.

"Only for the deserving," she adds prettily.

"Eve is a veterinarian," I put it.

"Well, that makes sense." His hands grip the arms of his chair as he turns to me with a grin, but I head him off.

"If there's a dog in this company, it's you, Phineas."

"Never was a truer word spoken," Matt agrees.

Eve laughs, and Fin protests, though the reality is he's as happy as a dog with two dicks that he's amused my pretty guest.

Wine is ordered and poured, when Eve slants me a provoking look from under her lashes.

"I get to order for myself today?" Her gaze is feisty, her address playful.

"Oh, no. Tell me you did not," Fin complains. "You pompous ass!"

"I was being chivalrous."

"It's really not that bad," Eve puts in. "It was just a glass of champagne, but I could see how it could become a habit." She narrows her eyes, as though she's trying to see inside me. Thankfully, she's a vet and not a clairvoyant.

"Life would be easier if people listened to me."

"Says the megalomaniac with the superiority complex," Matt says, not hearing the suggestion in my tone. "The one we all know and like anyway. Mostly. So, Eve," he says, turning to her, "do you live in London?"

"Hoxton," she adds airily, which must be the place her flat was before she moved in with *him*. "And I work in a clinic in Knightsbridge."

"I bet you get a lot of pampered pooches."

"We get all kinds of pampered everything."

"Have we met?" Fin puts in suddenly. "I can't help but think you look familiar."

"Do you own a pampered pooch?" Her smile seems a little stiff.

"It'll come to me," he says with a shake of his finger. "I'm pretty good with faces."

"And terrible to pretty faces," Matt mutters, picking up his menu.

"Eve helps out at an animal sanctuary in her spare time," I add, heading off *that* topic of conversation. "This is a concept you won't be familiar with, Fin, but she does it for free. Out of the goodness of her heart."

"I think you're confusing you with me," he retorts, pressing his elbow to the tabletop.

"Oh, but Olly helped out recently." Eve reaches for her wineglass.

Matt chuckles. "No way."

"Olly?" A smile hovers on Fin's mouth, his gaze darting between Eve and me.

"I know he doesn't like being called that, but we all have our crosses to bear." She puts the glass to her mouth but doesn't immediately drink, her eyes sparkling a little maliciously. "About the sanctuary, he did say I should take a photograph because you wouldn't believe him."

"No, don't say there aren't photographs," wails Fin. "Proof, or he paid you to say that."

Despite Fin's protests, I'm not sure photographic evidence would be enough. They'd no doubt accuse me of doctoring any images, dubious that I'd haul huge bags of kibble from one end of the property to the other, then shovel shit—literally—ruining a pair of handmade Italian oxfords in the process. All at the behest of an elderly woman in Wellington boots and a cardigan, who would've given Mussolini a run for his money. But I did what was needed. The trip to Nora's wasn't a waste.

"Veterinarians don't lie." Eve's answer is a mixture of shock, mock offense, and disbelief. "Haven't you heard of the vows we take?" she asks, her brown eyes wide and solemn. Only I see the mischief in them.

"There has to be an angle," Matt puts in. "Oliver never does anything without there being something in it for him."

"Oh, there was an angle all right," she mutters under her breath.

"Yes, I was trying to impress you, darling." I press my hand over hers, applying a tiny bit of pressure.

"You shouldn't have." Though her voice is soft, her eyes hold an entirely different tone. *No, really. You shouldn't have.*

Chapter 20
OLIVER

A Little Bird Told Us . . .

news that makes a Little Bird's heart *and* wings flutter.

Evelyn Fairfax, our poor Pulse Tok bride and virtuous doggy doctor, is sitting in a swanky Kensington restaurant right now with none other than Fin DeWitt, the handsome darling of London's gossip columns.

Get you some, girl! If a Little Bird needed a broad shoulder to lean on, party-boy Fin's would be top of the list!

Check out the pics. She looks so happy!

#Finlyn

Don't mind me. I'm just trying out a new ship ☺

I slam my phone down, screen first, the grainy images of Fin and Eve lighting an inexplicable fire in my guts. *Fucking ridiculous.* My reaction is ridiculous! Four people dined at this table—I shouldn't be angered by some strategically cropped bullshit of an image.

Yet I am. In fact, I'm seething.

"You okay there?"

I slide Fin a glare. "Perfectly." *Darling of the gossip columns. Broad-shouldered darling. What does that make me—chopped fucking liver?*

"I like her." Matt's voice pulls me from my brooding.

It's true that the meal, and the meeting, went better than I could've imagined, with my friends and my . . . and Eve getting along like a house on fire.

A fast-burning, short-lived fire, scheduled to last what's left of our three months. Not that she won't leave her mark. I'm sure we'll all find ourselves a little scorched. *And Eve, by my use of her.*

"I feel bad she didn't order dessert before she left."

My lips hitch. When the waiter arrived to take our order, Eve seemed to be staring at the menu as though committing it to memory. *Or considering licking it.* I'd declined pudding in favor of coffees, Fin and Matt opting to do the same. But still Eve's head didn't lift.

"Ohhh." I don't think she realized how porn-worthy her hum sounded. *"Hmm, hmm, hmm."* She wiggled a little in her seat. It looked like anticipation. *"That's it,"* she murmured to herself, unaware of the lull in the conversation. *"That's what I'm talking about. Every girl's favorite c-word."*

Matt choked on a mouthful of his wine. *Is she serious?* his look seemed to ask. Fin's glance was more in the vein of *You lucky fucking dog.*

168

"*Cake!*" she'd suddenly spluttered, noticing our silent exchange. "*Oh, my God, you guys are such perverts!*"

Guilty as charged. And I would be *a lucky fucking dog* if I hadn't agreed to this arrangement without the benefit of sex. It was all I could think about as she closed the menu, insisting she'd changed her mind. That she was calling it a night.

We stood as she did, and then she slid her arms around my neck, bringing her body flush with mine.

"*I think I aced it,*" she whispered only for my ears.

She was right.

She even had my cock fooled.

We all watched her leave. Strange, but it felt almost unnatural not to leave with her, probably because we'd been doing the pretend-dating thing for a couple of weeks now. *And that's all it is—pretend,* I remind myself. Eve is a lot of lovely things, but she is, ultimately, a means to an end.

"So, do we have to guess, or are you going to tell us what tonight was all about?" Fin asks lazily as he puts his glass to his mouth.

"About?" I bite the word out, not yet ready to forgive him his unwitting part in that stupid photo. *Which makes me an even bigger idiot than him.*

"About Eve." He swallows his drink, then sets it down, his movements deliberate and slow. "How can I put this?" he begins, pressing a pondering hand to his chin. "Whatever that charade was about, I don't believe it."

"I'm flattered you're so invested," I reply, swirling the whisky in my glass, watching the light turn the liquid a fiery shade of amber. *Broad-shouldered fuckwit, more like.*

"Invested. That's a very particular word."

"Lads, come on," Matt, the peacemaker, interjects. "Why does it have to mean anything beyond a pleasant meal with friends?"

169

"Because everything he does has an angle." Fin points a finger gun my way. "Some kind of payoff. He hasn't suddenly taken a shine to Eve in the natural way of things."

"Natural?" I repeat coolly. Conversely, my blood boils.

"She's not your type."

"I don't know what to tell you. People change. Fashions, weather, hairstyles." My lips twitch as I think of Eve uttering those very words.

"What the fuck are you talking about?" Fin exchanges a glance with Matt.

"I'm merely offering the notion that nothing in life is static."

"Okay, Socrates."

"I think that one was Buddha," Matt puts in.

"Whatever. Eve is too good for him."

It's true. She's far too lovely to be caught up in my plans. But there she remains, snared. I say none of that, of course. "I do wonder where this sudden display of impassioned offense springs from."

"You don't fuck with women who don't know the game. Someone you meet in a coffee shop or who you bump into outside of the office. The one that takes your breath away, the one you can't stop thinking about."

"What bollocks are you talking about?" Matt looks at Fin as though he's grown another head. "Sounds like you've been bingeing a load of sappy rom-coms."

"The one you want so bad you pin her down by sliding a rock onto her finger," Fin continues regardless. "Not like in the movies but in *real life*—other people's lives. Don't expect me to believe real is what just happened here."

"I haven't proposed, if that's what you mean." But it sparks an idea. Quite a cruel one at the culmination of my plans. I couldn't. *Could I?*

"Stick to your models and socialites. They're more your type."

"I have a type? Thank you, Fin. I wasn't aware."

He leans back in his chair with a snort. "Yeah, you do." He makes an expansive gesture. "We all do. Hot bodies. Cold hearts. Low expectations."

"And I'm supposed to take romantic advice from a man who's fucked half the world's internet influencers?"

"That's it!" With a snap of his fingers, Fin jolts straight in his seat. "The internet—I knew I recognized her."

My shoulders tighten, and I clamp my jaw shut.

"That's her, isn't it? Atherton's fucking fiancée!"

I slam my glass down. "He doesn't *have* a fiancée."

"Because you have her?"

"You say that like it's a bad thing."

"Jesus, Mary, and Joseph," Matt mutters, dropping his chin to his chest.

"You fucking dog. What's your angle?"

"I've no idea what you're talking about."

"Is this about Lucy?"

Every atom of my being revolts at the unexpected mention of her name. "You will never—" I halt. Breathe in. Start again. "It's not as though I planned or schemed. I was in my car, minding my own business, when Eve climbed in, wearing her wedding dress. You tell me that's not fate."

"Fate." Fin's expression firms. "Try another f-word."

"I will. Mind your own *fucking* business."

"This is all of our business," he says, making an expansive gesture. "Scheming is bad for business—bad for trust."

"What's that supposed to mean?"

"I showed you the Pulse Tok, and you barely flickered. All this time, you've had her."

"Had?" I repeat dangerously low.

He narrows his gaze. "What are you up to?"

"You've met her," I retort. "Does it look like I could persuade Eve to do anything she doesn't want to?"

"I know you can turn on the charm like it's nobody's business when you want something, you ruthless fucker."

"You're confusing me with you." If only charm had worked.

"But when charm doesn't work, you turn dirty. Which is it? Northaby, or are you all about pissing off Atherton to avenge Lucy?"

"Does it matter? All you need to know is Eve and I are enjoying our time together while Atherton is, as usual, being a colossal prick. He has her belongings. She had nothing but the dress she was standing in." And the delights it concealed. "She didn't even have shoes." I've no idea why her pink-painted toes in silk stockings should still seem erotic.

"But she's living with you," he states flatly.

"She's staying in the hotel, yes."

"In your suite?"

"That's none of your business," I say, straightening my cuffs.

"You're not serious." Matt's mouth is an unimpressed flat line. I flick my shoulder in answer.

"Does she know that?" This from Fin.

"I am not the devil you'd make me," I begin, the words firing from my mouth like bullets.

"Oliver," he says sadly, "I don't make you anything. We all know there's very little in the world you wouldn't do for revenge."

Chapter 21
EVIE

"I need help," I whisper as my arms bounce against the mattress, mortification filling me with restless energy. "Psychiatric help. Who talks to themselves in a busy restaurant?"

I relaxed a little too much—I wasn't prepared to enjoy myself! And Oliver's friends were so cool. Total charmers, and I enjoyed watching him play the straight man of their comedy trio. Maybe it's because they were so nice that I let my guard down.

The wine didn't help. Or the drool-worthy dessert menu. Man, I wish I ordered that heavenly slice of gâteau. *Layers of almond sponge soaked in Amaretto liqueur, layered with featherlight Belgian chocolate mousse and topped with a mocha ganache.* My mouth watered just reading the description, and I hummed in anticipation of sliding all that deliciousness into my mouth.

Come to mama!

But when I glanced up, three pairs of eyes were staring at me like I'd just sprouted another head. I felt like such an idiot, so I left in haste. And now I'm repenting (and cringing) at leisure because all I can think of is how crazy I must've looked. *Maybe food obsessed?* Which is better than a country club clone, I guess. The girlfriend of a rich dude who doesn't eat real food.

I shiver, the ghost of my not-yet-dead mother shimmying over my not-yet-dug grave. *A minute on the lips, an inch on the hips, Evelyn. That's not how you get a husband!*

"Yeah, well, brownies not frownies, my skinny sisters," I mutter as I reach for the box of Maltesers stashed in my nightstand. Maltesers are like if a Whopper and a square of Lindt milk chocolate had a love child with a British accent. The only negative thing I have to say about them is their sharing boxes aren't fit for purpose. *Who shares candy?*

I give the box a shake—sad face. There's no telltale rattle. *I must've finished them off already.*

"Ah!" I have another idea as I jump up from my bed, ignoring Bo's unhappy glare. *Bitch, who disturbs my slumber?*

Pulling on my door handle, I peek into the living area. But then I remember Oliver went out. He had come back to the suite not long after me, tense jawed and not in the mood for conversation. *Jerk face.* At least he'd thanked me for coming to dinner, though he stopped short of saying the meal was a success. Next thing, I heard the door to the suite close as he left.

My mind slides to the notification I received about my visa. I can't contemplate what it might mean if I haven't convinced his friends. I need sugar, stat. Sugar is my stress companion of choice.

Maybe that's why I was ready to lick the dessert menu clean.

I make my way into the tiny, immaculate, and largely unused kitchen, not bothering with the light as I pull a bag of giant-size marshmallows out from a cabinet.

So I might have sugar stashes all over the place.

As I rip the bag open, I look up at the *tippy-tap* of claws.

"Nothing wrong with your hearing," I say to Bo as he appears in the open doorway. Whoever said dogs don't smile has never seen one near a rustling bag. "You got the munchies too?" He does an expectant little dance. "You know your cute face alone does not earn you treats."

As though understanding, he trots into the room and, like a busking magician, unpacks his bag of party tricks. He sits, offers me his paw to shake, then balances himself on his hind legs to beg.

"Impressive. Can you teach Oliver to do that?" The dog cants his teddy bear head. "I'd give you *all* the treats if you teach him to beg at my feet. Add in a little tongue and . . ." Well, I'd be done for. What that man and his tongue can't do is something I shouldn't be dwelling on.

Oliver Deubel = no Romeo.

Meanwhile Bo, impatient for his treat, spins twice in a circle before plonking himself onto his fluffy butt.

"You went for the whole shebang, huh?" Well, nearly. I make a gun with my fingers. "Bang!" Bo throws himself theatrically to the floor—dead dog. "Fine, you earned it."

Reaching into the overhead cabinet, I pull out a bag of doggy treats and pay up. Bo trots happily away with his chew, leaving me with the bag of marshmallows.

I've just shoved a whole bunch of pink and white into my mouth when the entrance door *beeps*. My heart trips over itself as I hear it swing open.

Oh, my fuckery! Bad enough that I'm out here in the communal area, stuffing my face when I said I didn't want dessert, but I'm also dressed for bed. *Kind of.* I'm not wearing pajamas like a sane person would—no super slinky or cute nightwear for me. Nope, I'm wearing a T-shirt and huge granny panties. "Novelty knickers," so Yara had called them when we'd met up for a coffee earlier in the week.

They're her contribution to my homeless status, apparently. She knows about Mitchell holding my clothes hostage and I told her, thanks to Lori, I'm holed up in some cheap B&B, the London

175

equivalent of a roach motel. I didn't want to drag her into this because I didn't want her thinking I'd lost my mind.

Anyway, she gifted me seven pairs of underpants—one for each day of the week—saying they were bigger than she'd anticipated (an internet buy), and she laughed when she added, if all else failed, they'd be good to camp in. Literally, because they're almost big enough to use as a tent. They might be perfect for sleeping in. Not so much for being *seen in* by hot men you've slept with.

Hot men who've been out doing God knows what. *Or God knows who?*

Not that I'm letting that bother me. Nope. Just ask me. I'm *fiiine*! Nothing to see here but a girl trying to swallow down a mouthful of sugary goo while straining to work out what Oliver's doing in the other room.

Please universe, direct that man away from here.

Lord, which panties did I pull out of the drawer? Was it a pair emblazoned with such witticisms as:

EVIE'S BIG GIRL PANTS

BOTTOM'S UP!

THESE ARE MY SMARTY PANTS

or was it worse?

"You should've ordered pudding."

My heart skips a beat as Oliver appears in the doorway, his body backlit, his broad shoulders almost filling it.

Why does he have no shirt on?

And why do running shorts have to be so short?

At least I know what he's been doing, rather than who.

And why would I order pudding?

I swallow thickly, the marshmallow goo having become glue in my mouth. "I'm not a fan," I say, giving my head a tiny shake.

He frowns slightly, as though confused rather than unhappy.

"Pudding. The consistency doesn't appeal to me. I know, it's weird because I like all other sweet stuff. Cake and cookies and pastries." My words fall faster as Oliver's expression lightens. *Was it the pair with the slogan on the front or across the booty? The pair that glows in the dark?* "And obviously, I like candy," I add, crinkling the marshmallow bag.

"Obviously." His smile makes it seem as though he's laughing at me.

"I thought you'd gone out. I heard the door close—not that I was checking or anything."

"Why are you creeping about in the dark?" The shadow of his arm moves toward the wall, and my breathing suddenly sounds like an asthmatic at a strip joint.

"Don't—"

Too late, the room floods with light.

"Ah. Now I see."

"More than I anticipated," I mutter, tugging at the hem of my T-shirt. I keep my gaze lowered before I realize it might not be the greatest plan, given he's wearing running shorts barely bigger than my panties. "Stop staring, Oliver!"

"I'm Oliver again, am I?"

"I have other words," I grumble, avoiding his gaze.

"I'm sure the last time I saw knickers that size, it was in the V & A Museum."

"Rude."

"But those were frilly."

I look up to find him grinning as he glides his fingers over the hard, bare planes of his stomach. Everything inside me tightens, and don't get me started on those thick thighs as he toes off his sneakers. As he bends to swipe them up, a valley cuts between his broad shoulders, slicing down to his waistband. A hook pulls at my belly from the inside as he straightens and twists, muscle and sinew flexing as he throws his sneakers into the room behind him. I don't know which of us is more flushed, more glistening, as he turns back.

"You're being greedy."

His smoky tone brings me back to myself, heat rushing up my throat along with my apology. "Sorry, I shouldn't have"—I realize he's pointing at the bag—"eaten so many," I add in a stroke of slow genius.

He crosses the small space, my skin prickling under the weight of his gaze. I swear I hate myself right now for taking sex off the table, because I remember how it felt when he lifted me onto it and . . .

And now I'm banishing it from my memory again.

"I'm not sure these are the best postworkout snack," I say as he reaches into the bag.

"I don't know. A little of what you fancy does you good." He slides the marshmallow into his mouth, leaving me wondering how he can make something so silly sound so sexual.

"Do you always work out this late?"

"Sometimes." The bag crinkles as he slips his hand into it again, though I relax a little as he comes to stand next to me, leaning back against the cabinet.

"I wouldn't have pegged you for a gym rat."

"I went for a run." I try to ignore the heat of his arm next to mine as he turns the marshmallow between his fingertips like he's studying a diamond's facets. "It helps me think."

"Dinner was that bad?" Disappointment blooms inside me.

"No, Eve." His leg nudges mine. "It went well. Very well."

"So they were convinced?" *My visa's safe?*

"Not to mention as jealous as all hell."

"I'm not sure about that," I murmur, ignoring a spike of pleasure. *I'm just relieved,* I tell myself. *About my visa and Nora's money.* But when he arches an elegant brow, for once I'm not driven by the impulse to shave that sucker off. "So you don't run when you're stressed?"

"Is that what you do?"

I scrunch my nose. "I eat when I'm stressed. I only run when being chased."

"That I remember." His lips fight the shape of a smile, and I find myself blundering on.

"I have a running endorphin deficit. I think it's genetic. I wouldn't know what a runner's high looks like if it tripped me and sat on top of me." I stop when he opens his mouth as though he's about to say something. But he doesn't. "Say it. I won't be offended." Jiggly ass, know thyself, right?

"I ran for another reason."

"Like what?" Honestly, I'm curious. People who run must be built wrong.

"Running keeps me from making unwise decisions." He pops the pink candy into his mouth, as though stopping himself from adding more.

"That's fair." I take another, considering his words as I chew. "But for mental clarity, wouldn't it be better to run in the morning *before* work?"

"Work isn't my issue." Reaching behind him, he grabs the countertop, his chest expanding, his biceps flexing.

In a not-unrelated topic, my knees might also give a little.

I can't help but notice how long and elegant his feet are. Houston, we have a problem, because I like his feet, and the only body parts weirder than feet are the wenis and the flagina!

He must've had a trio of fairy godmothers visiting his crib, because there had to be spells involved in the making of him.

I bless you with looks!

I bless you with money!

Though puberty will strike but once, you shall have the blessings of seven men—the kind that can't be hidden in running shorts!

I hope someone sent the wicked fairy a thank-you note.

"You've gone very quiet."

"I was just thinking," I answer. Some might say overthinking. "I guess I'm trying to work out what's troubling you."

"I'm not troubled," he says, looking exactly that.

"Fine. Talk in riddles. See if I care. I mean, it's not like talking a problem through helps anyway. A problem shared is not a problem halved, or someone would've coined a phrase or something." I go for a double shot of marshmallows to stop my mouth when Oliver takes my hand.

"Eve." The way he says my name is like the brush of velvet. "Every night this week, after we've gotten back from wherever we been, I've gone for a run."

"I didn't see you leave."

"I wait until you've gone to bed."

"Why?"

"Why wait or why run?" He doesn't wait for my answer, tugging me closer. And God help me, I don't resist as I step over his outstretched leg. "Because I can't sleep." Taking the bag, he drops it to the counter. "Which leaves me lying in a bed not so far from yours, trying very hard not to wonder if you're touching yourself while thinking of me too."

"Oh." It's as though I'm not expecting our bodies to clash, as though I'm surprised by every, hard, glorious inch of him.

"I can't sleep for wanting you, night after night. And tonight, I couldn't stop thinking how, in the restaurant, it didn't feel like pretend."

"That was our agreement," I whisper without a hint of consequence. Consequences would make me a hypocrite. Haven't I been trying not to think the same?

"I want you—that much is real. I'm going crazy wondering if I'd ever get to touch you again." Everything inside me clenches at his admission, and as he tilts his head, the air between us seems suddenly heavy, like a storm is about to roll in. "I can barely think when you're near." His hands glide across my shoulders and move down my back as he makes a plea of my name. Like I'm driving him a little insane. Honestly, I like that for me.

"If you kissed me, maybe I wouldn't stop you," I whisper, swallowing his breath and his words.

"If I kissed you, you know where it would lead. Darling, feel how hard you've made me." Heat blooms inside as he presses me between the *v* of his legs. "It's little wonder I can't think straight," he says as his lips suck over the beat of my pulse. "All my blood having drained to other parts."

"You can take care of that anytime."

His low laughter against my neck is a physical thrill. "Aren't you listening? I've wanked myself half to death since you moved in."

My brain short-circuits; the realization, that base word—those images—they're too hot to process.

"Does that shock you?"

I shake my head.

"And if I asked you to watch?"

Ho-ly heck. "I'm not sure how that would help."

"It wouldn't hurt either."

Innuendo. It makes me chuckle, at least until his hands slip under my T-shirt and up my naked back. His approval is a low hum as he realizes I'm braless.

"I'm not having sex with you." God, I *ache* for him. But torment and annoy. Maintain the upper hand—those were my plans. If I give in, everything changes. If I give in, it means not only that I can't trust him but also that I can't trust myself.

I shouldn't muddy the waters any more than they are—it's been hard enough to fight the brand of sweetness he's shown me this week. The peanut butter and the fancy-Italian-chocolate spread that appeared on my breakfast tray. In my book, there isn't a Monday that can't be faced because of the existence of Nutella, and I'm not sure where he learned that about me.

He made sure the hotel ordered Bo's kibble and arranged for one of the porters to take him for an extra afternoon walk. A little self-serving, sure, because a tired dog is a sleeping dog, not one disposed to crotch-sniffing antics. He didn't even make that big of a deal about waking in the wee hours on Tuesday to the sound of continual flushing water. That was the day we learned Bo prefers to drink running water. It's just a pity he learned to work the toilet and not the bidet. Not that it mattered, considering a doggy water fountain turned up in the suite that same day.

I know Oliver has a mile-wide determined streak, but it seems to be rolled into a sweet cinnamon bun. Unless it's all a ploy, and he's an expert at playing the long game.

But we don't have forever. Ten weeks at my last count.

"Who'd be having sex?" he purrs.

"You. With your hand, I heard."

"I imagine you watching. Every night." I feel him swallow and love that tiny contradiction to his tone. "Your eyes dark and your breath held, anticipating every slide and twist. The tiny gasp as I paint your neck and your chest."

I'm hot. Bothered. *Wet.* This is so wrong, but I want it. Want him. "Still sounds like sex," I hear myself say, ever his antagonist.

"It can be whatever we want it to be."

I press my hands to the side of his face. "Well, look at you, getting all persuasive."

"Because it doesn't have to mean anything?" That haughty brow spikes before I can answer as he adds, "Nothing about this is careless."

"I'm still not having sex with you," I answer as I bring his face to mine.

There are no words to explain this. I no longer possess the will to condense this heat and need into reason as my fingers tangle in his hair and our mouths fuse. The hot, hard feel of him is incredible as his lips weave the magic I so remember. Slow, slick slides and deep, dirty tongue. He kisses like he fucks, and I'd be lying if I said he's the only one who has trouble sleeping. *The only one who resorts to touching themselves at the memory.* I turn a little wild at the thought. This is madness, but I can't seem to stop myself.

"Not in the kitchen."

He doesn't seem to immediately register that my hands are still around his neck, that I'm pulling him. *Come with me,* my biting kisses say. He follows, and we stumble from the room. No sooner are we through the door than I find myself backed up against the other side of the wall.

"My room"—his hips press against mine, the thick length of him enough to make a girl swoon—"or yours."

"No beds," I rasp.

"Don't need one." He takes my hands, almost slamming them to the wall. He gives a slow, dirty roll of his hips, and everything draws tight inside me.

"Good." I push him in the center of his chest, stepping after him. "Because we won't be using one."

In answer, he spins me, lowering me swiftly to one of the pair of long couches.

"I mean it," I say as his body follows. "Not sex." I'm not at all convinced what my deal with penetration is. I want him. He wants me. But I'm still not giving in.

"She who holds the pussy, holds the power." His hands on either side of my head, he looms over me.

"Freak." My hand trails lower, plucking at the waist of his running shorts. "Take these off."

A slice of moonlight cuts across his broad chest as he straightens, his eyes turning silvery as he pulls on the cord at his waist. "Take off your T-shirt. Give me something to work with."

"Tit for tat?" But I'm already crossing my arms at the hem. I pull it up and over my head, then trail my hand between the valley of my breasts. "You're up. *Tat*."

He glides his shorts down his thick thighs, and I can't pull my eyes away. The sum of his parts is just breathtaking. Warm flesh, the supple sloping of muscle, ridges and angles, and the thick length of his cock jutting between us. His head rolls back a little as he wraps it in his fist. Veins stand to attention in his forearm, the muscles of his abdominals flexing at his slow slide.

With a blink, I glance up. "I lied. I do think your cock is pretty."

His deep chuckle doesn't last as I touch my palm to his thigh and sweep my mouth over the silken head.

"*Fuck.*" His curse is thick and husky as he tightens his grip, rubbing the pearly bead at the tip across my lips. My tongue follows the path, and he makes a masculine sound of approval as I take him into my mouth.

"Feels so *so* good." His words are husk over gravel as I lick and suck, savoring the taste and musk of him. Between my legs feels heavy as he gives himself over to me with a sweep of those dark lashes, his hands sliding into my hair. "That's . . . fuck. Yes, like that." His words are all aching need and want, his thighs trembling beneath my fingers. "You're so good, darling. So beautiful sucking me."

I swallow his words like the delicious compliments they are—savor them as I savor him, drunk on this power and his taste as he gasps.

"Wait, not like this." His chest rises and falls as his hands cup my face. "I'm too wired to be gentle." His thumb swipes over my bottom lip. "I want my mouth on you. Let me make you come."

I close my eyes for a beat, unable to speak, the hammering between my legs suddenly a frenzy. He drops to his knees in front of me, lifting the weight of my breasts in his hands.

"You're so fucking edible," he whispers, licking my nipple. Sucking wetly, tautening and tugging, alternating with languid licks. "One day, you're going to let me fuck these."

I shut my ears to the implication of other days, shivering as the central air turns over, the air brushing across my wet, tingling skin. He begins to kiss his way down my body.

Oh hell, Granny panties, I think the moment before he presses his nose between my legs with a deep inhale. I almost levitate from the couch.

"One hundred percent," he growls, hooking his fingers under the waistband. "Breakfast, lunch, and supper time. Elevenses," he adds as he slips the black cotton down my legs. "Afternoon tea. Midnight snack. A whole-day fucking buffet, because you make a glutton out of me."

His low rasps of appreciation make little sense, but maybe it's infectious, this madness, as I writhe under him.

I whimper as he blows a cooling breath over the ribbon of flesh between my legs. Cry out, my breath hitting the air in tight gasps as the point of his tongue slides over my clit. My eyes tighten as I undulate against him, seeking to deepen the contact from this torturous tease.

"You're so slick, Eve." His tongue circles slowly. Skims a filthy flick. "So shiny and pink. I could swallow you fucking whole."

"Please!" Spasms begin to rack my body, sparks of starlight flickering behind my eyelids. "Oh, God, please!"

"I love to hear you beg. I love you fucking wild. Come for me, Eve. Give it to me."

Heat courses through my veins, the riot inside me building to a crescendo. Waves of pleasure roll through me, bursting from my toes and my fingertips. But waves are supposed to fade, not be endless.

"Too much," I whimper, pushing at his head. He doesn't budge or let up, grasping my hands in his. Something inside me snaps, the threads of this orgasm tied so tightly to the previous. I cry out, my mind and body at war. My hips tip, my thighs closing around his head, "No, Oliver. I can't."

"Yes," he purrs. "For me."

The sounds of our pleasure fill the room; licking and sucking, filthy whispered encouragements. Whimpers of utter pleasure. And something else. Something obvious but out of sight. *Oliver's hand working his cock as he gets me there.*

I close my eyes, imagining the sight. Veins standing to attention in his forearm, the muscles of his abdomen taut as his hand slides from root to crown.

I sound like I might be running, my breaths tight and my moans unrestrained. My body suddenly bows as though lashed by an electric line. Sparks flood outward as I peak with a startled cry, arching from the couch. Oliver moves with me, determined to drain every ounce of my pleasure.

"You're so good, my darling. *Fuck, yes.*" His husky compliments turn to masculine grunts, his broad shoulders blocking the light as he presses his knee between my splayed legs.

There's no need to imagine now, my eyes falling to his right hand working slickly along his length. As he breaks, my insides pulse and contract as though to join him. I make a noise, one I can't classify, the sight of him covering me in pearly strands shockingly hot.

With a curse, he falls forward, catching himself on the velvet arm. Then I'm tasting my arousal from his lips as he kisses me like he's drowning and I'm his life raft.

"You." He drags in a breath, his words a rush of air across my neck. "Oh, God. You have no idea what you've done to me."

My laughter vibrates against him. "Have I broken you?"

"Eve—"

I press my finger over his lips. Smiling, he bites the tip.

"You can't be broken, because we didn't have sex."

And maybe if I close my eyes, I can pretend he's not here.

"Fine, we didn't have sex."

"So it doesn't count," I assert. "What just happened was nothing more than a . . . very personal workout."

"I should fire my personal trainer." Before I can respond, his body dips, his next words a low growl in my ear. "Sex or not, I agree with your underwear. I could eat you out forever."

I mean, sure. Go for it. Meanwhile, what?

And then I remember. I remember which pair.

<FIVE STARS>—WOULD EAT HERE AGAIN

I begin to chuckle, our skin sticking together. Oliver opens his mouth to speak, only, with a sudden spasm, he jumps up with a roar. His ass hits the floor, and I lean over the edge of the couch.

"What the heck was that all about?"

His jet hair falls across his forehead. It does nothing to detract from his thunderous expression. He inhales, blowing air from his nose like an angry bull. "That," he mutters, filling the word with such distaste, "was the result of your dog licking my arsehole."

Chapter 22
OLIVER

A Little Bird Told Us . . .

"Good morning." I steal a kiss to Eve's cheek as she turns her phone over to hide the screen, though not before I catch a glimpse of that ridiculous gossip column. I choose not to comment on her reading habits, perhaps distracted by her hair, which resembles a messy bush.

"Morning."

I smile at her reply as I pull out a chair at the dining table.

She swallows what appears to be a bite of melon before decorously pulling the sides of the branded hotel robe a little tighter. "I expect the coffee is cold now."

"I wonder whose fault that would be?" *Don't judge her for her reading habits, but you do judge her,* whispers an unwelcome voice in my ear.

"Yours, obviously," she retorts, her eyes sparking gold in the morning sunlight. "You who hauled me into the shower this morning."

Something powerful and heated bursts inside me as she slips the downy collar of her robe lower to reveal a sucking bite to her skin.

"*Hauled* is such a strong word." I push away the soft whisper of *hypocrite* as I swipe my finger gently over the evidence of my desire. Desire, yes, but how I felt in the moments before was more complex. I envied and I coveted. I wanted to punish. To possess. To own.

I wanted to swallow her whole.

"Oh, it was the right word, all right." Eve ducks her head, concealing her smile but not her pink cheeks as she adds, "Just look at the state of my hair."

I stifle a smile as I snag the coffeepot, pouring the lukewarm liquid into my cup as an image flashes in my head: Eve on her knees, her hair darkened by water from the shower, my hands tangled in the strands. Her lashes flutter, her gaze full of the power she holds over me.

Fuck. The coffeepot hits the stand heavily as I set it down.

It's just sex, I caution silently. *Not even* actual *sex—no penetration. Unless I count my tongue in her—*

My heart races, my thoughts chasing after it. It's just because she's here. Available. We're just using each other, enjoying the advantages of proximity. There's no power. No knowledge. No stirrings of love.

Because love gives someone the power to break you.

It's a timely reminder.

"I can't blame you completely," Eve adds, obliviously patting her hair. As she narrows her gaze on the mutt resting by her chair, I'm brought out of my head.

How is the dog to blame?

"He's cleverer than you give him credit for," she says, intuiting my thoughts.

I lift my cup. She attributes more intelligence to Bo than is due. "I don't quite know how to put this, but you do remember he licked my arsehole?"

"I didn't say he didn't have fetishes." She barely gets the words out for her giggles. "He is smart—I know he's hidden my brush. He probably confused it for his. He hates any kind of grooming."

Ah, well, that makes sense now. "So you're saying he's both devious and kinky." I try not to grimace at my mouthful of cold coffee.

"I'm saying those are traits he picked up here. You *did* drag me into the shower this morning."

"If you weren't such a Peeping Tom, you wouldn't have been there in the first place." It wasn't quite shower sex, more soapy fun. Fingers, lips, and tongues. Kissing and rubbing in all the right places. We'd showered together last night, once I'd stopped cursing and she'd stopped dying from laughter, then spent the night in my bed. I'm not even sad the time was spent sleeping, because Eve Fairfax is a delightful snuggler. It was the best night's sleep I've had in a long time, not that it means anything. Eve might be too good for Atherton, but she is not meant for me.

Reaching for the bowl of blueberries, she lobs one in my direction. I catch it in my mouth.

"Asshole," she says, not at all like she means it.

"Was that an offer?"

"What?"

I pat the table. "Bend over, and I'll tongue your delectable rear." *Fuck it too.*

"Oliver, don't."

"If you don't try, how will you know if you're into it?"

191

"I don't remember Bo inviting you to bend over the table."

"Funny. I prefer red-gold Americans over goldendoodles, especially ones whose taste I could drown in." Under the table, my cock begins to stiffen.

"We're not . . ." Her expression falters. "That was . . . a onetime thing."

I find myself smiling and frowning at the same time. I'm not confused. I just don't think she really means it. I thought we reached an understanding as she took my extended hand and stepped into the shower this morning. I thought we put *only tonight* behind us. Fuck it, I want more than last night. I want this morning, tonight, Tuesday next week. I want—

I halt the thought. Breathe. Pause. Reevaluate.

I want her. Want to experience every inch of her from now until I have the keys to Northaby House. *Because that's the way it has to be.*

"Tell me what the problem is, Eve."

"Isn't it obvious?" She twitches the linen napkin next to her plate.

"I like you, and maybe I flatter myself, but I think you like me too."

She slides me a skeptical look, but I push on, because fuck that.

"Why does sex between us need to be an issue?"

"We didn't have sex." Her denial falls quickly. "This isn't a relationship, or even a situationship—this isn't anything."

"You were happy not to define things last night."

"But I did define it. I had to. Because you didn't ask me to move in with you for those kinds of reasons. Hell, you didn't even *ask* me to move in. This . . . line crossing is dangerous. We're not friends, Oliver."

"I don't think that's true."

"We're not even roommates."

"Yes, okay, I forced your hand," I say, tamping back my frustration. "But hasn't being here with me worked out for you? I've given you a place to stay—"

"*Given* isn't the description I'd use."

"I've shielded you from Mitchell and gone to considerable trouble and expense to smooth over the issues with your visa."

"You aren't doing me a favor. At best, it was part of our agreement."

"All right, that's true, but at least I can be honest. I can admit to liking you. I like having you here." A thorned knot catches in my chest, and I know I sound like a petulant child.

"Well, there will be no more *having* after this morning," she says, snatching up the silver dome housing a toast rack. "This will be a strictly platonic arrangement from here on in."

"That's a shame," I murmur, as my brain refers to my earlier statement: fuck that. Sex is like that jar of chocolate spread her hand hovers over. Once the seal is broken, there's no stopping you from dipping back in. I frown as I watch her select the peanut butter instead.

"What?" she demands, catching me studying her.

The table is set with white linens and fine china, sparkling glass and silverware. There's even a tasteful flower centerpiece. It's all a little theatrical, and none of this is for me. Breakfast before Eve was usually something eaten on the go. These days, I find I'm happy to linger. She's a pain in the arse in a lot of ways: impulsive, slightly chaotic, and as stubborn as a box of rocks; but I find my day is greatly improved by watching Eve put things into her mouth. Her hair seems to have a light and life of its own in the morning sun shine. I enjoy watching as she slides it to one side before addressing her meal. The action reminds me of a barrister slipping on her wig or a chef strapping on an apron: a signal that she means business.

Maybe the breakfast theater is a little about me after all.

Her face is so animated, and I find I could watch her talk for hours just to see the shapes her luscious mouth makes. I even enjoy watching her garnish her toast. She has such elegant hands, and her fingers exhibit such grace in their application of the gloopy, sand-colored substance.

Yes, breakfast times are a joy. If only I could offer her the same pleasure, because it seems soapy shower time has not improved her mood.

"Stop watching," she murmurs, licking stickiness from her fingers.

"Today isn't a chocolate day?" I ask, ignoring my thickening cock.

She looks up without raising her head, her pleasure subdued but evident. "Creeper."

"I prefer *observant*."

"Observe that I wanted a change."

"Fair enough. Do you have an evening dress?" I ask after a pause.

"What for?" Her eyes turn suspicious.

"There's an event coming up in a couple of weeks we'll attend."

"Let me guess. I've passed the friends test, so you're stepping things up."

"If you like," I answer simply, forcing my thoughts from enjoyment to purpose. Just because I haven't issued her a written schedule doesn't mean we aren't on a tight timeline.

"And I guess with you being so forthcoming in the information stakes right now, this is about the guy with the house—the estate?"

"Yes." I give in to a smile. "How perceptive of you."

"Not even, because I still don't know how you think I'm going to be able to convince him to sell you the place. I feel like I'm missing something."

A pinprick of discomfort pokes at my chest. I rub it like an itch. "Just remember our backstory, and be yourself." I look down at my cup, twisting the handle twenty degrees. *The way I find myself watching her sometimes makes me think he won't take much persuading.*

Eve applies her attention to her toast again. With violence this time.

"Are you worried?"

"About lying to someone who hasn't done anything to me, anything at all? What would make you think that?"

"I'm sorry," I say impulsively. Worse, I think I mean it. "I'm sorry you got caught up in this."

"Sorry enough to let me leave?"

"Eve," I chastise. "You're hardly my captive. You can leave anytime."

"Back to Connecticut," she mutters.

"That would be your alternative." I'm not sorry about keeping her here. I can't see how I'll ever regret it.

"I guess you're holding up your part of this ridiculous bargain," she mutters, more like an insult than a concession.

"You're not going to have much toast left at this rate," I remark as she continues to attack the slice like it insulted her.

With a pointed look, she violently bites off one corner.

"I'm glad you aren't thinking of me."

Her throat moves with a deep swallow as she sets it back to her plate. "Mitch can't eat peanut butter," she announces, seemingly out of nowhere. At his invasion, an iron fist tightens around my entrails. "He's allergic."

"Very badly?"

She flicks a shoulder. "He carries an EpiPen with him wherever he goes."

"What a shame." *As in, what a shame I hadn't known this earlier.*

"The shame is I gave up more than peanut butter for him. I like peanut butter. I hate my ex."

"That's understandable." This is a first, the mention of hate. And a first for me, as I realize I've been unfair to her, simply because she hasn't been angry enough for my liking.

"I don't think I've ever hated anyone before," she says with a brittle smile. "But here I am, eating peanut butter while imagining him suffering a painful death."

I laugh, though turn it into a cough. I don't want her to think I'm laughing at her. I think it might be relief. It isn't all me—it might not even be half my fault.

Except, I've treated her little better than the arsehole did.

"That's bad, isn't it?" Her expression twists comically.

"No worse than death by cab."

"I love peanut butter, but not for the taste. I love it because of what it might do to him." She examines her toast, then slides me a provocative glance. "Aren't you going to ask why today?"

"I'm almost frightened to."

"Liar." Now satisfaction flickers across her face. "He cheated on me. Humiliated me. Wasted my time and my energy." *No mention of love.* "But it's only this morning that I feel like I could watch him choke."

"Delayed grief?" I hedge.

"Oh, I'm not grieving," she says. "I'm pissed." Reaching for her phone, she slides her thumb across the screen. She offers it to me. "This is the same gossip column you showed me."

"Yes, I know." No need to mention I've been keeping an eye on it.

A Little Bird Told Us . . .

Mitch Atherton, property developer and cheating Pulse Tok groom, suggests he might not have been the only one in the relationship up to no good.

"Remember the first day you turned up at the clinic? There was a woman there. A journalist." I nod, and Eve carries on. "Una Smith. I guess she decided, when I wouldn't speak to her, she'd get her scoop from another horse's mouth."

"Or in this case, a horse's arse," I murmur, returning to scanning the text, the crux of which is:

- Mitchell admits he cheated.
- He agrees he deserved being abandoned at the altar.
  Very big of him, especially when:
- He denies he deserved the level of humiliation he was served.
  The absolute wanker.
- He also implies that Eve might also have been unfaithful after he found her being whisked from the scene by another man.

He stops short of naming me. He knows I'd sue him just for the hell of it. But Eve. *Ah, Eve.* What a shit Atherton is.

"This is nothing to worry about. Anyone with half a brain would see this for what it is."

"I still hate him."

"As is your right."

"Did you see the post before it? Scroll down a little."

I do, though this time, I'm prepared. *Unlike last night.* My expression barely flickers at the image of Eve looking all kinds of lovely, her hand resting over Fin's. Despite my outward calm, internally I still feel fiery. Which is ludicrous, given she barely tapped Fin's hand in reprimand to some stupid comment he made.

"Silly, isn't it?"

"Absurd," I answer, surprised by the evenness of my tone.

"You're not worried it'll cause a glitch in our relationship matrix?"

"No." I try not to frown. "But it is borderline libelous."

"We should sue their asses, then make Mitchell choke on my dick!" Her fist thumps the table, making the silverware dance. Bo barks and jumps up, trotting off to investigate the phantom knock on the door.

"I told you he's not the brightest." I could be referring to Bo or her ex. Or both.

"He is such a . . ." Eve presses her fingers to her temples as though to stem a sudden ache. "This implies I am as bad as him. I am *nothing* like him."

"Of course you aren't."

"But people talk." She can't hide her concern as her eyes find mine.

"Gossip is the tax you pay for other people's insecurities." I reach out, cupping her cheek. "Your dignity can never be taken away from you, no matter what they say."

"I like that."

"Good, because it's true. Fuck them, and fuck what they say. As for this"—I hand back her phone—"don't give it another thought. Privacy laws in the UK are very strong. Perhaps my legal team can get an injunction. At least, stop them peddling more lies."

"Do you think so?"

"I don't see why not." I make the mistake then of swallowing another mouthful of now-very-cold coffee before pushing back my chair.

"I know what you're saying—that it doesn't matter—but if you could get this taken down, I'd appreciate it so much."

"Leave it with me." I press my hand to her shoulder, taken aback as she reaches for it, and a pleasant warmth spreads through me.

How strange. It does feel good to sometimes be a Romeo.

◆ ◆ ◆

"Andrew, get me Warner-Jones," I say, striding through the office an hour later, the embers of Eve's gratitude still warming my insides.

"She's on holiday, Mr. Deubel. The Seychelles."

"And that's supposed to interest me why?" I pause, turning back to face him.

"No reason," he replies. "I just thought I'd mention it. You know, in case you didn't want to disturb her and her new wife on their honeymoon."

"When you're the source of her income, therefore the person who paid for her wedding, you can make that call. Until then, Andrew. . ." I point at the phone.

I pay my lawyer an exorbitant amount for her expertise. And for her office to be available to me whenever I need it.

"Got it. Oh, she did send this through for your approval already."

I open the folio he hands me to find details of Eve's visa application, then snap the thing shut as another thought hits. A less pleasant one. One that makes her warmth dim.

"Wait." Andrew stills at my raised finger, unmoving as I process my idea. It's one that's very much at odds with what I promised Eve earlier. Romeo or not, this might prove a better payoff. "I want you to do something else for me instead. There's a journalist by the name of Una something or other." I wave away the details as insignificant. "She's a freelance digital journalist, I understand, though she claims to write for the *City Chronicle*."

While I understand Eve's concerns, away from her, my mind is clearer; my own objectives are more pronounced. While my body might argue the case for her gratitude, my brain knows I have more pressing plans.

"*City Chronicle*," Andrew repeats, noting the information in his iPad.

"I want you to set up a call with her. Today."

"I'll do my best."

"Which is why the call will be today, Andrew."

"Right," he affirms with a nod as I turn and make my way into my office.

"Well, good morning," drawls an ironic tone.

My gaze moves to Fin, sprawled out on the Eames-style leather sofa. "You should come in more mornings," I say. "It's doing wonders for your term of address."

"Want me to throw in a few *my liege*s? Come on, Oliver. No one likes an ass licker."

I bite back a smile at the thought of last night's events, striding to my desk.

"You're thinking about ass licking in another sense."

If he knew, I would never live it down. "Do you know that when your lips are moving, they rarely make any sense?"

"And when you're yakking, all I hear is *blah blah blah*. Except, last night. Things were so clear, you didn't have to use words."

"Strange. I didn't have a hangover when I woke this morning."

"What?"

"Pillow talk. I'd have to be blind drunk, because you're not my type."

"Ah, but Eve is a *whole* other story. The way you looked at her said you're down for licking her asshole."

200

"Who's licking whose hole?" Matt suddenly appears in my office, a company-branded construction hat in hand.

I drop the folio to my desk, tamping back a sudden sense of frustration. "Have you both confused my office for the playroom this morning?" I turn and lean back against it. "The crèche is on the third floor."

"Our offices are on the third floor," Matt returns.

"Exactly."

"Our tiny cubbyholes with no fancy view over the park," Fin laments.

"Your offices are vast."

"We don't each have a floor."

"I own the building," I mutter, lowering myself to the edge of my Linley-designed desk.

"Generational wealth is such a bore." Matt grins, knowing full well that I won't bite. Who'd complain about being left the kind of money you couldn't spend in one lifetime? Well, Eve, obviously.

"Speaking of, when are you moving out of the hotel?" Fin asks.

"When the renovations are complete."

"On which house? The shag pad or the place you just picked up on London's most expensive street?"

"I thought that was the shag pad?" Matt interjects.

"The one we know about," Fin taunts.

"Is today a national holiday?" I glance Fin's way. "Is the circus in town?"

"Every day is a circus, working with you." Sitting up, he reaches for his take-out coffee cup, allowing me a moment to study him. Fin's job involves late nights and very few early mornings. It wouldn't be the first time he's come into the office trailing the events of the previous night behind him. On this occasion, he seems neither hungover nor drunk.

"Get fucked," Matt mutters as I turn my attention to him. "I've been at work longer than the both of you." He gestures to the hat. "And I've had to deal with the shite Tragic Mike's been dishing out over at Westminster Council."

"If he hears you calling him that, we'll never get through planning." Fin grins.

"Well, the eejit shouldn't have stripped at the council staffers' Christmas party then, should he? That fucker's brains could explode, and it wouldn't even mess up his hair."

"Getting back to this morning," I cut in, "what's going on here? Did we plan a prayer meeting, or is this an impromptu circle jerk?"

"That's more his thing." Matt hooks a thumb in Fin's direction, who laughs into his coffee cup.

"I mean, I like you both," he says, setting it down, "but not that much."

"I'm thinking this is more like an intervention." With a frown, Matt drops to the other sofa. "I know that arsewipe Atherton deserves his head kicking in. And I was all for you putting the block on planning permission for the last three of his builds."

"I'd like to know who you fucked to stop him," Fin murmurs, impressed.

"I was even entertained when you had Fin swoop in and steal his Qatari investors," Matt adds, ignoring him. "Though personally, I'm not sure it was worth the cost."

"Because boy can they party," Fin adds.

"But whatever it is you're up to now, I can't—*we* can't," Matt qualifies, his finger working like a metronome between the pair, "agree with it."

Folding my arms across my chest, I stretch out my legs in a lounging sort of attitude. "Sadly for you both, I don't require your consent."

"What are you up to, Oliver?" Mirroring my stance, Fin lounges back, stretching his feet out. "Eve seems like a nice girl. She also seems far too levelheaded to get caught up in your bullshit. Willingly, at least."

I make a show of looking at my watch as I drawl, "You have no idea what you're talking about."

"Is it Mortimer's place?" Matt asks. "Last time we talked about it, you said he was running out of time. That he'd have no choice but to accept your offer."

That was bravado. And before Eve fell into my lap. It was an opportunity too good to miss. *An opportunity I'm enjoying more than I should.*

"It's taking longer than I'd like," I say, pushing all thoughts of Eve away. "There's also the risk some foreign-moneyed wide-eyed newlyweds might be struck by the romanticism of the place."

"Nah," he argues. "Just hang on in there. You'll get it before long."

"You're not even interested in the place. Not really." Fin shoots me a narrow-eyed glare. "But I bet you're still using Eve to get it."

"Ah, come on, Oliver," Matt gripes. "The lass doesn't deserve to be caught up in this."

"Doesn't she?" My tone is icy, the warmth in my chest subsiding.

"You know she doesn't."

"Then perhaps she shouldn't have put herself at risk by almost marrying that prick."

And there it is, back again. Cold hard clarity.

Chapter 23
EVIE

A Little Bird Told Us . . .

about an interesting listing on Bookface Marketplace. Check it out below, then come back and tell us what you think.

Link: bf.mrk.bite.ly

451 comments

HideYoKids: I think that cheating dick is selling the bride's belongings on BF Mkt Pl. Is that legal? Can he even do that?

FloozyLoosie: Bet it's bcoz of the pic of her and the hotty.

SashayYourWay: Man was fiiiiine!

TrixieBits: She didn't move on. Girl moved up!

HoppyGoLucky: What a scumbag! Girlies, bring veggies. Preferable heavy root varieties because WE RIDE AT DAWN!

Twerksneark: Is that a Moncler jacket on the top of that box? Asking for a friend.

Sumin.up.rosie: DIES! He's put her wand on the top of that :O

Twerksneark: O_o No longer interested in the jacket.

TheHallouminati: Is that a wand in her box or . . .

PixiChick: She's just pleased to see you!

Charlie09: That thing is MASSIVE!

SlitherIn: It's the wand that chooses the wizard, don't you know.

HufflePuff23: It's the magic in the wand, Charlie.

Zara_A: Is that even legal? He can't sell her stuff.

Jam.Jar: Oooh. I'd buy those Manolos!

Zara_A. @Jam.Jar have some respect.

Jam.Jar: A steal is a steal, babe.

◆ ◆ ◆

Another day, another stupid A Little Bird gossip column.

Maybe I'm also stupid for reading it, I think as I set down my phone. My stomach flips as it immediately lights up with a text from Oliver. My hand hovers over it, though I ultimately resist, pushing it away as though I'm afraid of Oliver cooties. I'm not as afraid as I should be. In fact, I'm kind of into Oliver cooties, and that's definitely *definitely* a bad thing.

I shouldn't have fooled around with him after dinner with his friends that night. And I certainly shouldn't have spent the night in his bed. It was a miscalculation—one minute, I was *It's oh-so comfy-cozy here. I'll just doze for a little.* And the next, I was stirring awake, wrapped in his arms. Bodies touching led to fingers stroking, which led to us fooling around. Again.

And then again in the shower. My God, the shower! I still find myself daydreaming about it, and it's been two weeks!

Two long sexless weeks.

It's little wonder I can't stop thinking about the experience. In fact, that's where my mind had wandered to right before I opened my phone to the Little Bird I'd happily strangle and Mitch's latest online goading attempt. That scumbag wasn't content trying to make me look as bad as him. Oh, no. He had to go and humiliate me too!

Well, he can tell the world I own a wand vibrator—I don't care. Hell will freeze over before he can force me to see him. I am done being manipulated.

At least by him. *But by Oliver?*

I guess I'll be done when I have my visa—my biometric card or whatever. This thing between us is strictly business, which is exactly why I can't have his dick "accidentally" falling into me again.

"Urgh!" I fold my arms on the table and pitch forward. *A softer surface to bang my head on.* "Stupid. Stupid. Stupid!" I don't know whether *not* having sex with him made things better or worse. If we'd done the deed, I might've gotten it out of my system, because all I can think of now is how powerful it felt, denying him. Taking from him. Making him shake with need. Not that I feel very powerful now because I'm hotter for him than ever. "I am such a sicko."

I jolt straight, brushing my hair from my face. I've committed to this. I have no choice but to push through. The latest update on my visa application was a notification of a ten-week processing time. Ten weeks, when there are just eight weeks left before Oliver's all-important auction date.

It'll be fine, I tell myself. How hard can it be to pretend lust is love? By the time Oliver gets his house and his revenge, my visa will be well on its way. We'll shake hands and part amicably. No need to hate fuck him out of my system.

Only I don't hate him. I'm confused by him, by his motivations and the things he said.

"I want you—that much is real."

"It didn't feel like pretend."

It would be so easy to be sucked into that. To be fooled again. But I won't allow it. I need to remember how unmoved he'd been looking at the online photos of Fin and me that night. Especially when a stupid part of me had hoped for a reaction. A flickering of jealousy, maybe.

Oliver runs so hot and cold, surely it can only be a matter of time before I become lukewarm.

I sigh as I reach for my phone, the browser already open to the A Little Bird column. I scroll past today's installment without bothering to follow the link to Bookface Marketplace. I wonder who took the photos that night. It's strange how they chose Fin, when any fool can see Oliver is the alpha of their little pack.

Weird. The previous posts seem to be missing. The one from the restaurant *and* the one where Mitch tried to bring me down to his (snake belly) level.

Wow. I slump back in my chair. Maybe Oliver did sic his legal team on the column.

"This is nothing to worry about. Anyone with half a brain would see this for what it is."

Oliver's response to Mitch's *she's a lying ho* pitch echoes in my head. But he didn't mention legal action until I showed him the photographs . . .

Does that mean he's into me?

Maybe I'm not the only one in this weird *love-to-hate-you-but-still-want-to-ride-your-face* place.

I push away the thoughts. Oliver cooties are an absolute head fuck.

Chapter 24
EVIE

"Well, that nasty mange has cleared up, cutie. You'll be curled up next to your forever love in no time."

"You think there's hope for me?" I say, leaning over the fence. With my vacation time over, I've worked twelve-hour shifts this week, and now I'm at Nora's. And so is Yara. Yay!

"Don't creep up on me," she splutters, then she giggles as the terrier she's been treating leaps forward and licks her nose. "Ew, stop that, Barney!"

I smile at the sight of her being overwhelmed by a tiny bundle of four-legged gratitude. Maybe there really isn't anything in the world that equals the love of a dog.

"You know what Nora would say."

"You know where 'er tongue 'as been?" Yara answers in some imitation of Nora's accent as she pushes the grateful West Highland white terrier mix away from her face. "The old ones *are* always the boot. You done with your list?"

"Like a boss." There's been no letup from Nora's these past weeks, not that I mind. Though now that I'm back at work, I'm seriously coming to miss my luxury spa days. "Old Bess's ears are looking much less sore, so I'd say the drops worked, and I've taken the cone of shame from the new Great Dane cross horse."

"Has he got a name yet?"

"Nora's calling him Scooby. No *Doo*," I add. "Oh, and that rash on the springer spaniel wasn't ringworm but beetroot."

"Beetroot?" Yara repeats, struggling to her feet. "Yeah, yeah, I'd love me, too, if I'd made my skin look brand new," she laughs, patting the still-bouncy terrier.

"From Nora's sandwich, apparently."

"Really?" She glances briefly my way as we gather the tricks of our trade together.

"That's what it looks like to me. I remembered how that day she was eating a sandwich, and it washed off." I wave my hands in a kind of *ta-daa!* "You know her eyesight isn't the greatest."

Yara stretches her head to the side, as though trying to work out a kink in her neck. "Think we need to broach the subject of her driving license with her?"

Now it's my turn to pull a face. "I think our duty of care in this instance—"

"—is not to the old dear who'd tear us a new one at the first sign of interference?"

"That's about the sum of it." Leaning over the gate, I slide the bolt open as Yara administers the last of her treatment—a liver treat—to her patient. "You've just got to know how to handle her."

"I defer to you, oh knowledgeable one, but I would just like to point out that she has just taken the *Dis*Astra on a trip to the bakery," she says, using the nickname we've given her ancient Astra station wagon.

"Let's add that to the list of shit to worry about later."

"Speaking of shit, did you get yours back yet?"

I smile at her back as she closes the gate. Not only does Yara not speak Pulse Tok, but she clearly doesn't read that stupid column. But neither would I if I weren't part of their current obsession.

"Not yet." Maybe I should get Oliver's lawyers to intervene here too. My wand *would* come in handy.

"Is Bitchell still giving you shit?"

"Eh. Not me. He turned up at Riley's again. Lori was not pleased."

"Boo-fucking-hoo." She drags a finger down her cheek to mimic tears, her mouth turning down at the edges. "She's completely the wrong person to ask to pass on a punch in the face."

"Especially on my behalf."

"You haven't seen him since . . ."

"Since the wedding that wasn't?" I shake my head. "And I hope to keep it that way, especially as he seems to be suffering from a case of main-character syndrome."

"He's what?" Her expression twists.

"He seems to think he's entitled to sympathy, according to an online article last week."

"*Women everywhere are cheering for you,*" Una Smith had said. To use a Yara phrase, instead, she's stitched me up.

"Sympathy!" Yara explodes. "That twat is *this close* to being strung up by a group of women in pink saris!" She holds her index finger and thumb half an inch apart.

"I was tempted."

"Say the word, and I'll put out the call. Because that Pulse video thingy is like an internet tutorial on how to get punched in the face by a stranger."

"He was chased out of Brick Lane Market by women throwing fruit."

"Excellent! Well done, the sisterhood! But that's exactly what I mean—why the hell is he prolonging this? What's he up to?"

Probably playing Oliver's games. Or is Oliver playing Mitch's games? It's like the chicken and the egg—it's hard to tell where the distaste and hate stem from. *Well, there's Lucy,* my brain unhelpfully supplies. Lucy must be some girl to get a cool customer like Oliver to react this way.

"Who knows what that man thinks. And frankly, who cares? I should be thanking Jen for fucking him—oh, and they're still seeing each other, apparently." Or was that another A Little Bird edition he thought might stir me to action? Asshole.

"Jen." Yara's mouth pinches. "Didn't anyone teach her 'hos before bros'? 'Breasties before testes'?"

"She can have him and his testes with my blessing. Without her lack of morals, I would've married a stranger. He never once mentioned he had money, that he owned that whole building he lived in."

"That massive warehouse in Shoreditch? I thought he just rented his place there?"

"That's what he said. But it's his."

"Wow, he must be minted."

"A fact he forgot to mention. And here's another thing that slipped his memory: he was on a dating show before we met."

"Like *The Bachelor*?" Yara retches for effect.

"Worse. It was hot singles in a huge house on a tropical island, strutting around wearing nothing but shorts and bikinis for a drama-filled fuck fest." I looked it up on YouTube and almost didn't believe it was him. He was the posh boy of the group—he had an accent like Oliver's!

I mean, who was that man?

The thought feels like a finger poking me in the middle of my forehead. Rich, posh, and manipulating, the pair could be twins. I mean, I'm stuck with Oliver, but at least he hasn't hidden his bullshit.

"It would explain the continued media interest," Yara says.

"Yeah." I blow out an apathetic breath. "I thought once the Pulse Tok died down, that would be it. But it must be a slow news month in London if they're chasing him as some kind of minor celebrity."

Just another thing he must've forgotten to mention, along with his wealth, the scope of his business, and his tendency to dip his dick in other women.

"I've never heard of him. Well, not before you."

"The show ran like, a decade ago."

"So a Z-grade celebrity that no one gives a stuff about."

"Unless they cheated on their fiancée and hit the viral algorithm on Pulse Tok."

"It wasn't his cheating that made the thing go viral. It was the way you handed him his arse at the altar."

"Sometimes I wish I'd just walked away when I got those texts."

"Ah, babe." She gives me a one-armed hug. "Fuck that man. You'll find someone else."

I guess now would be the ideal opportunity to let her in on my big news. My big, fat, fabricated relationship.

"That's the thing. I kind of have." *Yara, forgive me for making you part of the plot*, but I can't keep letting her think I'm living in squalor.

"So soon?" She doesn't say *you idiot*, but her face does.

"Even sooner. I climbed into his car in my wedding dress, kind of fleeing the scene."

Her eyes fly wide. "No way!"

"I know. He didn't even kick me out."

She starts to laugh, really laugh. But I don't mind.

"Evie, you *so* should've made your own Pulse Tok."

"Sure, that's exactly where my mind was at when I'd just escaped marrying a serial cheater." The dogs in the kennels suddenly begin to bark. "Now look, your donkey braying has set the dogs off."

"Sorry," she says, pressing her hand to her mouth, completely uncontrite. But her laughter is infectious. "In your wedding dress? You must've looked like a total mental case."

"I think the phrase you're looking for is *damsel in distress*."

"Babes, you showed me the video. The aesthetic wasn't *distress*, it was more *murderous maniac*."

"Thanks," I mutter with a slow shake of my head.

"Not that he didn't deserve it. But this guy, he must be one of the good ones. Men these days are allergic to women in white dresses, you know."

I bite my tongue. *Good* isn't a word I'd use to describe Oliver, unless we're talking about his bedroom skills. Or his proficiency at making me want to strangle him.

"It's not like I was out in the street looking for a stand-in groom."

"Because you've been there, done that, *and* worn the lacy dress. You must've looked like a complete bunny boiler."

"Remind me why we're friends again?"

"We're better than friends. We're mates. We keep it real, but honestly, that whole story is just ridic."

"That's me," I murmur, watching as Yara pats the pockets of her scrubs like she's looking for something. "Ridiculous. Or at least my life is."

"So, what's he called?" she asks, turning to rummage in the bag behind her. "This Romeo rescuer of yours."

"Romeo." My shoulders move with a snort.

"No way!" She swings around, her eyes as wide as dinner plates. "You know they wind up dead at the end though, right?"

Hmm. One of us might.

"His name is Oliver." Saying his name shouldn't cause me that tiny bubble of pleasure. The man is no Romeo.

"Speak of the devil . . ."

My heart goes *ba-dum* at the sudden sound of Oliver's smooth, deep tone. I whip around to find his playful eyes on mine. But there's an intensity there, too, a facet of him I'm coming to recognize. "What are you doing here? I know I mentioned your name, but I didn't say it three times."

"I think that's Beetlejuice," Yara offers with a slightly dazzled look.

"He's got the suit. What shade is this?" I add in a whisper. "Could it be morally gray?" My lady parts are all aflutter as I reach out to rub the lapel of a (charcoal-colored) suit that hugs him in all the right places. It has the finest pinstripes and a matching vest. His shirt is a brilliant white, his tie dark. He even has a pocket square.

Oliver Deubel, you GQ-worthy thirst trap, you.

"I'll have to take your word for it," he replies, bending to press a kiss to my cheek. *Oh, so we're playing it this way, still.*

"What are you doing here?"

"Checking on my bunny boiler, apparently." He leans around me, offering his hand to Yara. "I'm Oliver. Thankfully, I don't own any pets."

"You're harboring one," I mutter as Bo suddenly appears, sticking his nose in Oliver's crotch at the first opportunity available.

"Yes, he does seem to like me," he says, deftly sliding him away.

"A little too much." I begin to giggle, but that is not a tale I'm about to tell. "Sorry." I give myself a little shake. "Oliver, this is Yara, my friend."

"Hello." Yara's voice is suddenly very girly. "It's nice to meet you, Oliver. Evie was just talking about you."

"Was she?" He slides me a look that's hard to decipher.

"She was just telling me how you met."

"Really?"

"And I was just saying that not many men would've seen beyond the wedding dress."

"And I was just telling her—"

"That I'm not 'many men'?" He stares lovingly at me, but for the beginnings of a smirk lurking at the corner of his mouth.

"You're a one-off." Not a compliment.

"Are you also a vet, Yara?" He turns a pleasantly bland expression her way.

"Yeah," I answer for her. "She has all the good drugs," I add, because if he asks me later about this conversation, I'll blame her illicit drug usage. "Again, what are you doing here?" I slip my hands into the back pockets of my jeans, suddenly not sure what I should do with them. I shouldn't be touching his suit up, and given what I just told Yara, I probably shouldn't wrap them around his throat either.

"I was hoping to whisk you away, but you weren't answering your phone."

"Oh." I pivot, then swivel back. "I put it down somewhere. The question is, where?"

"She does this at least five times a day." Yara directs this Oliver's way.

"That's not true."

"I know," Oliver replies over the top of my head. "Her glasses, too, I've noticed."

"No, she definitely loses her glasses more."

"I do not," I protest. "I've been pretty good with them lately. I've lost them, like, once?" I look to Oliver for confirmation, catching the end of a satisfied-looking smile. It's weird that he thinks he can hide it by rubbing a finger across his mouth. "Okay, maybe twice."

"Something like that."

"I have them right here," I retort, reaching into my cardigan pocket.

"Then who do these belong to?" Yara bends to her bag again and pulls out a pair of glasses identical to the ones in my hand. "You left them on the table after we met for coffee last week."

"Weird." I reach for them, instantly knowing they're mine, though I put them on, just in case. The prescription feels the same—the same as the ones I've been wearing on and off all day.

"Do you have two pairs the same?" Yara asks, unworried by my confusion.

"No. Yes. Well, I bought two pairs because they had twenty percent off the second pair. It wasn't much of a bargain when you calculate how I had them only a week."

"Sounds about right." Yara grins.

"Strange." I balance the new or spare pair on the fence post, when Oliver reaches for them, slipping them behind his pocket square.

"I'll just hold onto these for you."

"Whatever," I mutter, unamused.

"Right, well, I suppose I'd better get myself to the clinic," Yara says, bending to scoop up her bag. "I have a meeting to look forward to with the advocates of a cocker spaniel I operated on yesterday."

My expression turns sympathetic. The downside of this job is handling the unhappy cases. "Things didn't go well?"

"Eh." Yara shrugs, then slides her bag higher up her shoulder. "Foreign-body obstruction. The surgery was fine. The issue is that the foreign body turned out to be a pair of silky knickers."

"Wouldn't be the first time. For a dog, everything is edible until proved otherwise," I say, mostly for Oliver's benefit.

"Yes, so I've heard."

I slant him a look that says *So you've experienced.*

"But it is the first time I've been asked to *produce* the foreign body," Yara adds.

I pull a face. "Ew."

"Good thing Rachel managed to pull them before they were sent for incineration."

"Double ew."

"That's what she gets for giggling over other people's problems," Yara says airily, no doubt a reference to getting caught watching a certain Pulse Tok video.

I shake my head and smile, touched by her support.

"The advocate, also known as the pet owner," she clarifies for Oliver, "asked me to describe them over the phone, and she did *not* sound very impressed when I did. 'Red!'" Yara enunciates in an accent much posher than her own. "'I *do not* own red undergarments!' Anyway, they've been bagged for this afternoon's appointment, and I have a very nasty feeling I'm only there as witness to her confronting him."

"I'd clear all sharp instruments from the room if I were you."

I feel the sudden weight of Oliver's hand on my shoulder. "Because there are better ways to exact revenge."

My face heats immediately, and Yara looks thrilled.

"It won't be much fun," I say, hurrying on.

"Maybe not for him, but I think I might enjoy it." Her fingers fold around the strap of her bag. "Nice to meet you, Oliver."

"And you. I'm sure our paths will cross again." Then, like it's the most natural thing in the world, he wraps his arm around my shoulder, absently pressing his lips to my hair. I rest the back of my head against his chest, angling it to smile at him.

Anyone looking at us would probably mistake this for adoration. And I guess I'm getting pretty good at pretending, because even my heart feels like joining in.

Chapter 25
OLIVER

"I've got to find my phone," Eve says as her friend disappears. Yet she doesn't move, and neither do I, enjoying the weight of her head against my sternum and the whisper of her hair under my chin.

"Maybe we should buy you a tracker." I frown slightly at my use of the plural.

"What about my glasses? I don't understand how I now have two pairs of them."

Four pairs. She has four pairs, all the same. She just doesn't know that Andrew set his assistant the task of discovering which London optician held her prescription. None, as it turned out. They had to be ordered from the United States from somewhere called Warby Parker. Once the extra pairs were delivered, it was just a case of planting them around the suite to prevent her from spending large parts of her days looking for them.

"One of life's mysteries," I offer as my free hand slips over the curve of her hip. "But not a very interesting one, unlike like this spot right here." My fingers trail over the tiny indent below her hip bone that seems to have been created for my thumb, before I explore the gentle curve of her stomach. *Nature's sweet slide into another wonderland.*

"Hey!" She squirms, twisting away.

"You're ticklish." I happily slot the knowledge away.

"What's Change of Heart doing here?" Nora appears around the hedge, her voice particularly strident for someone of her advanced years. "Come to ruin another suit, have you?"

"Nora, you know his name is Oliver," Eve laughingly returns. A pleasurable pang resounds in my chest as she slips her hand into mine. "And no, you can't rope him in to help today. He's here as my ride."

If only.

"Done already?" Nora asks, unimpressed.

"Yep, all finished. Yara already left for the clinic."

The older woman sniffs. "She won't get her treat, then. Here, this is yours," she says, pulling a white paper bag out of her battered leather purse. A number of envelopes flutter to the ground.

"These look important." Eve gathers up the mail before taking the proffered bag. "This one is from the council," she asserts, sorting through them. "This one, I'm not sure. Want me to open it to see what it's about?"

"Nah, chuck 'em on the pile. I'll read them later. Take this." From the pocket of her green pants, she pulls out Eve's cell phone. "You left it on the hedge again."

"Oh! So that's where it was."

"You'd forget your head if it wasn't screwed on tight," Nora adds.

"Probably, but it would turn up soon enough. Don't leave these too long," she adds, brandishing the envelopes. "You might have a long-lost relative that's kicked the bucket and left you millions."

"Doubt it," the old woman grumbles. Her eyes then narrow, as though just remembering something. "Although we did have a windfall late last month."

"Oh?" Eve's surprise isn't feigned.

"Some company in the city paid off the outstanding vet bills." She sniffs. "Apparently, we get a year's free meds and stuff on top of that."

"Well, that's great!" Eve is the picture of enthusiasm, her expression one of puzzlement as she turns to me. I paint on an air of boredom. It was just a partial payment. Nothing to lose her mind over.

"I reckon someone somewhere is paying the piper," Nora says dourly.

"Don't be such a party pooper—the universe just filled your well!" Eve says happily as she eyes me suspiciously. *No change there, then.*

"My well's got a hole in it," Nora grumbles. "Things never last. You get nothing for nothing in this life, girl."

The words of a sage. Eve knows it, too, but she throws up her hands anyway. "Who cares where it came from?"

"Or who?" Nora sends a suspicious glare my way. "Here, I suppose you can have this. It was for Yara," she mutters, almost begrudgingly placing one of the bags into my hands, whether I want it or not. I murmur my thanks.

"Hell's bells and buggeration, my knees are killing me," she complains, leaning her weight against the pen's fence. "Reckon the clinic would let me book in for new knees with that money?"

"Even if they said yes, you wouldn't use it," Eve scoffs. She leans in as I part the paper bag with my forefinger, her voice lowering to an amused purr. "Remember every woman's favorite c-word?"

"What was that?" the old woman demands.

"I was just telling Oliver these are your favorites," Eve replies.

"Hark at her!" Nora pulls a face. "I'm not deaf, you know. Or dead. In fact, I used to like a bit of c-word myself, back in the day."

"Cake, Nora! I was talking about cake!"

"At your age, joy shouldn't be limited to a bit of sugar, unless we're using it as a euphemism for a bit of the other." She gives a ribald laugh. "Enjoy plenty while it's available. Use it before you lose it, I say!"

Eve tips back her head, muttering something to the clouds. Seeking divine intervention, perhaps.

"And you?" The older woman scowls in my direction. "You eat that Hairy Mary."

"I beg your pardon?"

"Go on, get your laughing gear around it."

"I . . ." Have no idea what the answer is. That I'd love to, morning, noon, and night, if it were up to me? Should I point out we're no longer living in the 1970s, that Eve's preference is for deforestation? The truth is, I'd spend days between her thighs regardless of the pruning situation. But that's none of Nora's business.

"Oh, my gawd, look at his face!" The old woman cackles.

"Oh my gosh," Eve repeats, though not with the same level of amusement as her gaze dips to the paper bag in my hand. "I do not want to know where your mind just went, but Nora was talking about that." She points to the bag. "The cake is called a *Hairy Mary*." She enunciates the name very carefully. "A supposed London delicacy."

"I've never heard of it." I peer dubiously into the bag at something that resembles baked goods. While *delicacy* suggests something dainty, this feels more like a brick. Puff pastry, icing, and a sprinkling of desiccated coconut. I suppose the latter is the connection to its name.

"You thought I was talking about that other *other* c-word, didn't you?" Nora says, using the back of her hand to wipe away tears of mirth. "You've got yourself a proper dirty bird, my girl!"

"I think that was a compliment," Eve says to no one in particular.

I know which I'd rather eat.

"I'm just pleased someone remembers what a Hairy Mary looks like these days." Nora sighs. "Make the most of it, son, because when you get to my age, it all falls out."

"Nora!" Eve spins on her heel and tugs on my hand. "Really? You had to go there?"

The old woman's laughter follows us almost the whole way out.

◆ ◆ ◆

EVIE

"Hey, Ted. Sorry I'm covered in dog hair." I shift uncomfortably in the back of Oliver's pristine Bentley, brushing at my black jeans.

"That's all right, miss," the driver replies jovially. Other than the occasional nod, it's the first time he's spoken to me. "It's nothing that won't vacuum."

My phone buzzes in my pocket, and I pull it out to see a text from Yara.

Oh. My. GOD! Your new Romeo is giving me such hot daddy vibes.

Oh my God. She is delusional.

"Everything all right?" Oliver asks, but my eyes are glued to my phone.

Go get some, girl! Who needs a hot girl summer when you can have a slutty one!

"Yeah, it's just Yara." I turn it over. "She just forgot to tell me something."

Something: go be a big ole ho bag!

"You're sure that isn't coconut?" He leans and swipes his hand over my thigh.

I bite my lip as blood rushes to the surface of my skin. "I won't be able to look at one of those again without laughing." Or dying of embarrassment.

"Such an unfortunate name," Oliver ponders.

"What's unfortunate is where your mind went."

"It was a natural jump, considering the direction Nora seemed to be taking things. We are talking about the woman who brought up BDSM the first time we met."

"I only just realized something," I say, turning to him. "Neither of you have any shame. You just open your mouths and say what you like."

"And there the resemblance ends."

"Oh, I don't know. You're also both ruthless in your own way. Tyrannical."

He hitches a brow.

"Despotic, autocratic, know-it-all." Playfully narrowing my gaze, I ask, "You're sure you're not related?"

"That is a horrifying thought."

I glance out the window as I say, "You can also be nice, when the moment takes you."

"I don't know what you're talking about," he says stiffly.

"Fine. Lie to me." My eyes skate over him. "Tell me you didn't settle Nora's vet fees."

"It was merely an accounting decision."

"Whatever the reason, thank you. It came at a good time."

"The balance—"

I hold up my hand. "I get it. Nora gets it when you get it. The house, I mean."

"Precisely."

I turn back to the window and realize we're not heading in the direction of the hotel. "Where are we going?"

"Just to Mayfair."

Mayfair. Another of London's fancy boroughs. "Want to tell me why?"

"We have an appointment."

"*We* do?" I ask, half-amused. "Where?"

"It's a surprise."

"Huh." I flop back against the buttery leather, suddenly disconcerted. "Just pointing out the obvious here—I'm kind of a mess." Messy bun, messy black jeans and T-shirt, and a cardigan covered in dog hair.

"Hmm." Oliver's eyes run over me critically. "Actually, it might be a problem. You seem to be dressed like a burglar." He smiles to take the sting out of his word, but I am dressed head to toe in black. *Apart from the dog hair.* "All that's missing is a balaclava." His gaze slides over my hair. "With hair like that, you'd be caught in no time."

It's hard to ignore what is clearly a compliment. I try anyway.

"Thief or not, you can't go wrong with black. Except when you're dealing with white dogs," I add, plucking at stubborn, wiry hair.

"I like to see you in green," he murmurs. "Like the dress you wore to dinner."

"The one with pockets?"

"Yes, the pockets. Perhaps that's why I liked it so much."

Pleasure bursts inside me. His compliments. His words. The little in-jokes we're having. Until I remind myself I can't trust any of it.

"It would be very impractical for a day at Nora's."

"But perfect for greeting me at the door, a smile on your face and a martini in your hand."

"How very 1950s of you. Also, dream on," I add as his lips quirk. I ignore my phone as it buzzes.

"Oh, I do. I dream of all kinds of things."

My heart skips, then stutters. *He doesn't dream of this being real.*

"Nora told me Mitch turned up at the sanctuary this week." The words tumble in a panic from my mouth.

"Oh?" He reaches for my hand, and I recognize his response as a stalling tactic. "Did she say anything about his visit?"

"Just that she threatened to sic Lamb Chop on him."

"Lamb Chop?"

"The sheep."

"The three-legged sheep—not one of the dogs?"

"She wouldn't risk the local council or police involvement. I'm not sure she's supposed to have so many animals on the land. Plus, what kind of man would admit to being terrorized by a sheep?"

"How terrifying could that woolly creature be?"

"That depends on whether you enjoy swollen testicles or not," I offer happily. "Lamb Chop has a habit of headbutting men right where it hurts. She's also bitten the postman's ass a couple of times. Maybe Nora should've hung on to the llama. That thing would chew off your face just for looking at him the wrong way."

"A llama?" Oliver's tone is a touch incredulous.

"Llamas are very territorial creatures. They've been known to bite off the testicles of their rivals, ending their bloodline."

"I wonder if you can send someone a llama," he muses.

"As a gift?"

"Yes, let's go with that."

"Kind of brings a whole new meaning to Dick at Your Door," I say with a snort.

"A dick where?" He looks at me like I've completely lost it.

"Dick at Your Door." I take back my hand, sliding away a stray lock of hair. "You know, the company that sends your enemies a chocolate dick to choke on?"

Oliver laughs, the deep sound apparently eroding my brain cells, because, apparently, I'm on a roll. Of idiocy.

"I know a drug dealer in Hammersmith who used a snake in his business. A boa constrictor. He'd mail it to people who owed him money, obviously to frighten them. I mean, it was the snake I was acquainted with, not the drug dealer. And in a professional capacity." Why am I babbling? "It's not like I owed him money or anything. How do you suppose he hasn't turned up at the hotel?"

"The snake?" He blinks. "Mitchell." He glances down, then straightens his shirt cuffs. "Few people know I live there. Which is exactly the way I like it." He pauses. "Are you worried about seeing him again?"

"I'd rather never set eyes on him again." The low violence of my own answer surprises me. "Why else do you think I gave up on my belongings?"

"You should've allowed me to rectify that."

"I don't want you to. There's nothing I need."

"There must be."

"Leave it, please. I don't want to talk about it."

Oliver studies me silently before speaking again. "You know, your paths are bound to cross again at some point."

My mouth twists as I suddenly understand his reticence. "I should've guessed. Seeing him is somehow part of your game plan."

"I'm no friend of Mitchell Atherton's. You know that. How would I have arranged a meeting?"

I harrumph my distrust of his answer.

"That's not to say I think it shouldn't happen. And when it does, surely, it would be better if I were by your side."

"Why? You gonna play llama?" I almost expect him to say something crass, assert that one of us being acquainted with Mitchell's ball sack is enough.

"It's not going to be swords at dawn, if that's what you're worried about."

Because he doesn't like me that much.

Sometimes I forget Oliver isn't like other men. But other rich men? Yep, I see those similarities. I wonder if he does it on purpose—reminds me of our situation whenever we're getting along well. I should probably thank him for it.

"I'm not so dumb as to think you'd want to protect my honor." My answer comes out uglier than I expect.

"That's not fair, Eve."

"Nothing about this is fair." I slide him a look, my gaze flicking up, then down.

"I will do what I need to," he answers simply. "But I'm not the one that put you in this situation."

"No, you're just the one who took advantage of it," I say, plucking at a button on my cardigan. Rich men can't be trusted. I should put that on a card. Laminate it for durability. Read it aloud ten times a day and use it as a mantra. "I was stupid enough to accept his proposal. I was fooled by his lies and his empty promises." I need to remember, not repeat the mistake.

"Enough," his cool voice commands as Oliver hauls me onto his knee, without a thought for what either I or the driver think. "This self-flagellation does not serve. You deserve kinder treatment, above all from yourself."

"Do I deserve kinder treatment from you?"

"He will seek you out. And I will be by your side. That will be kinder."

"Cool sidestep." Whether I'm to blame for this situation or not, Oliver definitely took advantage of it. The strange truth is I can't not like him. But trust is another question altogether.

"Just imagine it," he says, his hand whispering through my hair. "I'll take you in my arms and kiss you, and whatever plans he's undoubtedly scheming will be crushed. He'll be crushed. Because I have you and he does not."

Such words. All pretend.

"You want to see him crushed, don't you?"

I shrug, turning away from him. "I mean, it's a close second to death by peanut butter."

Chapter 26
OLIVER

"Here?" Eve glances up at the building, the distinctive blue flag fluttering in the gentle breeze. "Really?" Her doubtful gaze returns to me.

"Yes, really," I reply, fastening the button on my jacket as I take her hand. "Come on. We're already late."

The door opens before we reach it, meaning that Eve stops tugging, hissing questions, and generally fussing. She's right; I might've mentioned we were visiting one of the world's most prestigious jewelers, but that would've spoiled the surprise. And created a lot of questions, more to the point.

"Mr. Deubel, Miss Fairfax, welcome to Garrard & Co." Our greeter, a Mr. Jones, slides his hand down his blue tie and a slight middle-aged paunch.

"Good afternoon."

"Hi. Hello." Eve's eyes widen as we step inside. The interior is stylish and luxurious, but I expect her reaction is more about the store's numerous displays of diamonds.

"Breathtaking, isn't it?" Mr. Jones, our consultant for today, seems enchanted by Eve's apparent wonder as she stares at the high

Edwardian ceilings, the chandeliers, the silk-lined walls. And the jewels, of course.

"That's one word for it." She gives her head a tiny shake, almost as though coming back to herself.

Relief expands between my ribs. Eve is, in so many ways, unlike any woman of my acquaintance, but I've yet to meet a woman who wasn't dazzled by diamonds.

"This way, please." Jones indicates we walk ahead, though we do so very slowly as Eve marvels at the display cabinets housing various necklaces, bracelets, rings, and even ancient archival records.

"What are we doing here, devil boy?" Eve asks from between gritted teeth. Or that could be a smile, I suppose.

"'Devil of a man.' If you're going to use my name, at least use it right."

"El diablo," she whispers in an exaggerated Spanish accent, making a discreet horned sign as though warding off evil.

"Get thee behind me, Satan?"

"No, because you'd just stare at my ass. Oliver," she complains, "why are we here? You said it yourself—I'm dressed like a thief."

"Just keep your hands in your pockets, and if the alarms go off, whatever you do, don't run."

"This is very confusing."

"Relax." I nudge her with my shoulder. "You should only worry if it looks like I'm about to get down on one knee."

"That's not even funny," she grumbles, but before I can answer, her head doubles back to where a number of illustrations hang on the wall. "Is that . . ."

"Yes, beautiful, isn't it?" Jones puts in, coming up from behind us. "It's a hand illustration of the Imperial State Crown, prepared for the coronation of George VI by ourselves."

"George VI, as in the king of England?"

231

"King of the United Kingdom and the dominions of the British Commonwealth, at the time, I believe. Emperor of India also, if memory serves. Now, this one here . . ."

We're not here to buy a crown, but I wait patiently as the pair discusses the members of royalty whose persons Garrard has adorned over the centuries.

". . . by royal warrant of appointment," Jones drones on. "Authorized to provide goods and services to the British royal family, dating back to 1735 by Frederick, Prince of Wales."

Eve, suitably impressed but obviously troubled, clings to my arm as we're shown up a grand staircase to where a door stands open.

"We'd better be here to buy a present for your mom," she whispers, crossing the threshold.

"That would be a pointless exercise," I whisper back. "She's been dead for years."

"Your secretary?" She looks slightly panicked as she thumps her fists into the pockets of her long cardigan.

"Andrew wouldn't appreciate this type of bonus. I could probably see Fin wearing a crown as he wines and dines our clients, but it would give him ideas." Releasing the button on my jacket, I lower myself to a sofa of muted gray.

"Here we are, then," Jones says, closing the door behind him.

"Come and sit next to me." I pat the cushion next to me, and Eve pulls her hands from her pockets, warily lowering herself. Meanwhile, Jones crosses the room, busying himself at a tall cabinet.

"I took the liberty of selecting a few pieces," he says, making his way to the sofa setting, having put on a pair of white cotton gloves. "Of course, if these are not to your liking, we have many other suites to choose from."

"Pieces?"

I stifle my amusement at Eve's reedy tone and the way her eyes appear glued to the tray Jones sets on the table before us.

"Rings?" Her eyes dart to mine, not without panic.

"Surprise! I thought you might like to choose something sparkly to wear until the fateful day I manage to pin you down."

"Too kind," she mutters, murdering me with her eyes.

"She's overcome," I murmur as I slide my arm along the sofa back, pulling her closer. "You see, she's yet to say yes. You like to keep me dangling, my darling, don't you?" It takes everything inside me not to chuckle as she slides her hands under her thighs as though to stop herself from strangling me.

"It is a lady's prerogative," Jones adds jovially.

Eve seems to forget her intended reply as he lifts a ring from the velvet stand.

"Oh, my," she whispers. "That's really something."

"Yes, it's quite an eclectic piece. Sapphire, aquamarines, topaz, tanzanite, and turquoise. Very striking, if I might say so."

Personally, I think it looks a little like something you might get out of a Christmas cracker, but I don't mention it as he proffers it her way. Eve slips it onto the middle finger of her right hand. Her face is a picture of loveliness as she turns her hand this way and that so it catches the light. "It's so sparkly."

It didn't take her long to ease into this, I think, glancing back at the tray as Jones begins to talk about carats and clarity. Then she cuts him off.

"What about that one?"

"A snake," I say doubtfully, staring at the ring she's pointing to. "It's not quite what I had in mind."

"I don't know," she says silkily. "There's something about it that speaks to me."

"It's not *quite* a snake," Jones carefully corrects. "It's a serpent and one of our popular cocktail rings. A striking piece. Aquamarine and diamonds in white gold."

"It's very . . . avant-garde," I say diplomatically. "But I believe Eve to have more traditional tastes."

"I think it's appropriate," she contradicts, swapping the first ring for the second.

"I can't think why."

"Can't you?" She smiles but not with her eyes. "Think *harder*."

Eve and the serpent weren't my aim. "What about that one?" I say, plucking a sapphire ring from the tray to turn it between us. The light from the chandelier turns it a shade I wouldn't have expected.

"You have excellent taste!" Jones exclaims. "One of our modern classics. A double cluster of diamonds and a violet sapphire of striking color and brilliance."

"It looks like an engagement ring," Eve says, quietly discomposed.

"Don't worry, darling. I wouldn't cheat you out of it when the time eventually comes." It glints as I twirl it between my fingers, my mind slipping to a long-ago memory. In the meadow at the back of my grandparents' garden, I twirled a buttercup under my sister's chin to see if it would reflect gold. *Do you like butter or not? So went the game.*

"Do you like it?" Our eyes lock, the huskiness of my voice twisting the question into something else.

"The color reminds me of your eyes."

A madness grips me as I move closer. As I offer it to her. As she tentatively reaches for it. It feels like it could be the first in a lifetime of moments—shared laughter. Loving, living hand in hand as our bones weaken and our skin turns papery. But then, I remember who I am. What I'm about. And it occurs to me that I could never love her as she deserves.

I swipe the ring away just in time.

"But this one is more my taste than yours. Let's look at the aquamarine again."

◆ ◆ ◆

EVIE

What the fuck?

Did that just happen, or did I imagine it? Because, for a split second, it looked like he was about to propose. Worse—I was not running for the hills! Did he think his shoelace needed tying and I misunderstood? Or did his brain misfire—or did mine explode, because I *know* I learned my lesson some weeks ago. Mitchell lied and cheated and manipulated. And Oliver, well, he's guilty of at least one of those.

I am not that girl. I can't be that stupid. Twice.

I resist the urge to press my hands to my cheeks. They feel nuclear-blaze hot.

Did anyone notice? Did anyone see my literal brain fart? I cast a quick glance in Oliver's direction. He looks like he normally does, and Mr. Jones is still waffling about stones.

What in the actual fish cakes is wrong with me? I'd briefly considered throat punching Oliver when he made a joke about proposing earlier. I knew it was all just for show. Maybe my brain suffered a power drain because a stone complemented his eyes.

I don't want to be here. I. Want. To. Run. Away.

"You look a little flushed, Eve."

"I'm fine." Or another f-word. My eyes dart to Oliver's but don't hold as I make a grab for the ring that looks least like a promise. "It's just a little warm in here."

"Let me adjust the air-conditioning." Jones makes to stand but stills as I shake my head.

"No, it's fine." I plaster on a smile, hoping it doesn't look too scary.

"How about a glass of water?"

Stop being nice to me, or I'll cry. Come on, Evie. Get ahold of yourself, for fudge sake.

Oliver turns his wrist, the rubies (garnets?) in his cuff links catching the light as he moves back his pristine cuff. Hallelujah, he's going to say it's time to leave. Sounds good to me. I'll feign an appointment—a meeting. Hit the nearest wine bar to drown this ick.

"I think we will have that champagne, Mr. Jones."

"Ah, hell."

"Sorry?"

"I said *ah hella* like this one?" Shit. I'm wearing the ugly ring again. The one I only said I liked because Oliver didn't. It probably costs a small fortune, even if it reminds me of a mouthful of broken teeth. But the other ring? The one that matched his eyes? It's perfect—exquisite. I almost feel like I should tell him to buy it, to set it aside for his future wife. Except, when I think of that happy occasion, I feel a little stabby. I guess I'm just not that nice.

"This one?" Our eyes lock, his filled with something I can't place. *Relief?* "All the more reason to celebrate."

"Wonderful!" Mr. Jones actually claps his white-gloved hands. "I'll call for refreshments." He bounds from his chair. He must work on commission.

"Why do I even need a ring?" I whisper hiss, leaning in as Mr. Jones leaves. "And why isn't he worried I'll stuff all these jewels in my pockets?" I gesture to the velvet tray holding at least a dozen rings.

"He must be expecting me to keep an eye on you."

"You," I scoff. "What makes you think he'd trust you?"

"Money," he whispers with wide-eyed glee.

"Exactly the reason people won't trust you." *Why I won't trust you.*

"Don't worry. I'd visit you in prison." He reaches for the tray, his fingers spread wide as though ready to grab.

"You're not stealing anything," I say, slapping his hand away. "I don't even want a ring. I have no idea why we're even here."

"To give people lots to talk about, of course."

"I don't see how wearing a ring will help unless you also want me to wear a pin that reads, 'Oliver bought this ring for me.'"

His fingers are soothing on the backs of my hands. "Just trust me."

"About as far as I can throw you," I mutter, making him smile. "Just so you know, when this is over, you're getting it back."

As Mr. Jones clears away the tray and sends off my lucky-bag ring, champagne arrives on a silver tray, and Oliver touches the rim of his glass to mine. "Here's to getting what you want."

"Yeah," I return flatly. "And not what you deserve." *The story of my life,* I think as I take a sip, ignoring the way his eyes stay on me. I get a ring, but what I need is to get out of here. Get this experience over with, get my visa, and get my life back on track.

I pretty much guzzle my champagne, and judging by the tiny-looking gift bag that appears on the table, Oliver paid for the gaudy bauble by sleight of hand.

"I hope you'll come back to visit us again," Mr. Jones says as we leave the room, and my panic seems to lessen. "Perhaps for one of our afternoon soirees. We call them 'tea and tiaras.'"

"Tiaras? Like a princess?" I ask, glancing over my shoulder to see Oliver's mouth lift in a slow grin.

"Princesses wear crowns, not veils." His tone strokes like a caress. *Our inside joke.*

"Princesses do indeed wear crowns," sings a high-on-his-commission Mr. Jones. "But they also wear tiaras. In fact, anyone can wear a tiara."

"Oliver would look fabulous in one." I snicker quietly. Mr. Devil of a Man. You are due some payback.

"You think so? Perhaps we should take a look at them."

"Oliver, no. I was joking!"

"Not for me," he says in the tone of *obviously.*

"When am I going to wear a tiara?"

"Indulge me," he says, taking my hand again.

Dammit. I nearly escaped. At least headwear isn't dangerous.

The room is blue and gray, with tones of silver and gold. *And so many twinkling stones.* I'm drawn to where dozens of tiaras twinkle iridescently from nooks set in the wall.

"The Lotus Flower Tiara," Mr. Jones begins, noticing my interest in a tiara festooned with pearls. "A replica, of course. The original was a necklace gifted to Queen Elizabeth, the queen mother, by her husband, the then-future George VI."

He had me at *queen*, not that I'm into the royals, but I do love history. And this country has so darn much.

"It's beautiful."

"It was made here at Garrard, and then remodeled into the design you see today. Would you like to try it on?"

"Oh, no?" I hold up my hand. "I'm fine."

"Do it," Oliver whispers tauntingly in my ear.

"No." I whip around to find him standing too close, his blue eyes blazing, goading me on. "I'm not—"

"Lift it down, Mr. Jones. I'm sure Eve would love to try it on."

"Stop making decisions for me," I whisper, conflicted. Of course I want to try on the damn thing, but I don't want or need his permission.

"When will you next get the chance to try on a piece of history?"

Does he know? Did I mention my love of old stuff to him?

"Not an actual piece of history," Mr. Jones puts in. He already has the thing in his hand.

What the heck. My fingers pull at my silky scrunchy, tightening it, hoping it's not too messy. I reach out for the tiara, when I find it being passed into Oliver's out-held hands.

"Allow me."

Something inside me twists needily as he sets it on my head. *He's too close. It feels wrong, more dangerous than before.* I spin away to face the mirror, finding myself blinking slowly into a face I don't recognize. I'm not some girl from the backwoods, but I've never been impressed by baubles and trinkets. I'm practical. Low key. Yet here I stand, in the middle of moneyed Mayfair, wearing diamonds on my head and *loving* it.

"All that glitters," I whisper.

"Isn't gold." In the mirror, Oliver appears behind me, his eyes not on the diamonds and pearls but on my hair. "It's champagne, with threads of copper, amber, and ruby red." His gaze meets mine in the mirror when he adds, "It needs no adornment because it's beautiful. Just like you."

Chapter 27
EVIE

After my reaction in the jewelry store, I spend the next few days making sure I'm around Oliver as little as possible. I go to work, take on an extra shift, and go to Nora's so often I think she must be sick of the sight of me. It feels like Bo and I walk the length and breadth of London, pausing only for coffee (a puppuccino for him) and snacks in outdoor cafés. We sit under a variety of trees and parasols as I try not to contemplate life and the mess I'm making of it as London bustles by. I'm not just avoiding Oliver; I'm avoiding the feelings that being near him bring. I can't think straight when he's standing in front of me.

Meanwhile, the ring from Garrard sits on the dresser in my bedroom, a daily reminder of the mess I've gotten myself into.

"This is for you."

I jolt at the sound of Oliver's voice, almost dropping my toast in shock. I know he already left because I waited until I heard the door click closed before leaving my room.

He sets a folder on the table next to my napkin.

"Visa stuff?" As I glance up, I find he's wearing black-framed glasses. I discovered last week that he wears them for reading. I'd smiled and squirreled away the tiny fact, imagining his vanity had kept it from me. This morning, it feels more like a reminder that we're not in a relationship.

"I thought you'd want to read through the paperwork." Sliding the frames from his face, he folds them and slips them into his jacket pocket. His chosen suit is navy today, his shirt open at the neck, his watch a chunky silver Chopard. "Ariana said she'd taken you through the gist of things before she submitted the application."

"Yeah, she did. And I got my receipt with the processing times. It seems you'll have your house before my visa comes through."

He nods, then adds, "That doesn't mean things have to change."

"What do you mean?" *Silly heart, please calm down.*

"That you don't have to move out."

My laughter sounds strange. "I was thinking I'd find myself a place way before then. I might start looking next week. You know, after the big meet." The big meet that might go so badly that he'll want to be rid of me, because I have no idea what he thinks I'll be able to achieve.

"No." One adamant word, his diction sharp. "That doesn't suit me. The agreement was three months, and we're barely one month in."

"Oliver, I need to pull my life together. I can't hide out here forever."

He folds his arms across his chest, staring down at me as though I'm some wayward subordinate who might be cowed by his magnificence. I'm not cowed, but I am appreciative. *Which is an issue in itself.*

"I have to get on with my life."

"If you leave before the twelve weeks is up, it's a breach of contract," he intones stonily.

"You know a verbal contract isn't worth the paper it isn't printed on," I counter in the opposite tone, all jokey and lighthearted.

"Eve." He steps closer, his finger under my chin as he brings my gaze to his. "Don't test me on this."

I make a derisive noise as I jerk from his hold. My heart shoots into my throat as, like a prizefighter knocked down, I'm on my feet as though my survival depends on it.

"You don't get to tell me what I should or shouldn't do." My tone is low and hard. Bo scrambles out from under the table, step-ping between us with a low growl. He hunkers down, hackles rising in his fur. "You think you're the only one who can be a pain in the ass? You think me being here can't get difficult for you?"

Oliver reaches for the remains of my toast, then Bo is chasing it across the room. My fair-weather friend's taste for peanut butter makes him a shitty guard dog.

"Don't tell me. You're going to withhold sex?"

"Having sex with you would imply I like you." My eyes glitter over him. "Or at least some part of you."

"If you need reminding which parts of me you do like, just let me know."

"I don't like any part of you."

"Oh, but you do. Read the documents, darling." Reaching out, he taps the folder with his index finger.

Wariness skitters down my spine. He'd better not have . . .

"No. My application is for a working visa." Ariana, the immi-gration lawyer said so. "I checked the paperwork before I signed it."

"And the supplemental documents? My signed affidavit? Did you happen to see that?"

"What affidavit?" *What the hell is he up to now?*

"We decided a settled relationship would be an extra layer of solidity to your application. So that's what we have, you and I. You wouldn't want to move out before you have your visa and prove that a lie."

I inhale a deep breath, but I will not resort to cussing him out. "We agreed my visa wouldn't be dependent on a relationship with you."

"It isn't. Not wholly. It's just an added safeguard. A man of my standing wouldn't commit visa fraud."

"I don't give a flying fuck about your standing. Take it out. I don't want it—I don't want any link to you."

"How would that look, given it's already been submitted? A canceled spousal visa followed by a failed relationship. Be sensible, Eve. Think of how it would look."

I don't feel sensible. I feel rage filled. I physically vibrate with a deep loathing for his interference, his underhanded manipulation. Why would he force me to stay longer? I just don't get it. "You are . . ." I growl low and hard.

"Yes. I'm all those words running through your head and more. But I feel like we've had this conversation before." He takes his glasses from his pocket, examining them briefly before slipping them on.

Glasses. The word pings in my head. I step away, putting a little distance between us as I think. The tiara try-on session. The ring. *No, not the ring. That was another step in his fucked-up plans.* Fancy Nutella, peanut butter, his driver at my disposal—a dozen other little things. I know Oliver is far from perfect. I know he's not even someone I should trust, but people aren't wholly good or bad. Human nature is a thing of duality.

Was the affidavit his attempt at helping? Does he want me to stay? Something flutters in my chest, but I push it away.

"You love it, don't you?" Cocking my hip, I fold my arms across my chest. "You love playing up to your villainous alter ego."

His response? A bored look as he fastens a button of his jacket.

"I know I said you were the devil, but I'm not sure that's really you." *Not really all of you.* "Were you even going to have me

243

deported?" I'm not grasping at straws, but this just doesn't make sense.

His mouth tips, and as he saunters closer, I force myself to stand my ground. "Your optimism is truly astounding." His hand lifts to cup my cheek, and my pulse skips a beat. "I know who I am, Eve. I know my own faults. In fact, I embrace them."

Up close, his hair is slicked back perfectly, his jaw razor sharp and smooth. He smells like cologne and Oliver voodoo. He smells like I should be anywhere else but near him.

"By buying me a half dozen pairs of reading glasses?" With a flutter of my fingers, I add, "By dotting them around the place for me to find when I need them?"

"Darling, you're confusing an act of convenience with someone who gives a fuck."

I blink, trying to process the truth over a piercing hurt.

"What's done is done. You're committed. You will stay, and you will play your part."

"Until the bitter end?" I snipe.

"Yes, until then." His hand slides down my arm and I watch as he pulls his phone from his pocket, passing it over. "Take heart, it's all part of the bigger plan."

"Not again," I whisper, staring down at an image of myself, this time with him. We're outside of the jewelers', hand in hand. My cheeks are flushed, and I'm laughing, high on tiara window-shopping and residual embarrassment.

A Little Bird Told Us . . .

our Pulse Tok bride is moving on.

The saga continues!

This is different. At the side of the column is a byline attributed to Una Smith, the journalist from the clinic. Looks like she got herself a whole new column. I glance up, though Oliver's expression gives nothing away.

"Una's gone up in the world."

"I think that all depends on your definition."

"Did you have a hand in her promotion?"

"How?"

"Are you asking me to guess?" *You twisty mother trucker.*

"If you read it, you'll find it all very self-explanatory."

That's not an answer, but lowering my gaze, I scan the text.

Doggy doctor Evie Fairfax, our infamous Pulse Tok bride, has been spotted out in Mayfair on the arm of one of Europe's most eligible bachelors, Oliver Deubel.

Spotted leaving Garrard & Co, the exclusive jewelry store, the hotel magnate and private equity bigwig cut a handsome figure in a navy suit.

No mention of what I'm wearing, though that's maybe just as well.

Meanwhile Evie clutched a little somethin' somethin' in her hand as the pair attempted to fly under the radar, making a beeline for his luxury car.

Was there something sparkly in the bag? Maybe something with a lot of carats on a platinum band?

A rep for Oliver, who's regularly named on European rich lists, insists the pair is just friends, despite Garrard being well patronized by the rich and fabulous for its wedding collections.

Are those wedding bells a Little Bird hears?

Join us in wishing Evie better luck this time around.

#Eliver

Under the column there's something else.

APOLOGY.

On the eighth, we published images of Evelyn Fairfax and Fin DeWitt together, implying they are in a relationship. The *City Chronicle* understands this is not the case. Mr. DeWitt and Mr. Deubel are friends and business partners. The images have since been removed, and we regret any offense or pain caused to those involved.

I suddenly feel very cold. "This is not what we spoke about."

"Sometimes plans change."

"No shit, because you said you were going to get your lawyers involved—this is not a legal injunction. This is just more manipulation!" I guess that means his lawyers aren't responsible for Mitch's alternative-reality story being deleted, along with the photos of Fin and me.

"This way was more immediate."

"Do you have any idea what it looks like?"

"Of course. It looks like lovers visiting a jeweler."

"It implies you bought me a ring!"

"A good guess," he says, tugging on his cuffs. "Because I did."

"You're sure she didn't get that from you?"

"No, Eve. I did not tell a journalist I was about to propose to you."

"But you want people to think we're getting married."

He shrugs and, as though bored, slides his hands into his pockets.

"You said the stuff on the internet wouldn't matter, because the guy with the house wouldn't see it."

"It was shortsighted of me."

"He has seen it?" Panic blooms in my chest at what this might mean for me. For Nora.

"No, not as far as I know. But there were other factors to consider."

"What factors?" I demand, throwing my hands up.

"Nothing that need concern you."

"Because you'd prefer to keep me in the dark." I swing away, take four rapid steps, then launch his phone back at him. He catches it with a scowl.

He ought to be happy I didn't throw it at his head.

"I haven't lied to you," he mutters, sliding it away.

"Not even by omission?"

"You're being very melodramatic this morning."

"That's not an answer, you total asshole!" I press my hands to the top of my head as it begins to pulse.

"It was simply a gift."

"A loaner," I insist.

"A friendship ring," he amends.

I bark out a laugh. I'm so far from being amused, so far from feeling like his friend. Duality, my ass. He's as twisted as they come. *Why can't I get this into my thick head?*

"No one is going to mistake that monstrosity for a betrothal," he adds.

"They won't need to speculate because of that . . . that fantasy from Una Smith!" *"Women everywhere are cheering for you," she'd said. Like she cares!* "I am so slow on the uptake."

"You're just built to look for the good in people."

"Like I said, 'stupid.' Stupid for agreeing to this scheme. Stupid for still being here."

"And here you'll stay," he replies silkily. "There's no backing out now, unless you'd like to stay in the UK at His Majesty's pleasure, thanks to a little visa fraud."

"My God, I made a mistake when I saw good in you."

"Yes, that's probably true. Sit down, Eve." He moves the chair a little, his words barely an invitation.

I cross the room, because what else can I do? *Start throwing things at him?* "I wish to hell I understood what you're getting out of this." I feel like I'm missing something. Whatever it is, I feel like it's there, but just out of frame.

"There's your reaction to this." He puts his phone on the table as he takes his own seat.

"You like seeing me angry?" If looks could kill . . .

His smile is measured, almost provocative. "Remember when I said Mitchell would become the poster boy for fuckups? That the impact will leak into his life, affect his decisions? This is what it looks like."

"It looks like you and me getting engaged?" I ask doubtfully.

"Think of his attempts at manipulating the narrative. A Little Bird's previous posts, dragging your name through the mud. His suggestion that you're as guilty as him, that he might be the true injured party. And making images of your personal belongings available on the internet."

My wand. Given my anger, you'd think I wouldn't have the emotional bandwidth for embarrassment. You'd be wrong.

"But that's all directed at me."

"Because he can't get at me. He's becoming desperate, and I want that. I want to see him frantic. I don't want to see you hurt."

Tears of stupidity prick in my eyes. This isn't even about me—I'm just the means to an end—this is more about the past. *More about Lucy.* She must've really done a number on him.

"So you went to Una," I assert, forcing back my emotions. "You made a deal with her."

"It seemed the better option. For one, a defamation claim isn't immediate. It might also have brought more publicity to his accusations."

"Isn't that what you just said you wanted?"

"I also said I don't want you to suffer as a consequence."

"That's a cold kind of comfort, Oliver." I can't look at him and resort to fidgeting with the linen napkin. *I don't want him to hurt you. But I'll hurt you myself.* "Because I still look stupid. One minute I'm about to marry him; the next, you."

"People will always have opinions. Caring about them is a choice." Reaching out, he loops a lock of hair behind my ear before I can pull away. "I don't care what people think. The only person I need you to convince is the man you'll meet this weekend."

"The house," I say flatly. At least it's not all about Lucy.

"The estate, yes."

"Will Mitchell be there?" A cold stone settles in my stomach at the thought.

"I don't know." It seems he doesn't care either way. Can't say I feel the same way.

"What if he chooses to retaliate? Or causes a scene?"

"While I enjoy reminding him what he's lost, I don't think he's that sloppy. Besides," he adds, bending down at the appearance of Judas—*I mean, Bo*—to scratch him behind his floppy ear. "He knows you've moved on with a better man."

I make a flat line of my mouth and keep my thoughts to myself. *A devil of a man.*

"I'm glad we understand each other. That we've cleared the air." He stands, done with these topics. *Me, not so much.*

"You could've just told me some of this. Said you were trying to help my visa, that you had a better plan or whatever."

"Yes, because you would've been so wonderfully receptive," he replies, not without scorn.

"You really are a piece of work," I say, standing. I neatly push my chair under the table before glancing his way. When our eyes meet, there's no regret in his.

"I'm glad you're seeing that now."

Chapter 28
EVIE

I walked out. I left him standing there. It felt necessary. Symbolic, with the quiet click of the door, when I wanted to slam it so hard, it would rattle the hotel walls.

I didn't even have to avoid him in the evening, as he had a business dinner to attend. The first since I'd moved in, apparently. Stay until the bitter end? I wonder how many dinners and evenings out I'll drive him to. Maybe I'll get a reprieve, have my sentence shortened. *Not even that thought makes me feel good.*

"Was it this one?"

I snap back from my morose speculations and smile at the pedicurist. She's holding a bottle of vivid, vampy red nail polish in her hand. "Sorry, I zoned out."

"I'm just checking that Dart through the Heart was the shade you chose."

"I'd settle for a knife."

Yes, officer. The nail polish did *make me do it.*

"Sorry?" Her lovely (but improbable) lashes flutter rapidly.

"Silly joke." I paint on a reassuring smile. "Yes, that's the one."

If this was a real relationship, I wouldn't be sitting here (in his spa) beautifying myself for a night out with him. I'd be camped out in my pj's, refusing to move.

Actually, no. If this was a real relationship, it wouldn't be a relationship for very long. But it isn't real, so here I sit, preparing for tonight—for the big one. The evening I'm expected to work magic when I don't even have a wand.

Or an idea of what I'm getting into.

The past twenty-four hours have been a mess. I felt lonely. Trapped. I've needed someone to talk to, someone to help me process this mess, but I can't tell Yara, and Riley isn't back yet. Not that I could tell him, because where would I start? How could I begin to justify my actions, explain this anger—at myself, at Oliver. At a woman I've never met but suffered for.

Lucy. I wonder if she knows how much she's hurt him. If she's aware of the lengths Oliver is prepared to go to get over her.

Well, screw him, and screw her! I'm out of here the minute this is over. I'm done with feeling like a fool. Done with men that can't be trusted. I'm gonna take up yoga, join a retreat in Goa. Detox. Become celibate. I'm going to—

"Can you just . . ." The pedicurist smiles hesitantly up at me. "You keep tensing your feet."

"Sorry." I force my toes to relax. No need to make her job difficult.

My pulse picks up as my phone buzzes in my lap with a text. I don't know what's with the flutter. It's not like I'm expecting any kind of apology. Besides, Oliver rarely ever texts. The freak of nature that he is prefers to call when he has a summons to issue.

Also, as far as I can tell, he never apologizes.

But it's from Riley.

Riley: Ruben. Croque Madame. Bánh mì.

Evie: Slightly random.

Riley: War of the world of sandwiches. You have to choose.

I smile. I've missed this goofball. But still, this fair-weather friend needs a little kick up the butt.

Evie: Sure. It's not like anything else is happening in my life. As far as you know, I might've been mauled by a pack of rabid dogs and have died a terrible death.

Riley: No rabies in UK. I thought the unicorn fckd the conversation out of you bcz I hvnt heard frm u, either.

Evie: A tip? Text in whole words if you want to get laid. Not an offer, by the way.

Riley: Tetchy! Wanna swap war stories? I'm back home waiting for surgery on this leg. Gotta have external fixators fitted, like a damned Frankenstein cage.

Evie: Ouch! Also, thanks for telling me.

I guess that makes sense why he hasn't been in contact.

Riley: I thought Lori would've.

Urgh! If she wasn't such a bitch, I might not be in this predicament.

Riley: I win in the misery mistakes. A broken leg and I miss real mayonnaise. The French stuff. Miracle Whip is like pasteurized hobgoblin jizz.

Evie: Did your mommy make you a sandwich?

Riley: An inedible one. She's driving me crazy. Can't wait to get out of here.

Evie: I'm sorry, Riley. Let me know how the surgery goes or if there's anything you want me to do.

Riley: Tell me which sandwich. I'm dreaming of food.

Evie: Pork belly bao from that place we went in Oxford Circus.

Riley: Nice! Hey, as you're offering, will you do me a favor?

Evie: Shoot.

Riley: Arrange to get my stuff sent from the hotel in France?

A friend in need is a pain in the ass, even when you're feeling sorry for him.

Evie: Send me the name of the hotel and I'll see what I can do.

I no sooner put down my phone then it buzzes again. I blow out a frustrated breath, though I make sure not to curl my toes again. I'm expecting Riley to have added something to my shit-to-do list. But it's Yara.

Yara: Just so I've got this right, Oliver is only *one* of Europe's most eligible men.

It seems someone's been reading the *City Chronicle*.

Evie: You can't believe everything you read in the tabloids.

Yara: I'm disappointed in you. You should've hung out for *the* most eligible man.

Evie: Ha. Funny. Just like my life.

Yara: Has he got any brothers? Step or otherwise? Second cousins twice removed, but not removed too far from the (I'm guessing) inherited wealth? Asking for your friend. Because I'm not jealous of the hot man in the snazzy suit. Or the Bentley I saw parked outside of Nora's as I got into my ancient Fiat Punto the other day.

Evie: Your Fiat Punto is better than my ride.

Yara: Your ride is a billionaire.

What follows is a row of laughing emoji, followed by eggplants.

Evie: How did the war of the red panties go the other night?

Yara: A seamless change of topic? No blood was shed though I did think of euthanizing them both. I also thought of you being railed enthusiastically by the hot billionaire when they were shouting at each other.

Evie: I don't know how to respond to that.

Yara. I wasn't imagining you going at it! More like . . . and here I am with this pair of fuckwits. The words DICKING and DOWN sprung to mind. Just so you know, as your friend, I am here for the vicarious living.

Evie: I'll bear that in mind.

God knows what she'd think if I told her the truth. Probably that I'm an idiot for fooling myself into believing that anything good could come of this. All he ever does is veer from sweet to asshole, then back again.

Yara: He let you into his car in a wedding dress. That man is down to be your rebound. And I KNOW someone who looks as buttoned up as that has GOT to be a little freaky under those fancy threads.

Evie: Those fancy threads are exactly what make him not my type.

Maybe I should have that tattooed to the inside of my eyelids: *I'm not into men with money.*

Yara: Said no woman ever.

She sends me another line of laughing emoji.

But it's true. Because men with money run roughshod over everyone.

Chapter 29
OLIVER

"What's this?"

Suspicion fills Eve's tone as she stares at the garment bag hanging on the brass luggage cart. She puts her phone on the table, still eyeing it suspiciously. A shoebox sits on the base, another containing a matching designer handbag.

"That's your outfit for this evening."

Her head turns to me slowly, her expression one of distaste and her answer one single word. "Nope."

"No?" I can't say I'm surprised, though I act as though I am.

"No, it's not. See this? This is me, tapping the brakes." The comedienne that she is, she lifts her foot as though testing invisible hydraulics. "I might have to go with you, but you can't tell me what to wear."

"I'm not trying to dictate to you. I just realized we hadn't discussed what kind of function tonight is."

"That's what struck you as strange about tonight?" she demands, folding her arms across her chest. "Not that you hadn't explained who I'm supposed to schmooze or what you expect me to do?"

"No. I purposely hadn't mentioned any of that." *As I purposely haven't mentioned that my deal with Una included making sure there were no images of Eve and Fin floating about the internet.*

She narrows her eyes, all kinds of epitaphs brimming behind her pursed lips. Not that I blame her—not that I'm trying to make it up to her with a designer dress. *As if a hundred dresses could.* I know I've been unfair, that I promised one thing and delivered another, as far as the gossip column goes. I know I should've told her about my affidavit. I might even have mentioned it was Ariana's idea. But I didn't.

I need her to be wary of me. After my fuckup in Garrard, I need her to be on her guard. I'm not talking about the planted photograph of the supposed happy couple but about what happened with the rings. About thinking, even for a split second, that I could deserve her. I could never deserve her, but that doesn't mean I don't want her.

I could never earn her trust, not after the position I've put her in.

So I revert to type. Worsen my treatment of her. Continue to use her as a tool for my revenge. *Because you're afraid,* a little voice whispers. *Afraid of your feelings.*

What does it matter? Even if it was true, in a few weeks, she'll be nothing but an experience. Memories wadded up to be stuffed into an unexamined corner of my mind. *I can only hope for this kindness.*

"For your information, I don't need your help. See?" Thrusting her arms out, she wiggles ten bloodred digits under my nose. "I also have a perfectly acceptable cocktail dress hanging in the closet. A little black dress is the friend to all occasions."

"Almost all," I murmur, turning the page on the report I'm supposed to be reading. "Just not to this one." I slide off my glasses, vain bastard that I am, and glance up. *My God, what is it about making her fiery that gets me so fucking hard?*

"Do I look like I have hay in my hair?" she demands.

I take a moment, as though I check before answering. "Should there be?"

"You think I need fashion advice?" She pins her arms across her chest.

"No. You always look"—*edible. It doesn't matter what you wear, because I always want to take your clothes off*—"nice."

"*Nice*," she repeats, but not in the same tone. "Listen, *friend*, I wasn't raised in some no-name backwater—"

"Yes, so you said. Country club, horses, nasty, horrible rich men." Leaning forward, I place the folder on the coffee table as I wave away her explanation—*blah, blah, blah*. Buying Eve gifts is a completely different experience than I've had in the past, but I can't say I don't prefer it this way.

But that's not why you bought her the dress, the little voice whispers. Not the only reason, at any rate. It's not a peace offering or an apology for the things I say but don't always mean. I know it makes no sense that I swing from adoration to resentment simply because Atherton found her first.

Like that's somehow her fault.

It's just something I saw. Something that stopped me in my tracks as I took a break from the office earlier today. I found myself wandering into the boutique, and before I realized what I was doing, I'd guessed her size and had my credit card in my hand.

"You know, it seems to me you want to sabotage tonight, because there's no way we're gonna look like a couple in love," Eve says. "We'll be more like that couple seven years married and on the way to a divorce."

"*Seven* seems a very particular number."

"That's when boredom sets in," she retorts airily but for the almost imperceptible pinch in her voice.

I could never imagine being bored of her.

"Wear it or don't," I murmur as I run my thumb over the edge of my fingernail, as though a possible rough edge might be more of interest.

"You think you can bend me however you see fit," she says, spinning away.

"Oh, what I wouldn't give to make you bend," I mutter under my breath. Gripping the back of the sofa, I give in to a full-body stretch. She doesn't bite, though her eyes devour. I do enjoy the way she pretends she's unaffected by my physical appearance. *Unlike my personality.* I sigh and ruffle my hands through my hair, and I pop my biceps for effect. "I thought I was helping."

"Railroading, more like. My God, I really need to move out. I hear the rent in Kabul is cheap and the regime a little more tolerant."

"If you like blue. And full coverage."

"At least I'd get to choose it for myself."

"Just humor me, and open the bloody thing." The words fall from my mouth with a rush of air. "I didn't even pick it."

"Then who did?" she demands.

"Your stylist. I haven't seen it, but she assures me it's perfect for an evening at Kensington Palace."

"An evening where?"

"Kensington Palace. Don't get too excited. It's not like we'll be dropping in on William and Kate. They no longer live there."

"Do you . . . know them?" she asks slowly. Suspiciously.

"The Prince and Princess of Wales?"

"Silly question?" Her brow flickers. *Hopefully?* I'm not sure.

"A gentleman never dines and discusses."

A little growl sounds from her throat, and she eyes me as though if she stares hard enough, I'll disappear in a puff of smoke.

"There's an exhibition taking place at the palace over the next few weeks, and tonight is the inaugural gala evening. Fashion, jewels, some link between Crown and celebrity is the theme, I believe."

"Okay." Eve lowers herself to the opposite sofa without loosening her arms. "So, kind of fancy."

"Yes. I imagine there will be all kinds of celebrities attending. Minor royalty, foreign dignitaries, that sort of thing."

"What will you be wearing?"

"Why? Do you want to choose my outfit?" I regret the words as soon as they fall from my mouth. "That was a joke," I qualify quickly.

"Don't you trust me?"

"Men's clothing is different. Boring. It's not like there's a lot of choice," I hedge. The way things are, I wouldn't put it past her to outfit me in drag. Not that I'm giving her the opportunity.

"Oh, come on," she says, suddenly crossing her legs, putting me in the mind of how a cat behaves right before it pounces. "What's good for the goose is good for the gander, right? I'll even take professional advice, like you have."

"You want to dress me?" *I'd rather you undress me.*

"Not tonight. Some other time. Tit for tat."

God help me. God help my thickening cock at the remembrance of the last time she said that.

"What kind of professional advice?"

"I'll consult your tailor." She flicks a shoulder. "Or whatever."

"You'll stop harassing me about the dress if I let you choose my outfit next time."

"If I like it and I wear it, I think that's a fair trade. Unless you're under the impression I can convince this important person of our *love* in one evening."

"It's unlikely to be one evening's work," I agree.

"I still think it's weird how most people just want the best price for their property, not to tell the buyers what to do with it."

"It's been in his family for generations. It has cultural and historical significance"—as well as some other things I've yet to mention—"but in essence, it's the place of his birth. It just happens to have seventy bedrooms."

"*Eish.*" She scrunches her nose. "Just don't say you want me to pretend we're going to fill all those rooms with kids."

"Just an heir. And perhaps a spare." I point my finger over at the trolley again. "Try it on, and you'll have yourself a deal."

"I get to dress you next time?" Her sudden excitement seems disproportionate to our agreement.

"Why not?" I answer as though she's worn me down.

She practically bounces up from the sofa. "Then I guess I'll see you in half an hour."

"Thirty minutes?" I repeat doubtfully, then watch as she pivots, changing direction as she crosses the space between us. "What are you doing?" My words come out low and rough, my entire skin suddenly pierced by a million hot, pleasurable pins as she loops her elegant fingers around my wrist.

"Six fifteen," she says, reading my watch upside down. "What time are we going out?" Her eyes lift. They seem so gold in this light.

"The car will be here at eight," I reply, rusty voiced by her proximity.

"You can take me out for a drink before it arrives."

"Dutch courage?" I feel the loss of her fingers as she straightens.

"A chance for you to persuade me I *can* pretend to like you." She steps backward out of reach. "You want the performance of a lifetime, right?"

I want you on your knees, right now, in front of me. I want all kinds of things I shouldn't.

"See you at six forty-five."

Her words penetrate my lustful haze, and I pull a doubtful face.

"Have you met me?" Her confidence and her playfulness and the way she touches her fingertips to her sternum make me smile. "Remember, you gave me only ten minutes to get dressed last time."

"And you took at least twenty."

"Just imagine what I can do with ten extra minutes." She throws the retort over her shoulder, leaving me alone in the room to do just that.

Chapter 30
OLIVER

Seven on the dot, and the door to her room swings wide.

"If only I'd put money on you being late," I begin, gesturing with my glass, "I'd be quid's . . ." My words trail off as Eve appears in a pool of midnight-colored silk. The halter-neck style bares her shoulders and arms, the neckline plunging between her breasts. The dark silk skims her hips like a lover's touch, dropping to the floor to reveal a hint of red toenail.

"What do you think?" As she crosses the room, the sinuous flow of the fabric parts like a wave, exposing her leg almost to the top of her toned thigh.

"I think . . . I'm lost for words." And sporting a semi at the sight of her, at the heady perfume she's wearing as she comes to a stop in front of me.

"Honestly, I feel like a Bond girl." Her pleasure is a sudden, shy smile, and I note how her fingers toy nervously with a tiny silver purse. "You look like a Bond villain," she adds, taking the glass from my hand. Her eyes hold mine over the rim as she sips.

"Would that be the one with the pussy or the one with the unfortunate teeth?"

"The one that looks like Henry Cavill." Reaching out, she runs her thumb over my satin lapel. "You scrub up good."

My evening suit is single breasted and shawl collared and fits like a glove. I can't think of my own clothing when all I want to do is slide my thumbs under those shoestring straps at her shoulders. *Would her dress snag at her hips or flutter freely to the floor?* Now is not the time to find out. Unless I want a punch in the balls.

"I try," I say, taking my glass back. I set it down and offer her my arm. "Shall we get that drink?"

◆　◆　◆

The hotel bar is busy this evening as we enter. I could procure a table (I do own the place, after all) but it's best we aren't tempted to stay long.

Tempted. What a joke. In that dress, Eve is the personification of enticement. Desire is the serpent in the garden, and Eve is the forbidden apple dangling from the tree. Sweet and ripe for the plucking. *But only if I have no regard for my testicles.*

My hand slips from her back as she turns, bare but for two thin straps crossing at her spine. "What are you having?"

You under me, your breath in my ear as your body yields to mine. "The usual. And you?"

Her lips twist briefly. "Something to take the edge off. A margarita, maybe?"

"You're nervous?"

Her lips twist. "Whatever makes you think that?"

"There's nothing to be worried about." I have every faith she's up to the task.

"Meeting a man I don't know to do what, I'm not sure. No biggie, right? But—" She halts and frowns, as though she didn't mean to say that.

"What is it?"

"Well, this dress is gorgeous, but I feel kind of exposed." She pulls her purse to her front, holding it with both hands.

I give a quick and very thorough once-over. "You're not, thankfully. There are too many men in this bar to fight."

A tiny smile catches at the corner of her mouth, but she turns her head to hide it. "Fight them for my honor? Remember, you're not the hero type."

I'm prevented from answering, thanks to the barman's appearance. I place our order, and Eve declines a seat, watching as my employee prepares her drink.

"I feel like we should've talked more about this," she says absently, pressing her chin to her fist as she watches the barman salt her glass. "Maybe filled out one of those online questionnaires or something?"

Turning to face her, I rest my elbow on the polished bar top and my left foot on the brass footrail. "I don't quite follow."

"I barely know anything about you." She spares me a glance. "What if people start asking me questions? About you? About us?"

"There are very few people who truly know me, so your answers won't matter. You can say what you like. Besides, they're not going to be asking questions about me." My eyes slide over the smooth skin of her shoulder and down her back, my cock pulsating as I take in the luscious swell of her arse.

"Stop staring at my butt."

I look up to find her watching me in the smoky glass behind the bar. "It's what lovers do. Watch. Touch. Kiss when they think no one is watching. Sometimes, even when they know they are, just because they can't help themselves."

"You aren't the PDA type."

"You know that's not true." Leaning forward, I press my lips to her shoulder. "I absolutely can be inspired to public displays."

"Smooth," she says, her tone indifferent as she turns her face away. It doesn't hide the flush to her cheeks. "But if my answers won't matter, then I've decided you aren't the demonstrative type. At least for the purposes of tonight."

"That's a shame."

"Maybe you're even born again. You're very respectful, and you keep your hands to yourself. You don't even believe in sex before marriage."

"I can't imagine what kind of people you think you'll be speaking to tonight, but I suggest you don't say anything like that in earshot of my friends."

"Matt and Fin will be there?"

"Yes." I frown at her response. Her genuine surprise—delight, even.

"Thanks," she says, turning her attention away. I'm almost jealous of the smile she bestows on the barman as he places her drink down in front of her. As he leaves, she rises to her toes, attempting to pluck a tiny straw from a container just out of reach.

"A little help here?"

"Sorry. I wasn't watching the top half."

"Rude," she mutters, as I pass her a tiny straw.

You have no idea, darling.

"But thank you for saving my lipstick."

"Do I get to spoil it later?"

"You know, now that I think about it, you've recently taken a vow of celibacy."

"Kissing isn't fucking. That might depend on what you're kissing, of course." I take a sip of my whisky, allowing that little memory to float between us.

"I think you're about to enter a monastery," she adds airily.

"Another time, perhaps. Tonight, I'm besotted with you, and there will be public displays of affection and adoration. Even a little manhandling."

Her mouth turns down at the corners.

"But I promise to leave that one up to you. You can be as handsy as you like, all as part of the role." I lift my glass in a toast. "Bottoms up."

"Even if Bo is about?"

"There's a lesson I won't need to learn again."

"Because that's not happening *again*." She smiles around her tiny straw, and my mind turns deviant.

"I'm not sure what you mean."

"You might have those baby blues," she says, "but that innocent look doesn't work for you."

"I've gotten away with it this far." I give an unmanly flutter of my lashes, prompting her to giggle.

"You should stick to that haughty brow thing you love so much."

"My what?" I murmur, doing the exact thing she's talking about.

Her smile is sudden, wide, and genuine and makes my heartbeats fall in quick succession.

"That's the one . . . that makes me want to shave the sucker off."

I almost choke on my drink. Coughing into my fist, I clear my throat, then set my glass down. "That would leave me in a predicament."

"Or looking like a groom after a bachelor party."

"There's little chance of that ever happening."

"How am I meant to convince people we're heading for big love when you say things like that?"

"Because I'm saying it only to you." As I also remind myself.

"You don't think it'll ever happen?"

"That I'll have my eyebrows shaved off at a bachelor party?"

"That you'll fall in love again."

Again. Another Lucy assumption I suppose.

"My life is already quite full. It's not something I devote a lot of thought to." People don't fall in love. It's a choice, not accidental.

"If it happens, it happens? And if it doesn't, we'll just murder your harem and bury them, and you, with your pots of money when you pass."

"No harem."

"And no Saint Lucy," she murmurs, quickly taking a sip from her glass.

"You wouldn't call Lucy a saint if you knew her." I wonder where this has come from.

"Well, I don't know her, and I'm clearly not her."

"And for that, I'm very glad." I pause, choosing not to correct her assumption. "If you want to know, you only have to ask." Not that she will.

"I'm not interested." She flicks her shoulder. "It's not like I can trust your answers, anyway."

"I'll tell you the truth. You just have to know the right questions to ask."

"Like I said. I don't care." She paints on a fake-looking smile, and I'm sorry for it. But what I'm sorry for, I can't bring myself to admit. "If I can't make you a celibate monk, who can I make you tonight?"

"Make me a love-drunk fool." *Who doesn't deserve you.*

"Yeah, right." Averting her eyes, she lifts her drink again. "Why are you looking down at me like that?"

"Physics, darling," I answer smoothly. "I'm simply taller."

"Right."

Wrong. I'm looking down at her like a lover, remembering what it's like to be drunk on her. "I would *love* to know what's keeping your breasts in that dress."

"Hey!" She presses her hand to her chest, her laughter a sudden bark around the word.

"Careful." I catch her by the elbow when it looks as though she might topple back. "One wrong move, and the patrons of this bar will get an eyeful, and I'll be forced to fight the lot of them."

"To protect my honor? Again?"

"Plain old jealousy, I'm afraid. If I can't look, no one can."

"There will be no nip slips in this dress." Leaning closer, she flicks her finger against my chest. "Womanly trade secrets. Don't ask. I can't tell."

"What is the probability of finding an enormous pair of knickers under that dress later?" I slant her a narrowed look. "The kind made from trampoline skins."

"I suggest you remove your head from my undergarments," she says with mock primness. "You won't find anything under this dress—"

"Daring."

"—because when we get back later, we'll be parting at our respective bedroom doors."

"Ah, yes. I forgot. My apologies."

"Sorry, my ass."

"Your arse should be sorry. For making me stare at it."

"Favorite color," she demands suddenly.

"No one is going to ask you my favorite color. They're more likely to ask you what I'm like in bed."

"*Oliver.*"

"I had a nanny once who used to say my name like that." Her expression softens. "*Had* being the operative word."

She rolls her eyes, unimpressed. "Siblings?"

"One. A sister. Younger. And you?"

She gives her head a quick shake. "Stepsiblings. We don't maintain contact."

"Your parents are divorced?"

"My dad passed, and my mom has been divorced twice." This she says without inflection but not without some hurt.

"Yet you believe in marriage?"

"If you'd met my parents, you'd know they aren't exactly the role model types. But I've seen happiness, love, and fidelity. I know it's out there. What about you?"

I sigh, indifferent to the whole concept. "I'm on the fence, which is probably odd for a man of my age."

"See? I don't even know how old you are."

"I'm thirty-six."

Her brows jump. "That pretty face must cost you a fortune in fillers."

"I am a whole seven years older than you." This I know thanks to her visa paperwork.

"Exactly. Old. But you were saying?"

"About marriage? I need to find the right woman first. I'm sure that's how the convention goes." But I've never seen love as the kind of risk I'd take a gamble on. "But you've been in love."

"Because the day we met I was wearing a wedding dress?" She shakes her head. "Can't love a ghost."

I open my mouth, but Eve cuts me off.

"He didn't love me, so please don't say it. And I couldn't have loved him, because how can you love a person who never existed?" She stares at her glass, and we both watch as she twirls the stem in her fingers. "I must be an optimist because I do believe in love, even if I haven't found it yet."

"What will it look like, do you think?" I swirl the amber liquid around the base of my own glass, almost worried to look at her. "When you finally see it."

"That's the million-dollar question, isn't it?" She glances up, then away. "Love is . . . choosing that person always." The stones in her ring catch the light as she gathers her hair in one hand, the spill of it like a sheet of red gold slipping over one shoulder. "I guess I need to see it to know it." Her hand falls away and she glances at the glinting gems. "One thing's for sure. It won't be someone who buys me a ring as a photo opportunity."

Chapter 31
EVIE

Oh, Lord. What am I getting myself into?

Well, Kensington Palace. The *actual* palace.

I guess if you're going to be a fake fiancée, it might as well be in a royal residence.

If my mother could see me now, she'd be in raptures. Actually, if my mother was here, she'd probably be under arrest for trying to break into the part of the palace where the royal family lives. Any of them. She's . . . something else, my mom. She's not a social climber, but she is obsessed with status, good breeding, appearances, and all that hooey. That she can trace her family's ancestry way back to America's Founding Fathers is a point of pride to her. Get her near *actual* royalty, and God only knows what she'd be responsible for.

Maybe shouts of *Marry my daughter! Somebody! Anybody royal will do!*

We pass through a security checkpoint, Oliver's driver following the path to the designated parking lot. Once we arrive, Oliver rounds the car while I sit like a woman of good breeding. In other words, one who's forgotten what her hands are for.

"Thank you." I place my hand in his as, knees together, I slide out of the car. Without letting go, Oliver lifts it seamlessly to the crook of his elbow.

"You hate that, don't you?" Humor loiters in the quirk of his lips as we make our way to a marquee denoting the entrance.

"Being handed out of the car like a china doll?"

"I think it's the waiting you object to over anything else."

"I've got hands," I murmur, biting back the offer to demonstrate. To throw hands.

"You're always moving." His eyes skate over me. "Even your face is rarely static."

I scrunch my nose, then frown as I point to my face. "Are you trying to say I could regularly frighten small children with this?"

In answer, he gently knocks his shoulder with mine. "It's endearing."

You can't trust a thing he says, I remind myself, ignoring the instant glow his words create. I might've allowed myself to forget for a moment or two back in the hotel bar, but he was quick to remind me of the man he is.

"I'll tell you the truth. You just have to know the right questions to ask."

Who the hell does he think I am? Frickin' Yoda?

The line into the building is covered by a marquee roof, though it doesn't take long before Oliver is handing over our invitations, which are exchanged for a pair of bright-blue peacock feathers.

"What's this for?" I run my fingers along the length of the one he hands me.

"Take a guess."

"Not to tickle your ass," I retort.

"It's for entry into the exhibition. Not *that* kind of exhibition," he adds, taking in my expression. "There are fashion and jewels on display in the palace's staterooms. The feathers are color coded to match a viewing time."

"Oh." I guess I should've paid attention at security, but I was too busy listening in to other people's conversations. Apparently, there are newspapers and magazines here to cover the event. The *Guardian*, *Vogue*, *Grazia*, and *Tatler*, but I heard no mention of Una whatsherface or the *City Chronicle*, thankfully. It sounds like an eclectic mix of attendees are expected: celebrities, members of the aristocracy, fashion designers, artists, and philanthropists.

With his hand at the small of my back, Oliver leads me into the former home of kings and queens, princes and princesses. While I'm not sure who lives here now, the event is being held in some of the public rooms.

"This is . . . modern." I state the obvious as we clear the marquee and enter what is, effectively, a huge garden room. Decorated in creams and gold, the tasteful palette allows chandeliers to sparkle and mirrors to gleam as huge arrangements of white flowers and foliage add to the general air of opulence. There are barmen dressed in velvet frock coats, and waitresses wearing dainty gold tiaras. And the guests? They are a stylish and, in some cases, an avant-garde bunch—cocktail dresses and evening gowns, velvet dinner jackets, and jeweled lehenga in a profusion of colors and styles.

I was so determined not to allow Oliver to dictate my outfit tonight, but when I slipped this dress on, I immediately knew I wouldn't be wearing anything else. It fits like it was made for me, but I guess that's the beauty of working with a stylist.

"Is this the kind of thing you regularly get invited to?" I find myself asking. I was relieved Oliver didn't pick the dress. I'm also very happy not to be wearing my boring little black one.

"Invited? Yes. Attend. Not so much. We're only here to pin down Lord Bellsand."

"Who?"

He sends me what Jane Austen might call a speaking glance. *Like I'm a ye olde worlde dumbass.*

"The man with the house is a lord?"

"An earl, actually."

My stomach flips. I thought he said we'd have common interests! I glower his way but then realize I'm wasting my time. The man has no scruples. Besides, glowering all night isn't going to get me my visa or help Nora.

"What do I call him? I'm not curtsying or kowtowing, no matter how badly you want this house."

"He'd probably find that hilarious," Oliver says, lifting his hand to acknowledge someone across the space. "I expect he'll insist on Mandy."

"Mandy. His name is Mandy?" My tone? *You are shitting me.*

"It's short for Armand." With a murmured thanks, he lifts two flutes of champagne from a passing tray, pressing one into my hand. "He's very informal. I really do think you'll like him."

"That sounded like a backhanded compliment."

"I thought we'd called a truce this evening."

Something in his tone tugs at me, which is just ridiculous. I'm not feeling sorry for him! Oliver Deubel is no one's idea of a Romeo.

"Fine. I'll try better, but just for tonight."

"Thank you," he says, his fingers brushing my cheek.

"So, this earl. Lord Bellsand. You don't like him?"

"I do, actually. It's his sentimentality, his lack of business sense that has been the problem. Ah, there's Fin." I turn to where his friend holds court—the drop-dead gorgeous blond, glass in hand. Seeing us, he excuses himself from the fashionistas and philanthropists.

"Eve!" He greets me with kisses to both cheeks. "How are you, beautiful?"

"Knock that off," Oliver grumbles.

"I'm good," I reply, completely ignoring him as I touch Fin's arm.

"I'm glad to see you're still putting up with this devil." He taps the rim of his glass to Oliver's shoulder. Oliver's expression is still . . . weird. Grumpy. Milk-curdlingly bleak.

"Oh, it's a struggle," I offer happily. I'm playing my part. I'm not sure what part Oliver is playing. "With Olly, every day is a struggle."

My nickname seems to pull him back to us. In a blink, he turns all suave and sleek. He lifts my hand to his lips, his thumb sliding over the statement-piece ring like a subtle reminder.

"A struggle to keep your hands off me, more like." His gaze sweeps over me, bold and possessive.

"That's true. Sometimes I want to squeeze you so hard and never let go"—thanks to my heels, it's easier to press my lips to his ear as I whisper—"of your windpipe especially."

"It only seems kinky the first time, darling."

"Hey, enough of that," Fin playfully complains. "No PDAs. You'll make a single guy jealous."

"We can't seem to help ourselves." Oliver grins. Two–one to him.

"Well, try harder," Fin says flatly, lifting my hand from Oliver. He says nothing about the ring. "You look stunning this evening." His eyes move over me appreciatively, encouraging me to do a little twirl. I giggle because it's silly but all in good fun. Fin is a flatterer, and I get the sense he knows how to treat (if not keep) a girl.

"Thank you, Fin. You can pay me all the compliments you like."

"You never say that to me," Oliver puts in, aggrieved.

"Maybe I'm just treating you mean."

"It's keeping him more than keen," Fin says with a chuckle. "If you ever get sick of this one . . ." He throws a thumb in Oliver's direction.

"It won't be you she comes looking for," my so-called beloved retorts.

"No, 'cause it'll be me." Matt arrives by my side and bestows on me a one-armed hug, I guess because his other hand is occupied with a plate brimming with food. "How are you, Eve? Want a little nibble?" He offers me his plate.

"For fuck's sakes!" Oliver complains.

"Food, man," Matt protests.

"I'm good," I answer with a soft laugh.

"Looking good, too, I see."

"Will you two stop ogling my date?"

"Ah, shut your face. How is it," Matt continues, "that out of the three of us, you're the one with the date?"

"I'm sure neither of you will be going home alone," Oliver mutters.

"A scurrilous accusation!" Matt complains like an old maid.

"One that lands like an arrow," Oliver bites.

"Don't begrudge us poor bachelors our little pleasures."

"My pleasure isn't little," Fin puts in. And if I wasn't laughing before, I am now.

"Honestly, have you seen the state of him?" Matt jerks his head toward a smiling Fin. "Fat chance of him finding love, dressed in a green suit. A green suit!" He gives a slow, sorrowful shake of his head.

"It's black, not green." Fin sounds wounded. "Who the fuck would wear a green suit?"

"You, clearly," Oliver drawls.

"I suppose he does have enough cheek for two arses," Matt says, which I take to mean Fin doesn't give a stuff for anyone's opinion, because he sure as heck doesn't look like a chipmunk. "God love him, he shouldn't be allowed to go clothes shopping himself." With a pitying glance, he adds, "He's also color blind."

"Defective," Oliver adds.

"I wasn't alone. My tailor was there."

"No." Oliver's gaze flicks over him critically. "That thing is off the rack."

Fin swears, and I laugh again, and so begins our evening.

◆ ◆ ◆

For all the fancy setting, once the opening speeches are over, the night is quite informal. Guests mill around table settings, chatting and laughing before moving on.

The food is buffet style, but quite upscale. There's a lobster and oyster bar set on mounds of glittering ice, and another offering smoked salmon, beluga caviar, and a whole host of other things, none of which I find myself hungry for. I'm too nervous to eat.

What am I supposed to say? *Hey, I hear you've a house for sale. Wanna sell it to me and my hunk over here? I promise I won't install feature walls or shabby chic the whole damn place.*

"Get off!" Matt slaps Fin's hand away, shielding his plate with his body as Fin chomps on a piece of chicken. Or, according to the server, poussin in jerk seasoning served on a bed of fried plantain. "Watch him," he warns. "He's light fingered. He'd steal the eyes out of your head."

Fin begins to laugh, coughing a little as he swallows the piece of pilfered chicken.

"Serves you right. Choke, you bastard. I'll write your eulogy. *Phineas choked the chicken often enough,*" Matt begins in sonorous tones, "*but in the end, the chicken got its own back. And that is how he met his sad end.*"

"I will be castrated by paper cuts before you read my eulogy," Fin retorts.

"Sounds like a painful way to go, but you do you," Matt retorts.

"When my time comes, I plan on being in my own bed with a bellyful of whisky and a maiden's mouth around my"—he halts briefly, his gaze sliding my way—"nether regions as I disappear into the darkness from whence I came."

"He came, and he went." Matt presses his hand to his chest and gives a sorrowful shake of his head.

"You guys are too funny," I say, chuckling again.

"Yes. They're hilarious." An unamused Oliver offers me his hand, and like a good little fake girlfriend, I stand.

"See you guys around."

"Are you off to have a look at the posh frocks?" Fin asks.

I look to Oliver. *Are we?*

"Would you like to?"

"Who doesn't love fashion?"

"Him," Matt pipes up, nodding toward Fin and his green suit.

"I'd love to look." If Oliver had mentioned the exhibition much earlier, things might've gone much easier for him. "If you don't mind."

"Of course I don't," he answers like a good boyfriend would.

"We're pretty good at this," I say as we walk away. I find my thoughts to have mellowed a little. Blame the dress, the champagne, or the other side of Oliver I see when he's with his friends.

"It's not hard." His fingers tighten on mine. "I like you. A lot."

"I guess I must be drunk, then."

"Because you don't like me?"

I sigh, because I know what's coming next. *There are parts of me you like.* And he'd be right, but I can't afford to think of them. "You're like Jekyll and Hyde."

His smile seems out of place, considering what I've just said. "Can we talk about this later? The man we're here to meet is just ahead."

Oh, hell.

I just know this is not going to end well.

Chapter 32
OLIVER

"Argh! No! Deubel!" I feel Eve stiffen beside me as Armand Mortimer, Earl of Bellsand, throws up his hands in a show of mock horror as we cross paths. "The devil will have his due! He bloody well finds you everywhere!"

Eve relaxes instantly, pressing her hand to her mouth to stifle a giggle as the men at a nearby table break out in loud guffaws.

"The devil is off duty this evening, gentlemen. If you'll excuse us." I make to pass the table when Mortimer's gestures turn conciliatory.

"Now, don't be so hasty," he says. "Introduce me to this lovely creature, Deubel."

There's no fool like an old fool. It's not my presence that reminds Mortimer of his manners.

"My lord, this is Eve Fairfax. Eve, this is the Earl of Bellsand."

"None of that," he says gruffly, preening like an aging peacock as he slides his thumb into the embroidered silk cummerbund straining around his portly girth. "It's Mandy, and I'm delighted to meet you, Eve."

"Likewise, my—Mandy."

While Eve might have much to say about the evening later, my conscience is clear as far as Mandy is concerned. I didn't mention he's an earl because I didn't want her ferreting out the name of his estate. I know she has a distrust of wealth. *Of wealthy men.* She would've prejudged, possibly even concluding she didn't like him before this moment. Which would've been a shame, because I was telling the truth when I said I thought they'd get on.

As Mandy invites us to join him and his companions—the table of elderly chortling buffoons—Eve and I exchange a glance.

Mine: Be good.

Hers: What have you gotten me into?

Introductions are made, and more champagne is served before Mandy turns his attention to Eve.

"Have you visited the exhibition yet?" he asks, directing the question Eve's way.

"No, we were just on our way." Eve slides a loving glance my way, and my chest fills with warmth before I remember. It's all pretend, right down to the ring she's wearing. "I am looking forward to it. I love history and fashion, of course."

History. That's something I didn't know. I slot away the insight for examination later.

"What woman doesn't love elegance and jewels!" Mortimer chortles. "I myself am here as a patron. Our family have loaned a number of outfits to the exhibition."

"Oh?" Eve turns her attention to the older man, though she doesn't let go of my hand.

"Yes, a number of eighteenth-century pieces. Keep an eye out for the butter-colored mantua. It will make you glad to live in this century."

"I'm not even sure what a mantua is," she admits, much to his delight. He spends the next few minutes explaining with the zeal of a seamstress that it's a sort of overdress and that this particular one is almost three meters wide at the hip.

"It would only be worn here, you see, at the palace. During that period, the seventeen hundreds, you didn't need an appointment to meet the king. You needed to put your best foot forward, so to speak. Turn up in your best threads."

"A bit like tonight?" Eve answers with a smile, as the old fool fiddles with his cummerbund again.

"Precisely. But then, you'd put on your best outfit to impress the guards, or else you weren't allowed to pass on to the King's Staircase. Have you seen it yet? The staircase?"

Eve shakes her head.

"It's very famous. The walls were painted by William Kent. I daresay you'll enjoy looking, but then imagine trying to pass through a crush of people in a three-meter-wide dress!"

The pair gets on so well, I feel almost surplus to requirements. It's not a complaint so much as an observation, as Eve commits to her role beautifully, smiling my way and laughing into my shoulder. I might not be a large part of the conversation, but I fool myself I'm at the center of her thoughts. Every smile she slides my way makes me want to pull her onto my knee to kiss her; every touch she bestows makes me wish this was real.

It won't ever be. I've burned my bridges—razed them to the ground.

"How do you know this devil, then?" Mortimer slides me an uncomplimentary look that Eve doesn't see, as a range of emotions flickers across her face and fades. I briefly regret not exploring our backstory better, wondering what she's thinking. What she might say.

"A long story, then?" Mortimer asks kindly.

"No." She shakes her head, her smile sweet and her eyes a touch watery as they find mine. "Not really. We haven't been together long, but I feel like I know him so well. How can I explain this? Well, I guess Oliver rescued me."

"Really?" The man's bushy gray brows bounce like aging caterpillars.

"Yes. I don't know what I would've done without him. I just feel like the luckiest girl in the world." Her cheeks turn a delicious pink from discomfort or embarrassment; it's hard to tell.

"Well, we really don't often hear of this side of him."

"We?" I repeat mildly.

"People of our mutual acquaintance. You haven't got the best reputation, have you, Deubel?"

"That's people though, isn't it?" she says sweetly. "They like to dwell on the negative. Anything else isn't gossip worthy."

"Don't tell me you're not a fan of gossip," he says, chortling, and for a minute I think he might consider chucking her chin. "I never met a young lady who didn't love to hear a snippet of a rival's personal affairs."

"That's not a strictly female pastime," she says. "If you ask me, men are just as bad."

"Worse, sometimes," I put in. "Eve isn't one for gossip. She doesn't really have the time."

"You don't work for him, do you?" he asks, suddenly looking worried.

Eve smiles. I can see where her thoughts have taken this. *Only when I can't help it.* "No, I don't work for Oliver," she says with a spark of devilment in her eyes. "We're friends."

I gaze at her like a lovesick pup as I rub my thumb back and forth over the ring. "We have a very particular kind of friendship. I have hopes we'll be very much more one day very soon."

"Only you haven't asked yet," she singsongs.

"You can ask me. You already know my answer."

"No, no." Mandy chuckles. "That's not the way things are done."

"I know," I reply. "And I have just the grand gesture in mind."

For a minute, I think Mandy might be about to begin clapping.

"The problem is," I murmur confidentially, "pinning Eve down. She has a very demanding day job. And in her spare time, she volunteers her skills."

"What is it you do, my dear?"

"I'm a veterinarian." Only I can see her discomfort in the admission.

The old man's face lights up. I find myself once more wondering if Atherton knew what she did for a living before he asked her out. It wouldn't be the only reason for his interest—Eve is so much more than convenient—but he must've thought he'd struck gold when he discovered she was a vet. Unlike Eve, I don't wonder if he ever loved her, because I know it would be easy to do so. But love is a choice, and loving Eve is not something I've planned for.

"How wonderful!" Mortimer's gaze is degrees warmer as it meets mine. "Deubel, I insist you bring Eve out to the house."

And there it is. The bull's-eye.

◆ ◆ ◆

EVIE

Lord Bellsand, or Mandy, as he insists, is fascinating. He's a bit of an old roué, though I get the sense he's put himself out to pasture. Which is good for Oliver, because if I thought he'd brought me here as bait, he'd find himself in an awkward place. *Like explaining to a paramedic why his testicles are lodged under his ears.*

Anyhoo, Mandy seems to have lived one hell of a life, and I'm happy to let him chatter. It seems a huge part of my role, if I'm honest.

"Elizabeth Taylor?"

"My lips are sealed." He makes a show of locking them and throwing away the key.

"Was it the lions, the tigers, or the bears?"

"We don't have bears, my dear." Mandy pats my hand where it lies in the crook of his elbow. "We've never had bears at Northaby."

When he offered to escort me to the palace to look at his inclusion in tonight's exhibit, Oliver was all for it. He said it'd give me time to work my charm on him. Sucks to be Oliver, because it's worked the other way around. I kind of love Mandy already.

"I had hoped to introduce them to the park at some point, because my heart does ache at the barbarous conditions bears are kept in in some countries. Circuses and cages. And don't get me started on them being farmed for—" He halts and sucks in a deep breath. "Excuse me. I'll just put away my soapbox."

We are kindred spirits, Mandy and me. He's my mister from another sister, and we sing from the same song sheet. "I'm with you on all of that, Mandy. As you can probably guess, the topic of animal rights is very close to my heart."

"I knew you were a good one," he says, squeezing my fingertips in solidarity. "As for bears, the fact is, I haven't had the means to maintain the house, never mind expand the safari park. We've been operating on a shoestring budget for years."

Yep, that's right. It's not as bait that Oliver has me tagging along. I'm here because the house that Mandy is trying to sell has a mother-freakin' safari park attached to it. It's not just the house that's his heritage; it's the park and animals too. And I am going to kick Oliver's ass when I get him alone next, because this is the reason he's been so vague about it all. The potential Mrs. Deubel is not just a pretty face!

"You likely have lots in common" and *"Just be yourself"* were just Oliver speak for *I don't want you to ask too many questions.* Oh, and I have questions. And I have fears. And if I don't get the answers I want, then . . .

I don't know what I'm going to do about it, but I'll think of something.

I already feel guilty about being here, about taking part in this. I mean, I'm here for Nora, as well as for my own benefit, and I know I can't champion every cause, but I also can't lie to this sweet man.

"Eve?" Mandy's expression is full of concern.

"Sorry," I say, pulling myself from my thoughts. "I was just thinking about a documentary I saw."

"Bears?" He frowns. "I think I know the one you mean. A nasty business." He pats my hand again like I'm a delicate flower.

Northaby House Safari Park was created by Mandy's grandfather, who turned part of its vast grounds into the kind of place the local populace could, for a price, see lions and tigers and giraffes. He was a man ahead of his time, Mandy explains, because most men of his generation would've settled on a grand hunting tour where the only animals brought home would've been the ones they shot. *Shot, stuffed, mounted, and set behind glass.*

"Sadly, I'm getting on in years. I love the place, but it's time I looked to the future. The sad fact of the matter is, Northaby requires an influx of cash to keep it going. Quite frankly, my dear, I feel like I'm standing in the middle of a house of cards." He laughs but not with humor.

"It must be very difficult for you."

"It's been a trial trying to find someone who has both the means and the interest to keep it as it is." He sighs. "I thought I'd found someone, but he seems to have dropped off the face of the earth."

Mitchell, maybe? It's so ridiculous, the lengths that both Oliver and that prick will go to get their hands on Northaby. Mandy should probably look elsewhere, because neither of them are worthy of his legacy. And Oliver can barely cope with one dog!

How the hell did I get myself embroiled in this? I can't lie to this sweetheart, and I won't commit to anything that harms his wildlife.

"Quite honestly, I've been avoiding Oliver," Mandy admits. "He's someone who is known for making money from things he takes apart. He makes things shiny, new, and profitable, and safari parks are a lot of work. I didn't want to see my animals shipped all over the world and the house turned into a hotel."

"I understand," I answer quietly.

"But if you were to tell me—"

"I still can't quite get my head around a safari park in rural England," I announce, cutting him off.

"You should visit. Both you and Oliver."

"We'll buy tickets."

"Nonsense!" he exclaims. "You're welcome anytime, and you'll be at the ball, of course."

"Oh, yes. The ball . . ." The ball I know nothing about. *Thanks for nothing, Oliver.*

Mandy chuckles. "It's just my little fundraising attempt. My annual gala charity ball. Perhaps Oliver didn't mention it?"

"He likes to keep surprising me," I answer, with a smile that feels weird.

"Smitten!" Mandy announces, like he's genuinely delighted. "We might not be the only safari park in the country, but I think we're the finest." It's like he's trying to impress me.

"I'm sure."

"And it's not so strange. Think *safari* and your mind goes to the Serengeti—the great plains, dry heat, and Maasai warriors. But the animals don't mind our gray skies, thatched cottages, and old ladies at the bus stop complaining about the rain."

"I'm sure they wouldn't have it any other way," I answer fondly. "I love living here." Though I do prefer it when my life isn't unraveling at the seams.

"Do you know the savanna means a treeless plain?"

"Does that describe your land?"

"Not at all!" he scoffs. "Northaby has extensive woodlands. But lions fare just as well in the rain and wind. And the monkeys at Northaby will snap off your windshield wipers just as easily as they would in Kruger National Park. Ah, listen to me, boring a pretty girl with tales of my menagerie and me."

"Go for it. I'm loving this." Plus, it's easier when I don't have to lie.

"You're too kind, but for now we're here. The grand entrance to the King's State Apartments."

"Wow!" I tip my head back, scanning the space for full effect. "It looks like something from *Bridgerton*."

"From where?" His thick gray brows flicker, as though trying to place it.

"Never mind." *Bridgerton* is pretend old-world luxury. People like Mandy live in the real thing. "So, this must be the King's Staircase?" Mandy nods in the periphery of my vison as I gawk at the imposing structure. The gilt and the splendor, the high, high ceilings, and the painted faces staring down at us from the walls. "They look so real."

"In some cases, they were."

"The paintings are of actual people?" I glance his way, struck by the pleasure in his expression. It feeds mine, but then I remember my genuine enjoyment is adding to this falsehood.

"Some of them, yes. For almost three hundred years, those faces have stared down at all who ascend the staircase—characters from an eighteenth-century royal court. Those identifiable are King George's page, Ulric, and his Turkish manservants, Mehemet and Mustapha. And those characters dressed in red are the royal guard."

"The people you had to impress to gain access to the king and his crew."

"Yes, exactly right."

"Ye olde fashionistas?" Or door bitches in old-fashioned britches.

"Perhaps they were," he says, with a small smile. "And up there on the ceiling, looking down on us from a cupola, wearing that very dapper red turban, is the artist himself."

"Gosh. Do you suppose that's the world's first selfie?"

I made it clear I didn't want to be here, that I didn't want to be part of this, but the evening delivered on more fronts than I ever could have expected. The exhibit is amazing—a walk through the ages that includes outfits worn by powerhouse Hollywood names at the Emmys, the Oscars, and the Met Gala.

Beyoncé, Rihanna, Audrey Hepburn—the names go on and on. There are shoes, and jewels, and hats, and other headpieces, but my favorite part of the whole exhibit is the look back into fashions from the past.

My Lord, I love all this history. Georgian court dresses made of delicate silver tissue, embroidered mantua, and gentlemen's silk knee suits with matching frilly cuffs and high heels. I could spend hours just staring at them, wondering who wore them. Imagining what their lives were like, and whether court visits afforded them business or pleasure.

"You're very quiet, my dear."

"I don't think I have the vocabulary to say how much I love this." I smile Mandy's way, though I'm thinking of Oliver while also feeling a little sad. I'm sure he'd fit right into court—all lethal good looks in that cloak-and-dagger lifestyle.

"Charming," Mandy murmurs. "Just charming. But I have a little tickle in my throat that I think could only be helped by a glass of champagne."

"Then let's go and find you one." While his manners are exceptional, I'm sure he's had enough of staring at things that he can probably lift out of a closet any time he likes.

As we make our way out of the Pigott Gallery, I promise myself that one day very soon, when the exhibit is open to the public, I'm going to buy myself a visitor's ticket and ogle until my heart is content.

Back in the pavilion, we help ourselves to champagne as I crane my head for some sign of Oliver. He doesn't appear to be here, so when Mandy suggests a turn around the gardens, I agree. I'm pretty sure I'm not in any danger of Mandy getting handsy in the bushes, but I do hear music drifting in over the terrace, and I think I can see a dance floor.

"More *Bridgerton* memories," I murmur as we make our way out into the late-setting summer sun to where a string quartet is playing contemporary pop songs.

"Would you care to cut a rug with an old man?" Mandy asks, giving a comical shimmy of his shoulders. "See if I can't give Deubel a run for his money?"

"Why not?" I say, setting my glass down on a low wall.

"You know I can't give him a run for his money," he adds more seriously. For a horrible minute, I think he's going to tell me *not without the aid of some little blue pills*, but thankfully that isn't the direction he takes. "I have too many houses," he laments. "Too many roofs to repair and too much damp to prevent. Sadly,

Northaby is the only house not entailed, so I must sell it to prop up the rest. I'm honor bound to keep the title's property in tip-top shape, and the cost is Northaby."

"I'm so sorry, Mandy." And I mean it. We drop down the sandstone steps on our way to the flower-festooned dance floor.

"I'm too old to fight for what the animals need. I must start thinking about a time when I will no longer be here."

"That's a long way off." I squeeze his arm in reassurance.

"There's certainly a lot of life left in this old dog, but I'm tired of worrying about the future of the place. But I don't want to sell it to find it turned into a bloody hotel."

"That I understand." What the heck am I supposed to say?

"Tell me that's not what he'll do."

"Who, Oliver? All I can say is he's talked a lot about Northaby, but he never mentioned the animals."

"Oh." His brow furrows, his mouth turning down.

"No," I add quickly. "What I'm trying to say is I think he wanted the safari park to be a surprise." *Or maybe a shock to keep me on my toes.*

"Oh!" The same sound. Not the same tone. And may God strike me down for fooling this man. I need to speak to Oliver—find out what his intentions are. And if they are what I think they are, then . . . then I'm screwed.

"I can tell you're very special to him." At the edge of the dance floor, Mandy takes my hand, but before he lifts it to his shoulder, he stares down at the ring on my right hand. "Because this is one of the new pieces from Garrard, I believe."

"Yes, that's right," I reply, allowing him to move us into the dancing throng.

"A man doesn't buy a woman eighty thousand pounds' worth of sapphires, aquamarine, and diamonds for no reason, my dear."

Eighty thousand! I break out in a literal cold sweat, but then I remember it's only on loan. That it doesn't mean anything. I clamp my lips together, worried about what I might say as my heart begins to race. It's one thing to turn up, to play my role; it's quite another for me to suggest Mandy's animals will be safe.

"I'd go even as far as to say that you, and Oliver, of course, might be Northaby's future."

"Mandy, I don't know. Who knows what goes on in Oliver's head?" I prattle as panic begins to flutter in my chest. "I love all animals—"

"And history, quite obviously."

"Yes, and history. And while animals are a huge part of my life, my experience isn't in zoological medicine."

"It doesn't need to be," he says, patting my back. "The place just needs money and love, and I have a good feeling about all of this. I'm a great believer in intuition."

This is bad. Really bad. What the hell am I going to do about this? Oliver isn't the type of man who'd want the responsibility for those creatures. Meanwhile, Mandy is like Nora on crack! Except Mandy is a nice man who has manners and seems to like people as much as he likes animals.

"Whoops." Amusement makes his eyes sparkle and the apples of his cheeks lift.

"Sorry for your toes," I murmur, panic having forced me into a misstep.

"My fault entirely."

"You're too kind."

"And you're too lovely to wear that frown."

I guess there's nothing I can do about this situation right now other than concentrate and try hard not to crush any more of his toes.

The music changes, the tempo a little more upbeat, and Mandy totally gets with it as we swirl around the floor.

"I haven't had this much fun in ages. If Oliver hadn't put a ring on it, I might've been tempted to do so myself."

"It's a friendship ring, Mandy," I say with a laugh, "not that I expect jewels in exchange for my friendship."

"Oliver is more than your friend. We both know that, my dear. The way he looks at you . . ." His words trail off, and then his eyes slip over my right shoulder as though snagged by something unexpected.

A second later, revulsion zips down my spine, anger quickly following at the familiar and unwelcome sound of Mitch's voice.

"May I cut in?"

Every fiber revolts, my emotions rioting inside my chest like a storm. I want to yell, *No you may not. You may go to hell. Eat shit and die. Swallow peanut butter and swell while I run away with your EpiPen.*

Sadly, none of that is appropriate. This man has brought me to disgrace in a public setting one too many times.

"Yes, of course," Mandy replies, taking my unease for I don't know what. But etiquette dictates he step aside. "One dance, and I'll be back again. One dance," he repeats, this time for Mitchell's benefit.

As Mandy turns away, I do the same in the opposite direction. Until Mitch's fingers fold around my upper arm.

"For old times' sake?"

"Get your hand off me."

"One dance," he demands, yanking me bodily against him. "Unless you're planning on running again."

"Say what you need to, and get the fuck out of my life," I grate out, assuming the position—submitting. Short of the physical violence I still harbor for him, what choices do I have? Causing a scene might jeopardize everything.

"How are you, Evie?"

"I'm feeling kind of murderous."

"Fiery." His eyes skate over my hair. "I love when your temper brings out the redhead in you."

"And I love it when you're on a different continent."

"Evie," he says, twirling us around the floor, despite the fact that it must feel like he's dancing with a corpse. "You'd think I was the only one in the wrong."

I grit my teeth, refusing to bite.

"This was originally my plan, you know. Getting you to meet the old bloke."

"So you could get your hands on his house. Yes, I know." *Now.*

"But it wasn't the only reason I asked you to marry me. I love you."

"Great! I'm so happy to hear that. Let's leave, run off together, and be happy forever."

"But you'll do it for *him*."

"Are you kidding me right now!" Because Mitch put me in this position! My feet come to a stop, and I push him, manners be damned. I swing away, when he grabs my wrist. "Let go of me," I grate out. The dance floor is packed; I'm not sure if I'm relieved or panicked that no one seems to notice our scuffle.

"*Loved you*, I should say. Past tense. I wouldn't have you back, not after you've been fucking him."

"That upsets me . . . not one bit."

I try to move away, but he yanks me to him again. I guess, torso to torso, we must look like we're dancing, but I get right in his face, refusing to be cowed.

"I thought I was in love with you, but how could I be? You were nothing but a ghost."

"Better a ghost than the devil, Evie. What was he doing there that day? You tell me that."

"Like the man said, it was an act of fate. And I thank the Lord above for sending him when he did. Is that even your accent?"

"What are you talking about?"

"You're a posh boy." My eyes flit over him in distaste. "You can't even own it."

"That's rich coming from you—you and your *I'm so sick of the bourgeoise narrative*," he mocks. "*Rich men aren't worth the pain*. But look who you're fucking now."

"At least he doesn't pretend to be someone he's not."

"You're nothing but a lying slut."

"I wasn't, you know." My tone turns silky as I whisper in his ear. "But on our supposed wedding night, I turned slut for him."

His hand suddenly tangles in the back of my hair, like a lover holding me close.

"You ruined everything," he growls.

"And you fucked your way through half of London."

"Hardly," he scoffs.

"Did you think I wouldn't find out that you were screwing Jen? And I know you were fucking his PA."

He laughs quite suddenly. "Ah, the lovely Lucy. Is that what he said she was to him?"

"I don't care who she is or that you were fucking her." I try to pull away, my pulse jackhammering in my throat when he holds me there.

"There was a slight overlap, I'll grant you that," he says, sounding quite proud of himself. *Yara was right. The dude is smug.* "You didn't expect me to say faithful, did you, love? Not when we went months without seeing each other." He sickens me. I can barely believe this was the man I was about to marry. It's all so clear now.

I ignored who he was in favor of being right about him—about our marriage.

"Get your hands off me."

"Come with me, and I'll confess every dirty detail."

"I would rather dry hump a cheese grater," I mutter, pulling away, pushing my hands against his chest, and not caring a jot if I end up with a bald patch. I stomp my heel into his foot, and he curses. I spin away, two steps, and I'm out of his reach. But then, like tendrils of cold dread, his fingers grip my wrist again. He squeezes, and I wince, my words hitting the air on a pained breath.

"You're hurting me."

"That's the idea, though breaking your wrist would be a poor substitute for your neck."

"People are staring," I say, catching the eye of one half of a waltzing couple. I'm not lying—she did see. She just refused to make it her business. *So much for sisterhood.* "They'll alert security. Let me go."

Against my back, Mitchell's chest moves with an inhale, but the voice that speaks isn't his.

"I suggest you do as the lady says."

Chapter 33
OLIVER

"Ah, there you are!" A fourth joins us, Matt throwing his arm around Eve as we stand in the middle of the dance floor, Mitchell and I snarling and circling like dogs.

That bastard has his hands on her. He touched what he doesn't deserve.

"I said let her *go*." At my demand, Matt's gaze drops to where Mitchell's fingers make a manacle on Eve's wrist. He frowns. He knows people are staring, knows the press is here. Painting on a sloppy smile, he drapes himself around her like this isn't an altercation but a drunken conversation. *In the middle of the dance floor.* But I suppose the intoxicated rarely make sense.

"I bet he's like a bus with no wheels," Matt begins, his Irish accent thicker than I've ever heard it. "You get on, but it doesn't take you where you want to go. And when it's time to get off, he leaves you sorely disappointed." Somehow, he slides between them, disconnecting Mitchell's fingers. He whisks Eve to his side, and then the pair is gone.

The fist wrapped around my heart eases, the music seeming to pick up as, in the periphery of my vision, couples seem to whirl like dervishes.

"Come to save her?" he sneers.

"Not for the first time."

"Fuck off. I know you were having her all along." With his accusation, flecks of spittle fly from his thick lips.

"You really don't know her at all."

"Don't fucking lie to me."

"Not that I wouldn't have, though your anger strikes me as ironic, given you're the one in the wrong." As far as Eve is concerned, at least.

"Bastard," he growls, his accent betraying him, all round vowels.

I almost answer that we're one and the same, but I'm not like him. I don't have to be, I decide, as I turn away. I want Eve. I also desperately want to kick seven colors of shit out of the man, but I know that kind of satisfaction rarely lasts.

What does feel good is winning.

I have his fiancée.

I'm about to own Northaby House.

He'll be seeing my face in his nightmares for decades.

"Fuck it," he spits before I've taken a step. "What do I care if you want her? It was good pussy while it lasted. But then, so was Lucy. Easy come, easy go, if you know what I mean," he adds with a wink.

I see red—bloodred—and swing around to smash my fist into the middle of his face. Violins and viola screech to a halt, and waves of people part like the Red Sea. Mitchell lies in the middle, splayed out on the floor. Blood oozes from a nose that's probably broken, judging by the throb in my knuckles. My chest heaves as I stand over him. His eye is already swelling, and I want so badly to stamp my heel into his fucking face.

"Easy. Yes." Breath rushes down my nose, and I swipe my hair back from my head. "You set the bar so low, you make it a cakewalk." I'm surprised how calm my voice sounds as I kneel, ignoring his worried wince. "Let me give you a little advice," I say, examining my swollen knuckles. "Sometime in the future, when you're feeling lonely or nostalgic and pining for Eve, you might think about whipping out your pathetic cock to abuse yourself to some old memory." Grabbing his lapels, I jerk him up from the floor, bringing us face to face. "But just remember, while you're pretending, imagining, I'll be the one fucking her mouth." I push him away like the garbage he is, and he falls to his elbows. I stand and adjust my cuffs. "One other thing. If I ever see you near either Eve or Lucy again, I will fucking end you."

I stalk away, ignoring looks and judgment. My blood runs alternatively hot and cold as I think about my actions. Punching him was out of character, but I have no regrets and will face any possible consequences with a grin, because it felt good. It felt necessary. Like a release.

But now I need to find Eve.

Ah, Eve. The shit I just said.

My heart sinks. I'm no better than him. She deserves so much more.

I make my way toward the pavilion, scanning faces and the backs of heads before I see them, a trio huddled furtively on the other side of the terrace. My legs eat up the space between us, and the reason for their huddle becomes apparent: a bottle of whisky, no doubt swiped from the bar. The wealthier Fin gets, the more brazen his light-fingeredness seems to become. It doesn't matter that tonight is an open bar. It's the challenge that calls to him.

I pause for a moment, partly to calm this raging bull inside me, but also to see what this lot is up to.

"Her?" Matt squints into the gardens.

"Yes, you should go and speak to her," Eve says.

He tugs on his ear, then swings the bottle up to his lips. Wiping the back of his hand across his mouth, he says, "She's not my type."

"But she's gorgeous!" Taking the outstretched bottle, Eve takes a sip, then grimaces. "I don't know why anyone would drink whisky."

"Because what whisky will not cure, there is no cure for."

"I'm more concerned for what it might break." She gives in to a whole-body shiver. "You're sure this stuff hasn't ruined your eyesight? That girl is smoking hot."

"My eyesight is grand. I've just seen more meat on a spider's knuckle."

Eve's attention slices Fin's way, but he can't answer for laughing. "A spider's what?" she says, turning back.

"I mean, she's so skinny, one eye would do her. I'd probably break her," he adds reluctantly.

With a tiny but incredulous shake of her head, Eve passes the bottle to Fin. "It's official. Whisky made him blind."

I find myself smiling. I don't think my friends are much interested in Eve's matchmaking skills, but they are keeping her mind occupied, because Matt likes women, period.

"Well, whatever tickles your pickle is a personal thing," Fin says, pointing the bottle at our friend.

"You leave my pickle out of it." Matt smirks. "Oliver's already riled enough."

"He looked so pissed." Eve's expression turns pensive.

"Don't worry about it," Matt puts in. "That gobshite's face will look like he did the hundred-meter dash in a ninety-meter room right about now."

"No, that's not Oliver's style," Fin argues. "He'd say—"

"Rage is good, but revenge is better." It looks as though Eve is chewing the inside of her lip.

"Sounds like something he'd say," agrees Matt.

"Well, it seems I don't know myself," I begin, stepping into the trio's line of sight.

"Oliver!" Eve takes two quick steps, then pauses, her actions suddenly tentative. *Like her head and her heart have opposing opinions.* I wonder which wins as she throws her arms around my neck. "I've been so worried."

"That I might've killed him?"

"You wouldn't do that, I know."

"Do you?"

"Yeah, because I didn't bring peanut butter." She takes my face between her hands and adds, "Because you're too pretty to go to prison."

My laughter rings out as my friends make their goodbyes, but I barely lift my head.

"You're all right?" I ask, stepping away for the benefit of perspective without surrendering my hold on her.

"Yeah, I'm fine. He was just . . ." She rubs her fingers around her wrist. I lift her hand, and my stomach twists at the red marks I find there.

"That fucker." Every ounce of me wants to tear him limb from limb. He touched what isn't his—he touched what is dear to me.

"Oliver." Her hands cup my face, bringing me out of that haze. "It's okay. I'm okay. I'm just relieved that it's over."

"Over?"

"Seeing him. It won't matter if I see him again, because the worst is over. I should've faced him, gone for my stuff. I guess I didn't want to face the truth."

"Which is what?"

"I'm as responsible for that day as he is."

I open my mouth to protest when she cuts me off.

"I don't mean his infidelity. There's no excusing that. But I was fooling myself. I knew it, but I didn't want to face it."

I gather her into my arms, hugging her tight, filled with a sudden relief. "I understand." Finally. She really doesn't give a fuck about him. I hate that he knew her first, that she almost married him, but beneath all that resentment and jealousy, there was real fear. The human psyche is a strange thing, because only now do I realize I've been fighting these thoughts, this terror that she might walk away with him.

She suddenly rears back, slapping my chest. "But a safari park? Are you kidding me?"

"Eve." I graze my lips across her head. "Let's get out of here."

◆ ◆ ◆

We skirt around the palace gardens, taking pains to avoid the entitled, noisy throng—those drunken revelers swigging champagne from the bottle and staggering into hedges.

"It seems to have gotten a little wild," Eve says as high-pitched laughter cuts through the hedge.

"Yes," I agree, my heart kicking up a notch as though that were a suggestion.

"Do you know where we're going?"

"Home."

"Well, duh." She laughs, her fingers tightening briefly on mine. I'm almost surprised she's allowing me to hold her hand. "I meant, do you know where the car is?"

"Can't be far."

She falls quiet again, concentrating so her heels don't sink too far into the damp evening grass. Since the sun has set, the air has taken on a distinctly cooler feel. It's almost autumnal.

"So, tell me about this safari park," she says with a carelessness that must cost her.

"What do you want to know?"

"Oliver." My name sounds like disappointment. "I was so angry at you earlier, but I don't have it in me to fight with you right now."

I wheel around to face her so abruptly that she stumbles back a step. My heart hurts that she would, even for a split second, think that I might hurt her. But the truth is, I have. Perhaps not physically, but hurt is hurt.

"I'm sorry I didn't tell you. I don't want to fight with you."

"You're not. Not really." She gives a slow shake of her head. "I can't do this, you know. I can't in good conscience lie to that man about his animals."

"I haven't asked you to."

Her trill of unhappy-sounding laughter fills the night air.

"Not directly," I amend.

"You didn't even tell me who I was meeting—you wouldn't tell me the name of the house, and you certainly didn't mention the estate housed the inhabitants of the Serengeti!"

"Because you would've asked questions I wasn't ready to answer."

She rears back as though slapped, but I don't give her a chance to speak.

"I didn't mean it that way. I just honestly don't know what I'm going to do with that side of the place."

"So why buy it?" She looks at me as though I'm suddenly alien. "You can't expect me to believe it's purely to spite him?"

"It's also a sound business proposition," I answer defensively. Words twist in my throat, though I force them back, swallowing over guilt and anger. "But there was a time I would've burned the place to the ground if I could."

She looks away, horrified.

"Not with the animals in it, for God's sake."

Her expression falters. Is that pity I'm seeing? "You really hate him that much?"

"Yes, I hate him." But perhaps not as much as I admire Eve. *But that can't be true, can it?* "I hate him even more after tonight." I take a step toward her, cupping my hand to her silky cheek. "I'm sorry I wasn't there, so sorry I—" She silences me, her forefinger pressed to my lips.

"Like I said, I needed to see him. I needed confirmation that I don't truly know who he is."

"I should've been with you."

"Well, you weren't." She pulls away, begins to walk again. But then she turns her head over her shoulder, the tiniest of smiles playing on her face. "And then you were there." I hang onto that smile, store it inside me as we walk in silence for a while. "The animals," she begins again. "I know I can't defend every cause, but I can't help you if you've no concern for them."

"Do you really see me that way?"

"Honestly, I don't know what you're thinking from one minute to the next." She folds her arms across her chest. Perhaps a defense? But the night is also cool. And that *is* a very thin dress.

"Right now, I'm thinking you look a little chilled," I say as I slip off my jacket and drape it across her shoulders. "I'm also thinking you misunderstand me. Even without the weight of the law, I would never condone animal cruelty or mistreatment. I can't honestly say what will happen to the park, but whatever the outcome, you have my word that their fate will be a good one."

"I'm glad. I didn't lie to Mandy, just so you know. I mostly skirted around the truth."

But he would've made his own assumptions, and that was the whole point.

We fall quiet again, making me very conscious of her breath and the phantom swish of her dress.

306

"You looked so fierce." At her sudden whisper, I glance down. "How did it feel, playing the hero?"

"Instead of the villain?"

"You aren't all bad, Oliver." Her words sound like consolation.

"Or even half-bad?"

"Let's not get ahead of ourselves," she replies, fighting a twitch to her lips.

Is it my mood or hers that I find so bewildering?

"Oliver Deubel." She gives a slow shake of her head. "My hero."

"You're not meant to be flattered." My words are hoarse, and my feet slow to a stop all by themselves. "Standing up for you should be nonnegotiable. A bare minimum."

"I guess I wouldn't know."

"Because you don't need anyone to look after you, do you?" I shouldn't be sliding my hands through her hair. I should be frightening her off, because this feeling in my chest doesn't belong to me. This need. This . . . fear. What could've been.

"You're the one who intervened."

A noise stems from my throat. Not quite a scoff.

"The proof is in the pudding." I suppose she thinks I'm being noble as she twists my hand, exposing my swollen knuckles. "But let me ask you this," she adds soberly. "Did you do it for me or for Lucy?"

I'm not so noble, and her jealousy is unnecessary. I should tell her what happened, but I can't bring myself to utter the truth. What I owe Lucy comes before my own happiness. What I owe Eve . . .

"I did it because he deserved it."

Not enough. Her gaze drops. "Well, that's not flattery, but I'm not sure it's the truth either." She turns and makes to pass me. My fingers slide around her upper arm, stopping her in her tracks.

"I'm no one's idea of a hero. If you knew the things I said to him, things no man should ever utter about any woman, let alone a woman he respects." *A woman he longs to kiss.* "A woman he's supposed to protect."

"I don't need your protection."

"Perhaps it's protection from yourself you need."

"Why? What could you possibly have said?"

She shivers as I lean closer and bring my lips to within an inch of her ear. I can't bring myself to tell her about Lucy, but I can frighten her off. For her own sake. For mine. *Because I want her too much.*

"I told him he should imagine you sucking my cock." Her shoulders lift with her tiny inhale, not quite a gasp. "Because it's the nearest he'll ever get to having you again."

"Nice." She twists from my hold. "Thank you for putting those words out there." Her eyes flash, her gaze slicing over her shoulder. "For putting that image in his head."

"I've warned you time and again who I am."

"Yeah, I get it. I'm the idiot." Her eyes flash with defiance, and she begins to move. I grab her elbow and step into her, my shoulders blocking the moonlight from her face as she lifts her chin with the hauteur of a queen.

"Eve, you see the good *and* the bad in me, and you've yet to look away." Her lashes flutter as I press my thumb to her pulse, knowing full well I might never get this chance again.

"This is a very bad idea." She whispers her only protest as I angle my head, ghosting my lips over hers. I'm not to be trusted, that much is true, but I don't think she can trust herself either. "But then, bad ideas seem to be our specialty."

"Eve Fairfax. The only woman I know who can slice me apart with one look, only to seduce me with the next."

She gives a soft gasp as I suck over her pulse, her words less steady than she'd like, I'm sure. "Which do you deserve right now?"

"Only you can decide." I'll never deserve her, but fuck it, I would die trying.

Her lips are as clever as her comebacks when I press my mouth to hers. I kiss her deeper, my hands slipping under my jacket, making it slide from her shoulder in my quest to touch.

"Oliver, not here," she rasps, catching the slide of fabric. "Getting arrested won't help my visa."

She's right, but I'm not thinking straight. I just want her. No, I need her.

"I can't wait."

"And I can't be arrested."

My hand molds her hip, sliding higher, her breast a delightful weight against my palm. *No bra.* I swallow her groan as her nipple pebbles under my thumb. "Then it's a pity your body is such a raging flirt."

Her answer is the kind of noise that echoes at the base of my cock. Why must she be so small? Sweet like a peach, and so utterly beautiful. As though hearing my thoughts, her nails suddenly dig into the flesh of my arse, closing any space between us.

A thought drops into my head, and I take her hand, beginning to move us in the opposite direction. "Come on." Once, a long time ago, I remember there being a building nearby. An old folly.

"Where are we going?" Her exhilaration is as clear as the flush in her checks.

"It's a surprise."

"Not as much as you'd like to think," she says with a soft snicker.

I was right, anticipation tightening my skin as I spot the small structure though the trees. It's a little off the beaten track and has perhaps been overlooked in security terms. I send out a silent prayer anyway.

"Ladies first." I almost swing her ahead, only to wrench her back against me. A deep groan rises through my chest. I'm as hard and as hot as a poker, and her dress and underwear offer little in the way of protection. "Get your delectable arse in there."

Eve swings around, her gaze dark but bright as she steps backward into the darkness, and I follow her.

The folly smells of damp grass and misuse, the ground underfoot chalky as I step closer. I wrap my arms around her back, dipping my knees to bring me against that hot, tight piece of heaven between her legs. The taste of her mouth and the feel of her in my arms are like stepping into a dream to find it real.

"Let me . . ." I cradle my arm between her bare back and the cold, damp wall, my hand slipping between us. My fingers trailing the soft pout of her inner thigh, her breath a heated burst against my neck. "I pressed my teeth here, remember? God, I can still hear your whimper." The noise she makes seems involuntary, swallowed back, lips closed around it.

She won't close for me.

"And here." I press my palm to her pussy, the heat of her enough to make a man lose brain cells. "Ah, Eve. I still dream of your taste."

Her next sound is more guttural as her hands slide into my hair, pulling my head closer. I groan as she licks the salt from my neck, curse as she sucks.

"Touch me," she demands. "Please."

I slip my fingers under the gauzy excuse for underwear, a silky string thong. Twisting the fabric between my fingers, I give it a sharp tug. She gasps as the fabric gives, both sounds witness to our need.

"Two for two. You're going to owe me."

I don't answer. Offer her no preliminaries, her own body showing no resistance as I press two fingers deep inside her. Her fingernails dig into my biceps, the lewd sounds of her pleasure and her sharp, needy breaths an aural aphrodisiac.

"Oh, darling, listen to how much you need this. To the mess you're making of my fingers."

"Stop," she pants, beginning to ride my hand.

"Such a lovely girl. How sweetly you take my fingers."

"Stop. Talking." She buries her face in my neck. Her teeth scrape. Bite. I suffer the sensation through to my aching cock. "Yes. *Yes!* Less talk."

Her breathy demand curls around me. Her resistance, her fuckable mouth, dialing my pleasure to a ten.

"So demanding," I rasp, curling my fingers inside her. "But you know I don't take orders." Though I do love to hear her try, all the same.

"How about directions?" Her hand on my shoulder, she pushes. With my fingers still inside her, I shuffle back when she pushes again. Lust addled as I am, it takes me a moment to realize she's moving with me, turning us until our positions are reversed. The length of my back pressed against the wall, my legs slightly splayed. Grabbing my face, she presses her mouth to mine, her words, like her kiss, hot and sweet. "Oh, yes. You're a good boy. I see you can."

My laughter echoes through the dark space. Maybe I do like Eve's directions after all.

"Wait." Her eyes glitter as they meet mine, as she makes to slide my hand from between her legs.

"No, let me—"

She shakes her head. "Don't disappoint me, baby. It's my turn now."

As she slides down my body, every inch of my torso tingles in anticipation. Her movements are quick and rough as she pulls my shirt from my pants.

"Eve." I'm not sure if her name is a warning or a plea for more as she rakes her nails lightly down my chest, but the look in her eyes as she slides my shirt higher is nothing but triumphant. I groan as her tongue circles my nipple, convulse as she covers it with her teeth.

"Hmm." Lashes lowered, she hums, then licks her way down my chest. "I like it when you moan for me."

"Eve." A warning this time as I slide my hand into her hair.

"You want me to stop?" My answer is another garbled curse as her teeth scrape the side of my ribs. "What was that?" As her finger trails over my fly, my cock strains for attention.

"No." My answer sounds all ache and gravel. "Please don't."

My God, her expression as she presses her smile to my abs. Her hands make quick work of my belt, her touch warm and sure as she lifts my cock free from the confines of my pants. The position is awkward, my thighs straining from this half squat, but I wouldn't move for the world as her delicate fingers wrap my girth. Pale skin to ruddy, cool to red hot.

"Oh, darling boy, you're leaking." She pouts as she squeezes my aching cock, the bead at my crown pearly in the moonlight. I swallow back a curse at the mixture of emotions I suffer through. Elation, need, a sinfully wicked discomfort.

Her lashes are the sweep of an angel's wing, her lips full and luscious as she presses them to my aching crown. The wet heat of her mouth as she swallows me down feels like heaven.

She swirls her tongue as she sucks me with a hum of pleasure.

"Fuck. Oh, fuck!" My body jerks, my thighs trembling.

"Pretty." Her gaze makes a slow sweep up my body. "I love the way you're shaking for me."

Christ, I adore this look on her.

"Less talk, more cock sucking." I apply the slightest pressure to her head, using some sense of her own words.

"So bossy," she murmurs before she takes me in her mouth again.

"Sweetheart." I swallow over the desire to take control, to hold her there, as I loosen my hands from the silky strands. Her tongue, her lips. This feels like sheer bliss. "God, yes. Like that."

Her mouth comes off the head with a wet *pop*, her eyes sparkling in delight, in the knowledge of her power over me. Over the moment. "Now who's giving orders?" she purrs, dragging her thumb across my glistening head.

"How about pleas?" Something inside me snaps as I take her beneath the arms and bring her mouth to mine. "I'd beg to be inside you."

"I'd like to hear that." Her smile pressed against mine, our mouths turn hot and messy, all gasping, broken breaths, kisses and half-formed words. My hands slide over her shoulder, thumbs slipping under the strap of her dress. We both groan as her breast is bared, her nipple hard against my palm. Down my hand travels, over the swell of her arse, two fingers spearing inside her.

She garbles a noise, her walls clenching.

"Let me taste you." My fingers are wet as I take her wrist, moving her hand from my cock as I press up from the wall. I stagger like a drunken man in the shadows, knowing if anyone passes by, we'll be spotted by virtue of my white shirt. But I can't think of that now as I spin her around, my words a supplicant's prayer in her ear. "Eve, let me, please."

Her body answers, her fingers splaying against the wall, her bottom thrusting out. My hand falls to her hip, my other gathering her dress to reveal legs, thighs, the delicious roundness of her arse.

She turns her head over her shoulder, and moonlight hits her just right, making an old master of her. Eve. *Temptation in the Shadows*.

"What are you waiting for?"

"I'm not waiting. I'm appreciating." I press my lips to her shoulder, inhaling the scent and warmth of her. "Appreciating perfection." I kiss my way down her spine, whispering my want of her, then press my face between her legs. She cries out, the sound raw and intoxicating as I lap, delicately at first. Then less so, until her thighs begin to tremble and her gasps are all vowel sounds.

Ah—Ah—Ah.

I feel like a king as her orgasm hits. Her legs begin to buckle, and I hold her there, growling into her very center.

"Oh, God. Oh, God." Eve gasps, swallowing down air.

I pull myself to my feet, her arousal sticky and sweet between my lips. As I press my cock to her, we both gasp at the contact. Her body undulates, her heat brushing my throbbing crown. *Heavenly. Torturous.* Our breaths echoing in the dark space.

"Oh, fuck. Eve. Please, let me . . ."

"Oliver?"

I swallow, force myself to still, my abs tightening, my nerves taut with the need to rut and fuck. If she doesn't want this . . .

"What you said earlier, about him watching?"

"Yes." I swallow again, my muscles seizing. *Waiting. Wanting. Aching.*

"Watching me suck your cock." Her lashes flutter, and she whimpers as I scrape my teeth across her jaw. "Am I wrong to want that?"

Relief feels so sweet. I groan with a quiet agony as her body surges, my bare cock slipping along the heavenly ribbon of her flesh.

"No, darling." I tighten my grasp on both her dress and myself. "No worse than wanting to see him choke on peanut butter."

Her laughter is soft, and it's strange how he doesn't matter to either of us anymore. With a tiny groan, I push forward. *Her heat. Her sigh.*

"I hope the image haunts him for the rest of his life."

"Fuck, darling, yes." *She's so slippery.*

"Yes." Her fingers splay wider, her sigh an invitation. "Please."

"Oh, Eve, I'm going to ruin you."

"I want that."

We'll call it payback, *because you have plucked me apart at the seams.*

There are no words to describe the sensation of her body accepting mine. Raw. Bare. My whole being aching and desperate, I pull back. My gaze falls to my cock, glistening and wet. *Fuck.* Screwing my eyes tight, I drive my way inside her. She cries out as our bodies meet, whimpers as I wrap my arms around her. I hold her there, my heart beating against her back as the pulse of her body makes me unspool.

"Oh, darling. I want my mouth on you, sucking at your sweetness if I could be two places—everywhere at once." Such is my desperation for her.

"Your mouth," she whispers with a slow undulation. "It's so filthy."

"You love it." I pull back, then again take her to my hilt, her moan ragged and breathless. "Say it. Tell me you love my filthy mouth," I demand, punctuating my words with my thrusts.

"I l—love . . ."

My heart expands, my body taking over.

"Your mouth on me."

"*Fuck.*" I torture us both with shallow jabs and deep punches of my hips until we're both panting and desperate. "Tell me you'll stay," I demand, my feelings too twisted to express any other way. "Eve, I need you." *I don't deserve you, but I can't let you go.* I feel desperate, unhinged. Unable to get close enough, deep enough, feel enough of her. *Of this.*

She cries out, grinding against me as I whisper how good she feels, how close I am. I move my fingers to her clit as she peaks, her body beginning to milk me for all I'm worth. As it turns out, I'm not worth a great deal more as I pull out just in time, white heat spurting into my hand.

"Oh, God." Eve slumps forward, her palms keeping her face from the stone. "I don't think I can feel my legs."

Swiping up my abandoned jacket, I pull out my pocket square and clean up as best I can. "Come here," I whisper, pulling her away from the wall. "It's probably damp."

"You're worried about my health?" She buries her nose into my chest, her skin dappled with gooseflesh now.

I worry more about her, about this, than I'm prepared to admit. I press my lips into her hair in lieu of an answer, draping my jacket over her shoulders again.

"Thank you," she murmurs, pulling the sides closer. She gives an embarrassed giggle when I pull a handkerchief out from the pocket and swipe it under the hem of her dress, pressing it between her legs. "The full service, huh?"

"You deserve nothing less." After what we've just done, should this feel so intimate?

"So you're a two-handkerchief guy, like a Boy Scout."

"One for show. One for blow."

"Oh, my gosh." She ducks her head with a soft laugh. "That is not a Boy Scout motto."

"Depends on the boy. We're not all created equal, you know."

"That is true." Pressing her head into my shoulder, she adds, "Some boys are so bad."

"Some boys are trying to be better."

"Oliver?" Her head lifts, her expression softening as her eyes find mine. "I'm not sure what you're trying to say."

"Eve, just be with me," I whisper, lifting her hand to my cheek. My heart pounds so hard, I wonder if she can hear it. "Be with me, not because I said so, but because you want me." I turn my face and press a kiss to her palm. "I'm not asking you to promise me anything. Just be with me because you want to be. Because I want to be with you."

Chapter 34

A Little Bird Told Us . . .

Gather round, my flock, and let me tell you a tale that, once upon a time, would've landed a man in the stocks. I suppose some people might get off on that, but not on Crown property, surely!

gasps

clutches pearls and yells

"Orf with his head!"

And it sounds like that *almost* happened when a Pulse Tok cheating groom met doggy doctor Evie's new man. Or so rumor has it, as no party will confirm. Though Mitchell Atherton was seen to be sporting a magnificent black eye soon after.

Also lacking confirmation? The (alleged) shenanigans later that evening when our London lovers (looking *quite* disheveled) were spotted being escorted to their car by an armed policeman.

Was that a gun in his pocket?

Not the policeman. His was in his hand. But a Little Bird does ponder, What *could* that have been about?

Surely not a little alfresco naughty . . .

554 comments

Sassie_Sarah: Good! That dick had it coming to him.

TheHallouminati: I ordinarily don't condone violence, but I reckon I could punch him all day without my arms getting tired once.

TrixieBits: Women everywhere are cheering right now!

RageAgainstTheWashingMachine: Yas! Payback! You go get some, girl!

SashayYourWay: I'd do that man anywhere. Call me anytime, Olly, babe!

FloozyLoosie: Public sex. If you're getting caught, you're not doing it right.

MadShagger: Unless you're into that. #exhibitionistrus

FloozyLousie: Got caught giving a blowy on the Tube to Cockfosters once.

HoppyGoLucky: Username checks out.

Hells.Bells: Love a bit of al fresco nookie, myself.

Slayz4Dayz: One time me n my man got frisky at St Mary Mags cemetery behind Sir Richard Burton's mausoleum.

TrixieBits: OMG! Is he dead? RIP cheap Virgin Holidays.

Twerksneark: That's Sir Richard Brandson. Burton is the Karma Sutra dude.

Sumin.up.rosie: I've done it in the bushes in Regent's Park

Pennies4Molly: Back of Ikea for me.

Twerksneark: The Royal Courts of Justice on his desk. He even let me wear his wig 😉

PixiChick: In a phone box

Charlie09: Up the bum!

This article is no longer accepting comments.

Chapter 35
OLIVER

We made no promises, and we swore no vows, throwing ourselves headlong into the enjoyment of each other over the coming weeks. In some ways it was inevitable. We're like two magnets with poles that attract and repel, depending on the way they're held. I'd like to have told her I'd hold her always, but I know I'm not worthy of the honor. She deserves better, but for now, she'll make do with me.

I'll admit that I half expected Mitchell to kick up a legal stink following our altercation, but perhaps he realizes the longer he chases trouble, the more trouble will hound him. Or he could just be regrouping. I don't really care. He's not the sole focus of my attention anymore.

That's not to say I've forgiven, forgotten, or even changed my plans. I suppose I'm just much happier. It's true that Eve is unlikely to move far from my side as I negotiate Northaby's purchase and beyond. But she'll be there because she wants to be, not just because she doesn't trust me with the animals' welfare. She's taken an interest in the outcome, of course. It's just who she is. She will always champion those who have no voice.

Meanwhile, she continues to frustrate and beguile me in equal measure. But I'm not alone in my suffering, as I see she's had a similar effect on Mandy. I find my mouth lifting reluctantly as I recall Eve's malicious glee the morning of our very first visit. As I emerged from the walk-in wearing a tweed jacket, she laughed and said I looked like I was cosplaying a farmer. She wasn't too impressed when I bought her a matching outfit for our next visit. *But she wore it.*

While I've more or less danced around the future of the safari park with Mandy, the old duffer seems certain that Eve will be the making of the place.

"It's not on you," I've reassured her. "I've promised him nothing, and neither have you. It's not your fault he plays on deaf ears."

She sees it. She knows it. Yet still she spends her evenings on her laptop (curled on the sofa or next to me in bed) investigating rehoming possibilities at other zoos and wildlife parks. It's not an uncommon practice, thanks to facilities expanding to include new species or provide genetic diversity to existing ones. I think she finds comfort in that.

"They're just preliminary investigations," she'll insist. "Nothing concrete. I know it really has nothing to do with me."

But I see it troubles her. So I'm quietly conducting my own analysis for my eventual ownership.

My phone begins to ring, pulling me from my contemplation.

"It's yours," a gravelly tone barks down the line.

"I beg your pardon?"

"Dammit, Deubel. You know what I'm talking about."

"Mandy, what a pleasure." Satisfaction expands beneath my ribs as I process his unhappy declaration.

"Yes, yes." His exhale whistles down the line. "Let's just get to it. It's time, I'm afraid. I can no longer hang on to Northaby. So, assuming you still want the old place, it's yours for the asking price."

"That's such wonderful news." My lips tip, and I find Atherton to be the last person on my mind. "Eve will be delighted." *At least, I hope she will be. Eventually.*

"I'm disappointed you haven't fully committed to the safari park, but I'm going to trust your young lady in the application of her thumbscrews. I am assured you will be cognizant of their welfare, in the meantime."

"Of course, my lord. May I ask why the change of heart?"

He huffs, then sighs. "The roof is about to fall in on the Norfolk house. Do you know how much a new roof costs these days, Deubel?"

"I have a fair idea."

"It's bloody annoying that I can't just off-load the place." But his Norfolk estate is attached to his title. It can legally only be passed down to the next in line.

"I'm sure you understand safeguards will be set as a condition of the sale."

As much as he can control them. What happens following the sale will be none of his business. Not that I intend to release tigers on the inhabitants of Surrey.

"Of course." But I find my own pleasure suddenly short lived, a cold dread settling in my stomach. I'd foreseen Eve remaining by my side, at least for the animals' welfare, but when she finds I have Northaby, will she insist on moving out? Her visa application is moving along. Ariana tells me she expects it to be complete within a couple of weeks.

"I have my back against the wall." Mandy Mortimer's voice pulls me back from my dread. "There's nothing else for me but hope."

But hope is not something I trade in.

The call ends, and I slump back in my chair. This is what I wanted—my ultimate goal. Why don't I feel like I've won?

"I must be fucking crazy," I mutter, dropping my head into my hands.

"Crazy in love?"

I sit up to find Fin leaning against the doorframe. "I'm certain that door was closed."

"I heard you talking to yourself. Thought I should come in and check."

I stare at him without answering. Maybe if I do it long enough, he'll get the hint and piss off.

"I was speaking to Lord Bellsand," I say when it becomes apparent I'm not that lucky.

Fin smiles like he doesn't believe me, and, crossing the room, he drops into a chair on the far side of my desk.

"I thought only babies smile from wind."

"Cute. You have babies on your mind."

"What?"

"I can't say I've ever imagined any of us as dads. I like playing daddy in the bedroom, but that's kinda my limit."

"You astound me," I say. "And that's not a compliment."

"Don't try to make out like I'm the only deviant here."

"As usual, I have no idea what you're talking about."

"No?" He plucks his phone from his pocket. Bringing his fist to mouth, he theatrically clears his throat.

"*A Little Bird Told Us . . .*" He looks up, not bothering to hide a shit-eating grin.

"Fucking hell," I groan. "What now?" I may have created a monster in helping that woman get her name on the column.

"Already cursing." Fin tuts playfully.

"Just get on with it. The quicker you read it, the quicker you leave."

He clears his throat again, making me want to punch it. *"Our London lovers were recently spotted coming out of a property in Chelsea looking a little worse for wear—"*

I sit up straight. "Drunk? When? That is absolute rubbish and borderline libelous."

"—coming out of the exclusive club, Century."

"Oh. That." Eve *was* a little tipsy. Delightfully so. "And this is what constitutes news these days?" I mutter, pulling my laptop closer, feeling suddenly a hundred years old. "They ought to be careful with their language usage."

"Oh, they were. Listen to this. *The besotted businessman and his American love were described as clinging to each other like honeymooners, their chemistry electric and their hands everywhere, before they were whisked away in a chauffeur-driven car. This Little Bird is still clutching her pearls, because she makes that, allegedly, alfresco naughty twice in two weeks!"*

So we'd gotten a little handsy. But it was dark; there was no one around. *Or so I thought.* The strap of her top had slipped from her shoulder and . . . "Is there an accompanying photograph?"

"No."

"Good." Una Smith must be bloody unhinged. This was not the deal we struck. At least she's naming no names. *Not that she needs to.*

"Sounds like the real deal," he teases.

"Sounds like a load of old rubbish. Speaking of deals, Northaby is done."

"You got it? Well, that's great."

"Your enthusiasm underwhelms me, Phineas."

He shrugs. "That place has been your hard-on."

"The prospect of making money doesn't excite you?"

"Money doesn't make a person happy. Love does."

I snort. Then frown. "How many glasses of wine did you have with lunch?"

"Oliver." He draws out my name. "You've gotta admit the way you've been since Eve walked onto the scene is like night and day to how you were last year."

"Last year was . . ." A fucking mess. Atherton. Lucy. So much pain in those two names. I'm glad to finally feel as though I'm putting one of them behind me. *Not that I'll ever get over* . . . "Well, trying," I say, settling on the word and banishing the rest from my thoughts.

"Oh, you weren't irritated. You were a fucking beast. But I get it—you were under a lot of stress. But now? Now you're a teddy bear."

"Don't be asinine." Speaking of lunch, I think mine has given me a case of indigestion. I press my palm to my sternum at the sudden discomfort.

"Eve's had a real calming influence on you."

"Now you're just being ridiculous. Eve makes me feel anything but calm—the woman is like a whirlwind."

"I didn't say she was calm. I said she made *you* calm. Anyway, what are you gonna do with the place?"

"Northaby?" I should be relieved in the change of conversational direction, but this ache . . . "What I always said I would."

"I think turning the place into a hotel is an amazing idea. It'll be like a whole holiday venue. Luxury for the parents—pool, spa, and fancy restaurants—and then animal entertainment for the kids."

"Yes, come and feed your offspring to the lions. Sounds like a lawsuit in waiting."

"Not if it's done right. You'll keep part of the place private though, right?"

"What for?"

"For you. Eve. And maybe later, a few little Olivers and Eves."
He mimes the pitter-patter of little feet with his fingers. *Arse.*
"Imagine living in that place."

And I do—just for a moment. A moment of bliss. Bliss that's
short lived.

I used her for my own means. For revenge. I'm no better than
Atherton, though it took me a while to admit that to myself. Aren't
I still using her now? Stringing her along, knowing I'm incapable
of love? *Unworthy of* her *love?*

"You okay?"

"No. I don't feel too well." When this is all over, I probably
won't ever want to look at Northaby again.

"What is it?"

"I think I'm coming down with something." I suck in a deep
breath. "My chest hurts." I can't be having a heart attack at my
age. *Can I?*

"You were okay a minute ago."

"And now I'm not," I snap. I don't remember the last time I felt
unwell. I have the constitution of an ox—I'm never ill.

"Your chest, huh?"

"Yes." I rub my sternum with my knuckles. "What *is* that sensation? I feel like something has burrowed into it."

"Into your heart?" The corner of his mouth kicks up. "It's
not—gasp! Horror!—love?"

"The heart is not some mythical vessel—it's a muscle! What are
you laughing about? I might be having a heart attack! *Oof. Fuck.*"
And now, I suddenly feel short of breath.

"Haven't you ever heard the song 'Love Hurts'?"

"Yes, and I've also heard the song 'I Do Like to Be Beside the
Seaside,' but I'm not sure what that's got to do with anything."

"You should just admit it. Works for me. Eve is cool. She keeps
you on your toes, and you need that."

327

"Admit what? That we're enjoying ourselves? That one minute, we're at each other's throats like cat and dog, and the next—"

"You're the same species?"

"We are completely unsuited. She's ethical, good, and kind. She's a vet, for fuck's sake! She fixes things, while I tear them apart."

"For money."

"Which she has no interest in. She deserves better than me."

"Huh." He brings his hand to his chin, stroking it pensively. "Don't you think that's a question for Eve?"

"What is that?" I circle a finger, indicating his face. "Are you playing at therapist? Because you can fuck right off! I don't even want a safari park."

"So why have you been chasing it?"

I usually have an immediate answer, but right now, it's like that answer no longer makes sense.

"People have done worse for love."

I'm not sure I like what he's implying, even if it does strike a chord.

"You know, Van Gogh chopped off his ear."

"Then gave it to a prostitute," I enunciate, leaving him under no illusion about what I think of his advice.

"Maybe she showed him a real good time." His eyebrows waggle.

Meanwhile, mine appear to be perspiring. I slick my hands over my face. "He was probably clinically depressed. Or suffering a mental break."

"People have murdered for love, faked their deaths, tattooed lovers' names on their skin. And you know why?"

"Because they're idiots."

"Because love is worth that risk. It makes a person feel euphoric, like they could take on the world. I hear it's like being off your face on coke."

"Well, that settles it." I throw up my hands. "I'm definitely having a heart attack because I feel anything but euphoric."

Fin frowns. "I'm not finished. When we fall in love—"

"People don't fall in love," I grate out. "Oops! Deary me, I nearly tripped and fell face fucking first into a love puddle?"

"Don't tell me you don't do that," he says with a small grin.

"What?" I pull at my cuffs. Yank off my cuff links. Tug my shirtsleeves up my arms. I feel like I'm frying!

"Eat pussy. Only assholes don't reciprocate."

"Why do I even bother?" I mutter, pulling at my tie next.

"I read a study a while back," he continues, completely ignoring my distress. "It said our prefrontal cortex, our brain's control center, drops into low gear when we're in love, and the amygdala, our brain's threat-response system, shuts down."

"So we fall in love because we turn into driveling idiots? I'm not sure how that helps."

"Maybe that's *how* you fall. All those warning systems turn off. You behave differently. Unlike yourself."

"I'm not sure that was a scholarly peer-reviewed article. Sounds more like a Pulse Tok."

"You think it's bull?"

"What I'm questioning is if you can read at all."

"Are your palms sweaty?"

I look down and fold my fingers inward. "A little. Could Andrew have turned off the air-conditioning?"

"Does your heart feel like it's beating fast? Are you lightheaded?"

Yes and yes. "Could it be a virus?"

"It's more like your fight-or-flight responses. You know why. You're panicking because you're in l-o-v-e," he says, spelling out the word gleefully. *Bastard.*

"No," I bark, using the tone reserved for Bo. "Don't be an idiot." Not that it works on him either.

"You've got all the classic symptoms. And I'm not just talking about how you're feeling."

"I have no idea what you're talking about."

"The ring from Garrard."

"It's a fucking monstrosity." A manipulation. No need to mention how, for a split second, I saw an alternate life spilling out before me.

"The dog you've got living with you. Eve's dog. I bet you've never had a pet, never wanted one. Not even a goldfish growing up."

"So?" I frown.

"Tell me that's not bending for love."

More like bending for Eve's manipulation.

"Punching Atherton out. Worrying about Eve. The donation to that dog sanctuary. Ha! You're not as sneaky as you think!"

"Not sneaky at all, considering it went through accounts. It was a tax write-off."

"You're sure it wasn't for love? To impress your love."

"Idiot. I am clearly coming down with something. I need a doctor, not this pseudotherapist shit!"

"What you have, there's no remedy for. Fight it, or give in—makes no difference. The bottom line is, there's no escaping love."

Inhaling a deep breath, I force myself to sit with his words, to stop denying them but rather feel what they do to me.

Fight or capitulate.

"Just be with me." It's what I asked her that night in the folly, my heart beating so hard that it hurt. A lot like now. *"Be with me because you want me."*

I couldn't look up at her, couldn't take a denial. Instead, I turned my face and pressed my lips to her palm.

"I'm not asking you to promise me anything."

"Be with me because you want to be."

My heart spoke the words that my head was too fearful to give. *Because I love you.*

I sit straight in my seat. "Well, fuck!"

Chapter 36
EVIE

As the summer days begin to shorten and the evenings cool, my connection to Oliver—our tentative relationship—takes a turn into ridiculously cute. We walk Bo together in the evenings, often stopping for an ice cream as we stroll through one of London's royal parks. On weekends we drink coffee by the river, and after dark, you can find us drinking cocktails at exclusive rooftop bars.

We kiss on street corners, canoodle under lampposts, and sneak smooches wherever we can, not caring who might be watching. It's like my life has become someone else's Instagram feed with a filter that might well be called *new beginnings*. It's not a highly curated feed—there are no fakes. I'm not a woman standing in front of a man asking him to take a dozen shots just to get one perfect one. Each moment has its own kind of perfection, even the ones where steam of frustration seems to shoot from Oliver's head. Moment after moment, everything between us just seems so natural.

Not to be confused with naturism.

My mind bends to that night at Kensington Palace. The night we gave in to our attraction and ultimately agreed to be together without fear of expectations. Oliver, my inadvertent hero, was so sweet, even if the sequence of events wasn't exactly perfect.

Oliver's sweet kisses and words. His tender touches with his handkerchief.

Then one of London's finest tactfully clearing his throat.

My panic as Oliver unhurriedly righted my dress.

My hand in his as he shielded me from the officer's torchlight . . . nimbly stuffing my ruined panties into his pocket.

The frightening size of the police officer's tactical weapon. (Not a dirty joke.)

And the imagined headline in my head: VET CHARGED WITH PUBLIC INDECENCY FOR HAVING SEX IN THE KING'S GARDEN—SHE'S TO BE DEPORTED!

That would be so much worse than a lousy Pulse Tok video.

But then to my absolute relief (thanks to Oliver's charm), the police officer directing us "lost souls" to our car.

I like Oliver. I like him a lot. I tried not to, and I didn't trust him. But we're working through that now. On those long walks, we've had a lot of time to talk, because I won't make the same mistake as before. I refuse to get ahead of myself, no matter how my heart skips when he's near.

No more power games.

No more telling me after the fact.

No more making decisions for me, even if he thinks it's the right one!

I will be present this time. I won't be the slow-boiling frog, losing herself in the watery soup.

Beyond that, things are good. Uncomplicated. We're just enjoying each other, without plans for the future. Or maybe I'm fooling myself because I do think about Lucy more than I ought to. I can't seem to bring myself to ask what happened. Maybe I'm not as cool as I think. But then, I did almost marry a man who'd been screwing half of London. "One bitten, twice shy" is an understandable position, I think.

But sometimes I catch Oliver looking at me like he's tracing the shape of my face, committing it to memory as though I might disappear. And when we make love, he trembles with such intensity, it seems almost like fear.

I could be imagining things. Maybe it's my own feelings I should be examining.

"There you are." Over the back of the couch, Oliver's face appears in my line of vision. I don't hear what he says; rather, I read the shape of the words on his lips as I pull my Beats from my ears.

I make to sit up when he presses me back with a kiss. "Stay where you are. I'll come and join you." Rounding the couch, he slides off his jacket and drops it to the chair, then his fingers move to his tie.

"Slowly," I purr, dropping the headphones and my phone to the floor. "Give a girl a moment to watch the devil strip from his workday skin."

His tie slides from his collar with a *slick*, and Oliver continues his saucy striptease. He halts when he gets to his belt. "Want to help?"

"Oh. I see we're having dinner in."

He laughs, low and dirty. "We're meeting Mandy at eight o'clock, but a snack between meals never harmed anyone."

"I could go for a little something," I purr.

His lips twist at my words.

"Okay, not so little, then."

"Wait. Where's the fluffy terrorist?" he asks, as his fingers move to his belt.

"In my bed, I expect." It's where he sleeps. Mostly. Somehow each night, he winds up in bed with me and Oliver. Which Oliver loves . . . not a whole lot. *But he tolerates.*

"Don't move," he mutters, heading for my room. A moment later, the door closes, and then he's back, climbing over me, his knees bracketing my thighs, such wickedness sparkling in his eyes.

"Now, where were we?" His tie is suddenly dangling from his fingers as he lifts my wrists over my head.

"Where? I think the devil was about to take me to heaven."

◆ ◆ ◆

"That is *not* how you get your dick sucked."

I almost choke on my latte, and I'm pretty sure some of it comes out of my nose. "Yara!"

"Oops. Sorry. Did I say that out loud?" Her gaze slices left, then right, then she gives a shrug, satisfied she hasn't offended anyone's sensibilities. Mine apparently don't count. "Take a look at it," she adds, flipping her phone around to face me.

"At what—ew, Yara! Put that thing away."

We're catching up over coffee in a fashionable Italian coffee shop after work, though it's arguably almost Negroni time. Unless you're a fluffy labradoodle, when all day is puppuccino time.

"I bet he's heard that before." Yara gives a dirty laugh. "He says I can have it all night long."

"Oh my God." I press my hand over her phone until the screen is facing the table. "Do you want the poor woman behind me to have a heart attack?"

Yara eyes the blue-haired octogenarian over my shoulder, taking in her twinset and leather pants.

"She looks like she can handle it. Not his dick, obviously. That's a UTI in the making." She glances at the screen again. "But I think you're right. She can probably see it from over there." She sets down her phone, folding her arms against the table. "All night long," she says almost wistfully. "A few years ago, I wouldn't leave a rave until

335

six in the morning. These days, the only thing I want to *do* all night is sleep. The prospect really excites me."

Unable to resist the lure for long, she picks up her phone and taps the screen back to life. "That thing must be nearly a foot long. I mean, what does he expect me to do with the other six inches? It's not a Subway sandwich you can halve and wrap up for later."

I drop my head between my hands. "Online dating is a cesspit."

"It's all right for you, sitting in your ivory shagging tower."

"My what?" My head jerks up.

"Not that I'm not jealous or anything," she says, narrowing her eyes for effect. "I'm totally jealous," she adds, leaning closer. "I reckon this one only has holes in his pocket. And you know what the holes are for."

"It's his. He can play with it as often as he or his Tinder date likes." I pick up my cup and take a sip.

"This isn't Tinder. He's a man my parents want to meet. They found him on one of the matrimonial sites."

"You're considering an arranged marriage?" My eyebrows ride high with surprise.

"Blame my recent reading choices." She leans back in her chair, running her finger through a dusting of spilled cocoa powder. "Though I don't think there are many billionaire-mafia bad boys on the apps the parentals are viewing."

"*Apps* plural. Wow."

"It keeps them occupied," she says with a shrug. "It was, apparently, the least I could let them do when my biological clock ticks so loud my mother isn't getting any sleep."

"But you don't even live in the same city."

"Which is exactly my mother's point." She blows out a long breath. "There's no harm in looking, right?"

"I guess not."

"If you ever meet my mum," she says, flicking a lazy finger my way, "never mention you picked Oliver up wearing your wedding dress. She believes in manifesting."

"It's not like we're in love," I say with a laugh.

When I look up, Yara's lips are pursed. "Methinks the lady's prickly protest is too much. You two are so cute. He makes you happy, and he punched that twat out, saving me the trouble of setting up a GoFundMe to pay for the aunties' flights."

I wonder if she'd think him so great if I told her what he said to Mitchell. Not that I would. It's kind of weird that I wasn't offended. *Weirder still that I was a little turned on.* But I've since decided I like the idea of Mitch's erection shriveling when he thinks of me. Second best to his dick falling off, of course. Speaking of dicks . . .

"Do your parents know this guy is sending you dick pics?"

"I'm not sure it would make a lot of difference, given my vagina is about to close up for good. Plus, he is the cream of the crop. He's a real doctor."

"Oh, a doctor." My answer is the verbal equivalent of an eye roll.

"Yep, that top-tier individual." She grins. This is a conversation most vets are familiar with. "Because it's not like we have to learn the pharmacology, physiology, and anatomy of literally a million species."

"Well, not literally. More like a hundred or so, but our education covers animal behavior, internal medicine, surgery, dentistry, and ophthalmology. I mean, just who are the true general practitioners?"

"Preach!" she says holding up evangelical hands. "Good thing other people's opinions don't stop me loving my job."

"Me either." But it doesn't stop my blood from boiling sometimes.

"So, how is tall, dark, and drop-your-knickers hot?" Yara asks, reaching for a tiny sachet of sugar.

"Oliver?"

"Unless there's someone else you're currently dropping your knickers for?"

I wouldn't have the time. Or the energy. The man keeps me very satisfied. "Oliver is good."

"And . . ." She draws the word out, her eyes dancing.

"And I'm good, thanks for asking."

"And . . ." She gives an excited little wiggle in her seat.

"Together we're really, really good." And that is the truth, the whole truth, and nothing but the truth. It's also ignoring all the icky stuff like *Where is this going?* and *How much do you really like me?* along with *Can you see yourself falling for me?* and *Do you want to have kids, and, if so, how many?*

"That's so exciting! I told you this was going beyond rebound status," she says, skimming a sugar packet my way.

"I'm not really thinking about the future," I say with a perfect disregard for the truth. How can I not think about it? I sometimes obsess. "After what happened with Mitch, I'm taking things as they come." And avoiding those mistakes. The way I see it, my visa is just around the corner, and then I guess we'll see where this goes.

"That's fair," she agrees. "But don't close your mind to opportunities. He did buy all those glasses for you, remember?" She presses her hands over her heart, doing that cartoon-heartthrob thing.

"Such a dork," I mutter, smiling as I think of all the things he's done for me. The denials he's made when there really is no arguing with how sweet he can be.

"How is Riley, by the way? Have you heard from him lately?"

I nod. "I spoke to him a couple of days ago. The surgery went well, the external fixators are hell, and he's starting physio."

"Ouch." Yara shudders, then reaches for her cup. "If you ask me," she says, putting it down again, "a man doing anything for you is the pinnacle of manhood—the hottest version of said man."

"You mean Oliver?"

"Who else?"

"Yeah, you could be right." Not that I plan on telling him or anything. He'd probably accuse me of being up to something.

"Also, love and happiness have been known to spring from stranger wells."

Yara doesn't know the roots of this thing sprouted in blackmail. But can I really shout *blackmail* when it's suited my purposes too?

"Stranger wells." I harrumph.

"What?"

"Name a relationship with a stranger beginning than a woman in a wedding dress hurling herself into a stranger's car."

"Okay." She drops her hands to her lap and appears to think for a little while. "So, my cousin, Sam. She was out with some bloke on a first date, a blind date. Anyway, she said he was a horror, that the only way she'd get through the date was with alcohol. So, there she was, ordering a drink at the bar, when this other dude, off his chops, barged up and pretty much ordered over her. Jumped the queue!"

If there's one thing that will make a Brit pissed off, it's queue (or line) jumping.

"She was well annoyed and elbowed him in the guts as she turned around to give him a mouthful. The bloke got in her face, and her date got up from their table to defend her. There was a massive fight, and to cut a long story short, she's been happily married for three years now."

"To the horror of a date?"

"No. He was a conspiracy theorist—one of the tin hat brigade. She married the policeman who carted her off to the station.

Brawling in a pub is a public-order offense." She holds out her hands as a kind of *ta-daa!* "The lawman and the lawbreaker. Stranger wells."

"Cute." But not quite as convoluted as my own meet-cute and all that's followed. A tale of cheating exes, blackmail, a fake relationship turned kind of real, a stately home grab, lions, tigers, and . . . puppies!

My love life is a zoo. But it's about to get worse.

Chapter 37
EVIE

"Honey, I'm home!" I call ironically, kicking the door closed with the sole of my sneaker. I slide my purse from my shoulder and drop Bo's leash when I freeze at the high-spirited echo I was not expecting.

"Honey, we're here! How cute," I hear next, pitched lower for her audience. "I just love how darling you both are."

What in the actual fish cakes . . . *My mom is here?* I guess it figures that she's already decided Oliver is the man of my dreams. She wouldn't even come to my wedding—she hasn't even seen us together, not that any of that would matter to her! *Like attracts like, she would say.*

"Mom, what are you doing here?" I try not to sound accusing as I find her, my stepfather, and Oliver cozied up on the couches.

"There's my girl!" She rounds the coffee table, her arms outstretched, though not for a real hug. Hers are more of a let's-not-let-our-bodies-touch gesture, accompanied by a superficial peck on the cheek. On this occasion, there's also a high-pitched squeak. "Oh, there's a doggy here too."

"This is Bo," I say, redirecting his nose from her tasteful cream pants. "He's kind of friendly."

"Some might say a little *too* friendly," Muffy murmurs as she edges away. I can feel her eyes running over me as I settle Bo by the chair, pulling an emergency distraction chew from my jacket pocket.

"You look well." *Well* is a pass in her book. Hell, it's almost a compliment. "Have you been to the gym?"

Do I look like I need to? No, I decide. That wasn't a jibe. This time.

"No, I was at work. I stopped off for a coffee with a friend on the way back." She glances at Bo as though she's not convinced. "When you're a vet, bring-your-dog-to-work day can be every day." And when you don't want to keep annoying the chef in the hotel belonging to the man you're in a . . . *whatever* with, you take him with you.

The cardinal rule of diners? Never piss off the server or the kitchen staff.

"Oh." Her gaze drops. "It's just leisure wear?"

It's just that she can't help herself.

"Activewear is the new day wear." *Mrs. Stepford.*

Margret Elizabeth Hadley Winthrop—was Carrington for a while (that husband was old money but too tightfisted with it) and before that, Fairfax—is an absolute gas. *Or maybe I mean that she makes me want to gas myself.* She's gorgeous in a way I'll never be. Where I inherited my dad's auburn cast, Mom's hair is like liquid gold. Her delicate beauty will never fade, thanks to a host of regular tweakments. Sadly, her outdated attitude is here to stay too. I love my mom. I do. It's just easier for us both that I love her from afar.

"So, what are you doing here?" *Unannounced and uninvited— surely that's a social sin on your antiquated planet.*

"Todd surprised me with a trip to Paris." She twists away, her hand swooping around like the host of a dating show.

Meet my stepfather, Todd Winthrop, a sixtysomething self-made millionaire and an old money try-hard. And boy does he try hard. *My nerves, mostly.* Despite being married to my mother for almost seven years, he hasn't picked up on the fact that people in her set aren't slaves to designer labels. Meanwhile, old Toddy boy is dressed from toe to toupee (or maybe hair transplant) in Loro Piana, Canali, and Cole Haan. Quiet luxury that screams *I have money!* very loudly.

"Hey, Todd!" I wave, then trudge my way over to him like a dutiful stepdaughter. One not in the mood for his conceited bull. "You know, it's still technically summer here in London," I tease, tweaking his cashmere sweater. I bet there's a Moncler gilet lying around here somewhere too.

"I found the weather a little cool," he says, wiping a palm over his sullied threads. "How are you, Evelyn?"

"Just peachy." And waiting for the other shoe to drop.

"Sweetheart." Oliver takes the pause as an opportunity to remind me he's here with a kiss to the cheek.

"Sorry." The smile I send his way is genuine, my heart doing its usual pitter-patter in the face of all that handsome. But I wish he wasn't here, because these little meetings rarely end well.

"How was your day, darling?" *Handsome and domesticated. What a catch.*

"Busy but good." I apologize with my eyes. *Make no promises* surely included no meeting of the parents.

"How about a drink?"

"Yes, please." Make it a bucket.

"Muffy?" Oliver turns, but she cuts him off, holding out her glass. It would be highly unfitting for my mother to *have* another drink, but she will allow her glass to be *refreshed* until the cows come home. Vodka, club soda, and a twist of lime. She swears it's what keeps her trim and once suggested it was a tipple I should adopt. At the time, I felt the same about cookies. *If you weren't opening a new box, then surely one more didn't count.* I suppose the only issue with her dieting advice was I was fifteen years old at the time.

Drinks are poured, and we settle, Mom and Todd on one couch, separated by her beloved ten-year-old Birkin purse. I sit next to Oliver on the other couch, Bo at my feet, and the coffee table a line drawn between us.

"So, when are you guys off to Paris?" *Please say soon.* These family meets are always as comfortable as a pelvic exam.

"Tomorrow," Todd says. "We flew into London just to see you."

"Lucky me." And I mean it. Only one night! Still, my smile feels like one on a ventriloquist's dummy. *As in, painted on.*

"I'm sorry we couldn't be here before." My mother cants her head to one side in a look that's maybe supposed to convey regret.

"When? Oh, you mean the wedding!"

Her head jerks up, not quite so dignified.

Yes, Mother dearest, I went there! "Don't worry. It's not like it's a secret. Oliver knows I was about to marry another man. He did pick me up at the venue, after all."

"Quite literally, as I recall." Lifting his glass, he presses his smile to it. I love how he's playing along. "It was quite the experience."

"You were at the wedding?" Todd looks disturbed.

"When are you going to get around to asking what happened? Quick recap?" I offer, talking fast and with my hands. "My fiancé cheated. I left during the ceremony."

"I'm sorry to hear that, sweetie," my mother says. "It was very unkind of him, but I'm sure it happened for the best."

Him screwing multiple women was for *my* best? That's because she was under the impression (as was I) that Mitchell had no money. *No name. No prestige to bring to her bridge game.*

"How come you knew where to find me?" We haven't spoken for, what? Four months? Since she'd decided to inform me she couldn't make my wedding.

"Now, Evelyn, I know you were upset, but we had the Tregar benefit that weekend."

"So you said." Such a perfect excuse and bound not to cause offense—my own mother choosing to attend an annual fundraiser over her only daughter's wedding.

"We RSVP'd last year, before you said you were getting married. I don't know why you had to plan things so late." She glances around as though expecting agreements.

"Mom, it's fine." The reality is, it's good she was absent.

"I'm sorry for what happened, though I'm still not really sure what that was. Riley said—"

"You've spoken to Riley?"

"Chelsea did," Mom says. "He told us where you were staying."

Because he has the hotel address, since he'd asked me to arrange to have his belongings sent from France back to London. *Not that they'll do him any good now that he's back in the States.* He also knows about Oliver. *The unicorn.* The rest Chelsea and my mom would've ferreted out for themselves, hence this visit and apparent approval.

"Chelsea is my daughter," Todd explains for Oliver's benefit.

Todd is very proud of his daughter, to the extent that he funds her life choices. Or *lack of action,* as I prefer to call it. It's not that she doesn't work, because she helps out from time to time at an art gallery on the Lower East Side of Manhattan. Muffy has convinced her it's the best use of her time while waiting for her Prince Charming to arrive, because it's not like she can spend her whole day drinking cocktails at Soho House.

"It's good that Chelsea caught up with Riley." At least, I hope it was good for him, because that had to be a booty call. At least

345

they didn't see the Pulse Tok. I'd know if they had. I would've heard my mother's screams.

"Poor Riley. It was good of Chelsea to visit him, wasn't it?" Mom says.

Good for him *and* his penis.

"How is Parker?" I ask, then turn to Oliver. "Parker is Todd's son. He's studying to be a doctor."

"Very admirable," Oliver remarks pleasantly.

"A plastic surgeon." Todd nods, proud. "Great money in that game."

I note the tiny twitch of my mother's right eye. Good breeding prevents the talk of wealth, but she understands there are some things she can't control. *Forgive him, Lord, for his new money ways.*

"A family with two medical professionals," Oliver says.

Todd snorts, but my mother cuts in. "What is it you do, Oliver? If you don't mind me asking?" If I didn't know her, I'd say she was just being polite. But I do know her. She probably knows where he buys his underwear, along with his net worth.

"Private equity," Oliver replies. "Some property development, and so on."

"Smart." Todd taps his nose. "Fingers in lots of pies. That's the way to go."

"Are you renovating?" Muffy asks next, doing that game show—hand thing again. "Not that this isn't a very beautiful suite."

"Thank you," Oliver replies. "We're not staying at the hotel. We live here."

Muffy looks confused. She'd probably frown but for her last (lightly done) facelift. "You live in a hotel?"

I almost laugh because the shock of *live in a hotel* has negated the inclusion of *we*.

"Yes. Well, I own it."

346

I can see Mother dearest is thinking that's some bougie bullshit. Or maybe she's running through her mental Rolodex of people who've chosen this lifestyle. Will she recount to her bridge partners how it was good enough for Tennessee Williams, Byron, *and* Salvador Dalí? *Cynthia, dear, Evelyn's young man is a billionaire, after all!*

The poor get labeled crazy. The rich, meanwhile, are just eccentric.

"It's really quite convenient." I curl my hand around Oliver's knee, and his fingers cover mine.

"I like to think so."

She's shook—so shook she forgets to have her drink refreshed. Then talk turns to dinner plans, and Oliver insists they must stay and dine with us.

"We couldn't possibly impose. A busy man like you must have plans."

No mention of me, of course. My profession registers only as a weak blip.

"I insist. If you'll excuse me, I'll call down and arrange things." Oliver stands, leaving us to ourselves for a few minutes.

"Evelyn, he is just *lovely*." Muffy folds her hands in her lap, her expression flushed. "Such beautiful manners." My mother is concerned with status and culture, which I guess makes Oliver look like the jackpot. "Oliver told us you recently dined at Kensington Palace!"

"With at least three hundred other people. It was a thing. An event."

"Patronized by the royal family, no doubt."

"I wouldn't know." Wouldn't care. And I'm not about to tell her I'm playing tennis with an elderly peer of the realm next month. I can't wait to meet the lions again. At a suitable distance, of course.

"Aren't you going to get dressed?"

347

"Dressing to dine at home is a little too *Downton Abbey*, don't you think?"

"But in a restaurant, Evelyn."

"I guess I wasn't planning on dining in Adidas." I really wasn't, until it became an issue.

"Oh, good." She smiles, relieved.

"What's he worth?"

"What?" I turn to Todd, returning his rudeness easily.

"Money," he grunts. "What's his net worth?" I guess Mom hasn't shared her findings.

"I don't know. I don't care," I say as I stand with more dignity than I feel.

"Honey, Todd is just looking out for your welfare," Mom says. "We both want to make sure you're well taken care of."

"I don't need anyone to take care of me. I have a job and a decent income." I ignore Todd's derisory huff. "I have money in the bank and more than enough to live on. I'm content with my life."

"Until you're not. Until you're calling, asking for us to bail you out," he mutters gruffly.

"I think you're confusing me with your actual daughter." With my retort, I waltz off to the bedroom, Bo trotting behind me.

I say nothing to Oliver when he pops his head around the bedroom door five minutes later.

"Everything all right?" There's a careful note to his tone as he steps into the room. "You seem a little off."

"*Raging* is the word you're looking for." I blow out a breath as I tie the elastic at the end of my braid. "I'm sorry. This isn't your fault. I can't believe they just turned up."

"You've nothing to be sorry about."

"Debatable."

He slides his hands into his pockets as he saunters closer. "I think this is worse for you than it is for me."

"Todd is an opinionated ass. He just rubs me the wrong way. What the hell was my mother thinking when she married him?"

"I'm sure lots of people would question your sanity for being with me," he murmurs, plucking at the end of my braid.

"Then I'd just have to set them straight. Tell them you gave me no choice."

"Yes." His brow furrows, but before he can step away, I link my fingers through his.

"I'll tell them you're a beast who forced me to live with you in your castle. But I would've moved in anyway if I'd known you'd always help me look for my glasses."

"That is a very low bar you set."

"Of all your smiles," I murmur, touching my finger to the corner of his mouth, "this is the one that annoys me the most."

"Because it's suave and enigmatic?"

"Because it makes me want to kiss it from your face." I pull his head down to mine for a kiss. When he pulls away, we're both smiling.

"We'd better get back."

"Urgh." My shoulders collapse. "I'd rather stick toothpicks under my toenails and kick a wall."

"I think I've heard that from you before."

"An evening with them will be just as painful."

"They do seem an odd match."

"Not really. Todd is rich, and my mom likes money."

"Ah." There's so much said in that tiny noise.

"I'm being unfair. She isn't some aging gold digger. She was raised to believe she'd be little more than an ornament in her husband's life. I don't think she's worked a day in more than thirty years, but that's the path she chose."

"Family. That other f-word. You look lovely, by the way, and I know you're hungry—"

"I was," I say with a frown. "They spoiled my appetite."

"You'd better get it back, because I've just booked the chef's table experience."

"Is that one of those meals where we have to prep our own food?" I give an unimpressed twist of my lips.

"No, but that might've been a decent alternative."

"What is it, then?"

"It's a culinary experience and includes enough people coming and going to take the onus off you."

I press my head to his chest. This man. Sometimes I can't believe I ever said a bad word about him . . .

◆ ◆ ◆

It turns out, Oliver is a genius.

We're greeted in a private dining room I didn't know the hotel had. There's a plate glass window—with a view of the hotel's industrial kitchen—that's thick enough to drown out most of the explosions of swear words. *Must be a chef-y trait.* The sommelier arrives almost immediately to serve us champagne, the head chef appearing next to introduce himself. We're offered canapés from a selection including wild-mushroom tarte tatin with tarragon and rillett of duck with plum pickle. *I'm not even sure what a rillett is, except delicious.*

From there, we're served a meal fit for a queen and taken through all four courses with explanation in the finest detail. The food is classically simple, but the flavors delicious.

"They just melt and meld!" Muffy is in raptures, though that could be the result of the numerous wine pairings and also the heat of the kitchen when we're given pristine white aprons and invited to join the crew as they prepare our mains.

The experience is something else. I've never seen Todd so relaxed or my mother so flushed. When it comes time for petits fours and coffee, a sixty-year-old brandy arrives as an accompaniment.

"Well, Oliver, it's quite a place you've got here," Todd says, awarding the evening his seal of approval in the understatement of the year.

I loved seeing this side of Oliver. He riffed with his staff, fitting in like he's always popping into their fiery domain.

"Thank you, Todd, you're very kind."

Todd is certainly something. I'd thought, when Muffy first introduced us, that he'd be different. A self-made man who'd worked hard for what he had, but he was just as arrogant as the rest. Maybe even worse, because he seems to be under the impression that he's better than everyone else—smarter because he got where he was by himself.

I despise the level of arrogance the rich have. I hate how power and wealth seem to make for a distinct lack of empathy. I see it at the clinic almost every day, and I've learned that it has nothing to do with where the money comes from. Inherited or earned, the more money you have, the bigger a dick you seem to become.

I know I'm guilty of a prejudice, and I'm conscious that not all wealthy people are terrible humans. There are good rich people out there, and maybe, underneath that starched, bossy surface, Oliver might just be one of them. It seems almost weird how I'd pigeonholed him when we first met, putting Oliver in the same category as the people I knew growing up. People who wanted for nothing, who grew up rich and spoiled, rarely hearing the word *no* in relation to their desires. Those who assumed they could do what they want, get what they want, because family (and money) would always bail them out.

"I'm so pleased you've looked after Evelyn," Muffy says, nursing her brandy, "given her recent problems."

"What problems are those? Almost marrying the wrong kind of man or almost marrying a man who was cheating on me?" Oops. The wine seems to have loosened my tongue.

"They're the same, aren't they?" Todd retorts.

"Sure." And not at all. It wasn't a sense of prescience that kept them in Connecticut.

"Some people are very good at hiding who they are," Oliver begins. "Eve was unlucky, that's all. But I think you'll find she does a wonderful job of looking after herself."

My mother titters, and Todd huffs a laugh.

"What's funny?" I demand, with a tilt of my glass. "Guys, share with the class."

"Eve." My name is a caution as Oliver settles his warm hand over mine.

"No, I want to know what's so amusing about my life."

"You're almost thirty years old," Todd says. "You don't own a house or a car. You bounce around from place to place. And have no responsibilities."

"Not to make it a competition," I say, "but don't you pay the rent on Chelsea's loft? And her Uber account."

"Chelsea is twenty-five," he says gruffly.

"A whole four years younger than me. Meanwhile, I've worked in Sri Lanka, Indonesia, Spain, and the UK. I support myself, and I do just fine."

"Volunteering isn't working," Todd scoffs. "You spent all those years studying, and for what? So you can flit around the world with nothing but a backpack, volunteering and living in hovels, only to eventually settle for a job that pays less than fifty thousand a year."

"Pounds, not dollars," I snipe, hating that I'm justifying myself.

"That's not a living, Evelyn."

I pin my arms across my chest and let out a slow, calming breath. "Because I should've studied human medicine?"

"It would've paid better," my mother adds carefully. "You'd be a doctor. It's not just about money. Your standing would be better. You'd be treated better too."

"By whom?"

My mother blinks back at me, wide eyed. It wouldn't occur to her that the only people who disrespect my job are the people that are supposed to support me.

"I'm not interested in accolades," I add wearily. "I'm doing what I was born to do. I love my job. I love animals, and I fell in love with treating them."

"Yes, I know that, honey, but—"

"You can't know. Not really. It's tough some days. I see so much suffering, but there's not a job on this earth that could surround me with such love. Animals devoted to their owners or loving on their rescuers. Owners who dedicate themselves to their pets. People can be hard to deal with because some people are just assholes." I try not to look Todd's way, just as I ignore my mother's soft chastisement. "But in my little treatment room, even the assholes are redeemed in my eyes through their love and care for their pets."

"Love doesn't pay the rent." Todd looks to Oliver, maybe expecting manly solidarity.

"You don't pay my rent, so no worries there." No love lost either.

"You never asked," he grumbles.

"I prefer to control my own strings. Purse strings," I tag on quickly.

"I don't understand how you live the way you do," he continues, needling me.

"In a luxury hotel?"

"You could've been anything," he retorts tersely. "But you wouldn't listen to your mother."

Because my mother listens to you.

My throat is suddenly tight, a wash of acid aversion sluicing up from my stomach. Words burn and boil in my throat, ready to explode from my mouth, whether I want them to or not, when, under the table, Oliver settles his hand on my thigh.

"I think you're missing the point, Todd. Eve doesn't want to be anything but what she is—*who* she is. That in itself is beyond admirable, isn't it?"

Todd opens his mouth, but gets no further than a complaining huff.

"Not everyone is driven by money, and so many of us wired that way do so by hustle, by insincerity and deceit. But the people who truly keep this world spinning are people like this amazing woman." He turns to me, his beautiful eyes so fierce. "She nurtures, she heals, and on behalf of others, she kicks arse when it's needed. I won't sit quietly as you denigrate her choices. You should be honoring her for the woman she is, not griping about what she is not."

My heart swells with an emotion I find hard to contain as the table falls deathly quiet. Then, in a show of manners particular to only him, Oliver calls the server's attention as he asks, "More brandy, anyone?"

Chapter 38
OLIVER

I wake suddenly in the dark to the sound of my hammering heart. Disconcerted and not yet fully in the land of the living, I stretch my arm across the bed, reaching for my anchor. My Eve. My . . .

Something brushes my face. I'm certain it's not Eve's hair because it doesn't remotely smell like flowers. "Jesus Christ, Bo! Get your arse out of my face."

The dog's head jerks up, his eyes shining in the darkness. He gives in to an unhurried, tremorous stretch before jumping up and shaking his head.

"Ergh!" Saliva hits my face. "Get the fuck down, dog!" He just stares at me. Swallowing my frustration, I modulate my tone to tactical negotiation levels. "Bo, get down off the bed. There's a good dog." I'm not sure that's true. It's more that he's good at *being* a dog. But he makes a noise that I'm sure is triumph before he launches himself to the floor, his toenails tip-tapping all the way out of the room.

In the darkness, I strain to hear if Eve is near.

What a night. And what a pair of fuckwits Eve has for parents. From the moment they arrived, it was obvious their presence was to be a trial, not a comfort. Eve's whole demeanor screamed *anxious* around them, and when she didn't hold back, it was more like she couldn't help herself.

I'd called down to the concierge to book the chef's experience, thinking it would distract them and fill any taut conversational spaces. Only, the reservation had already been taken for that night, along with all the nights between now and the new year, I was pleased to hear.

Natalia at the concierge had explained that tonight's booking had been made for an anniversary, that the party were staying the night in the hotel. So in a display of . . . well, I don't quite know what the fuck that was, or what madness possessed me, I took the guests' room number, knocked on their door, and introduced myself. Then I offered to exchange their chef's experience for an all-inclusive week's stay in our sister hotel. In Saint Kitts.

It had even been worth the trade for a while, until her arse of a stepfather began to tear her down. I couldn't stop myself from getting involved.

"Oh, fuck it," I mutter, flinging back the duvet. I'm going to find my girl.

◆ ◆ ◆

EVIE

"Are you gonna take that shot?"

I look up, dragged back to the present and out of my messy head.

"I went to sleep with my eyes open," I say, smiling across at Bob, the night porter.

"I thought you were studying which was the best shot." He turns back to the beer tap he's tinkering with. "I'd pot the red in the middle pocket, myself."

"Thanks." I pick up my glass, the whisky warming my throat and my chest. It's an acquired taste, whisky. It's also a taste I'm not sure I've yet acquired, but it's better than the warm milk I'd convinced myself might help me sleep.

I'd tossed and turned after Oliver dropped off to sleep, but given there was no milk in the suite's kitchen, I thought I might sneak into the hotel kitchen instead. At least until I found Bob in the hotel residents' bar, complete with a pool table. Although, according to Bob, the hotel's owner prefers *billiards*. I didn't mention I could shake the owner awake to check.

I set my glass on a nearby table, having already been frowned at for putting it on the edge of the pool—*billiards*—table. It's gone two in the morning, and I pick up my cue and the square of blue chalk as I distract myself from the thoughts I don't want. I take aim, and the balls go *thwack* as they fly across the baize, the red ball tipping into the middle pocket.

"Well done." I slowly straighten at the compliment that's not in Bob's voice. "We have a pool shark in our midst."

"I believe it's called *billiards*." My gaze slides Bob's way as my mouth tips apologetically. The old man shakes his head, amused.

"*Billiards shark* doesn't quite have the same ring to it," Oliver says.

I find myself chuckling, though I wince as the weighted end of the cue strikes the floor harder than I'd intended.

"What's so funny," he asks, strolling closer.

I scrunch my nose. "You have bed hair."

He reaches up and slides his hand through his hair, a sudden warmth rising in my chest. For once, it's not the tight flex of his physique. It's the affection in his eyes and the way that he's dressed. The eccentric billionaire, wandering his hotel, his hair askew, dressed in navy pajama pants. *And a T-shirt too.*

"I left you a note. I couldn't sleep."

357

"I didn't see a note. It was probably victim to Bo's rear end."

"Oh, no."

He comes to stand next to me, adopting a low, confidential tone. "I almost mistook his tail for your hair."

"Yikes." I pull another face, though it softens as his hand cups my cheek.

"You should've woken me."

"So we can both lament my parentage?"

Oliver's expression flickers into sympathy, and I tighten my grip on the cue as my heart tip-taps.

"Families are complicated."

"Are they? Mine seems pretty simple. Toe the line, or get ridiculed. Why do they have to be so . . ."

"Set in their ways?"

"Obsessed with money. So arrogant. Why do the wealthy think money makes them better than everyone else?"

His mouth cants, and he half turns, leaning back against the table. "Arrogance lives at all levels of financial status," he says carefully. "Wealth is just an amplifier."

"Oh, I'm aware," I say, adjusting my grip on the cue. "Have you ever had to deal with a plumber in the depths of winter? The attitude? Immense. Huge! But my experience is, the wealthier the person, the bigger the asshole."

"By that edict, I'm not quite sure *where* to adjust my monocle."

I huff out a laugh, tipping forward to rest my forehead against his shoulder.

"What about Nora? She's quite arrogant."

"Nora's a special case." I stand straight again and reach over for my glass. Taking a tentative sip, I offer it over. "Besides, I'm not sure she's arrogant as much as she is a grump."

"Eve," he begins over the rim of the glass, "you know she looks down on everyone."

"Unless you're wearing a fur coat and have four legs. She's had a hard life. Of course she's going to be prickly around people. She gets a pass from me for all that she does."

"What about me?" He sets the glass on the table, *tsk, tsk,* and turns to me. "Do I get a pass?"

"No matter what I've accused you of," I say, my tone turning soft, "there's no deficit in your empathy. What you said earlier . . ." My words trail away. I feel like if I speak, my heart might overflow, and my tears might never stop flowing. And I hate crying. It makes me feel weak—makes me look like a frog!

"I only spoke the truth."

"I've never had someone stand up for me like that."

"That is not what I wanted to hear."

"It is what it is." The words. I can barely force them past the ball in my throat. "Can't help the way I was made."

"Bob." His gaze holds mine as he pitches his voice just loud enough for Bob to hear. "Would you leave us, please?"

"No worries, boss." A clink of metal against wood, the shuffle of shoe leather, and the doors to the bar close with a quiet *thunk.*

"It must be nice when people do as you say," I whisper, even though we're the only ones here.

"I used to think so. Recently, I've revised my opinion."

"Liar," I say, biting back a smile.

"It's true." Warmth licks at my stomach as his own lips tip.

I inhale deeply. I've never told anyone what I'm about to say. Never said the words out loud, at least. I mean, who'd want to hear the poor little privileged girl lament her upbringing? But I feel full, like there's no more space for this bottling up. "When I was growing up, we had a Labrador. Dilly. She was amazing. I was an only child with a four-legged sibling, and she was my best friend. We would run and play together, and she'd let me fall asleep on her like she was my pillow. I told you my dad died, but my parents divorced before that. I was seven, and the night they decided they'd had enough, I just hid in my room with Dilly, burying my tears in her fur as they shouted and screamed, their unhappiness reaching its climax. Losing her a few years later was almost unbearable. I've never cried like I did that night, and I still miss her every day."

"Dilly is why you became a vet?"

I shrug. "Animals were easier. It's the people around me that I found difficult. There was a time Mom used to be proud of me. For what I was studying, for what I'd planned."

"I'm sure she's proud of you still."

I shake my head. "No, she isn't. I mean, she's always been critical about my appearance, frustrated that I don't make the best of myself. But it was never about the best for me and more about getting myself a man. If I'd taken her lead, I would've snagged a husband at college and not worried about my GPA."

Oliver surprised me earlier with the strength of his defense, and he surprises me again when he doesn't speak, just takes my hand, offering me a silent comfort, allowing me to purge.

"Marry a rich man—that's always been her focus. Like it did her any good. They divorced before dad came into his inheritance, so there was little of their wealth that came her way. Her next husband was a skinflint, and the reason I lost my dog. She didn't die of natural causes. They had her euthanized while I was away at camp." His eyes turn soft, but I rush on. "She was old, I get that, but Martin, Mom's ex, said the vet bills were too much. But they didn't even give me a chance to say goodbye."

"I'm so sorry."

"Then Todd came along. By then, I was old enough to see that the issue was and always will be money. Money makes Mom compliant. She twists and bends to a mold because of it. It's been hard," I say, swiping at silent tears. "But it's also been a good lesson. Wealthy men have the power to ruin you."

"But not you," he says quietly, staring down at our linked fingers. "You have an iron rod running through your spine. You're strong, and you're brave, and when you bend, you do so only out of love."

"I'm sorry I lumped you in with them," I say, tears falling freely, my words partially choked. "I didn't give you a chance."

"Hush now." Everything seems tangled by my thoughts as he lifts my hand, my body comprehending his actions before my brain does. His lips are soft as he kisses each of my fingertips in turn. "Do you know, I adore you." By his tone, he might be discussing the weather. "I suppose I'm just a little slow on the uptake when it comes to love."

"Oliver?" Loves. *Loves me?*

His answer is a hum that's not quite a confirmation as he presses a kiss to my palm. "Your eyes look so soft. Is it tears, or is it wonder?"

"Try *shock*?"

"Eve." My name is a chastisement that feathers across my lips as he lifts my hand to the back of his neck.

"Wait." My hand slips to his warm chest, the scent of him, of soap, spice, and man, calling to me on some level I don't understand. "Wait just a minute. Are we talking *strong levels of affection* here? That you love having me around?"

He smirks, yes, smirks, with intent, and my heart begins to dance like a highly strung Chihuahua. On crystal meth.

"Well, I love *having* you, yes. But this is much bigger than that. Perhaps I should tell you how I admire you . . . ardently."

A smile catches in the corner of my mouth. I can't stop it from spreading. "Have you struggled in vain? Your feelings can't be repressed?"

"This will not do," he murmurs, pressing his hand over my mouth. "Sweet, lovely, frustrating Eve, I love you."

His declaration brings emotions I never could've anticipated—feelings I've never experienced before. My hand clasps the back of his neck as my vision blurs, my heart overflowing with joy, with tenderness, with desire, and with every related emotion possible.

"You." He breathes the word, gathering me close. "Do you remember telling me what you thought love would look like?"

"Yeah," I answer, recalling the conversation and my harsh words.

"Love is choosing that person always, you said. That made sense to me somehow. I've never believed people just fall spontaneously in love. It has to be a choice. A choice to love or not. And I stand by that, because I didn't *fall* in love with you, Eve. It didn't happen by chance, and it wasn't a mistake. My heart chose you, my darling." He sweeps the hair from my face and presses his lips to my head. "And when you're driving me up the wall, when we argue and snipe and can't seem to agree on anything, my heart still chooses you. Again and again, over and over, without doubt and without fear, because even at those moments, I would still rather be with you than anyone else in the world."

I begin to laugh softly and give my head a slow shake.

"Was that not romantic enough?" Oliver asks, lifting my watery gaze to meet his bemused one.

"That's not it." This man loves me. He loves *me*. And I am tired of fighting my feelings. The good, the bad, the ugly—the ugly pretty—I want every part of him as desperately as I want his kisses. "It just occurs to me that, by that explanation, I must love you too."

"Eve." His voice breaks over my name as he pulls my body flush with his. The pool cue falls from my nerveless fingers, clattering discordant and ignored to the floor. His lips are so tender, and I taste whisky from his tongue as we kiss and we kiss, as we share love and joy and relief. Until that unseen corner is inevitably turned, and our kisses change in strength and depth, becoming deeper and desperate. My moan vibrates through us both, his hands beginning to roam—the base of my throat, my ribs, my waist—when he pulls back, his face made of shadows and determination. He takes my breast full in his hand, plumping lushly, rolling the pebble of my nipple between his fingertips.

"You have become everything to me." Our mouths meet again, our touches turning frantic, our tongues tangling and our teeth clashing. We kiss as we live, wild for each other.

His T-shirt comes off, mine next, his hands framing my breasts, my nipples aching peaks that he sucks into his mouth.

"Oh, God!" My body bows and twists, his fingers echoing the sucking pull of his lips, liquid hot pleasure bursting through me.

"Darling, I need you."

"Yes." With my whispered assent, his hands slip under my thigh, lifting me onto the pool table. Lifting my knee, he drives himself between the clasp of my thighs. We both groan as hard meets soft. "Take these off." I tug at the waist of his pajama pants, sliding my foot against his thigh.

"You drive me insane." His words are all ache and gravel, the rasp of his stubble making me pulse and shiver. "You make me the happiest I've ever been."

"Same," I pant out, my thoughts fragmenting at the threat of his teeth.

"Kissing you makes me feel I could explode with happiness." His arm at my back is a brace, balls clicking and rolling as he lays me against the green baize. "Fucking you feels like a religious experience."

"Hallelujah. But less talking, more worshipping."

"Shut up," he rasps, playfully biting my shoulder. "You know you love what this mouth can do."

He's so right. I think it will always be like this between us. Give and take, push and pull, driving each other crazy all day long.

And just when I think it can't get any better than this, Oliver pulls back, and for a moment, he just stares down at me. I swallow hard, overcome by the love in his eyes. Love and maybe a little surprise, like he's not sure how he found himself here.

I close my eyes, screwing them tight, imprinting the moment behind my lids. *I love him.*

"I knew it wouldn't take long." He smirks.

"For what?"

"Before you'd look at me again. I know you can't help yourself," he taunts. "It's a curse being this handsome."

"Pretty, you mean." Reaching up, I pull his mouth to mine, our kiss urgent and brief, as though we're frightened we might miss something. My fingers coast through his thick hair, glide over his broad shoulders, his muscles flexing and bunching beneath his heated skin.

"Yes." I arch into his hand as it glides down between us.

"You smell fucking edible." His compliment is hot and rough as he makes short work of my pajama bottoms. My body jolts as he brushes the pad of his thumb across my clit. I can feel how wet I am through the mixture of cool air and the heat of his breath. "You're so pretty. And all mine." My breathing turns ragged at the press of his tongue, pleasure pulsing through me.

"Oh, yes!" I anchor my hands in his hair as his mouth lays claim to my pussy, the brush of his stubble and the pull of his lips making my whole body tremble. I cry out in surrender. I cry out in love. I give in to this most delicious of torments as I come undone.

A minute or a lifetime later, Oliver is standing above me. His eyes are dark, and his mouth and chin shine obscenely with my pleasure.

"Tell me you want me," he demands.

"More every day." I swallow, overcome by the moment. Overcome with the notion that this is our love. *Our call and response.*

"Tell me again. Tell me—"

"I do." My hips tilt in a silent plea. "I love you, Oliver."

"Yes, thank God."

He lines himself up, and we're both done for.

Chapter 39
EVIE

A Little Bird Told Us . . .

that wedding bells could be sounding in the distance after a lovestruck billionaire begged residents of his hotel to give up their reservation so he could impress his future in-laws. The besotted businessman exchanged their table for four for a week in a swanky six-star Saint Kitts hotel!

Oh, Mr. Deubel, I have a table for six at Chipotle I'll happily swap.

Call me!

I'm not sure which is crazier. The image of Oliver in a Chipotle restaurant or the idea we could be getting married, which is not even a little funny considering how we met.

I text Yara a quick thanks for sending me the link to the column's so-called news. She thought the mention was hilarious—she didn't even ask if it was true. But I guess the way rich people live is so fantastical, they might as well be aliens.

I try not to read the column these days, and I would've liked to have avoided any reminder of my parents' visit. I'm still having cringey flashbacks weeks later. The things they said . . . *Urgh!*

As I slide my phone back into my purse, I find myself wondering why Una Smith has such a hard-on for us as a couple, because according to Oliver, he had no hand in this. And I believe him. It's too early to say he's hugely reformed. I guess his heart is in the right place. *Mostly.*

Mine too. *Mostly.*

"I feel very suspicious when you're sitting there, smiling to yourself."

"Sorry?" I glance across at Oliver as the Bentley slows for a corner.

"Especially as we drive around Dalston. Care to explain why we're here?"

"All will be revealed," I reply mysteriously. If being mysterious includes giggling behind your hand and trying to disguise it as a cough.

He wants to know what I'm up to, meanwhile I've given up trying to figure him out. I know he still wants Northaby, but I'm confident he'll do right by the animals. *It's no good taking them on if his heart isn't in it. Better they find new homes.*

Meanwhile, I know he won't truly change his spots. He'll always be up to something—it's the nature of this man. *This man I love.* But I know I'm no angel either.

"I forgot to ask you." I turn to him in the vein of someone just remembering something. "Did you bring your passport?"

"What for?"

"Well, this is unfamiliar territory."

"Dalston or the fact that you're in charge?"

"Oh, I'm always in charge. I'm the girl behind the curtain."

"Pulling strings? That sounds frighteningly familiar."

"Does our intrepid traveler have his passport as he sets out on his quest to explore the deepest, darkest corners of East London?"

Oliver spikes a brow at my deep-toned nature-documentary-style narration.

"Oh, come on! When was the last time you ventured farther than Shoreditch?"

"Sometimes I forget you think you're hilarious," he says, turning to the window as the Bentley stops at a red light. He eyes the pub on the corner, baskets of brightly colored begonias teeming from it.

"But then I remind you."

His chest expands in preparation for a deep sigh. "Yes. Yes, you do." But he can't *quite* hide his smile. "I have a creeping suspicion this has something to do with my outfit for Mandy's ball."

"Perceptive." It is only a few days away.

"Perceptive enough to know you're going in the wrong direction. My tailor is nowhere near here." His gaze slides doubtfully to the window again.

"Here's the thing. We're not going to your tailor."

"Shock."

"I thought you'd feel like that about it." I almost wiggle in my seat, excitement bouncing around my insides like bubbles in a pop bottle. "But fair is fair. I so dutifully wore the dress you chose for me." I slide my hand over my thighs, straightening a rumple in my skirt.

"Frankly, I thought you'd forgotten about it."

"Hoped, you mean."

"I distinctly remember you agreed to speak to my tailor."

"So fussy. Relax! I have everything in hand."

"That's not as reassuring as you might think."

"I called in to your tailor," I say, patting his thigh. *Yum.* "I picked up your measurements."

"For something off the rack?" he says, as though holding it at arm's length between a pinched finger and thumb.

"Don't make me spoil this surprise." I give a slow, disappointed shake of my head.

"The surprise in Dalston," he deadpans.

"I think you'll love it." *I know I will.*

I've put a lot of thought into this afternoon. Undertaken a lot of research, and as the car slows to a halt at the address I've given Ted, I turn to take in the full effect on Oliver's face.

"A charity shop?" His expression is as dark as thunder.

"We call them Goodwill stores back home." At this, his head jerks my way, and he looks at me as though I've grown a second head. A much uglier second head.

"My goodwill is something that's diminishing by the second," he mutters.

"It's one of the biggest in London," I say, ignoring him to look at the window display. *Wouldn't do to laugh at him.*

There's a leather sofa in the long window, a fluffy afghan throw over the back. The aging credenza next to it houses a tea set with a garish pattern, white crocheted doilies sitting under each piece. There are literally hundreds of stores like this around London, but some of them—especially the ones closer to Oliver's hotel—are too fancy for my current purposes. For example, the thrift store in Notting Hill had a Boss suit in the window for seventy quid!

So I expanded my search to include anywhere that might stock the opposite of designer wear in my quest to get him back for the dress. The very lovely dress that made me feel like a supermodel, but that's not the point. Because the point is, he's not supposed to make decisions on my behalf. Even if he thinks those decisions will benefit me. I choose my own clothes and pay my own way.

This is just a small reality check for the man, especially as I've received notification that my biometric card is in the mail. I've been granted my visa—weeks earlier than the forecast. I haven't told Oliver, and if Ariana, the immigration lawyer, notified him, he hasn't said.

We haven't ironed out what happens after. Maybe we're both trying not to burst this bubble. But we need to discuss what our relationship will look like. I'll tell him about my visa. Soon. I'll have to. But today, I guess I wanted to prove that things won't change.

"This is unacceptable, Eve."

"Too bad, so sad. Get your butt out of the car."

"This was not what we agreed."

"I don't remember agreeing you could pick out a dress for me, and don't invoke the stylist, because that's just a technicality."

"I was trying to help."

"Hello!" I singsong. "Same here."

"No, Eve, you are shit stirring," he growls.

I press a hand to my offended chest. *Moi?*

"Yes, you! Causing trouble. Having fun at my expense and—"

"Sir, we're parked in a loading zone." Oliver frowns Ted's way as he adds, "I reckon we might get clamped, maybe even impounded?"

Good one, Ted. Oliver climbs slowly from the car.

"You're so tetchy." That sounded a little too gleeful. The way he glares at me says he heard it too. "It's not like I'd let you go to this thing looking stupid."

"The fact that I'm here does not mean I will be wearing clothing purchased out of . . ." He turns his head, glances at the storefront, and apparently pretends not to know what it is. *"That place."*

"No." I hold up a finger. "No givesies backsies. You said—"

"In this instance, it would be *takesies backsies*," he utters with a ghost of a smile. "It's starting to rain. Let's go inside and get this over with."

I almost break out the happy dance when I remember something. "Wait." Oliver turns, his hand on the door handle. "Say cheese!" I snap a pic with my phone.

"What was that for?"

"Pictures or it never happened, Mr. Fancy Pants."

"The only thing I fancy is getting this over with." An old-fashioned bell chimes above the door as Oliver pushes it.

This is going better than I ever imagined.

Shit stirring?

Troublemaking?

Enjoying the heck out of myself?

Yes, yes, yes!

"Hi." I greet the assistant with a bright smile before I almost bump into Oliver, whose feet seem to have turned into concrete. "What the f—"

"Fabulousness!" I shout, drowning out his growly dissent with enthusiasm and a sudden jazz-hands movement.

"You're not the first person to be taken aback by the size of this place," the store assistant offers happily, glancing up from the counter.

This place is huge. I guess this floor must be for homewares, as lounge and dining settings are dotted about the space, the rear wall filled with racks of plates and bowls and kitchenware.

I kind of love thrifting, though I don't get to do it often. But when I do, I always come back with at least one gem. Which is why I stick my hand into a nearby wire basket overflowing with chunky glassware. *Is that a novelty sherry glass?* I yank my hand back, because nope. That thing looks more like a butt plug.

"Is there anything in particular you're looking for?"

I turn my attention to the woman, her hair a shade of gray closer to lilac. I love how stores like this are almost exclusively manned by older friendly women. Trendier thrift stores, those run by hipsters and retro-loving cool kids, seem to have the vibe all wrong.

There's something comforting about thrifting, not just because I'm doing my bit to fight fast fashion and landfills. And who doesn't want to do their bit for curing cancer, helping the homeless, and saving animals? But it's more than that for me. It's the idea of the unwanted finding a new home, being recycled, reused, and reloved. Or maybe it's flipping the bird to how I was raised. *Who knows?*

"Could you direct me to the men's section, please?"

Oliver grunts, and the poor assistant's eyes fly wide.

"Pay him no mind. He's just stressed. You know what it's like when you're time poor but you need a new outfit for the weekend. Worst feeling in the world, right?"

Oliver glowers.

"No need to explain, dear. My Arthur used to sulk like a sullen baby when he had to go shopping with me." Oliver's attention spikes to the woman. "That's it," she says. "That's the exact face he used to pull. I bet he's still pulling it in his coffin. Anyway, menswear is in the basement." She looks down at her ledger, and I swear she adds under her breath, "Same place as Arthur went." However, it's not her ledger that draws my attention but the laminated cards stuck to the front of the counter.

No Backpacks. No Shopping Bags.

"We've had a lot of theft lately."

My attention shifts back. "In a charity shop?"

"Times are tough," she says with a shrug. "Also, people are bastards."

372

"Well, I just have my purse."

"Wait." Oliver reaches to his back pocket, pulls out his wallet, and peels out a fifty-pound note. "Consider it insurance," he says, putting it on the counter. He turns his dark look my way. "Let's get this over with."

"That was generous of you," I say as he wanders ahead.

"What do you suppose her title is?" He throws a thumb over his shoulder. "Door dragon? Member number one of the unwelcoming party?"

"Be nice. This is a *charity* shop."

"My charity extends to that fifty and to ten minutes. That's how long you have to torture me."

"Sounds kinky."

"If I get flea bites—"

"Such a snob!" I say as we approach the staircase down. "Bo's fleas seem to know better, so I'm sure you'll be fine. Your blood is probably too bitter for flea tastes."

"But not for yours," he says slinging his arm around my waist, hauling me against him. "Do you think your sweetness and light balance me out?"

"Of course. Aren't you glad you found me?"

"Oh, I count my lucky stars daily," he whispers, making me shiver when he presses a kiss behind my ear. "Let's get this over with."

"Stop! This will be fun, and no different to an hour spent wandering around Harrods or Harvey Nicks."

"I don't shop. I have people who do that for me."

"Well, you're shopping today, crabby ass, like it or not. You're so stuck up."

"Refusing to rake through other people's castoffs in a place that smells like mothballs and old socks does not make me stuck up."

"Shut up," I snipe, grabbing a random item from the nearest rail. I thrust it at him. "Go and try that on."

"On?" His brow spikes, then he glances at what turns out to be a gray T-shirt. It's going to be too small, I can see, but it serves him right.

"Yes. Take off posh threads, and put on T-shirt." *Asshole,* I add in my head.

"And this is what you want me to wear to an exclusive charity gala?"

"Wouldn't that be perfect? Double-dipping in the charity stakes. Triple, if we count the fifty. Think of all the angels in heaven right now, smiling down at you."

"A. Charity. Gala. Ball." He annoyingly enunciates each word.

"Try. The. Frickin'. T-shirt. On."

"This is like a bad dream."

"Go, drama queen." I point in the direction of the dressing rooms.

He doesn't say *fucker,* but his expression does before he saunters in the direction of my outstretched finger.

I don't particularly want to see him in a boring old T-shirt, but it beats having him follow me around, complaining. Grabbing this opportunity, I flick through the racks of shirts and sweaters, pausing to consider an ugly Christmas jumper for a moment but ultimately putting it back. I'm not quite sure what I'm looking for, but I'll know it when I see it. I turn from the rack when I see something hanging from the end of an aisle.

"Oh, my gosh! These are perfect!" All this moment is missing is a beam of heavenly light and a celestial choir! And just the right size. *At a squeeze.*

I'm almost giddy as I make my way to the men's dressing rooms.

"Are you in here?" I whisper, not wanting to trespass into that (slightly feet funky) no-woman's-land.

"Against my better judgment," comes a familiar voice from a cubicle at the far end.

"Glad you didn't run away."

"I did think about it but decided you weren't winning this one."

Oh, but I am, I think, hooking the hanger of my prize over the door next to his. "Knock, knock! Are you decent?"

"I'll never understand why people say *knock, knock* when they can just . . . knock." The door opens wide to Oliver's unimpressed face. "As for decent? That depends entirely on your definition."

I don't answer or make a peep, mainly because I have both hands pasted over my mouth. Who would've thought a gray T-shirt could be so funny!

"What's the verdict?"

I am *loving* what I'm seeing. I don't know why, but I thought he'd still be cranky and maybe put it on over his shirt or something. But not so. His shirt and jacket are hanging from the peg in the wall, the T-shirt on his actual person.

This is *such* a beautiful moment.

"Is it bring-your-twink-to-the-office day?" I burst out, unable to stop my laughter. It could be the combination of those pants and those highly polished shoes that brings the thought to mind. I press my hands to my stomach. The icing on the cake of this outfit is the T-shirt, which is a mite too small. It doesn't so much hug the bulk of his biceps as expose them, while revealing more than a sliver of skin at his waist. There's also a cherry on top of the icing in the form of a chest pocket with a cartoon Japanese-style lucky cat peeking from the top. "You look so . . . *kuwaī.*"

"If you say so."

"That's Japanese for *cute.*"

In answer, he tugs at the pocket to reveal a hidden message: SHOW ME YOUR KITTIES.

I feel my mouth twist. "I don't know what the Japanese word for *less cute* is."

"Personally, I think it adds a little something."

"You would."

"Go on, then." He hitches an expectant brow.

"What?" I press my hands over the girls. "Not even!"

"I think I deserve a little something for my compliance."

"And I think you might've bumped your head." I make to swing the door closed, when Oliver begins to make chicken noises.

"I am not flashing you in the Goodwill!" I hiss, swiping a look behind me to make sure no one is listening. And it's *then* I hear the celestial choir. What a perfect accompaniment to that shirt.

"Kitty will be very disappointed," he purrs. Unironically.

"The kitty wants to see my titties?"

"Let's go with that."

"What's it worth?" I ask, swinging the door to the cubicle back and forth a little. *It wouldn't do to show my hand.*

"Oh, God." He straightens, his expression suddenly firming. "What are you up to?"

"Why do I have to be up to anything?" I answer innocently.

"I ask myself the same question. Regularly. And the best I can come up with is this is your version of pulling my pigtails." His voice goes husky as he reaches out, the backs of his fingers a gentle caress against my cheek. "In other words, this is your love language."

In the name of a tap-dancing Jesus, he might be right. He's turned me kinky! I've never wanted to tease or torment men before—I've never experienced the levels of gratification I do when I'm driving him up the wall. *God, I love this man. So much.*

My eyes turn soft, my insides suddenly warm and gooey. All I want to do is hug him . . . but I also really want to see him in this outfit. So I give my head a quick shake, bursting my little bubble of love forcibly.

"Want to try a little experiment?" I murmur, hopefully temptingly.

"Flash me your kitties, and I'll think about it."

"That just sounds wrong."

"You could flash your pussy instead?"

"Keep your voice down! Honestly," I mutter, pulling the hanger from the other door. Turning, I wind the fabric around it for concealment, and as I step into the cubicle, I the drop bundle to the floor and my bag on top of it. "If teasing is my love language, what's yours?"

"This," he says, hooking his finger to flash the message in his pocket again. "I'm waiting. Show me your pretty, pretty kitties."

"Demands are your love language?"

He makes a chiding click of teeth and tongue. "Words of affirmation."

My eyes on his, I undo the top button of my shirt. "Take off your pants."

Oliver frowns. "I don't think—"

My fingers flick another button open as I arch a little from the door. "If I'm putting up the goods, you should at least reciprocate a little."

His throat works with a deep swallow as I languidly trail my hand over the (promising) bulge in his pants. He also eyes me doubtfully.

"Just a little peek," I pout as I slip open another button on my shirt. "Who would've thought getting you out of your pants would be so hard."

His mouth pinches in one corner, yet he reaches for his belt. Meanwhile, I unfasten the rest of the buttons until my shirt lies open at my sides. I glance down, my insides contracting powerfully at the sight. The sides of his pants are folded wide, his thick cock exposed, his hand wrapped around the root.

More than I bargained for, sure. But I am not *disappointed.*

"This is as far as I'm going," he says. "I can't believe we're about to risk arrest for the second time."

"It's at least the third time. Besides, no one will see."

He bats my hand away, making me realize I'd reached out.

"No touching," he commands. "It's my turn to affirm my love language." He steps a little closer. The space is already limited, but when I hold my hand out, it's not to stop him. "Your tits are amazing," he says as his hand brushes up the sides of my ribs. Fire spreads across my skin as he takes my breasts between his hands, his thumbs swiping over my nipples, cursing as I echo his movements over the satin head of his cock. *I know, I know. But is it any wonder I'm getting sidetracked?*

"I'm so obsessed." His thumbs hook into the fabric of my bra, and my breasts spill out. The heat of his mouth is shocking.

"I allow it," I whisper shakily at the soft burst of his breath. I close my eyes, desperate for him to take me into his mouth again.

He doesn't disappoint.

"Words of affirmation, physical touch, quality time, and acts of service. I have so many plans for your breasts."

"I'm not sure how you'll manage all that." I swipe my thumb over his silken crown, making him groan.

"By fucking them. Coming all over them." His words pound inside me in the sweetest of percussions, even as I reply. Though what I'm saying is anyone's guess.

"That's"—*deliciously graphic*—"specific," I finish. I try to hang on to my wits as he unpicks them one by one, his tongue circling my nipples in shiver-inducing circles.

"Can I?" His voice is low and rough. I lick my lips, but before I can answer, he ups the ante a little more. "In the park in your T-shirt and your navy dress in the evening breeze. When I can see the shape of your nipples, it drives me to fucking distraction."

His words, the picture he paints. I can't help but see it too. I try to hang on to my plans, but it's almost an impossibility.

"All I can think about is getting my mouth on them," he whispers into my ear, "sucking them until they're glossy and pink. I think of how good you'd look with my cock wedged between your fabulous tits." Hot breath, hotter words, as his fingers coax and tease, making me leak more than brain fluid.

"Oh, God." My body jolts. No, it's not possible. I'm not about to orgasm from a little aural and some boob action! Yet my spine bows from the door as my insides pulse emptily. I roll my lips inward to contain my pleasure when from beyond the door, there comes a rattle of metal coat hangers and a weary-sounding huff.

"Here, John," a woman mutters. "I found you a forty-inch waist. You might as well take them in with you."

John's response is unintelligible, though it's in the tone of one who is long suffering. Not that I'm paying attention as Oliver covers my mouth with his. He pushes my hand from his cock to wedge his thick thigh between my legs. The door begins to rattle at my back as I burst from my skin. Oh, my good Lord. *I am a deviant,* I think as I pulse and twist, as I come apart before the backdrop of a mild domestic argument. In a thrift store!

As I sink back into my skin, every inch of me seems to tingle.

"You know how I love you," Oliver whispers, kissing his way across my jaw.

"When you're so cruel?" My whine sounds a little hoarse.

"Inspired by it, more like."

"You play dirty."

"Says the woman who just got off in a charity shop."

Urgh. That sounds so bad. I push his body from mine. *I'll show you embarrassment.*

"What are you doing?" he asks as I yank his pants to his knees. He chuckles out my name as I slip my hand around his heel and lift. Unbalanced now, he slams his palms against opposite walls to stop himself from falling. "You really are determined to get my pants off, aren't you, darling?"

"Yep." I flip off his other shoe and tug his pants clean off. Meanwhile, Oliver can't seem to do much for laughing. I scramble for my purse then thrust the mystery hanger at him.

His hands clutch the leather to his chest, and he stares at me as though I might've lost my mind. "What the—"

"I don't want to hear another thing from you until you put those on." Flipping the lock, I push the door open, slip out, and pull it closed before he can answer. As I turn, I realize I didn't think this through so well.

"Hi!" I give a nervous wave to my audience, the motion brushing air across my bare midriff. "Oh." Glancing down, I pull the sides of my shirt closed, relieved I'd at least put the girls away. "I like this one so much, I'm gonna wear it right now. It's nice, right?"

The man standing in his boxer shorts just inside the door of the opposite cubicle closes his mouth, then nods dazedly. The woman pushing another pair of pants at him seems less invested in my babbling as her eyes fall to Oliver's pants bundled in my hands.

"He needs a different size," I say. "I'll just go check the rack."

"Your rack is perfect," calls a cheerful Oliver from behind the door. "Kitty can verify!"

When I burst from my skin a second time, the sensation is not so pleasant.

I fasten my shirt, then loiter around the miscellaneous bins as I wait for the henpecked and henpecker to leave. I'm pretty sure Oliver won't be going anywhere before then. I duck my head as they pass, then happily make my way back.

"Come out, come out, wherever you are," I whisper, tiptoeing into the men's dressing rooms for the second time. Before I reach the door, it swings open. An invitation I take, practically jumping into the open space.

Oh the joy! The immense happiness. He's not leaving but . . .

"It looks like you might be!"

"Be what?"

"Coming out!" I clasp my hands to my cheeks as I take him in. "Who knew you'd look this hot in leather pants!" Joined with a little crop top, it's fair to say he does not look like himself. But it turns out an alternative-universe gender-fluid Oliver still revs my engine.

"Almost in leather pants," he gripes with a small, uncomfortable jut of his hip. "They're so tight, I can almost taste them. Do you realize how hard it was to get into these? They're like fetish wear," he says, turning to look at his ass in the mirror.

"I think I'm developing a fetish." Because the leather hugs *all* the good bits. "Yes, turn around," I demand, unable to wait as I press my hand to his hips. "Let me see that booty properly."

"Stop that," he mutters, slapping away my hands. "The only time you should see a man wearing leather pants should be when they've misplaced their motorbike."

"How do you feel about assless chaps?" I ask. "You'd look amazing at a charity ball in them."

"If you think I'm going anywhere in any kind of leather that isn't footwear—"

"But I ordered you a crushed-velvet jacket in red to go with them! Bow tie too. Why did you think I got your tailor's details?" This is the phrase that breaks me as I collapse against the cubicle doorframe, laughing so hard, I worry I might pee myself.

"Are you quite done?" Oliver asks, unmoved. I nod, wiping away my tears. "I can take these off?"

"I can't believe you put them on."

"What was I supposed to do? You buggered off with my trousers. I was only putting them on to follow you until . . ." His gaze falls to his highly detailed crotch, and I start laughing all over again.

Chapter 40
EVIE

I'm still laughing about the leather pants two days later as I hop off the bus on my way to Nora's after work. *Can't ride with Ted all the time.* Watching Oliver rip the seams to get them off was hilarious. I'd chuckled all the way to the counter, carrying the silly T-shirt he insisted I buy for him, where the cashier was pricing up items for Halloween. Oh my gosh, I really did think I might pee myself on the spot as we'd watched her fit a ball-gag rubber mask to a mannequin. Even after I'd composed myself, I didn't have the heart to tell her it wasn't exactly holiday appropriate.

I make my way merrily down the street when something in the distance catches my eye as it glints in the afternoon sun. I realize what it is before I'm even close. Six-feet-high industrial fencing has been erected in front of Nora's old fence, the weatherworn wooden one. It's exactly like the kind of stuff you see on building sites. There's even a gate that looks more like a door. It's ajar, though a padlock swings on the latch.

I pull it open and do the same for the regular gate next, and the dogs set off barking. Everything else looks normal as I make my way through to the shed, where I spot Nora sitting on the wonky blue office chair.

"What's with the new fence and gate and stuff?"

She shuffles in the seat to face me, and I immediately know something is wrong. Her hair looks like a bird has nested in it, and her shirt is buttoned wrong. My stomach sinks when our eyes meet, my mind rushing ahead of my feet. Is it a TIA—a ministroke? Her eyes are so dull, and her face seems sunken. She looks like she's aged a dozen years since I saw her a few days ago.

"What is it? What's happened?" As I crouch down beside her, my mind registers her movements, how her arms lift without issue. I realize belatedly she's warding me off. Nora is not a hugger, and she will sit you on your butt for even trying. "Thank God." I press my hand over my hammering heart, and it takes me a moment to process what she's saying.

"They're locking me out—they're gonna take the place away from me."

"What? You mean the fences aren't yours?"

"I just came in this morning and saw them—and that notice." Her chest heaves with agitation as she points a bony finger in the direction of the hedge.

"I didn't see any notice." I put my bag down on the old table.

"'Cause I tore it off! This is his fault. I know it is!"

"Whose fault? Is it the owner?" I ask, bringing my gaze level with hers. "Has the place been sold?" I don't help with the accounts, but I know Nora pays only a nominal rent. Or at least she told me she was the tenant here, not the owner.

"No, he's dead. Been dead for years." Her lips purse with annoyance, and she gives an exasperated shake of her head.

"Then who are you talking about?"

"That rich prick you brought here!" The forcefulness of her words almost knocks me on my ass. "I got that letter after you brought him. I'm gonna shove that silver spoon of his right up his arse, you see if I don't." She balls her hand into a fist, banging it against her thigh.

"I brought? Do you mean Oliver?" For all her insults, it's clear she's frantic, but what on earth?

"Yeah, him. I saw him snoopin' about the place that day he moved the dog food. Talking on his phone, he was, looking shifty and up to no good."

"Oliver didn't do this." I find myself standing because, even as I reassure her, a little voice inside me says, *He wouldn't, would he?* But that's ridiculous. He wouldn't be interested in a scrappy piece of land in the middle of—

I halt. That's not the direction my thoughts should've turned. Except I know him. And I know he's all about frying bigger fish.

"No one ever said nothin' about the place before, and I've been here donkey's years! He comes here, and all of a sudden, I get that letter. It's him, I'm telling you!"

"Nora, please calm down. Do you have the letter? Can I see it?"

"You pulled it out of the postbox weeks ago. I just shoved it on the admin pile without looking at it." Her expression turns mulish as guilt pokes a thin finger at my chest. I've long suspected Nora is dyslexic. She's old enough to have been raised at a time no one knew or cared about so-called word blindness. That she can read at all is probably testament to her stubborn attitude. Given my suspicions, I'd more or less wheedled my way into being her unofficial admin assistant a couple of times a month. I generally open the mail to stop it from stacking up, and we go over its contents together.

"If I gave it to you, it doesn't mean I knew what was inside."

"I didn't say that." Her chin juts out.

"Well, can I read it?"

Her hand shakes as she reaches for her pocket, and my heart gives a little pang at how frail she suddenly looks.

"You're on my side, right?" she asks, crushing the letter to her chest.

"Always."

"I told you toffs are no good, but you didn't listen."

"Nora, please. I wouldn't let anyone do anything to stand in the way of your work."

Suspicion seems second nature to Nora. I have no idea what she's suffered in her life or why she's turned from people. She hasn't been the easiest person to get to know. While I get the sense that her experiences led her to this path, she's no animal hoarder trying to fill the holes in her own life. She's a genuine advocate and puts all her energy and efforts, the entirety of her focus, into saving the animals no one else gives a damn about.

"I'm sorry I haven't been around." That I've been so caught up in my own life and my own problems and, let's face it, caught up in Oliver. "But if you don't want me to read it, how can I help you? Shall I call Yara instead?"

"No." She thrusts out her hand. "You read it, then tell me it's not from him."

I unfold the crumpled paper. It's from a lawyer, and as I scan the text, my heart sinks to my sneakers.

A notice to . . . what the hell is the law of adverse possession?

Hereby notify . . . application made to the Land Registry. Such security measures as deemed applicable. Continued use for the foreseeable future . . . demonstrating exclusive possession.

"Nora, who owns the land?"

"Levi Blau. But he's been dead for more than twelve years now."

"But you pay rent though, right?"

"I used to, but he died, and no one asked for it after that. I used to put the rent money to one side, just in case, but there didn't seem much point after a while."

"No one reached out to you about it?"

She shakes her head.

"You didn't try to find anything out?"

"How? By séance?"

"I don't know. His wife? His kids?"

"He had a sister who went to live in South America, I think, but she was even older than him. What was I supposed to do?"

Oh, I don't know, maybe try not to stick your head in the sand. I blow out a breath, glancing down at the letter again.

"The question is, who owns it now? Whoever put the fence up says they're applying to the Land Registry office, but that doesn't mean they own it, right?"

"I don't know, but they're not gettin' me out."

"No." Reaching out, I curl my hand over hers. "Not if I can help it."

I leave Nora and go through the motions of my visit—health checks, meds, and I call and schedule a scan for a newly arrived pregnant whippet. Once done, I get out my phone and search the web. It would appear that William the Conqueror, the king of England way back in 1066, has a lot to answer for. Apparently, in this country, you can just proclaim yourself owner of land (or property) that you can prove has been abandoned by its owner. There's a little more to it than that—time frames and hoops to jump through—but that is the crazy crux of it.

It looks like a company by the name of Atterir Limited recently discovered the land the sanctuary stands on is ownerless and claimed it for its own.

Well, Atterir Limited, hold my beer.

Chapter 41
EVIE

Maven Inc. I pull Oliver's business card from my purse, remembering my mild amusement as he handed it to me weeks ago. I called him a relic, asked if he'd kicked and screamed when his company dragged him into the digital age. He smiled and said, if nothing else, it would save me googling him again. He also said I could drop by the office anytime. He probably had a little *afternoon delight* in mind.

I hadn't. *Yet.* Had sex on his desk. And it's not happening on my inaugural visit, I decide, as I pull out my phone to call an Uber from Nora's to take me to swanky Belgravia.

When Nora accused Oliver, my mind said: this land is not worth his time. But shouldn't I have sprung to his defense? Thought something like, *He wouldn't do that* or *He's not so underhanded.* Only I know otherwise. He's never hidden himself from me—I know he's capable, but that doesn't mean I think he's behind the letter or the fence. Not that this makes me feel any better.

I give myself a shake. Mitchell lied to me from the moment we met. At least I know what I'm getting with Oliver. He's not a devil. *Except between the sheets.* I love him despite his faults because that's how love works.

The office building is Georgian, four stories high, with a white stucco facade. If I'd given any thought to what Oliver's office would look like, this is exactly what I would've imagined. No chrome-and-glass tower for him.

I report to the elegant reception desk to hear he's unavailable. Not *not here* but *not available.* I turn away, unsure what the distinction is, and I'm about to call him when I hear my name.

"Eve, hey!" At Fin's exuberance, I swing around. "How are you?"

He crosses the space in long steps, and I turn my head to receive his kiss, laughing as he moves to kiss the other cheek, and we almost bump noses. "Sorry, I forgot. The European way."

"We can shake hands, but it seems a little cold blooded, given the news."

"The news?" I repeat.

"Oliver and you?" he begins in confidential tones, whether because he's concerned about being overheard or for the sake of my blushes, I can't be sure. "The big L-word confessions?"

Not my blushes, then.

"Ohmygod." My words fall in a rush, my cheeks pinking with happiness, not embarrassment. "He told you?"

"Eh." He shrugs. "Not in so many words. Not that I needed to hear them. It's so obvious—he's gone from being regular-level tetchy to next-level asshole, then to sublimely happy."

I laugh as Fin's hand gestures make a jolting map of Oliver's moods.

"Hey, I'm serious. He's suddenly like this transcendental being."

"Have you considered the Oliver that's coming to the office might be an alien . . ."

"He's something else all right. But what are you doing here? Coming or going?" he adds.

"Going. Oliver isn't here. Or isn't available." My eyes move briefly to the reception desk again. "It was just a visit on the fly, nothing arranged."

Fin snaps his fingers. "He's out of the office all day. I remember now. Out of London, in fact."

"Oh." He never mentioned it, but then we don't much talk about his work, though he likes to hear about my day. "No worries. I'll catch him later."

"Got time for a coffee?"

"No, that's fine. You must be busy too."

"*Got time for a coffee?* as a pretext for me teasing out all the juicy details Oliver's not sharing?"

"Nope!" I reply with a laugh.

"So you don't want to hear how he's skipping though the office, singing Disney songs, and sniffing tulips?"

"He is *so* not the skipping type." I eye the flower arrangement on a nearby table. No cheap and cheerful tulips there.

"But wouldn't that be something?" Fin says, rubbing the sandy bristles on his chin.

"Something freaky," I sort of sing under my breath as Fin turns and indicates a nearby door with raised brows.

"That coffee?"

"Sure." I shrug. "Why not?"

"Fancy," I murmur as he closes the door behind us. I'm not sure why I say it, other than that it is. It's not an office—more like an informal meeting room. The room is decorated in muted tones and dark wood, the decor simultaneously masculine and soothing. Abstract art hangs from the walls, a coffee bar taking up the whole back wall.

"How d'you take it?" he asks, standing at the fancy inbuilt coffee machine. "Latte? Cortado? This baby does them all."

"Flat white, please."

I take a seat as Fin pushes a couple of buttons, producing a perfect-looking coffee in an elegant white cup and saucer.

He takes a seat opposite me, crossing one long leg over the other. "What's funny?"

"Just the malicious gleam in your eye."

"Not malicious, more . . ."

"Mischievous?"

"Gotta have something to entertain me," he says, sipping from his cup. "Seriously," he adds, setting it down on the marble coffee table between us. "I'm really happy for both of you."

"Thank you." I'm oddly warmed and more than a little embarrassed as I reach into my purse and pull out my glasses and my phone.

"I don't know what you've done to him, but he's really happy."

His words make me glow. "He makes me happy too."

"That's good. I mean, I had my concerns. Oliver is a complicated man."

"Aren't you all?"

He huffs a laugh. "We're simple creatures, Eve. Essentially big house cats."

"Because you pee on things to mark your territory?"

"Not me," he says as he laughs. "Not sure about Oliver."

"Oliver is *not* a house cat." Fiddling with my glasses, I slide them on.

"We just want to be looked after. Loved on. Maybe get the occasional belly rub."

"That's not a cat. That's a dog."

"*Men are dogs* doesn't have the same ring to it." He grins. "I'm glad you're both happy, though . . ." Fin stands and leans over the coffee table, actually plucking my glasses from my face. Stunned, I let him.

He peers through the lenses, then hands them back. "Just making sure they aren't rose tinted."

"And he's your friend?" I laugh as I fold the arms, then rest them in my lap.

"It's a hard job, but someone has to do it."

Hard and *do* are not two words I intend to discuss with Oliver's friend.

"You know . . ." He pauses as though weighing his words. "I swore he was up to something that night we met you for dinner. I don't know if he told you, but I might've accused him of stringing you along. What with Atherton and all that crap that passed between them and Lucy."

"Yeah, Lucy." I stare down at my cup as I suffer that familiar sinking sensation. He loves me, but all the trouble, the stuff he put me through, was on her behalf. I know she was more than his PA, but I can't bring myself to ask about her. My pride won't let me.

"He told you about her? Wow."

"No," I add quickly. "I know about losing the land at tender and what Mitch did. But, honestly," I say, painting on my *I don't give a fuck* face, "I'm not interested in going over old ground." He shoots me a doubtful look, but I just raise my chin. "He'll tell me if he wants too." No way I'm lowering myself to ask him.

"Oliver swore he'd crush Atherton." Fin pauses, his attention turning inward for a beat. "I can't say I blame him. I guess I worried he was making you part of that."

"I think he's got his closure," I say, lifting my cup, not about to mention our troublesome beginnings. Like Yara says, love has sprung from stranger wells.

"I told him months ago he should've set the guy on his ass. But I might've also suggested the pair hate fuck it out."

"What?" I splutter, worried my coffee might shoot out my nose.

"Shock tactics," he adds with a grin. "I'm glad he's getting over it, though God only knows what he's going to do with that monstrosity."

"Northaby? I kind of love the place."

"I said he'd look at home there, playing lord of the manor."

"He's got the tweed," I add with a giggle.

"I told him he should move out there, give running that giant petting zoo a shot."

"I bet he loved that."

"He replied, 'I'm a businessman, not a philanthropist,'" Fin says, mimicking Oliver's cut glass tones. "Then he shot me down when I tried to turn the conversation to breeding."

"Oh my gosh. I am *not* touching that."

"You should persuade him."

"No way. As long as the animals aren't destined for some exotic-animal trade, I'm happy for him."

"Oliver's a lot of things, but I know he wouldn't do that. Think about it, though. Access to your very own safari park."

"Actually, it's animals I came to speak to Oliver about."

"Oh?"

"Well, I wanted to pick his brains about the sanctuary I volunteer at."

"Will I do? I'm on my fifth coffee of the day, so I guess now is as good a time as any."

"Do you happen to know how I can trace the owner of a company in England?"

"Depends. What kind of company is it?"

"A limited company, I think." Slipping on my glasses again, I flip over my phone and bring the touchscreen to life. "Atterir Limited is its name."

"You can find the owner of a limited company easy enough." Stretching out his long legs, he pulls out his own phone. A few taps on the screen, then he rounds the low table to sit next to me. "So, this government website makes the names of limited companies available. And this company, Atterir—do I have it spelled right?"

I glance down and nod. "Yes."

"Well, its owner is listed as another company," he says, tapping a little more. "And it looks like *that* company is registered outside of the UK in an offshore jurisdiction."

"Can you tell who owns that company?"

He gives a quick shake of his head. "The second company is registered in the Marshall Islands. Companies there aren't required to disclose their shareholders. It's basically an offshore haven for shell companies. Mind telling me what this is about?"

So I tell him about Nora and the new fencing and how distressed she is. "It seems kind of ridiculous that there's an ancient law still in force that allows people to just claim land."

"That's not strictly how it works. The land must have been abandoned and due diligence undertaken to make sure there are no other claimants. And even then, it takes years."

"Nora thinks the owners are all dead. What would that mean, do you think?"

"She needs to know, not just surmise. That's what this company will be doing in the meantime—finding out. I guess Nora could also claim it's not abandoned, given she's maintained the land for those years."

"She could do this herself? Get in before whoever this is? I mean, she fenced it first."

"It's possible. Why don't you leave this with me, and I'll do a little digging."

"You wouldn't mind?"

"Of course not."

"My next idea was to engage a lawyer, so yeah." I draw my shoulders up. I guess I wasn't expecting his help. "I'd appreciate it."

"Let me see if I can trace the company, then find out what Nora's legal standing is."

"Thank you so much, Fin."

"Hey, what are friends for?"

"In my experience, big knickers and inappropriate text messages." I bark out a laugh. "Sorry, I was just thinking of my friend, Yara."

"Should I be buying Oliver underwear?"

"He'd just *love* that."

"No, he wouldn't. But I think I'd like to be introduced to Yara, Eve's friend."

"That is not happening," I say, sliding my phone away. "She's looking for a husband."

"Doesn't mean she wouldn't enjoy a good time while she waits. Is she pretty?"

"She's pretty fierce."

"My favorite kind."

"Like a flavor of milkshake?" I say in the vein of *Don't you dare.*

"Eve, come on. I don't have a date for Northaby's charity ball."

"Take Matt," I say, laughing as I swing my purse onto my shoulder. Yara would probably ask if his dick is decked in diamonds. Maybe ask for visual proof. Seriously though, I don't know Fin well enough to get involved, and there are the aunties to consider. If he didn't treat her right, he'd likely find himself impaled on one of the Gulabi Gang's sticks.

"Come on, what do you say?"

I pat his arm like an elderly aunt. "Honestly, Fin. I don't think you could keep up with her."

Chapter 42
EVIE

A Little Bird Told Us . . .

Our billionaire London beau was seen at a Surrey safari park, but not to look at the monkeys. He was at Northaby House with the earl, who recently put the whole shebang up for sale. Coincidence or not?

This Little Bird wonders if a safari park might be a veterinarian's perfect wedding gift . . .

A Little Bird only hopes, on the big day, they're not planning on releasing a cage full of lions in the place of butterflies!

◆　◆　◆

"And here's Eve Fairfax!" I make a fist around my invisible micro-phone as I interview my pretend red-carpet self. *"Who are you wear-ing tonight, Eve?"*

"Oscar de la Renta." I begin to bounce on the spot as, from across the room, Oliver gives a slow round of applause.

"Oscar de la Renta and every man's eyes." The look in his eyes is borderline predatory.

"You like?" I give in to a delicious little shiver. My dress is a rental, but I'll never tell. Who has twelve thousand dollars to spend on a dress they'll wear only once? *Oliver, I guess.* But we've already been down this path. I recently lamented losing my wedding shoes again, because I totally could've dyed them to match this beauty. Instead, I picked up an inexpensive pair of gold strappy heels and a tiny matching wallet on a chain from a local consignment store. But the dress is a piece of luxury. A gold-sheath minidress under a festooning of black tulle, adorned by embroidered golden leaves.

"I like *you* in it," Oliver says, his legs eating up the space between us. "You look amazing." I love how he gives his head a little shake, like I've stunned him.

"I told you I could dress myself." I try his brow move on for size, but I can only make mine arch together. I probably look less enigmatic and more like Bert. *From Bert and Ernie.* "I can also dress you." My gaze flickers over him, full of suggestion, not that he needs the help.

"I prefer it when you undress me. Leather pants really aren't my thing."

"Leather pants *love* you," I whisper, cupping his smoothly shaven cheek, almost anticipating the brush of bristles later. I slide my hand over his satin lapel, not shawl-collared tonight but pointed. His jacket is double breasted and has a classic feel about it.

"I have something for you, and I'm so pleased to say I think it'll work."

"Oliver . . ." My body language turns to that of an embarrassed teen as he moves to the table behind him, sliding a shiny black box from it. "You shouldn't have," I whisper as he balances it on his palms. "But can I tell you the truth?" My gaze lifts, and he nods. "I'm touched that you have, no matter what this is."

"Even if it's that leather mask with a pink ball gag?"

"You went back to the thrift store!"

His laughter is so deliciously deep it almost resonates through me. "I told you thrifting is addictive," I add.

But I can breathe easy, because this is not a piece of jewelry. The box is way too big. Plus, it's made from heavy embossed card. It's not that I don't want jewelry; it's more that I'm not comfortable with receiving expensive gifts. I'm pretty sure he's gathered this by now.

"The only thing I'm addicted to is you."

"I knew it all along. You were never going to have me deported." He slides me an amused look. "You love me *and* my ridiculousness."

"Are you going to open it?"

"Yes!" My answer is an excited hiss as I press my hands to the sides of the box and shimmy the lid off. There's another box inside. Smaller. Black again. "Is this going to be a Matryoshka doll joke? Box after box after box, and a pack of Tic Tacs in the last one?"

"Yes, because I'm evidently that much fun."

"I think you are," I murmur, sliding the lid under my arm before reaching in. My fingers brush the tactile feel of velvet, and suddenly, I know. I know, and I don't care as excitement wells inside me.

"Let me help."

I throw the cardboard lid behind me, and Oliver discards the rest, holding out the black case like an offering. The velvet has worn bald in places, but that makes this feel all the more special. *Reused. Reloved.* Somehow, Oliver has picked up on this.

I press my thumb to the tiny brass button. The lid creaks open, and I gasp.

"Oliver." I look up to find him smiling down at me. Meanwhile, my eyes must be a little dusty, because my vision is suddenly hazy.

"Do you like it?"

"It's a tiara," I whisper, awestruck. Bandeau style—that much I remember from our trip to the fancy jewelers. It sparkles so brightly, and though quite dainty in style, those are such a lot of diamonds.

"So it is." His mouth hitches. "It's Victorian. An heirloom piece, I'm told. I saw it, and I just thought, that belongs on Eve's lovely head."

Stop before I explode with pleasure.

"It looks like flowers." The setting is a row of graduating *V* shapes that look like fronds. Tiny stones sit at the base, each frond holding a bigger, much more stunning stone. *But still delicate, like a flower bud.* I touch my fingertips to the cool, glittering stones.

These can't be diamonds, can they?

"Of course they are."

"I didn't mean to say that out loud. But real diamonds?" My gaze lifts again, my brow furrowed with worry this time.

"Almost four hundred of them, a mixture of old and rose cut. It also converts to a necklace, which is quite a statement piece for all its daintiness. Want to know how many carats?"

"Dozens, I'm guessing," I say, shaking my head. The eighty-thousand-pound ring is already too much.

"Let's say several dozens."

"But why?"

"Because I saw how much fun you had at Garrard. I wanted to see you smile like that again. And also, because this is the kind of gift no one else can ever give you. Well, apart from Mandy."

"Mandy is not going to give me a tiara."

"He's enamored enough. You do know he was called Randy Mandy in his younger years."

"That's so funny. I love that for him."

"But not so much for his chambermaids, I'm sure."

"He's too much of a gentleman. But, Oliver, I can't take this from you. It's too much."

"Nothing is too much for you. Not from me. Especially when I have plans of seeing you wear it and nothing else."

I press my hand to my hip as I answer. "Well, there he is. Regular-programming Oliver."

"The one you love."

"I kind of like the one who buys me tiaras too," I answer shyly. "And the one who loves to be the big spoon to my little spoon. I also like the one who feeds me chocolate for breakfast. But the Oliver I love best is the one I have right here."

His hand snakes around my back, and he kisses me like he doesn't want to let go, but all I can think is *Don't drop my damn tiara!* Kiss broken, I make my way to the mirror, and Oliver helps me attach this loveliness to my head.

"I had the jeweler put the velvet band on to match the color of your hair—no easy feat, given its brilliance."

"If you ever get tired of property, you could always consider a career in hairdressing," I say to our reflections as he fits the final pin. "Or a lady's maid."

He pauses, his eyes meeting mine in the mirror. "Doesn't that mean I'd get to help you from your clothes every night?"

"Like you don't already."

"Tonight, I'll leave the tiara." From behind, he presses his lips to my neck. My breath quickens as my thoughts blur, everything inside me turning molten at the touch. "There, the lily is gilded."

I inhale shakily as his hand slips down my shoulder. I look like a princess. *Cinders in her borrowed dress.* "It's beautiful."

"Not quite as beautiful as you." His voice is rough as his hands slide around my waist. "I don't think I've ever thanked you for helping me get to this point."

"Northaby?"

"With everything. I wasn't joking when I said you were the best thing to fall into my lap this year. I just didn't realize at the time how lucky that made me." My heart fills, but he's not done. "I know we had a less than promising start, but I can't wait to see what life brings us."

"Me too." I cover my arm with his, and his smile spreads sweet and slow like spilled honey.

"We should probably leave." Yet his arms tighten. "I'm sure your second-most-ardent admirer is pining for the sight of you."

"Bo?"

"That dog loves no one but himself." He's out for a walk right now with one of the porters. They're going to keep him company tonight when we're out charity *ballin'*. "You know I mean Mandy."

"Too funny," I say as he takes my hand.

"Who's laughing?"

I turn to the back window, still marveling as Ted maneuvers the Bentley through Northaby's entrance. "I love how it's like a mini Arc de Triomphe." I turn back as the road opens up to the miles-long driveway, flanked by rolling green lawns and majestic trees. And not a lion in sight. "I'll get to see the animals tonight, right?"

"Was it not enough that the monkeys almost destroyed Mandy's Land Rover last time?"

"They were rhesus macaques, and Mandy's Land Rover is built like a tank." That's not to say the other cars there that day fared so well. The macaques chewed on aerials, pulled off windshield wipers, and chewed anything they could snatch.

"I'm afraid alcohol and beasts tend not to be a good mix. Add in a safari park full of wild animals, and it'd be a health and safety nightmare."

"Har. *Har.*"

"But I have seen the keepers walking the grounds with some of the less fearsome animals at events before."

With Lucy, I'll bet. The thought curdles my mood like sour milk.

"What kind of animals?" I ask, trying for an upbeat tone.

"I think I saw koalas last time. Snakes. And I'm sure there was a baby alligator. Yes, someone made a comment about it being the ideal handbag. Mandy wasn't very pleased. In fact, I'd never seen him so fierce."

This warms my soul. "Mandy is on my list of favorite people."

"Long list?"

"Just four people. Don't worry, I am considering adding you to it."

Oliver laughs.

As we draw closer to the house, the topography changes to reveal a lake and a quaint-looking boathouse. Beyond, straight lines of manicured hedging hints at a formal garden setting. Ted turns the corner, and we get to view the house from another aspect. Tall, the buttery stone gleams in the setting sun.

"What is it?" Oliver turns. Maybe I gasped in surprise or delight.

"We didn't come this way before."

"No, we went to the other entrance."

"I just realized you're buying a Pemberley." In this light, at this moment, Northaby House looks like something out of a Jane Austen novel—made for TV!

"I'm buying a Northaby," he says with an amused shake of his head.

"Shut up!" I sound almost offended. "A safari park *and* Pemberley? It's good for you we met before I got to know Mandy."

He looks at me like I'm the funniest thing ever. He obviously doesn't know that bitches *love* a Pemberley.

◆ ◆ ◆

Ted joins the queue of fancy cars waiting to reach the red-carpeted entrance. Honestly, when your house looks like this, a red carpet is overkill. Not that it stops me from feeling like a princess as the door is opened for me by a for-real, live, liveried footman.

And the house. Oh, my gosh. Mandy was so patient with me at the palace, but my first time here, I saw how mundane being there must've felt to him. Like wandering around his kitchen in his slippers. Northaby is so swanky, I'd totally wear my tiara to breakfast if I lived here.

"At the risk of repeating myself," I murmur, leaning into Oliver. "Wow. Wow. Wow."

"You like the place, don't you?"

"Who wouldn't?" I answer, taking it all in. "Imagine living in a house so grand, you have a staircase that goes in two directions but leads to the same place."

"Imperial."

"It must feel it," I agree with a nod.

"No." Oliver's lips twitch. "That's what it's called. An imperial staircase."

"It's what I call *over the top*. Do you think Mandy would mind if I dashed up there so I could swan my way down? I have the dress for it." I demonstrate a little swing of my hips, which Oliver seems to appreciate.

"You'd have to ask him."

It's cordoned off with a velvet rope, so I decide to wait.

"It's just so . . . historic," I say, trying not to look like a hick as I stare at the paneling, the rococo ceiling, and that chandelier.

We're served champagne, and we begin to mingle, Oliver stopping to exchange small talk with people here and there. I flush with pleasure as he introduces me as his girlfriend, his better half, and once simply as "the woman I love."

Swoon!

Given that I've already seen bits of the place, I'm happy to pay attention to the canapés. Grilled scallops with lobster sauce and herb-crusted tuna on seaweed. *Mm-mm!* I make it my mission to sample at least one of everything on the passing sweet trays too. *Tarte au citron, tiny brownies, and lavender-and-lemon meringue. Just delicious!*

It isn't long before Mandy finds us, looking very dapper in a tuxedo jacket of claret-colored velvet.

"Don't you look handsome." I try very hard not to let Oliver catch my eye, as I recently threatened him with a red crushed-velvet jacket and matching bow tie. But at least Mandy isn't wearing leather pants.

Oof. Quick, someone hand me the brain bleach.

"Likewise, my dear. Your beauty is outstanding." Lifting my hand, he presses a kiss to the back of it.

"Mortimer," Oliver playfully chastises, lifting it away. "Stop trying to steal my girl with your flattery." My skin flushes with pleasure. It's such a tiny reference, but it feels like a huge statement.

"Flattery is all I have left these days, old boy." He glances at the pretty ceiling for effect. "Oh, but it's grand getting old."

"Better than the alternative," I offer.

"Yes, that's true. I'm not ready to push up daisies yet." He hooks his elbow out. "Care to allow an old man to steal you for a while?" He looks to Oliver. "I'll have her back before the auction starts. Why don't you go and spend some of that money of yours?"

"Subtlety isn't your strong point, my lord."

"Can't take it with you," I put in, my hand lifting unconsciously to my tiara. "But don't buy anything for me."

"My dear," Mandy chastises, "that's a gentleman's prerogative. Indeed, some would say it's the only thing he's good for."

"Oliver has his uses," I demur, instantly aware of how that might be taken, and a blush creeps up my neck.

I slip my arm into Mandy's as Oliver politely coughs.

We commence our grand tour—it's not my first, but I don't care. I could spend a year wandering the halls and still not know the place. We stroll through elegant drawing rooms filled with landscape art and portraits, a long saloon (with tapestries), an octagonal one (with ornate plaster and blue silk walls), an immense library, and parlors for every occasion. And everywhere we tread, Mandy has a wealth of information to share.

"This part of the house was modernized in the Palladian style in 1630 by Inigo Jones."

"So modern."

"And in the following century, the gardens were redesigned by the famed Capability Brown."

"Mandy, are you making up people's names just to impress me?"

"Silly girl." This earns me a slap to the wrist and a chastising *tsk*. "Of course you're impressed."

"The origins of the house go back farther than that, right?"

"Four centuries," he confirms as we step out onto the terrace through a set of outsize French doors.

"I am so beyond impressed. Not everyone has a safari park in their backyard. Are those kangaroos in the distance?" I squint through the oncoming darkness.

"We do have them, wallabies, too, but no. The marsupials should be in their enclosure. Unless they've escaped. Though I hope not. The bucks have a lethal kick, and I could do without being sued this evening."

In the cooling air, we stand in silence for a beat before Mandy speaks.

"Not everyone would be suited to a safari park in their back-yard, as you say, but I believe it would you."

I smile his way. "Sadly, I don't have the cash."

"But you know someone who does," he says softly.

Someone who has trouble sharing his space with a dog. Though Oliver objects mainly to sharing pillow space with Bo. *Pillow-butt space?*

"Someone who is very in love with you."

I glance his way, wondering where he's going with this. "You're sure I can't see the tigers?"

"Another day." He pats my hand fondly. "Summer is at an end, and the evening is already too dark to be wandering about in a safari park. Unless you want to be dinner."

"Eat dinner? Yes. Be dinner? Not so much."

"My lord." We both turn to the creak of a door and a man's voice from inside. "I'm sorry to intrude, but could you spare a moment?"

"Would you excuse me, Eve?"

"Of course. But maybe you could show me the way back to the great hall? It's that or send out a search party after I get lost."

Mandy laughs. "You'll get used to it." *Not sure I'll need to, but okay.* "The simplest way is to stay outside and to walk along the terrace here. That will lead you to the front of the house, and then the hall."

"Just remember what I said about the search party," I call as Mandy and his aide disappear through the door.

"No bears," I whisper, my heels crunching over the red, shiny gravel. "Silly me. I never once asked about wolves."

But it turns out it isn't either of those creatures I should be worried about.

Chapter 43
EVIE

"Ow, dammit!" Spike heels and crunchy gravel are a recipe for a rolled ankle or a skinned knee, I decide, as I clutch the edge of a stone urn for the second time in as many minutes. As my phone begins to ring, I slip it out from my purse, half expecting it to be Oliver wondering where I am.

"Hello." The line crackles, so I repeat my greeting. "Hello?"

"It's him!" The words burst down the line. "I told you it was him—he did this to me."

"Nora? Are you okay?" The line hisses ominously again. I really wish she'd get a better phone. I might have to buy her one and disguise it as my old one. "Hello?"

"I said it's him!" Her voice is so shrill, I pull the phone away from my ear with a wince. "I told you he was up to no good, sneaking around the place, taking pictures."

My heart sinks, my will along with it. "We've been over this, Nora." After the fence went up, I explained that I had a friend looking into things. I told her not to worry, and I meant it, because I'll fight tooth and nail for her. "Oliver doesn't own the company who put that fence up." The company name didn't register with Fin as familiar. Besides, Oliver wouldn't do that. *I hope.* Things have just been busy, and that's why I hadn't mentioned it to him. "We'll know who's responsible soon."

"I know it's him, and whatever that fifty grand was for, I hope it was worth it."

She got the money? Strange that he never mentioned it, that he didn't wait until the sale was complete. But I guess there's no point in denying it now.

"Nora, please. Listen to yourself. It was a gift, not a conspiracy." Wouldn't I have gotten the fifty grand in that case? Maybe the worry of the money has pushed her over the edge. Maybe I should call Yara.

"I don't want his filthy money!"

"Then take that up with him," I say, stalling. She deserves it, and I'd do it again—I'd do it for me, and I'd do it for her. I'd do it for Oliver. Haven't we all benefited from those strange beginnings?

"Talk to him when he's trying to get me shut down? Are you having a fucking laugh?"

I am so very far from laughing. I'm more like exhausted with this.

"You're not getting closed down." My tone is sunnier than I feel. "Like I said, I've got a friend looking into it."

"Yeah, nice friends you've got," she jeers. "Not sure I'd accept their help."

This is getting ridiculous. "Listen, Nora, I haven't got long. Can we talk about this tomorrow?"

"Are your ears painted on? We can't talk about this tomorrow because everything is *not* all right. That is what I'm trying to tell you. That . . . that *man*. Strutting around like the cock of the walk, well he can take a running jump if he thinks he's kicking me and my dogs out of this place. I'll do for him! You see if I don't."

"Then who'll look after the sanctuary?" I ask evenly, wondering if she's in the middle of a mental break. "Let me call Yara, sweetie.

I can't come around right now." She sounds so distressed, maybe I can swing by later, when we're done here. Leave early, maybe?

"You can't come 'round here no more," she says, the words spilling with force. "Not when you're with the enemy."

This seems worse than I thought. Should I call an ambulance?

"You remember Duggan?" she demands.

"The skinny kid with the bad skin?" He'd recently been sent to help as part of a community service order or something.

"That's him. He hacked the school's computer, that's why they sent him here. I saw him yesterday, told him about the fences. He said he'd help me look into it."

"Nora, that kid is fourteen. Please don't say you encouraged him to break the law."

"You're not listening. He said he'd help, and he did." The accusation stings. "And what he's found out doesn't surprise me one bit because that . . . that bastard you're with is at the end of the daisy chain of fucking companies, and he's trying to steal this place from under my feet!"

"Nora, that's not true." It can't be.

"I'll go to the council—the newspapers. You see if I don't! I'll tell them about the man who gave me fifty grand for God knows what, and I'll tell them that *you* brought him 'ere."

I know she's scared, but this is really too much.

"That is unfair, Nora. I've only ever helped you. Oliver isn't behind this." He can't be. *Can he? Not after everything we've been through.*

"I knew she wouldn't believe me." Nora's words turn distant, like she's moved her mouth from the phone to speak to someone else.

"Is Duggan there with you?"

"He is," she retorts pointedly.

I take a deep, calming breath and push away her angry vibe. "Let me speak to him."

"No, I won't. But he says he'll send you a screen thingy with the proof."

"Okay, whatever." This is ridiculous. I'm tired, and I don't want to believe this, yet there's a tiny part of me that says I've been in this place before. Like the flicker of a flame, I know it's there. That I should heed it. But I know it might hurt.

"Then you'll see," Nora states with satisfaction.

"Yeah, I guess I will."

As an autumnal breeze picks up, I shiver and rub my arms. The sensible thing would be to move indoors, but I refuse to take this . . . *whatever* inside the house. I need to know what she's talking about before I see Oliver, because I don't have what you might call a workable poker face. I do a pretty good line in *Drop dead* and an excellent *Go fuck yourself* when I'm feeling it. But what I'm feeling right now is uneasiness.

I stare at my phone again, swiping my thumb across the screen. If Nora's little juvie pal has been lying to her, I will, in her words, do for him—I'll throw him to the macaques and let them teach him some fucking manners!

His text doesn't arrive after five minutes, so I make the decision to take my gooseflesh inside and call her back, when the weight of a jacket suddenly drops onto my shoulders.

I'm far from thrilled.

"Give me a break," I mutter, recognizing the scent of infidelity. *It could easily be the name of his cologne.*

"I remember the first time I slid my jacket onto your shoulders," Mitchell says. "Remember? We were coming back from—"

"What do you want, Mitchell?" Memory lane isn't a place I'm visiting with him.

"You weren't always so prickly." His words are softer than his expression.

"Wish I could say the same for you," I mutter, yanking at the fabric and thrusting his jacket back at him. "Wait. Sorry. I just confused *prickly* with *prick*."

"Evie." He shakes his head slowly, as though I've said something funny. His smile used to make me feel noticed. Now it makes me feel nauseous.

"Go away, Mitchell. I have nothing nice to say to you." Understatement of the year. I'd rather wrestle a tiger with catnip tied to my nipples than have any kind of discourse with him.

He catches my arm as I make to brush past him. I flinch, hating that tiny tell.

"Evie, please."

"Let go of me," I grate out, relieved when his hand retracts.

"I'm sorry about last time, at the palace. I'd been drinking, and I was just so angry. I'm not proud of what I said or did."

I blink, momentarily stunned. This isn't the direction I was expecting him to take, not that I accept his apology. He can stick it where the sun doesn't shine.

"I should've told you about the business, about the building being mine."

I huff an unhappy laugh at where he chooses to start.

"I just wanted to give you the chance to like me for me." His words fall quickly, like a train speeding up. "But then you said all that shit about wealth, so, well, I didn't say."

What the hell? "As if that's a valid excuse, or even the most hurtful thing you've done."

"No, but it's where it all started."

"Yeah, your line of fuckups is pretty long."

"I'm sorry I didn't treat you the way you deserved. I really loved—"

"*No.*" I point my finger in his face, and it takes everything within me not to poke it right in his eye. "I don't want your apology. We were getting married, Mitch! Making promises, all the while you were lying, screwing women behind my back."

"But you weren't living in London when it started."

I actually laugh. "Are you for real?"

"That didn't come out the way I meant it to."

"No shit. Maybe you should've written it down. It might've helped to stick to a script."

"What?"

"This is all such bullshit. But I really don't care anymore." All things considered, I think I'm being quite restrained. I haven't once mentioned peanut butter, his EpiPen, or the wooden onesie I sometimes dream of putting him in. "What you did was lowest of the low."

"No, not the lowest." The words are expelled on a burst of ugly laughter. "Not by a fucking mile. I know I was wrong. I screwed up—didn't tell you the truth."

"Stop. I don't care!"

"Evie, fucking Deubel?" He shoves his hand violently through his hair. "I'm nowhere near as bad as *him*."

What is it with this pair?

"I'm leaving." Done with this. I push past him—properly this time, hating how my bare shoulder brushes against him.

"What did he tell you about me and Lucy?"

"Urgh." With a harsh shake of my head, I keep moving. It always comes back to frickin' Lucy!

"But I bet he didn't tell you his part—I know he didn't say who she was."

Every atom of my being revolts at his words. I know I should push on, that no good can come from hearing this, yet my steps begin to slow, like I can't help myself.

"Spit it out," I demand, canting my head over my shoulder. "What are you trying to tell me? Did she die?" Could this be why Oliver is so cut up?

In the darkness, Mitchell shakes his head. "No, she didn't. Not that she didn't try."

"How do you *try* to die?" I throw my arm out in a careless gesture as I turn, my brain catching up a split second too late. "You're full of shit," I say, my blood turning icy cold as I pivot away.

"I fucked her, and I shouldn't have. I lied to her. Pretended I was into her more than I was. I got her to tell me about his business, then I screwed him over, snatched the land out from under him. It was just business."

"Unbelievable," I whisper, horrified anew. *I almost married this man.*

"I was wrong, and I own up to that, but don't tell me he's done the same. I don't know how he can sleep at night."

"Go away, Mitch," I yell, but the gravel behind me crunches anyway.

"He told her he'd never forgive her." His hand grips my shoulder, and he spins me to face him. "He said things he couldn't take back. I made her cry, but his rejection made her want to die."

But that's not how a mental break works. Besides: "You can't even admit your own part in it."

"Because it wasn't my fault!"

I blink, disbelief echoing through me. Whatever Oliver did, maybe he pegged Mitch right. Maybe he is a narcissist.

"I wasn't meant to look out for her—she's not my fucking sister."

Like a clunk of gears, everything suddenly drops into place. Lucy wasn't just his employee. "My God. *His sister?* No wonder he hates you."

"Not as much as he hates himself. I might've fucked her, but he was the one who fucked her over."

I turn away. I'm not cold anymore. I'm numb but for the swirl of sickness in my belly. *Why didn't Oliver tell me?*

"He disowned his own sister," he calls after me, his poison continuing to pour out. "Sent her packing because she made a mistake. Because she had a relationship with me behind his back."

I spin around to face him. "His back? What about mine?" A slight overlap, so Mitch had said last time. But this right here is a different tack, so what does he hope to achieve this time around? Make me run from Oliver like I ran from him? A huff leaves my throat. This isn't the same. It hurts that Oliver didn't tell me—that maybe he felt he couldn't trust me at one point. Maybe it hurts him to remember. Whatever the reason, we'll talk it over. *Because his heart chooses mine.*

"It just sort of happened."

My laughter rings through the night air. "Give me a break. You planned it. Just like you planned to use me. You strung us both along—her for some land, me for this fucking house!" I shout, glancing up at the ancient stone. This place, I bet it's witnessed some scenes over its long years, but nothing as bizarre as this.

"Yeah, for this house—the one you're lying for right now. Why, Evie? Why him?"

"Make up your mind. Last time, you accused me of sleeping with him while planning our marriage. Which is it, huh?"

"I don't fucking know!" he yells. "I can't make it out, but what I do know is I'm not the one who drove his sister to try to kill herself."

"Nothing is ever your fault, is it?"

413

"It's not like I gave her the pills!"

As I reach the door, I push my way inside the grand hall, not caring about the crush of people or whether Mitchell follows me.

How can he not see his part in this? He treated me like he treated Lucy. When I turned to Oliver on our wedding day, *he* helped me when he could've kicked me out of the car! *I* pushed at the hotel elevator when he would have left me alone.

He must've thought I deserved it.

I'm no longer jealous of Lucy. It's no comfort when I feel hurt, when I see this for what it is. What happened with his sister must've crushed him, whether he sent her away or not. But people who try to end their own lives aren't in their right state of mind—it's called a crisis for a reason. Oliver isn't to blame. *Except maybe in his own mind.* I have to find him—tell him I know. That I understand, and that it changes nothing.

My phone vibrates, and I look down, realizing it's still in my hand. The number is unfamiliar but brings my mind back to Nora. My stomach coils tightly as I make my way to the side of the room to open it. I thought the last few minutes were a lot to take in, to process, but this makes my head *hurt*. Makes my heart feel chilled. Screenshot after screenshot, some with notes scrawled in a childish hand, others with roughly drawn arrows and highlighted text.

As the party swirls on around me, as people drink, and eat, and laugh, I stare at my phone until I'm sure of what I'm seeing. A web of offshore holding companies with assets valued at over three hundred million, largely in real estate, ultimately own Atterir Limited. *The same company who fenced off Nora's place.* From reams of documents, with lawyers, accountants, and corporate entities named, to what looks like information pulled from a data leak, I find the answer I most dread. The ultimate owner's name.

No. *No.*

This isn't the man my heart softened for.

Chapter 44
EVIE

Am I the stupidest woman in the world?

Could he just not help himself? I can't believe it—I want to believe *none* of it, to put it down to coincidence and the ramblings of a teenage would-be anarchist.

My stomach knots as I set out to find Oliver. I need to hear him deny it, to listen as he explains why he didn't tell me about Lucy. I need to hear that he loves me, that this isn't some sick kind of payback.

As I move from room to room, my skin feels as though it's burning, yet my blood feels like ice water as it pumps through my veins. There's no sign of him in the ballroom, or any of the places where people gather. In the long gallery, outsize portraits of Mandy's ancestors witness me freeze.

"A little bird says," a woman's voice trills.

I don't recognize the plummy accent, but my stomach still sinks. *A journalist?*

"Who'd bid on that?" asks a second female voice.

My gaze shifts left, and I take in the tables running along the wall; this is where the silent auction is being held. I edge my way to the nearest lot as though interested, though my aim is to listen in. A plastic stand holds the details of one of the auction lots, blank tickets scattered across the table to detail bids for . . . *a balloon ride over Northaby*. I move to the end of the table, edging closer to the voices as I pretend to consider bidding on an ugly painting this time.

"Haven't you been keeping abreast of the news?" the first voice demands.

"That thing in Whitehall?"

"No one is interested in the government, Caro. I'm talking about the feud between Oliver Deubel and that slice of naughty, Mitchell Atherton. His love rival." She draws the latter out salaciously, not giving a damn who might be listening. "It's all been rather scandalous, not that I usually follow such things."

"No, of course not." Her companion doesn't sound convinced or much interested.

"A love triangle, I gather."

I'm pleased someone is enjoying my drama-filled existence.

"Who's the lucky girl?"

"Screw her! It's the other two I'm interested in. Oliver especially."

"Oliver . . ." The second woman draws out his name as though rifling through a mental Rolodex. "Oh! That wicked-looking dark-haired beast? The one with the eyes!"

Yes, bitch, he has two of them.

"Yes, that's the one. He looks like he could break a girl in two."

"And make you say thank you."

I turn my head, but I can't see who's speaking for a stupid statue and the crowd of people milling around in their stupid evening wear.

"But what has a bird to do with it?"

The first woman tsks. "Just look at lot sixty-eight."

"'Tea at Claridge's and then a night in the West End with the Earl of Bellsand.'"

"God, not that one."

Sounds like a good time to me.

"It must've been lot sixty-nine," she adds with a smutty snicker. "A Little Bird is the awful gossip column I've been following. It's been bleating on about him being head over heels in love with some American vet. It sounds as though they've been tweeting up the wrong tree, so to speak, because take a look what's on offer."

"A night in London with Oliver Deubel," the other woman says. "Drinks, dinner, and an evening in his hotel."

"If that's not an invitation to fuck him, I don't know what is." The pair cackle like witches over a cage full of chubby kids.

I drop my head, muttering a litany of insults under my breath. But I have to see this for myself. As I edge closer to the table, the PA system squeals, and I wince.

"My lords, ladies, and gentlemen," Mandy's voice booms. "And the rest of the riffraff at the back." The crowd chuckles. "Thank you for taking time from your busy schedules to grace us with your presence. If you could just stick around long enough so we can relieve you of the contents of your wallets, that will make me, and my menagerie, very happy." More laughter, but I can't look as I edge my way to the next table, slipping around the statue. "It's all for a good cause. Northaby's animal kingdom, of course." A round of applause. Then, "And I have some very, very exciting news about the safari park's future coming soon."

I block it all out. I feel bad enough about my lies of omission, but I suddenly feel more than complicit. *Did I try my best, or did I just not do enough?* Those poor animals. Will Oliver screw them over too?

"Excuse me," I whisper, moving against the tide of guests heading away from the makeshift stage. "I just need . . ."

No, not this. Oliver does have an entry in the silent auction. *He is the entry.*

A heavy weight drops to my chest, the discomfort somehow appropriate. It reminds me to breathe, at least, because this is too much. What's real and what isn't? It's hard to tell, because each breath is a trial, each thought a memory. A truth. An untruth. Oliver kept telling me he was no good. Did I ever really believe him? Should I believe him now?

". . . introduce my special guest, our kind patron of the evening, Oliver Deubel."

Mandy's voice pulls me back to the moment, to applause and a crowd that suffocates.

"Good evening."

My stomach turns over at the sound of Oliver's deep tenor.

"If I could beg your indulgence for a moment. Eve?" His gaze skims the crowd, but I don't respond. *I can't.* "I know she's in here. I'm sure I saw her tiara sparkling."

Laughter swirls around me as I become aware once more of the gold and diamonds on my head. A gift so very special, though not because of its value—its dollar cost—or even its provenance. But because I thought he understood me.

"Eve Fairfax, could you make your way to the stage, my darling?"

The crowd starts to shift, one or two people looking in my direction. People he introduced me to earlier, I realize.

So, maybe this is where I get the booby prize. *The award for most gullible goes to Evie Fairfax.* Maybe this was his endgame all along. One final humiliation before he gets what he wants and puts the whole matter to rest. Only, he doesn't look like a man up to his neck in nefarious intrigues as his gaze finds mine. And Mandy is looking on with such fondness.

Is this . . . no. He can't be about to . . .

A realization drops inside me like a bomb.

He's going to propose.

I want to believe the events of tonight are one jumbled mis-understanding. That maybe he kept Lucy from me out of some misplaced sense of responsibility, that Duggan is an idiot, that the auction entry is someone's idea of a sick joke. And the way he's looking at me, I could believe all that and more. But this feels wrong. Too much like another manipulation.

No more lies. No more power games. No more railroading. These were what we agreed.

Part of me wants to heed the warning and run, but the other part is both sickened and stirred as I find myself at the base of the metal steps. As I hear the *clink, clack* of my heels. Feel eyes burning holes in the back of my fancy dress.

Just like last time.

I don't fit in here. I never did. I should've remembered my mantra. The rich care for nothing but themselves. Yet my leaden feet still cross the stage, and I allow Oliver's arm to slide around my waist. He presses a kiss to my cheek and whispers a soft greeting I can barely make sense of. His arm tightens as he turns to the audi-ence, their faces obscured by the glittering chandeliers.

"As Mandy says, there's to be an important announcement con-cerning Northaby and its animal kingdom. But first I'd like to take this opportunity to . . . well, it's rather personal, but something I find I want to shout from the rooftops. Short of that, you lot will just have to do."

How can he understand me if . . . How can he do this?

Time slows as he turns to me, the audience sucked away as though by a sudden vacuum. A look crosses his face, and for a moment, I'm in Garrard, on that damn sofa again, my heart lifting as my brain cells shift into negative numbers.

"Eve," he says huskily, as his hand slides into his jacket pocket. He pulls out a tiny velvet box, the light catching its tiny golden clasp.

"I almost did this a few weeks ago. I'm not sure if you noticed." Uncertainty flickers in his expression, but it's so fleeting, it might be a trick of the light. "I saw before me the first in a lifetime of moments—shared laughter, loving, living. Hand in hand. And then I chickened out."

Canned laughter. A hoot of encouragement. My chest feels hollow, my heart pounding like the warning beat of a drum. He moves to open the box.

Chocolate and peanut butter, umbrellas held over my head in the rain. His jacket over my shoulders, his strong arms wrapped around my waist. Tiara dress-ups and thrift shopping for tight leather pants.

I open my mouth to say something, but nothing comes out.

I tried to fight my feelings, didn't I? I think, as a sense of something washes over me. It's not déjà vu. At least, not in the traditional sense. More like an insight.

My heart just ran ahead of itself.

I'm not the slow-boiling frog this time. I jumped into the steaming pot with my eyes wide open. I threw myself into the idea of him, the idea of us. We love, yes, but this feels wrong. How can his heart choose mine if this is how he would seek to tell the world? This is not a moment to be shared as part of a business deal.

"Eve, my darling." The lid pops, diamonds glitter, and my apprehension tilts to certainty.

This isn't like before, because it *hurts*. I need to trust myself. Trust him. But how can I?

This is a mistake I can't risk twice.

"Stop." My voice surprises me, ringing out, my fingers curling against his shoulder. "You're making a mistake," I whisper.

The collective inhale seems almost familiar.

"Eve?" Oliver's brow furrows. That flickering expression from before? It settles this time.

"I can't marry you."

"Darling—"

"No. I can't." *This is not honesty. This is not our moment.* "I'm sorry," I say, turning away. Sorry for Mandy. For the animals. Sorry for making Oliver look at me that way. "Check out lot sixty-nine," I say as I step away. Something wet trails down my cheek. "Bid big, ladies. Oliver Deubel is a heartbreaker, but he really will show you the time of your life."

Chapter 45
OLIVER

A Little Bird Told Us . . .

it's business as usual for our ditched billionaire London beau as he returns to his swanky office. But what happened to his American vet?

One man jilted at the altar. One man's proposal publicly rejected at a charity gala.

Is it her? Is it them?

One thing's for sure, this Little Bird has to admire her style of public breakups.

#EliverNoMore

Like a scab on the skin I can't help but pick, I scour the digital news daily, wondering if I'll find a hint of her. In the days that follow, the tabloid press seems to haunt me, hanging around outside the office, shouting my name as I leave the hotel. It used to be I found A Little Bird's inclusions a trial, but those now seem like simpler days.

A sordid love triangle and a stately home? The media has made a meal of our lives.

"I see you've shaved."

I pinch the bridge of my nose, not bothering to look up. "I decided a beard wasn't really my style." At first, a beard was easier. Especially as I couldn't stand the sight of my own face, but it made me so itchy, I wanted to rive it off.

"Agreed." Matt's feet sound against the carpet, the leather barely creaking as he lowers himself to a chair on the other side of my desk. "It's not like it hid how shit you look anyway."

I lift my eyes from my laptop. "I'm not in the mood for another pep talk."

"Good. I'm not in the mood for giving one. And that was an insult." A pause. "Any news?"

"News?"

"Don't be an eejit."

"No." I inhale until my lungs ache. "No news. Just old news. She left." She left me. I can still see her walking from the gallery, head held high, the horde parting like the Red Sea for Moses. Then closing over her absence.

Love is the most exquisite path to self-destruction.

Why do I miss her so much?

Matt clears his throat, and I blink, coming back to the present. *It's really shit here.*

"It's what you do now that might make the difference," he begins.

"The fact that she left says it all. She doesn't want to be with me. And let's face it." My seat creaks as I lean back in it. "Who would blame her?"

I fucked up so many times, and then I let her leave when I should've chased her. I let Mandy lead me off the stage and into a private room. Brandy was what was needed. He even muttered something to the butler about sweetened tea. I came back to myself suddenly. I wasn't catatonic, but I was fucking dazed. But I wasn't about to let her run away, not without a discussion. Not without reminding her of my love. I found Ted had taken her back to the hotel, and by the time I reached the place, she was already gone.

Afterward, I learned about the auction lot. None of Mandy's staff could explain where it came from. But that wasn't what made Eve run.

She would've wanted to throat punch me first.

The chair creaks again. There was Northaby, of course. Did her conscience ultimately get the better of her? The irony is, if she'd waited just a few more minutes . . .

No. There would've been little point if she'd already come to the conclusion she didn't want me.

"You're as thick as pigs' shit."

"What was that?" I blink, my focus returning to the office once more.

"Is that a letter opener?" Matt half stands, swiping the antique silver knife from my desk. "I'll just look after that for a wee while." I frown as he shoves it down the side of the chair.

"You think I might stab you?"

"More like you might stab yourself when you hear what I've got to say. I can't believe your plan is just to sit here and mope."

"I'm not moping. I'm working."

"I switched your Wi-Fi off hours ago. Unless you're conducting business telepathically, you're fucking moping."

"What am I supposed to do? You tell me, because I've tried—I've looked for her! I went to the clinic, to Nora's, the house in Chelsea she'd stayed at before. The clinic wouldn't help, Nora's place appears to be on lockdown, and the one time I managed to get the old woman by phone, she was most succinct in her reply when she told me to '*fuck right off.*' And the girl at the Chelsea house just muttered something about not being Eve's messaging service before she slammed the door in my face."

"So, hire someone to track her down?" Matt shrugs. "Discreet, like."

I consider lying. But what would be the point? So I debase myself.

"I did. Almost immediately. She got a cab to Heathrow Airport, and it seems she got on the first flight she could find, which was to Dubai. From there, she flew into Singapore, then on to Brisbane. Where she is now, I'm not sure."

"But you're going to find out, right?"

"I haven't made up my mind yet." I'm torn between wanting to find her at all costs and being conscious of the fact that, though she said she never wanted to see Atherton again, she didn't leave London to avoid him. Moving to the other side of the earth isn't exactly subtle.

"Pussy."

I look up to find Fin walking into my office. "Oh, good," I mutter with a glower. "Tweedle Dumber."

Ignoring me, he takes the seat next to Matt. "You can't just let her go. You'll regret it, just like you did Lucy."

I glower his way, wishing Matt had left the letter opener. "Are you suggesting Eve has gone somewhere to take her own life? Because that's the most ridiculous thing I've ever heard." Not Eve. But then again, I would never have imagined that my sister would . . . I shiver as though someone is dancing on my grave.

No, Eve would be more likely to take a knife to my throat.

"That's not what I meant. Lucy was ill. Her actions were a cry for help."

"It wasn't a cry for help. She tried to *kill* herself. A distinct difference, I think."

"You're not paying attention. You argued. Shit was said. Ultimately you let her walk away, which is what you'll regret with Eve too."

"I *sent* Lucy away," I growl, my fingers gripping the arms of my chair. "I made her leave, and I don't need reminding, because I live with the regret of my actions every single day." I swore then that love wasn't worth it, because it gives another the power to break you. A lesson my poor sister had to learn on two fronts.

"Made. Let." Fin makes a weighing motion with his hand. "What does it matter? The result is still the same. You, torturing yourself."

"He fears love. It makes him think of loss." Matt's stab in the dark hurts like fuck.

"Get the fuck out of my office," I mutter. "Both of you." I'm tired of this. I miss her so much—her animated face, her laughter. Her fucking temper.

But she left, and that was probably for the best. She abandoned her ring, her tiara, and anything with a link to me. She also took the dog. I didn't even want him, yet I feel his loss badly. The suite is so empty. *Just like my fucking life.*

"Did you ever tell Eve what happened with Lu?" Matt cants his head.

I shake my head. "I used her own reluctance against her, her own pretense of not giving a fuck, because I couldn't bring myself to admit what happened." Lucy was truly devastated, heartbroken over that . . . waste of skin and bone. Atherton used her, then discarded her—he didn't even have the kindness to lie about why. She was a means to an end, and when she confessed that to me, I blew up. Said things I shouldn't have. Made her leave. If I'd had even a hint of how fragile her mental state was, I would've tied her to a chair. Locked her in a room. Gotten her to see a doctor before . . .

"It wasn't your fault," Fin says softly.

"I failed her." Like I failed Eve in so many ways.

"That's so not true," he says wearily, rubbing his cheek with his hand. "You were angry, that's all."

"I told her I never wanted to see her again." Anger blinded me. Lucy was more than my PA. More than my sister. I trusted her judgment, her business acumen. I withheld nothing from her. She knew about the tender, knew my bid would blow the others out of the water. She had no idea of the ramifications of sharing this with Atherton. But that didn't matter to me, not in that moment. "Because I'm a bastard who couldn't see beyond the money I was about to make."

"You're just a hothead," Matt puts in. "Lu knew that. She would've realized you didn't mean it if she hadn't been in the middle of a mental health crisis."

"It's depression that kills, not idiot brothers," Fin adds.

"But I should've realized she was on the edge—I should've known way before she'd gotten to that point."

"She didn't even tell her doctor," Fin says, throwing up his hands. "You and Lucy are so alike, it's fucking scary. Never show weakness. Never admit you might need help. You didn't break Lucy or drive her to hurt herself, asshole."

"I wasn't there for her." My words bleed. I bleed. Hurt and anguish and anger spill from me. "Don't you understand? I wasn't there to stop her from swallowing those pills."

"This is old fuckin' ground. If Lucy was here, she'd slap you for being such an idiot."

427

"Was there anything in Mortimer's note?" Matt demands. "About the house? The animals? Anything?"

I shake my head. She took the time to write him a note, scribbled on a piece of hotel note paper.

> I'm sorry.
>
> Oliver was never going to keep the animals.
>
> Please forgive me for my part in this. I have no excuses. I wish I could stay to tell you myself.
>
> Take care, Mandy.

"There was nothing in it for me."

"Well," Fin says, "I suppose she wasn't pissed off at him."

"The animals weren't supposed to be part of the plan. Northaby was meant to be made into a high-end country hotel. The luxury crowd expects a pillow menu, spa days, swimming pools. Cocktails on the terrace and long walks through lush woodlands that don't involve outrunning Sumatran tigers."

"But then you changed your mind." He holds out a hand, palm to the ceiling, like his words are a comfort oh-so reasonable.

I changed my plans for her—to have her look at me with something like admiration, maybe. And now . . . "Now I own a monstrous great house with fucking safari park in the back garden. Do you have any idea how much their food bill is?"

"You need something to spend your billions on," Fin says with a laugh.

"I don't fucking want the place!" Not without her. "I didn't want it in the beginning—I just wanted Atherton's miserable head on a plate!"

"Ah, sure, but you might enjoy it," Matt says tugging his ear.

"He could get a ringmaster's hat and a red tailcoat," interjects Fin.

"That's a circus, not a zoo, thick arse."

"It's a fucking safari park!" I yell, my sanity hanging on the thinnest of threads.

"But it wasn't the house, was it?" Fin says casually, curling his finger to flick invisible lint from his pants leg. "I know we call you the devil, but I really didn't have you pegged as the type to sneak property out from under a senior citizen."

Mandy? I frown, not sure what he's talking about. But then I do understand. Did I leave the paperwork on my desk? "What do you know about this?"

"More than I want to," he mutters. "Especially given the crowd outside."

"What crowd?" But I'm already on my feet, moving toward the window. It's hard to see what's going on down there, but someone seems to be waving something white with red lettering. "Is that a placard?"

"Multiple," Fin says. "Some of them even have the correct spelling."

◆ ◆ ◆

I take the stairs two at a time, my employees scattering like beetles exposed from under a rock as I reach the marble floor of the foyer. *Almost skidding across it.*

"What's going on out there?" I ask the receptionist.

"I'm not sure, Mr. Deubel, but Andrew is trying to find out. He said not to call the police yet."

I nod curtly, recognizing the pattern of footsteps behind me. Fin and Matt, no doubt come to watch the circus. *Maybe I should've gotten those ringmaster's tails,* I think as I pull the door open.

"Down with the bourgeoisie. Down with the oppressive class! Down with the bourgeoisie. Down with the oppressive class!" On and on the chant goes.

"They could've chosen a catchier slogan," Fin says over my shoulder.

As it turns out, there are a dozen or so protesters marching up and down in front of the office, mostly younger people in sweatpants and hoodies, scarves pulled over their faces as though they're highly wanted criminals. They seem oblivious to the open door, to us standing in front of them, perplexed, as they merrily chant on.

"*Peace, bread, land,*" Matt reads. "Was that the name of the bakery on the corner?"

"Lenin, actually. And that one over there was something Stalin said." Fin points to a placard made from a broomstick and one side of a cardboard packing box, with red paint that dripped like blood before drying. "Though it's supposed to read, *You cannot make a revolution with silk gloves,* not *slik gloves.*"

"Oliver?" Matt turns to me. "Have you been pissing the Communists off?"

"Not so I'd realized," I answer, still scanning the crowd. "Though I'm not sure *Fuck dis noise* is part of *The Communist Manifesto.*"

"It would make more sense for one of them to read *Down with Atterir.*" Fin slides me a look.

"It isn't what you think," I mutter with a frown. "Why didn't you mention it before now?"

"Not my circus," he grunts.

"Safari park," Matt corrects. "I think what he means to say is he thought you were cleverer than this."

"Clearly not," I say, turning back. "Though I'm bright enough to know that one is meant for me." I point to a placard and the holder with a familiar face:

NEXT TIME I'M BRINGING THE LLAMA

"That's a rare old set of balls," Matt says, impressed at the sign's accompanying artwork. "Very . . . anatomical. Is this about llamas at Northaby?"

I shake my head. "My planned castration, I imagine." I smile weakly at Yara. In answer, she holds her placard higher and chants louder. She wouldn't speak to me when I called at the clinic. Haunted, more like, *waiting for her to arrive for a shift.*

That day, as Yara had climbed from her car, I almost sprinted to reach her before realizing she was pulling a long stick from the back seat. As she brandished it, she was kind enough to deliver her insults in another language, though probably for the benefit of the clinic's clients, rather than me.

Next to her stands Nora, and on the end of a loose leash is my former fluffy bedmate. *Not the one I'm in love with.*

"Down with the bourgeoisie. Down with the oppressive class!" Nora's voice carries above the rest as she spots me looking. In the place of a placard, Bo wears a doggy-size sandwich board with the words of their chant.

"Bo! Hey, boy!" I call out, patting my knees enthusiastically. One *woof*, a strong pull, and he's free, bounding over, his tongue lolling happily. I laugh aloud—it feels strange—as he heads straight for me . . . then dodges to run right by me. I feel my expression fall. *Rejected by a fucking dog.* But then something warm hits the back of my calf.

"What the hell!" Matt pushes away, Fin following.

"Of course he would." I nod, not bothering to move as Bo uses the back of my leg as a lamppost.

Chapter 46
OLIVER

"Nora." I make my way through the mostly teenage protesters. "What's this about?"

"There he is, lads! The man who's trying to put my poor animals out on the street!" She grasps Bo's leash as he trots back to her side.

"I'm what?" My reply sounds tremulous with laughter, though I don't feel so amused as the chants turn to jeers.

"Bastard!"

"Eat the rich—it's all they're good for!"

"Death is the solution!"

"Don't say that," complains a voice from behind a red scarf.

"I can say what I like," a spotty teenager retorts.

"I can't get arrested! My mum doesn't know I'm in the city—I'm supposed to be in double geography this afternoon."

But there's something familiar about the teenager with the unfortunate case of acne. "You," I call out. "You tried to slash my tires on Tuesday." The car was parked outside the hotel. Ted chased after him, but he got away, dodging through the busy afternoon traffic.

"Can't prove it." He puffs his chest, all hot air and attitude.

"Yes, I can. I have it on camera."

"Ha! Your fat bastard driver couldn't catch me."

"Lucky for you. He might look like your portly uncle, but he's ex-SAS and French Foreign Legion." That seems to knock the wind from his sails as he slinks to the rear of the grumbling group.

"Nora." I turn my attention her way. "Truly, I'm confused."

"Down with the bourgeoisie!" she yells in response. *And right in my face.*

"Why don't we go inside? We can deal with whatever this is calmly. Perhaps over a cup of coffee."

"You got any cookies?" The kid with the scarf jerks sideways as he's elbowed by the girl next to him.

"No fraternizing with the enemy," she hisses with a scowl.

"I'm going through a growth spurt!"

This is like a fucking circus, I think as I gesture to the building. "Shall we?" *Please leave your monkeys behind.*

"No." Nora juts her chin pugnaciously. "Anything you have to say, you can say out here."

I shrug. "I'm not quite sure what it is I can help you with, though I'll try my best."

Next to her, Yara snorts. "You could start by telling her why you put up that industrial fencing."

"I . . . put the fencing up?" There was new fencing when I visited last, I recall. The place was very secure, but I didn't pay attention beyond the fleeting thought that how Nora chose to spend my donation was up to her. "I'm not responsible for any fencing."

"Must've been the fairies, then." Nora's fingers tighten on Bo's leash, their color livid. "I ain't got money to spare for fences."

"Though she did use some of her most recent donation to buy a new padlock," Yara puts in. "And motion sensors. And an alarm."

"Very sensible," I hedge. Not that I'm about to break in.

"The rest she's going to give to a lawyer to rip you a new arsehole."

Both women seem like they're looking forward to the prospect, and my adamancy begins to wane. Choices I made. Directives I issued. The sinking realization that things might not have gone quite to the timeline.

"Turns out, he is that stupid."

My attention twists sharply as I realize Fin is speaking to Matt. "What the fuck, Phineas?" I demand.

"Eve came to me. I told her I'd help her find out who was behind the fencing. I just didn't expect it to be you."

"You told her?" *No one was supposed to know.*

"Sure. Along with making money and drinking expensive whisky, I told her puppy abuse was your favorite thing." His expression twists as he adds, "Asshole."

But my mind has already moved on. Perhaps she . . .

No. Eve wouldn't leave me over a misunderstanding. Would she? *Oh, fuck.*

I whip around to face the crowd, a surge of adrenaline coursing through my veins. Not *just* a misunderstanding, but perhaps it was the final nail in the coffin. I'd told her I was no good—proved it to her again and again. *Before I fell in love, and everything changed.* If only she'd waited. If she'd come to me. Except, on that stage, I hadn't given her that chance.

"This is a misunderstanding." More like a clusterfuck I've brought on myself.

A wave of dissent sounds through the rabble's rank.

"Let me explain." I can absolutely explain, even as words crowd my throat. I swallow over them. I doubt I've ever wanted to account for myself as much as I do now. *I must get her back.* "You see, you were in jeopardy of losing the sanctuary."

"Is this bloke a few sandwiches short of a full picnic, or what?" Nora turns to her jeering crowd. "That's why we're here—I'm at risk of losing it to you!"

"No, you don't understand—with the owner dead and no living relatives, anyone could've claimed the place."

"But no one did," Yara says simply. "Not until Nora got your threatening letter."

"It wasn't threatening." Or it had better not have been. How the hell has this happened? My instructions were explicit. "But it was premature. My legal team weren't supposed to act on it until I'd spoken with you."

"Spoken with me!" Nora shrieks.

"That letter all but said they were chucking her out." Yara's words might be impassive, but her expression is anything but.

"I'll blow the place up before I give it to you."

"You're not listening." I try very hard to keep a grip on my rising frustration, my panic at this glimmer of hope. If there's a chance to learn where Eve is, I'll do whatever it takes. "I don't want your land. I was simply trying to protect it."

Nora's face twists, and Yara huffs in disbelief.

"On Eve's behalf. And, yes, I was trying to do something that would impress her."

"To earn boyfriend points," Matt adds in solidarity.

He gets it, at least.

Yara juts out a hip, leaning her weight onto it. "Explain."

"Someone made a mistake."

She snorts, and someone else shouts "No shit," but I carry on. "I made a mistake—I was trying for the element of surprise."

"You bloody well achieved it!" Nora incredulously puts in.

Heads will fucking roll for this. "The land belongs to no one at the minute."

"No, possession is nine tenths of the law—that place belongs to me!"

"Nora, nine tenths are worth nothing when battling someone with more money. Someone ruthless." A hiss goes out, and the remains of a store-bought sandwich are aimed at my head. "Yes, I am ruthless," I admit, glaring at the perpetrator as I pluck lettuce from my hair. "But I am also in love."

Catcalls and jeers of disbelief follow, but I push on.

"I did this to prevent anyone else from doing so, because that would've upset Eve. She hurts to see her friends suffering, to see animals suffering. She lives her life for others, and I wanted to do something for her to show that I understand. That I see *her*. I would never do anything to hurt her." *Not now.*

"Only, you did." Yara's tone is without inflection, but the barb still twists. "And that letter brought us here."

"And Duggan!" shouts a young voice.

"You could've just bought it and donated it to Nora," she persists. "It would be small change to you."

"Yeah, we've seen your property portfolio!"

"Bought it from whom?" I run my hand through my hair, tamping back my frustration. "It currently doesn't belong to anyone. The timing of the letter was a mistake and the fencing wasn't due to go up for another month."

"Well, my lawyer says I have squatter's rights." Judging by the direction her gaze slid, Nora appears to be taking legal advice from the would-be tire slasher.

"Your ten years of usage does provide you with some rights. But I'd hoped you would transfer those rights to me, for a substantial sum, of course. It's complicated to explain, but with those years as mine, I could take ownership of the land and protect you. All of you." Eve, Nora, the animals.

"What a load of—" This time, I duck in time, avoiding a launched apple core.

"Why not just transfer it into Nora's name?" Yara demands.

"Why would I?" My frustration spills over.

"Because it's mine, you thieving git!" the old woman shouts.

"Let me finish!" I bellow. Nora's face falls, and regret pokes me like a hot finger to my chest. "I'm sorry," I add immediately, infusing my apology with the emotion driving me. *Apprehension. Irritation. Hope. God, I hope.* "I wasn't trying to take anything from you. I was trying to set the animal sanctuary up as a charitable foundation. To provide it with an income generated by the land value to safeguard your future."

"Why didn't you just tell Nora that?"

"I had every intention of doing so." Jesus Christ. Are they even listening? "But I had more pressing concerns," I add in the understatement of the year. "The letter was scheduled to be sent in a month to give me time to explain everything to Nora. It was to be a surprise for Eve."

"And those were the boyfriend points." Yara looks unimpressed.

"I was hoping Eve might take a role in the foundation." To my friends, I add, "That was before I saw how much she loved Northaby."

"When you decided to give her a safari park instead." Fin's mouth tips, seeming to imply I'm an idiot. But his eyes are warm, at least.

"I'd hoped she'd make that choice." I've already signed a contract with Mandy, one full of guarantees and stipulations that have ultimately made me the sugar daddy of dozens of species.

"It's not a ringmaster's outfit he'll need." Matt chortles as he adds, "It'll be wellies and overalls."

"My mistake was using one of my offshore registered companies as the legal entity to secure the land." *Please tell me you're getting this . . .*

The skinny anarchist's chest puffs. "Sounds suspect to me."

"How old are you?" I demand.

"Fourteen," he replies with a grunt.

"Come back in twenty years, and tell me what you wouldn't do for love."

"I'd better have a girl before I'm an old geezer like you."

"If you're lucky, you might. If you carry on the way you're going, your love might be your larger, scarier cellmate." Sliding my hand into my pocket, I pull out my business card holder and flick one his way.

"What's this?" he asks, eyeing it suspiciously.

I cast my eyes heavenward with a sigh.

"An opportunity to turn your skills to the light," Matt answers for me.

More like the morally gray.

"Is someone gonna take pity on this guy? Tell him where Eve is?" Fin claps a hand to my shoulder. "I mean, just look at the creases in his shirt. The bags under his eyes—the scruff on his cheeks."

"Please, do you know where she is?"

"I do." Nora infuses the words with extreme cockiness.

"If nothing else, I have to try to put this right. Would you tell me? Please?" I'll get on my knees if I have to.

Nora shrugs a shoulder. "I'm not sure if you're tellin' the truth about this land."

"If you want me to stop, I will. I'll provide you with a legal team to—"

"I want it—I want a proper charity."

"Yes, fine. We can do that. Start it right now, if you want. Just—"

"Swear it. In front of all these people."

Several phones are suddenly out and recording. "This better not end up on Pulse Tok," I mutter.

"Courts only," Yara says. "If you renege."

"Fine. I, Oliver Deubel, swear to set up an animal charity to support Nora's good work. I promise to provide for all legal costs and remedy any and all legal issues with the land her animal sanctuary currently stands on. Will that do?"

Nora shrugs, her sudden satisfaction settling around her like a cloak. "Well, I'll tell you, but she don't need you no more. She's got a new fella in her life. His name's Tucker," she adds with unconstrained delight.

"Sounds like a tool," Matt mutters.

"He's a big fella, so she tells me. We're all happy for her, right?" She doesn't seem to have realized that most of her protesters seem to be walking off in the direction of the nearest tube station.

"I would like to speak with her myself. Loose ends, you understand. So many things I have to say."

"Loose ends lead to nothing." Yara gives her head a tiny shake and begins tugging on Nora's arm.

"You want to grovel," the old woman asserts.

"Yes." My shoulders sag with a deep breath. "I suppose I do."

"Go on, then." Pulling away from Yara, she folds her arms across the front of her raincoat as her head makes a slight dip in the direction of the ground.

"Was that a   twitch?" I do hope so.

"A cue," she says, ignoring Yara's cackling laughter. "You wanna know? I wanna grovel out of you."

My smile feels acid, and judging by the flickers of unease among the remaining stragglers, I think it might look acid too.

Nora, meanwhile, remains unmoved. As cool as the proverbial cucumber, in fact.

"You misunderstand me, Nora. My groveling is for Eve."

"Ah," she says, in the vein of one who understands she holds all the cards. "So you don't really want to know where she is, then?"

Chapter 47
OLIVER

"Where to, sir?" Ted slams the car door, reaching for his belt.

"Papua New Guinea. That's in Melanesia, or so I'm told." I suppose it might've been worse. She might've chosen somewhere slightly less accessible. *Like the moon.*

"Sorry, sir?"

"City Airport," I amend, brushing aside Ted's confusion and the dirt from my knees. *Courtesy of Nora's insistence that I grovel.* As I dropped to that grimy pavement, I realized there was nothing I wouldn't stoop to for a chance to see Eve again.

Hope, it seems, is a much stronger motivator than revenge.

"Isn't Papua New Guinea rough? Dangerous, I mean."

My gaze meets Ted's in the rearview mirror as I make a vague noise from my throat. I'm trying not to dwell on the reality that Eve chose to move to a country where violent crime, kidnapping, and civil unrest are commonplace.

Am I really so awful?

Well, yes. I suppose I *was.* But that was before. Put simply, revenge blinded me, and there are none so blind as those who will not see. I only hope she'll forgive me, let me spend the rest of my life making it up to her.

As for the place being dangerous, Eve is no fool. She wouldn't have moved to the country recklessly. *But in a fit of despair?* No, nothing about this situation is the same as before. With the information she had, she put me in my place, there on the stage, and then moved to the end of the earth to avoid me.

"Sir?"

"Eve volunteered for an animal charity in the country." She's currently working out of a remote copper-mining town some hours flight from the capital. "I'm sure they're taking good care of her." It's the only answer I'm prepared to give as I swallow over the sudden ache in my throat. How could I have ever believed I could atone for Lucy by hurting Eve? *Enough.* I've wasted so much time on regret. My actions will be different this time around. I won't let Eve go, not without my love ringing in her ears. My love. My regret. How being with her, seeing life through her eyes, has made me a better man.

I can do this. I can convince her we're worth the risk, and I have twenty-two hours, according to Andrew's itinerary, to come up with the right words. I also have Nora's and Yara's blessings, of sorts. And my friends' best wishes for luck. *Did they wish me luck, or did they say I'll need it?*

Not that it matters. I won't waste this chance, Tucker or not.

A low grunt rumbles up from my chest. The man's name is like my own personal rain cloud, pissing on my hope. I don't believe Eve is dating already, though I'm sure it won't be for want of trying on his part.

Tucker the fucker.

Actually, no. Tucker better not be a fucker, or I'll twist his testicles off.

I wonder if I can hire a llama in Papua New Guinea.

But as my phone rings, my plans drift away like a daydream.

◆ ◆ ◆

"Peanuts?" The flight attendant smiles as she offers me the ridiculously tiny packet.

I shake my head. What kind of an idiot doesn't have a spare private jet? And what kind of fuckery is at play when an airport the size of Heathrow has not one first-class ticket available to Australia? Hell, business class! Instead, I find myself flying economy on some el cheapo airline. *In coach, for fuck's sake!*

Andrew tried to warn me against flying commercial . . . after I'd stopped swearing at his news that my jet was out of commission. A technical issue. Three days to fix. He'd sourced another, he'd added happily, no doubt anticipating my appreciation for his diligence. But a flight scheduled to leave in thirty-six hours was of no interest to me. Not when I'm crawling out of my skin to see Eve again.

I found myself redirecting Ted to Heathrow Airport, which led to this, a flight to Brisbane—with a small detour through hell—in a seat that doesn't recline, situated next to the toilets.

First world problems? I prefer the first-class kind. Private pods, china plates, and actual silverware in the place of school cafeteria trays and the indignities of a plastic spork. No one in their right mind would choose to travel this way, but I would go through worse, I know, just to see Eve again.

God, I hope she wants to see me, that she'll give me a chance to explain. To tell her how my life is empty without her.

"Did you really trade a week in the Saint Kitts for a dining reservation?"

"Sorry?" I look up to find the young woman next to me holding a baby—a baby who seems to have materialized out of nowhere.

"I heard you going through the other cabins, trying to get someone in business class to swap seats."

"It was worth a try," I answer in a tone much more even than how I feel. Which is impatient, bad tempered, and generally fucked off. A muscle in my left eye begins to twitch with tiredness as I watch the one thing that could make this journey worse: a grizzling infant.

"I'm holding this little one for my sister," my neighbor says, beginning to bounce him—her?—against her knee.

"Won't that . . ." I make a gesture similar to that of opening a lively bottle of champagne.

"Nah, she likes it. Don't you, Maisie?" the woman coos. "You know, if I'd been sitting in the good seats, I would've sold you mine. For a hundred grand," she adds with a grin.

"And I would've paid it." My answer melts her expression, her eyes suddenly wide. Not that it matters, because I'm here, and I would suffer through much worse deprivations. Not that I hadn't tried everything to avoid this particular one. Extorting the loan of a jet, bribing the ticket agents—I even tried the "do you know who I am" ploy, which only left me looking like a twat. "In fact, I would've paid double, because this experience has been—*oh, fuck!*"

And now I'm a twat covered in baby vomit.

Chapter 48
EVIE

I throw my bush hat to the tiny, lumpy bed and brush my sweaty hair from my face as the video call attempts to connect. I'm just about to hang up when a telltale tickle at my ankle draws my attention. And my slap.

"Eve?" A melodic, cut glass accent fills the air, and I spring upright, like one of those crazy inflatable dancers outside of a car dealership.

"Hey, Lucy!"

Yes, that Lucy.

"I'm good. Exceptionally good, actually." She smiles, and my heart twists at the familiarity. "What where you doing just now? When the call connected?"

"Zumba?" I answer, my voice rendering the answer a question. I was swatting at a mosquito, but the jumpy reaction was more about the sound of her voice. It's not deep like Oliver's, but the cadence is so similar, it caught me off guard.

"Ah. I thought Tucker might've been touching your bottom again," she says with a soft chuckle.

"We left Tucker in Port Moresby." Thank God.

"He is so sweet."

"Easy to say when it's not your butt he's feeling up."

"I do think my life could only be improved by some bum touching."

"I'll drop him by your apartment in Singapore on my way back home." Home. It's such a small word, but it fires a thrill through me. I can feel its pull, his pull.

Will he forgive me?

"You've decided?" It's not hard to see her pleasure, despite the grainy internet connection.

"Yes." My shoulders lift with a deep inhale. "I have." It's time to be brave. I shouldn't have left in the first place, but in that moment, I let fear rule me. I let it convince me that it was happening all over again—a proposal by the wrong man for the wrong reasons—that I was about to be made a fool of again. But I see things clearly now. Oliver isn't a thing like Mitch. He was acting out of love, not opportunity. Sure, his timing might not have been great, but I know his heart was in the right place.

"Eve?"

I come back to myself and Lucy's concerned expression. "Sorry, I zoned out." Oliver was about to propose, and I cut him dead in front of all those people.

"You're worried."

My stomach sinks to my boots. "What if he never wants to see me again?"

"He will."

"What if it's too late? What if he can't trust me again—it's not like it's the first time I ran." If only I'd trusted myself, listened to my heart and not my overcrowded head.

"Stop," she says softly. "You were overwrought. You worked against your feelings instead of with them, that's all."

We've talked a lot about what passed between Mitch and her. And what came after. We've gone over the similarities in our

446

experiences and how easily a betrayal, a loss of trust, leads to a cloud in judgment. It can make you feel like you'll never trust again—yourself or anyone else.

There isn't much we haven't shared. I've told her about my parents, the roots of this erosion. And she's confided how she wishes she could take back all that passed between her and Oliver.

"He'd be a fool not to listen." Lucy is so kind. Beautiful, serene, wicked funny too. She has this openness about her. I'd be lucky to call her a friend. *Or a sister?*

I found her email address on her company website while I was hiding out in Dubai. I reached out, not quite sure what to expect and already regretting leaving the way I did. I don't know what I was expecting. Certainly not understanding or friendship.

"Maybe you should come with me?"

"And play gooseberry?" she laughs. "No thanks."

"That might be a little optimistic. He might throw me out."

"Doubtful. It sounds like my brother is head over heels for you. And I think you're just the person to keep him on his toes."

"But what if—"

"Eve, love doesn't just go when your physical presence removes itself. It's just a hiccup, and hardly surprising, given your natures."

"Meaning what?"

"That you're both as stubborn as a box of rocks. Enough worrying. Tell me about your day. Mine was a nightmare of numbers and boring talk. Paint some color for me."

"Oh, I've got color. Green for the bushland to get to some remote village. Blue for triage and surgery tents we erected. Then there was a lot of red and brown after that, but I'll leave the sources to your imagination."

Her nose scrunches. "No puppies?"

"I filled my quota of puppy cuddling. Then I neutered a half dozen village strays."

"Did you think about anyone in particular while doing so?"

"Like Mitch?" I shake my head. "I don't get how *dog* can be a human insult. I've met more dogs I like than humans."

"You have a point, but I do think he should be neutered. As a preventative measure, if nothing else."

Before I can answer, a commotion starts up outside. The roar of an engine, the barking of dogs. Raised voices?

"Hold that thought," I say, pointing a thumb over my shoulder. "I need to see what's going on outside."

"What if it's trouble—the rebels or whatever they call them?"

But rebels don't have posh English accents.

Chapter 49
OLIVER

I press my hands to my hips and arch my back, which has more kinks than Fin, currently. With a murmur of thanks, I nod at Ronald, my driver. Not that he's paying attention as he stares at his newly acquired Patek Philippe. But at least we're here.

Unless I'm about to be sold to criminals.

I wonder if anyone would pay the ransom?

"Oliver?"

My head snaps right, and oh, what a sight. Eve stands in the doorway of a ramshackle hut, a million emotions flickering and fading across her face, none of them settling. She looks so lovely, her face dappled with freckles she didn't have before, her hair more golden than red, even in the fading light.

"Oh, thank God." I don't recall moving. All I know is I'm peppering her forehead and her face with kisses, my hands sliding over her as though she might not be real. "Darling, I've missed you so much."

"What are you doing here?" She begins to push at my chest as though just coming to her senses. A pity for her that I'm senseless to everything as I tighten my arms, not giving an inch.

"Everything okay over there?"

I turn my head to the deep voice and the pair of men looking toward us. They're wearing the same khaki-colored outfit as Eve, and just as crumpled, though one man has the addition of a pistol holster. I tighten my arms, pulling her impossibly close, because fuck that and fuck *you*, Tucker the nonfucker. Eve is mine.

"Yeah, it's fine," she begins. "This is Oliver. He's . . ." Her eyes dart to me, uncertain. "A friend."

My stomach pits. "Eve, I love you. And I swear to you, I'm not guilty of . . . well, not directly responsible for all of it." *So much for preparation of eloquent declarations.*

"You're guilty for crimes against fashion." Her eyes flick down to my nipple-chafing T-shirt.

"A baby vomited on me." Keeping one arm around her, I yank at the hem, which has a habit of creeping up. "This was all I had in my carry-on." *My talisman.* "You bought it for me in the charity shop, remember?"

"Yes, I remember," she answers softly.

"My jet was . . ." I make a gesture, my heart hammering as my words begin to tumble over themselves. "Then my luggage went to Guangzhou. Not that I blame it, because I wouldn't want to be seen with me—just look at the state of me."

"I am." She fights a smile, not quite giving in. "But what are you doing here?"

"Eve." Her name brims with emotion. "I've flown not only commercial but coach across the world, hurtled through a mountain range in a tin can piloted by a madman. I've endured a three-hour ride in an ancient Land Rover that has probably given me brain damage, thanks to a lack of shock absorbers and unpaved roads. I'm certain I've left the shape of my skull in its roof. I have a very nasty case of tropical swamp arse thanks to the heat, and—"

"Oliver?"

"—I'd do it all again because, well, because of hope. And love."
I take a breath, pulling it deep. "Eve. My darling, I have been such
an idiot on so many fronts."

"I know."

"You do? I shouldn't have kept Lucy secret from you. I'm sorry.
I was so ashamed."

"Of her?"

"Of myself. Of how I behaved. Through all of it."

"Think you can say that again?" she asks, pulling back.

"Yes, of course, I'll say it again and again, but please—" But
then her fingers are sliding into mine, and she's leading me to a
shack.

"You'd better come in."

My heart pounds painfully at her solemn expression. At what,
or who, I might find inside.

"You still there?"

My blood freezes as I steel myself. It doesn't matter. Tucker the
fucker could never love her like I will.

"Still here and glad to hear you haven't been carted off by the
raskols."

Lucy?

"I googled that," my sister adds, her tone tinny. "I suggest you
don't do the same. Please tell me you have an armed escort."

"Well, I have *an* escort." Eve reaches for her phone, holding it
up. "And he has arms. Say hi to your brother."

"Oh my God—you're there!" My sister's smile is so wide.
"How?"

"Brought to you by the magic of Google and an email or two,"
Eve says.

"And lots of telephone calls," Lucy laughingly puts in.

And then I'm looking at her, my sister. The internet connection is poor, but it doesn't stop me from noticing how glossy her eyes are. *Mine too.*

"How your ears must've burned," she says.

"You put in a good word for me, though, I'm sure." My words are all bluster as gladness rushes through me.

"I told her the truth."

"Which is what I deserve," I answer in a more serious tone.

"That you deserve happiness. You both do. I love you, Oliver. Now, stop being a prat, and give Eve a proper kiss."

"Luce!" Eve exclaims.

"I'm ending the call now, but I expect to hear from you both soon."

The call ends, and Eve puts her phone back on a grubby, makeshift dresser. "I like Lucy a whole lot."

"She inherited the good traits," I answer, swallowing thickly. I can't believe they've been in contact, that they're . . . friends? "I miss her."

"She misses you." She folds her arms, not exactly defensively—more like she's trying to hold herself together. "You have to get over the past, Oliver. Make things right."

My heart gives a little pang. Just like Eve, putting others first.

"I will—I am," I insist, desperation poking me in the ribs. "I got over Atherton."

Her gaze lifts, but not her head, as she eyes me skeptically.

"It's true. I was blinded for a while, but you brought me into the light. You're more important than revenge, more important than anything. I didn't try to steal Nora's land. I just made a pig's arse out of myself trying to impress you."

"Impress me?"

"I wanted to make up for all I'd done to you. Hell, it's not even that. You make me see things differently, Eve. You fucking inspire me.

452

You are so kind and so lovely." I close my eyes, not quite believing what I'm about to say. "Damn it, you make me want to be a better man!"

"Wow. That's quite an accusation," she says, her words as tremulous as her expression.

"Not that I'm *all* bad."

She pulls a face as though considering this. "Maybe not even half-bad," she eventually says with a shrug.

"Good." I blow out a breath. "I mean, thank you." She smiles, and I find myself rushing on. "That auction lot—a night with me? Does that strike you as something I'd ever be into?"

"Not for charity, at least. That was meant to be a joke," she adds quickly. "I know it wasn't you, but at the time . . ."

"I gave you a thousand reasons to worry, I know. Eve, I'm—"

"All I could see was how you'd manipulated me. You were about to propose, and even that felt the same. I told myself you were just like Mitch."

"—so sorry." But it isn't enough. Not after those words. God, I've made such a mess of things.

"I was so confused. I had so many thoughts swirling through my head. Everything you'd done, everything you'd said. The good and the bad, all of it."

"Darling, I'm so sorry. I was wrong about so many things."

"You're not listening, Oliver. I couldn't trust myself to stay, but I should have. I should've trusted my heart—it's there where I know who you truly are."

My throat aches, and my own heart twists, half with hope and half with agony.

"Leaving you was wrong. It felt wrong. Feels wrong now. I just didn't know what else to do."

Relief. Oh, fuck, the relief as I reach for her. "Give me this chance, and I'll never give you cause to doubt again. I promise you things will be different."

"That's just it, Oliver. I've come to realize that people don't change." She looks sad as she brushes the backs of her fingers across my cheek. "Their masks just slip a little."

"No, that's not true." I haul her closer, pulling her body flush with mine, my thoughts thundering, even as her eyes soften with a tender warmth.

"Oliver." My name is a soft breath on my cheek. "Your masked slipped. You were showing me glimpses of who you were all along. You're not just Oliver Deubel, the autocratic, blackmailing, asshole tycoon. You're also the man who loves me beyond anything else."

"Eve." Pure joy floods through me, my arms fusing in their hold. "Oh, God. Eve." *Finally.* "I love you so much."

"I know," she whispers, her eyes bright and wild, glimmering like stars in the night sky.

Our mouths meet. A touch. A slide. It's everything.

"Why didn't you come home?" I demand, taking her face between my hands.

"I needed space. Maybe I needed you to come for me. And you did."

"I've got the mosquito bites to prove it."

Laughing, she buries her face in my chest. I hold her tight, screw my eyes tighter. "I'm so sorry—I must stink. But I'm not letting you go. Not now, not ever."

Her laughter trembles, tears fall, as she pulls me to the tiny bed. Our legs tangle, and my heart feels fit to burst when I tip her chin. Brush her cheek, stare into the face of my everything. She is perfection and sees me, loves me despite my flaws. Fuck. Love might be the ultimate risk, but I understand now why people seek it, fucking die for it. The payoff is sublime. The connection . . .

And then her hand slides between us and connects with something else.

"Here?" It's not really a question, more a husky confirmation.

"Note how I pulled *you* onto *my* bed?"

"I love a decisive woman."

"Oh, yes, you do."

"But darling, I have one last confession to make before you can have your wicked way."

She groans and drops her head back to the mattress.

"I've done something."

"Please don't say I have to get Pieter to shoot you. Not after you've come all this way."

"Pieter?" My gaze shifts briefly. "I thought the other one must've been Tucker." I give my head a quick shake. "Actually, I don't want to know. I don't care what passed between the two of you."

"Between me and Tucker?"

"Not my business."

"You'd still have me?"

"In a heartbeat. Though the first time of *having you* might only last ninety seconds."

"That's the best you've got?" she whispers, drawing my lips down to hers. "Because Tucker is a hunk of loving no girl can resist."

"*Eve.*"

"He likes to pet my face while he curls his long tail around my butt."

"I don't need to—" I hold a finger between us. "Wait. His *tail*?"

"It's huge! So, so long." But she's chuckling.

"But is it pretty?" I demand.

"Not as pretty as—"

I slide my fingers under her shirt, and *oh, fuck*, her skin feels like silk, a moment later her breast filling my hand. And then we're kissing. God, how we kiss.

"Tree kangaroo," she rasps, pulling at my T-shirt. She yanks it over my head. "Tucker is a tree kangaroo."

"Deviant," I growl, making her laugh again. "But you still might need your friend with the gun."

"You're jealous?" Her eyes are bright as I push up onto my palms.

"I think I might have rabies. I'm definitely stark raving." I drop my hips, and we both gasp at the contact. "Because I want to spend the rest of my life with you."

"That's not . . . very complimentary," she rasps as she undulates against me. "Wait," she demands, pushing at my shoulder. "That's it? That's your confession?"

"That, darling, and I bought you a Pemberley."

Chapter 50
EVIE

A Little Bird Told Us . . .

Our London lovers are back on again.

PDAs. Knicker flashes. Wedding bells. We want to see them all!

"Now, where were we?" I purr as I slide my thigh over his, the flare of my robe settling over us like a silken flower bloom.

"I think you were about to kiss me." Oliver's smoky tone beckons me closer like curling fingers. *Like the sight of him isn't incentive enough.* His hair stark against the white pillows, the sheet lying low across his waist. I run my fingertips over his broad chest, admiring how a few days in the sun has turned him golden.

He hung around while I worked my remaining few shifts, fulfilling my commitment to the animal charity, and he used his time well (not once complaining about the lack of amenities) by surprising me with a few days on a luxury yacht before we left tropical Papua. A gift, he'd called it. Not a case of making decisions without me. A little time and a little space to reacquaint ourselves. And it was heaven.

Equally beautiful was our stop off in Singapore. Lucy and Oliver were so lovely to watch together. I left them alone to talk and heal old wounds. When I returned, it was like meeting the siblings together for the first time. They were so different. So smiley. So . . . ornery in their love language.

And now we're back to reality. To London and whatever our future together might bring. And I cannot wait to experience every moment of it. We have so much to look forward to. Helping Nora get the sanctuary's charity up and running. And I'm pleased to find Yara is coming on board, especially as Oliver and I are going to be a little busy with Northaby.

We have so many plans and so much to learn about running a safari park.

I won't own Northaby outright, because that would be madness. It'll be held in trust, securing it for future generations to love.

All because of *his* love.

It's not so much a Pemberley that he's provided me with but a legacy. There's still going to be a hotel, because Oliver wouldn't be Oliver without making money. The place is getting a whole new lease on life and an influx of billions. And we're going to have an apartment there. Maybe even a wing . . .

As special as that is, it's not what made my heart sing.

Northaby is set to become a new kind of vacation, one that's accessible for families of all incomes. We're preserving everything, sharing everything—the animals and the history as we open the whole place up to the public. It'll be a place of learning about the past and the future as we aim to educate our visitors in conservation. It's the best gift in the world. One I get to share with the world.

"What are you waiting for, darling?"

What I won't ever share is this man. He is so wonderful, so handsome, his eyes bright and expectant, a sultry smile playing on his lips.

"Don't rush me," I whisper, cupping my hand to the back of his neck, my finger teasing the soft hairs there. "It's not like we have anywhere to be." He makes a noise of masculine contentment as I press myself closer, my breasts rubbing his chest through my thin robe.

"Eve." He's all ache and want as I rock my body over his, barely touching the sheet that's not exactly covering his—

"Oh!" He whips it deftly across the bed, pulling my body down to his. Hard meets soft in an instant, and I whimper, my insides turning molten.

"You are so beautiful." His compliments turn me pliant as his fingers slide the robe from my shoulders until it pools at my waist. "Your freckles," he whispers, trailing his finger across my skin. "So pretty and just begging to be kissed."

"Sweet talker." I sigh as his lips trail across my skin, as he lifts my breast, his eyes turning languid as he sucks my nipple into his mouth.

"Sweet is watching you ride me." He blows a cooling breath over the hardened peak.

"*Yes* . . ." I push up onto my knees, my hand sliding between us to slip across my hot center in a bare caress.

"Fuck, yes. Touch yourself. Let me watch. Eve, in the garden of temptation."

"Lady garden," I half rasp, half laugh, undulating over him.

459

"You look like my fantasy brought to life. All lush curves, wet pussy, and pleading, fuck-me eyes."

His words are a filthy kind of reverence as I slip my fingers inside. As I writhe. "My Romeo has such a dirty mouth," I whisper, loving his eyes on me.

"I'll let you ride it in a little while." His voice rasps like sand-paper as he grasps the base of his cock.

"God, I need to feel you inside me." Pleasure pulses through me as his tongue moves over my nipple. I buck. I break. Come apart, just a little bit, there, against him.

I feel so utterly owned and loved as he presses himself to my opening. Our breaths hold as I take him inside, as he holds me there, his eyes never leaving mine. We are wild and unrestrained as we express our love this way, our pleasure too great to prolong as my love spills at his words.

I can feel your heart beating for me.

You are so fucking perfect.

"Oh, God!" A ripple of awareness courses through me and I fall apart in his arms. Oliver follows me as I reach my peak.

Our arms drape around the other, our lips reluctant to part as we whisper promises of love and devotion, when we're rudely interrupted as Bo bursts through the door.

"Ew, Mr. Bo!"

"Bugger off, Bo! Stop hogging my woman."

We collapse in a heap, Oliver shielding me with his body. And pulling the sheet with him, because you can't be too careful where that dog's tongue is concerned.

"Get down," Oliver complains when Bo's slobbery doggy kisses are interrupted by a knock at the door. More accurately, a series of thumps that sets him off barking.

"Ignore it," Oliver says, bodily rolling Bo from the bed.

"It might be important," I protest, pitching the other way before he can stop me. "Yara said to expect the paperwork today."

"Bloody Nora."

Ignoring my love's grumbles, I right my robe and squeeze out through the door, managing to leave Bo behind as the hammering starts up again.

"Coming!" I call, crossing the space.

"What, again?" Oliver shouts. "I am fucking amazing!"

"Shush," I shout, not sure why I'm bothering. Whoever that is can't hear over the noise of their own racket.

"Where's the fire?" I call, yanking the door open.

"Evelyn Fairfax?" A woman in a gray pantsuit stands on the threshold, a guy in business casual next to her. He has one hand sunk into his pocket; in the other he's holding a leather folio.

"Yes, that's me."

"My name is Rebecca Brown, and this is Vernon Hall. We're here from His Majesty's Immigration Department."

Oh, shit! My brows bounce; my mood too. "Hi! Hello! How can I help you?"

"We're here for your appointment. Your visa inspection?"

"I . . ." *don't know what they're talking about.* "I already have my biometric card, notification that everything is hunky dory. A done deal?" *Hunky dory? Where in the heck did that come from?*

"Not quite," Rebecca says. "It has come to our attention that the relationship aspect of your visa might have been breached."

"I'm not sure how," I answer, fixing on a smile. "Mine is a business visa, not a relationship one."

"Well," the man by her side mutters gruffly. "There appear to be some discrepancies. It's a favor to you that we're here."

I give myself an internal shake and turn a dazzling smile on the pair. "Well, then I guess you'd better come in." Moving back from the door, I grasp my robe at my chest. "Please excuse the state of the place," I demur, eyeing the clothing explosion on the sofa. Oliver and I might've gotten a little frisky on the couch last night. "We've just gotten back from a trip," I say, stuffing a pair of my panties behind a velvet throw cushion.

"Yes, we're aware," Vernon says at the same time Rebecca says, "Anywhere nice?"

The pair then exchanges a look that seems like a *whole* conversation. I cannot for the life of me decipher what it means as their gazes return to me.

"Nice?" I nod as a myriad of images flash through my head. Some of them sweet. Some of them sexy. And none of them suitable for public consumption. "Yes. At least, I think so."

The door to the bedroom opens, and Bo bursts out, shortly followed by an absolutely beautiful but very naked Oliver.

"Eve? Who was at the . . . oh, hello." I begin to giggle as his hands move to his junk at warp speed. He shuffles sideways behind one of the sofas. "I didn't realize we had guests," he says, ridiculously half crouching behind it.

"Oh, I think we get that, honey." I turn to Rebecca with a small shrug. "Well, I guess you now know I'm not with Oliver for his money. But where are my manners! Please, take a seat. Can I offer you something to drink? We have wine and whisky . . . I think there might be some vodka in the fridge?"

"It's ten o'clock in the morning." Not only is Vernon grumbly, but he's also very judgy.

"Sorry, we're still on vacation mode, and it's always five o'clock somewhere!"

"Let's get on with this, shall we?" the man mutters.

I decide I like Rebecca better, even if she's pink faced from ogling my man. But I direct them to the dining table, sliding last night's post-sex-recovery room service (club sandwich for Oliver, fries and mayonnaise for me) to one side.

"Can I just ask," Oliver begins, swiping up a throw pillow from the couch to use as a modesty shield, "who are you, and what are you doing here?"

"This is Rebecca and Vernon. They're here about my visa interview." With a shrug, I mouth, *"What the fuck?"*

"Eve's visa was arranged with an immigration lawyer. It's been awarded already. What exactly is this about?" Oliver asserts with as much dignity as a naked man can.

The pair looks at the paperwork. Heads shake and mutters are made.

"The application is for a spousal visa," Rebecca murmurs, still red cheeked.

"Your second visa application," Vernon adds snidely.

Gee, thanks for the reminder, Vernon.

"No, there's been some mistake. That's the wrong category of visa."

"That's all you have to say?" Vernon demands. "Nothing to explain the reason for two spousal visas?"

"No, not really." I narrow my gaze, suspicious. Is Vernon from the immigration department or the morality police?

"Not that it has anything to do with Eve's visa or, quite frankly, anything to do with you, but Eve is in a settled relationship." Oliver adopts a superior tone, eyeing the pair as though they're underlings.

"What about the Pulse Tok video?" Rebecca asks meekly.

"And the media interest?" Vernon demands. "Do you have anything to say about that?"

"Just that they're very intrusive," I reply, aggrieved. "They were already camped outside of the hotel when we got back yesterday."

"I'd love to know who's feeding them information." Oliver fumbles with the pillow, and Rebecca squeaks at his inadvertent dick slip.

"Listen," I say, trying very hard to master myself. "That pack of sharks has gotten most of it wrong. We didn't split up," I add in my most innocent tone. "I had volunteering commitments. On the other side of the world." Totally plausible, right?

Vernon's gaze slices my way. "I'm not sure I believe you."

"Really? Well, last week, I spent hours applying ointment to that man's infected mosquito ass bites while we were in Papua New Guinea."

Oliver turns and flashes his taut, tanned buns. They're still dappled with red, raised welts. Naked sunbathing will do that to you in the tropics—the mosquitos are on steroids over there.

"Enough of this," Vernon gripes. "You need to prove to us that this is a legitimate relationship."

"Hello!" I hold out my hand to indicate Oliver's undressed state. In response to their blank stares, I add, "The man is butt nekkid."

"Sex doesn't constitute a relationship."

But I can see Rebecca disagrees.

"What's his favorite color?" Vernon demands.

I fold my arms with a sigh, then send Oliver an *I told you so* glare. "Remember this conversation? Didn't I say we needed to go over this?"

"This is highly irregular," Vernon puffs. "Miss Fairfax will be detained, likely deported, if we don't see evidence that this is a real relationship."

"You want evidence?" Oliver demands, Frisbee-ing the throw pillow across the room.

Rebecca gasps, and I squeak as all that gorgeousness eats up the floor between us. *Swinging free, if you know what I mean.*

Oliver whistles and Bo barks, bounding between us with a box between his teeth. Oliver takes it and drops to one knee.

"That was clever." Really clever, though I'm not sure where I want to look most.

"The benefits of jet lag. We've been working on it while you slept, haven't we, Bo?"

"I hope you kept your pants on."

He doesn't laugh, though his chest moves with a deep inhale. "I know it's probably too soon, but when you know you want to spend the rest of your life with someone, you just know. I might not know your favorite color, but I know mine is the red gold of your hair. I know you to be fierce and loyal and loving, and I'll spend the rest of my life trying to deserve you."

My heart lifts, my whole being turning weightless. I glance down at my feet, not sure how they're still touching the floor.

"I swear to love you with all that I am, over an engagement that spans years, if that's what you want. Because my heart chooses you, my darling, from now until my very last breath."

I have no hesitation. My heart is filled with nothing but certainty and love. His heart chooses mine, and mine his.

Tears course down my face as he flips the box open to reveal the ring of my dreams. A violet sapphire, almost the color of his eyes, a dainty row of diamonds circling it. My hand trembles as he slips it onto my finger.

"Eve, my love. My heart. Will you marry me? Sometime? Anytime? Just say you'll always be mine."

Epilogue

A Little Bird Told Us . . .

She said yes!

Have you seen the *City Chronicle*'s Pulse Tok scoop?

Did it bring a tear to your eye when our London billionaire (big boy) beau, Oliver Deubel, showed his American sweetheart, Eve Fairfax, (and the rest of the world) his *naked* love?

This Little Bird had reporters on the spot when it happened, and we have the original uncensored footage (more like *foot*-age). It brought both a tear and a wince to our eyes!

Jealous? Of course! All that man and money off the market for good.

But his Maven Inc. partners are still single. The gorgeous Fin DeWitt and the mysterious Matías Romero.

Can anyone hook a Little Bird up?

Meanwhile, this Little Bird wants to know where these lovebirds are tying the knot!

We've heard it's somewhere tropical, and we're paying big bucks to find out!

ACKNOWLEDGEMENTS

I am eternally grateful to the women who hold me up and support me in the kindest of ways. To Lisa Staples, thanks for being the best sounding board, my medical expert, and for traveling the globe to visit. Thanks to Michelle Barber, beautiful soul and keeper of the Lambs. To Elizabeth Barr for her eagle eyes and for accepting the title of Keeper of the Rear End.

Thanks to the Lambs (the lovely people in my reader group) for still being around when I emerge from living in a fictional world.

To my children, undoubtedly my best work! You come up with the best lines but the worst book titles. You entertain and delight me to no end and are the best cheering squad in the world. I'm just so bloody proud to call you mine.

To Tee. Just because you're amazing.

To Amazon Montlake and their amazing editing team, thanks for the opportunity and the experience.

To Mike, a brilliant tea maker and the best husband around, thanks for not putting me in the nuthouse.

Finally, my sincere thanks to the person holding this book in their hand. My job is amazing. Thank you for letting me do it.

Read on for an exclusive extract of

No Ordinary Gentleman

Things not on Holly's bingo card:
Being propositioned to a threesome by an older attractive couple in a swanky London hotel.
Being saved by the handsome stranger who'd been listening in . . .

Annika and Lukas are nice people, and I do like older people, but I don't want to screw them! I don't have daddy issues. Or mommy issues. I haven't even managed sex as a twosome in eighteen months, so a threesome is way out of the question.

Universe, you have your wires crossed!

"I think we've shocked you a little," Lukas says . . .

I clamp my jaw shut. *How about no shit, Sherlock?*

"Annika and I love to travel," he continues smoothly, "and when we do, we like to take a little holiday from monogamy to spice things up."

"That is . . ." That is TMI, right there. Just too much information for me. I'm happy to share a bottle of wine or a cheese platter, but that's where I draw the line. I can't even share a water bottle with my sister without feeling a little unsettled by the my-mouth-where-her-mouth-has-been thing. Am I giving some kind of unconscious DTF vibes? Because, seriously, I am so *not* down to f—do *that*.

A threesome! What the fluff?

I lean back in my seat as Lukas moves forward in his, like a snake about to strike. *Or a deranged car salesman with a crazy deal to pitch. This is a car I'm* not *taking out for a ride.* But then a large hand appears in the space between us. A large hand attached to a strong wrist, which, as I look up—and up—appears to be attached to the devil in his Sunday suit.

I recognize those eyes—I met them over the edge of the *Financial Times* just a few minutes ago. Who knew the devil had such cool-colored eyes, amusement dancing there instead of fire and brimstone?

"It is *you*," his deep voice intones, its buttery warmth catching me off guard. I find myself pressing my hand into his. He pulls me to my feet and almost into his chest. His hard, unyielding could-rent-the-space-for-advertising chest.

I exhale a breathy "Yes" because, up close, this is a lot of man. A wall of man, you might say. Older, sophisticated, and so dang sexy. *I like older people,* a little voice inside me squeaks. And then I realize I'm just staring at him. "I—I am me," I stutter. "I mean, yes, it *is* me! And it's you . . ." *You handsome devil, you.*

He stares playfully down at me, one eyebrow quirked almost in a question mark. Up close, his eyes seem a deeper shade of blue, but maybe it's thanks to the dark blue of his suit. Whatever the reason, the result is striking, even with those crow's feet. Not the kind that need *Botox, STAT!* It's more like a serious expression could be his default face. But right now, his gaze hooks mine like he's daring me to play along.

"It's Cousin Lyle!" I belatedly announce. Fictitious Cousin Lyle, otherwise known as the hot man who just recently vacated his seat to rescue me.

"How are you, *Olive?*" His mouth quirks in the corner, his tone a tiny bit sour. I try not to laugh, unsure if it's the name he's christened me with that I find funny or that he doesn't like the one I've given him.

"Olive?" Lukas, the other (much older) man asks. "You said your name was—"

"Who were you this time?" The stranger sighs, staring balefully down at me. "It was Candy again, wasn't it?"

"If your parents had named you Olive, you'd be making up names too," I counter happily. Oh, my. I do love a man who can think on his feet.

"But you'll always be Olive to me." Fake Lyle's reply is smooth as silk, or at least the synthetic kind. *For all our insincerity.*

"Lyle, you're such a tease," I murmur, finding my fingers on his chest somehow. "So, how are tricks?"

"Tricks are . . . tricky." If temptation had an expression, I'm looking at it.

"And you need my advice," I assert with just a hint of fake sympathy as I turn to grab my purse. "You've got boyfriend trouble again, haven't you?" I waggle an admonishing finger at him.

"You know how it is," he answers, that sour note resurfacing again.

"I'm not sure I do," I answer, sweet as saccharine. God, I love that he's playing along.

"Come now, you know a hedonist rarely resists pleasure."

His purring response twists and coils and blooms in places it has no business being. The man has big-dick energy—wrapped in a silky, seductive coating of highly sexual energy—and I think I'm getting a contact high from the fumes.

"Thanks for the invite." I turn, quickly addressing the kinky folk on the couch, who seem too stunned to respond. "Rain check? I'm sure you understand—family should always come first." And with that, I take the arm my stranger doesn't quite offer and get the hell out of Dodge.

I almost drag him from the bar, not able to move away from the situation quick enough. Out through the hotel's stylishly mini-malistic foyer, down the front steps, and into the afternoon spring sunshine, all before you can say "straight-acting Cousin Lyle to the rescue."

"Oh my God!" I turn wide eyed to my would-be savior as we round the corner. "Can you believe that just happened?"

"I can't believe you made me leave my cup of coffee."

"I'd say sorry except . . . I didn't make you."

"It must be my good nature to blame." His lips quirk with amusement.

"Well, I, for one, am pleased you did. I mean, I know it's Wednesday."

"I'm not sure what the day has to do with anything." The man's head tilts as though to study me.

"Hump day?" I offer ridiculously. *Not an invitation. Not yet, at least.* But he just stares back without offering anything more. "Come on, Lyle, it's not even three o'clock!"

"I'm also not sure what the hour has to do with it."

"Are you telling me you're regularly propositioned on weekday afternoons?" My hands suddenly find my hips as I warm to my theme.

"Perhaps not to a threesome," he concedes, rubbing a hand across his chin. But I see the beginnings of that smile.

Boy, it must be some gene pool he's been swimming in.

He's too masculine to be pretty, and *plain old handsome* just doesn't do his looks justice. *Brutally good looking* might be a better description. The man in the fancy suit has an air of Viking about him.

I suddenly feel like I might need a good conquering.

But then his smile fades as he seems to come back to himself. To himself, the moment, and, judging by his change in manner, the ridiculousness of the situation. He straightens not only his shoulders but also the cuffs of his shirt under his jacket. Cartier cuff links, I note. The kind that say classy yet understated and high-rolling rich. Not that money does anything for me. In fact, no man has ruffled my truffle, so to speak, in more than eighteen months.

Rich might not do it for me, but that accent? Oh, yes.

"I trust I was in the right, intervening as I did." He's suddenly all business; crisp consonants and brows that pull together, where before they did not. It looks like I was right about that serious face.

"My God, yes!" I exclaim. *Way over the top, I know.* "A thousand times yes." One minute, my hands are in the air, and the next, they're planted squarely on his chest. Don't blame me. The damn thing is like a magnet. "Thank you for saving me, Lyle."

"That's *not* my name." His hands cover mine, lowering them to my sides, his small smile somehow a demonstration of his amusement and disapproval at once. "But I'm happy to have been of assistance."

"Well, Lyle did Olive a solid." Come on, smile a little more for me. "I literally had no idea how to get myself out of that."

"Rain check seemed to cover it." His eyes narrow once more as though regretting the comment. Or maybe he's remembering how I made him my fake gay cousin.

"I was being polite! Trying not to make them feel uncomfortable. I just had no plans of taking them up on their offer."

Something flickers in his expression, almost like he's reached a decision. He inclines his head and murmurs that it was nice to meet me. The soles of his shoes scrape against the pavement as he begins to pivot away.

"Wait!" I call out, not ready for the exchange to be over. He's like a puzzle I haven't finished deciphering—a Rubik's Cube I haven't finished messing with yet. "Where are you going?" The words are out of my mouth before I can stop them, my hand moving too.

"I'm sorry?" His gaze slices up from where my fingers are curled around his forearm, cool blue eyes matching his tone.

I never was any good with a Rubik's Cube, not that it ever stopped me.

"Tell me you're not leaving me here." Which is clearly what he's about to do. "Lyle, you can't leave! I've got nowhere to go but back in there." I point exaggeratedly back the way we came. "I'm staying in *that* hotel."

"I don't quite see—"

"If I go back, Mr. and Mrs. *Let's Get It On* might think I've changed my mind."

"You could always go somewhere else," he offers, arranging his features into something that looks like polite confusion. But I'm not buying it.

"Somewhere else?" I'm not really worried about going back to my hotel room alone. I just don't want to. I also don't want to wander around London alone—it's no fun when you're by yourself. And I would know, having visited enough bougie cafés and drunk enough coffee to sustain a third-world country's GDP. I've wandered around London's museums and parks, and I've designer window-shopped till I've been ready to drop. Not that I'll say that to Mr. Viking here.

"But I might get lost." The words fall from my mouth without a flicker of remorse. I don't even get the urge to hitch my *liar-liar pants* higher.

"I beg your pardon?"

"I'm on vacation." It's not technically a lie. "Today is my last day in London, but my first away from the tour company, and I've already gotten lost three times looking for a CVS." His frown deepens, and I weave my lie a little tighter. "A pharmacy? I have the blisters to prove it. Want to see?" Tightening my grip on his forearm, I tentatively lift my foot.

"That won't be necessary. I really don't—"

"Honestly, I'm amazed I found my way back to the hotel." Oh, woe is me. I'm just a poor damsel lost in the big city and laying it on a little thick. *Did I mention I majored in drama in college?* "I have such a terrible sense of direction. Oh!" I add as though struck by a sudden thought.

"Why don't you let me buy you a coffee?" I say at the exact same time as he says "Perhaps, I can . . . escort you to the nearest coffee shop?"

"Great!"

"I'm sorry?" He shakes his head, a little dazed, I think.

"I can buy you a coffee as a thank-you and replace the one you left behind." I slip my arm through his and lean on him a little, but his feet aren't budging.

"I'd really rather not." He looks surprised, almost as though the words escaped from his mouth.

"Oh, do you have to go back to work?"

"No, but—"

"You have somewhere you need to be?"

"Not exactly." His brow flickers again.

Pity for him he's not as good at lying on the fly as I am. *What can I say? It's a talent.*

"I guess I must've overstepped the mark," I murmur, pulling my arm from his. "I forgot I was in a big city for a minute." I frown and bite my lip for good measure, then sigh. "I can't imagine the folks back home turning away a stranger. It'd probably make the evening news." I look up at him, all sad doe eyes, and even throw in a hint of teary glisten. "Come to think of it, it might even make the evening news here. Especially when I wind up lost. Or dead."

So I'm laying it on thick, but what the heck? *I just want to see what I can get away with* is my recently adopted motto for life. It's how I ended up in London! And something tells me *Lyle* would be good company. As well as excellent eye candy. And he was nice enough to save me from the terrible twosome threesome people, which proves he's a gentleman.

But no ordinary gentleman, my mind supplies.

"I guess you have a wife." If he answers yes, I'm calling bullshit. That hand doesn't look like it's usually home to a wedding ring.

"No. Why would you ask?"

"I just don't want you to get the wrong idea. I'm not making plans for your body." Even if it is a *really* nice body.

A glint suddenly replaces his narrow look, though not like the one he'd shot over the top of his newspaper earlier. That look hadn't made my insides feel like a ribbon curled on the edge of a pair of sharp scissors. Kind of fizzy but a little afraid. Not the boogeyman kind of afraid. It's more like the kind of sensation you get when you reach the top of a roller coaster, anticipating what's to follow.

Feels a little like an omen. An omen for a thrilling ride?

"I—I'm just being courteous," I stammer as he does that wicked eyebrow thing again. "I mean, if I were your wife or girlfriend, I wouldn't like to loan you out."

"Just to be sure I have this right," he begins, "you think it's my civic duty to take responsibility for you as a visitor to the country? But only if I don't have a wife or a girlfriend."

"I mean, isn't that what you just did in there?" I gesture back toward the hotel.

"I gather you thought you were in danger?"

"In danger of combusting into flames of embarrassment, yes. And now, according to the rules of my people, I should thank you. With a hearty handshake." The heat in my cheeks feels like a contributor to global warming as I take his large hand and pump it ridiculously. "And a cup of coffee." I pause. "Lyle, you're looking at me like you know what crazy is and that I'm it."

"I wouldn't say *crazy* exactly." This time, his frown seems in an effort not to give in to a smile.

"Relax. It's not like I'm going to get you drunk on pink cocktails before chaining you to my bed. I just have twenty-four hours to kill."

"Twenty-four hours?" If I'd tried to anticipate a reaction to go with his wary tone, I probably would've chosen dread. Not the almost speculative look that he slides over my body.

"I'm not even going to ask what that was all about," I mutter, ignoring how my skin reacts as though his gaze were a physical thing. The tingling flare between my legs is a little harder to disregard.

"*I* have twenty-four hours until I leave," I reiterate, bringing my hands to my chest. "And you," I reiterate, touching his very nice chest and custom-made suit again, "could keep me company for an hour or two."

"You know, a lot can happen in a couple of hours," his low tone rumbles.

Then for the second time in our short acquaintance, he lifts my hands from his chest. Only this time, he reaches his long arm around me, pulling me to his side.

ABOUT THE AUTHOR

Donna Alam is a #7 Amazon Kindle Store and *USA Today* best-seller. A writer of love stories with heart, humor, and heat, she aspires to sprinkle a little joy into the lives of her readers. When not bashing away at her keyboard, she can often be found hiding from her responsibilities with a book in her hand and a mop of a dog at her feet.

Follow the Author on Amazon

If you enjoyed this book, follow Donna Alam on Amazon to be notified when the author releases a new book!

To do this, please follow these instructions:

Desktop:
1) Search for the author's name on Amazon or in the Amazon App.
2) Click on the author's name to arrive on their Amazon page.
3) Click the 'Follow' button.

Mobile and Tablet:
1) Search for the author's name on Amazon or in the Amazon App.
2) Click on one of the author's books.
3) Click on the author's name to arrive on the their Amazon page.

Kindle eReader und Kindle App:
If you enjoyed this book on a Kindle eReader or in the Kindle App, you will find the author 'Follow' button after the last page.